SCORCHING SECRETS

THE PROPHESIZED SERIES

KAITLYN HOYT

Cover Design by Victoria Faye
www.main.whitandware.com

Formatting by Inkstain Interior Book Designing
www.inkstainformatting.com

Editing by TCB Editing
www.tcbediting.weebly.com

DEDICATION

This book is dedicated to my cousin,
Anthony Fogolini
May 10, 1993- August 17, 2012

We all miss you and love you.
Rest in peace and fly high with the butterflies!

OTHER KAITLYN HOYT BOOKS

SCORCHING
SECRETS

CHAPTER ONE

MY BODY IS NUMB. I can't feel anything. My thoughts are running a mile a minute. Everything is a mess. The pain in my stomach is gone. The only thing left is the hole in my heart. This isn't how it was supposed to end. I imagined so many scenarios of how that night was going to end, but this was not it. She's supposed to be here with us. She did something to change the vision. I know it. I wasn't supposed to come out of that alive. It was supposed to be me, not her.

Me.

Again.

Claire's gone. She left us. She's not coming back, and she knew that. In the hallway, she told me: *"You'll all be alive."* She didn't say we. I should have caught on to that. I should have known. I should have kept a better eye on her. That conversation keeps running through my mind. She said I was the daughter that she never had. That's why she was getting teary-eyed…because she knew that she was going to be leaving us soon.

"Ryanne?" I can hear Colton talking to me, but I can't respond. I can't talk to anyone right now. My mind won't let me leave. There are too many thoughts running through it to form any coherent sentences aloud. I keep my eyes forward, focusing on the road through the front window of the car, ignoring everyone. We're heading to our next location. Tom has decided to stop using houses the family owns. He thinks it'll be too easy to track us that way. He has a place in mind, but won't tell us its exact location. It's safer that way—safer if we don't know.

The sky darkened when we got into the car. Thunder keeps rolling, and lightning randomly strikes around us. I try to pull the magic in and control it, but controlling the weather is a lot harder than pushing thoughts back, and I just don't have the energy to do it.

Everyone else is distraught over her loss too, but I can't get her out of my thoughts. I can't stop thinking about everything. She was right there in the kitchen with us. I should have stayed and looked for her. I could have done something. Couldn't I? I know that I could have, but what? I glance at Colton and David. They just lost their aunt, their guardian, and while they look sad, they don't look as upset as I am. Why am I more upset than them?

I try to keep my eyes forward ignoring everyone's penetrating gazes. They keep glancing back at me to make sure that I'm ok, but I'm not. I'm not going to be for a long time. No one could replace my mom. However, for the first time in a long time, I felt like I had a motherly figure in my life. One who didn't want to be my best friend, but one that truly loved me like a mother should. One who would help me when I needed it and wanted to see me succeed. A motherly figure that would do anything to make sure I was fine—that I was moving on. Now, she's gone. Claire is gone, and it's all my fault.

Death follows me like a stalker, constantly reminding me that no one around me is safe.

"Ryanne, please stop thinking like that," Liam grabs my left hand with his right. Putting a hand on my chin, he forces me to look at him. "There's nothing you could have done differently."

Staring into his grey eyes, I see the worry. The worry for me. I feel the barrier I put up a couple of hours ago start to melt away when he looks at me like that. I don't know how Liam does it, but he always knows what I'm thinking. Either he's very perceptive or I'm just really predictable.

"She knew, Liam," I can feel the tears brimming to the surface. "She knew. She told me, *you'll* all be alive. She didn't say *we'll* all be alive. She didn't include herself." My lips start quivering. "She did something. It was supposed to be me that died. Not her. Me." I start shaking my head. The movement causes the water to spill from my eyes and slide down my cheeks. Liam wraps his arm around my shoulder and pulls me closer to him. With my head tucked into his shoulder, I let the tears fall. I fist my hand into his shirt and sob. He rubs my back, but doesn't say anything.

There's nothing to say.

After a while, no more tears come. I still feel like crying, but my body can't anymore. I close my eyes but remain tucked into Liam's side. All the tension in my muscles disappear and I slowly drift into sleep.

COLTON

TOM, BRADGEN, AND DAVID SEARCHED through the rubble of the home for Claire once the chaos from the explosion died down. There was nothing. Just charred wood and glass fragments. Pieces of furniture were haphazardly lying around, but Claire wasn't in there. It was as if she just disappeared. Liam, Logan, Emma and I stayed with Ryanne. She passed out in Liam's arms after she realized that Claire never made it out of the house. The cry she let out while looking at the house will never leave me. It keeps playing over and over in my mind—along with the sight of her small body lying limp in Liam's arms. She's been through too much recently. I don't know how much more she can handle.

After the battle, everyone went their separate ways. Tom promised to keep in touch in case more help was necessary. A day will come when we will all manage to come back and band together. The Prophecy states that Ryanne will end this supernatural war. I can't think of any other way to end a war than with a battle. When that day comes, we'll need to contact them again.

We loaded into the car and headed on to our next location. Tom wouldn't tell us where the house was. He decided that we aren't going to go to any family properties anymore. It's too dangerous. Ryanne needs all of our protection, and we're going to take every precaution to make sure that she isn't discovered so easily.

Sitting at an angle so I can see in the back, I keep my eyes on her. Between Liam and Emma, Ryanne stares straight ahead, refusing to talk with anyone.

"Ryanne?" Liam asks her. She doesn't move. She hasn't spoken a word to anyone since she woke up. We've all tried talking to her, but she just ignores us. She refuses to let anyone comfort her. It hurts me to see her like this. Liam glances up at me and shrugs his shoulders. Claire had taken a liking to Ryanne. We all have.

I still can't wrap my head around the fact that Claire is dead. My guardian for the last ten years is gone. I can't believe it. I knew that this was going to get tough, but every outcome I thought of had us all alive. Claire is supposed to be here in this car with us as we drive to the next house.

I can't think about it. I have to focus on something else. I look out the window and watch as a bolt of lightning strikes the ground in the distance. Ryanne's magic is causing this. Her emotions cause the weather to change.

I look around the car. No one seems to know what to do. I meet Logan's eyes. Like Liam, he just shrugs at me. Logan's the only one that knows... knows that...ugh. I can't think about that either.

None of us like to see her distraught. I want to yell at her and make her talk. She needs to get everything out. Bottling everything up isn't good. Being angry and upset isn't going to change anything. Claire's not coming back.

Hopefully when we get to the next house, we can train. Training always helps me feel better when I'm angry or upset. Releasing pent up anger on someone is very cathartic.

I pull my attention from the weather when I hear her talk. I can't hear what she is saying, but I can hear the sadness in her voice. It cuts through me like a knife. I turn around in my seat as she leans forward and curls into Liam's side. She starts sobbing into his shoulder, and I can do nothing but watch her tears soak through the thin fabric of his shirt. He's resting his chin on her head and rubbing her back, trying to comfort her. My stomach tightens as I watch them together. I understand that she feels comfortable around him, but I want to be the one comforting her. Not watching another man do it.

HITTING A BUMP IN THE road jolts me out of my sleep. I'm still tucked into Liam's side, but my body feels too weak to move. Despite Logan healing me after being stabbed, I still don't have enough energy to do much of anything. I keep my eyes closed and listen to the conversation going on around me. "She just needs time. Don't pester her too much," Liam says.

"There was nothing she could have done differently. She was stabbed, Liam," Colton's voice sounds in front of me. He pauses and during his silence, I can hear people shifting in their seats. "We all thought that Claire got out of the house. She wasn't in the kitchen with us."

"That doesn't mean anything, Colton. You know her. She's blaming herself. Dravin was there for *her*. What would you think? You know that she doesn't care about what happens to her. She cares about every one of you more than she does herself."

"Ok, we're here. Someone wake up Ryanne and Emma," Tom calls out from the driver's seat of the car.

"Ryanne. Ryanne. Wake up. We're here," Liam starts lightly shaking my shoulder. I deeply inhale and push myself away from his shoulder, avoiding everyone else's penetrating gazes. Liam is the only one who seems to understand—the only one trying to understand.

Everyone is out of the car except for the back row. "Can you help me? I still don't feel strong enough," I ask Liam when he moves to get out.

He nods and grabs my hand, slowly pulling me over to the door. Stepping out of the vehicle, he turns around and puts his arms out for me to hold onto. I grab his arm and take a tentative step out of the car. I sway when both feet are planted on the ground. Liam pulls me toward him and wraps an arm around my waist, steadying me. "Thank you," I whisper to him before turning and looking at the house.

The house is a little smaller than the previous one. Surrounded by trees, the two-story brick house blends into its surroundings. The dark brown bricks contrast against the lighter beige shingles. Four wooden steps lead to a small porch, shading the front door. Large rectangular windows adorn the two floors with white frames. Medium-sized shrubs line the base of the home, running under the windows. It isn't nearly as nice as the last cabin, but it is still nicer than what I'm used to.

Entering the house, the first floor looks similar to our previous places. A large living room is the first room I see. The room has deep red walls and dark wood flooring. A large flat screen television is mounted on the wall directly across from the couch. It's the large sectioned couch that instantly attracts my attention. Liam must have noticed me staring at it because walks me over to it and helps me sit down. David and Emma go off to look at the rest of the house, while Bragden helps Tom bring in our bags from the car.

Logan walks to the couch and crouches in front of me. "How are you feeling?" Without looking at him, I tell him that I'm fine. I'm not, but I don't want to be healed anymore. I want to feel as bad physically as I do emotionally. I need to feel something. Liam shakes his head at Logan, silently telling him to drop it. I could kiss Liam right now for telling everyone to leave me alone. Logan looks away from me and up at him and with a sigh, he gets up from his crouched position and walks out of the room. I pull my legs under me and lean over onto the armrest, closing my eyes.

I'M SITTING IN THE MIDDLE of a grassy field, picking wildflowers when the wind starts to pick up around me. It isn't me this time. I slowly turn around and see three gorgoths surrounding me. Towering over me by about two feet, their impending presence sends chills through my bones. I've seen these beasts once before when I entered the dream world unintentionally. Liam was with me that time. He was the one that fought it off while I initially cowered behind him. He's the one with the weapons. I don't have anything to defend myself with. I jump up and take a step back.

The wind intensifies, and the sky darkens, mirroring my mood. My emotions affect the weather. If I'm upset, it starts raining. When I'm angry, it begins storming. When I am happy, it's sunny. When I'm frightened, there's a combination of weather components. I look around the clearing for anything I can use as a weapon, but come up short. Just my luck.

I take a couple steps backwards as the gorgoths start coming toward me. Their piercing red eyes stare ahead, daring me to make a move. Jagged teeth are visible, giving the impression that they're smiling at me, knowing that they have me cornered. I turn to run into the forest when two more appear behind me, effectively surrounding me. I have a plan but need something to distract them. I just need enough time to call some of my magic to me.

I don't get that time though as all five gorgoths decide to attack at once. I try to call my magic to lift me into the air above them, but can't gather enough energy that fast. I turn and run toward the two off to the side. I'm not going to let them just attack me without fighting. I call small amounts of magic into my limbs as I swing out to kick the first one in the stomach. It anticipates my move and grabs my leg with its talon-like hands, embedding its pointed nails into my skin and throws me to the side. I land on the ground with a thud and roll a couple of times before I hear a loud piercing scream. Turning toward the sound, I see Liam yanking a sword out of the back of a fallen gorgoth.

"Ryanne!" I bring my eyes back to the gorgoths in front of me. They are stalking toward me again. I hear a second scream, which means that Liam has gotten another one. Hoping to hold them off long enough for Liam to finish and come help me, I run toward them again, knowing that I can't kill them, but I can find a way to possibly stun them.

I call more energy to me and visualize lightning striking the ground where they are standing. I close my eyes and concentrate on my magic, ignoring the throbbing in my leg. The wind increases in intensity again and thunder rolls more vehemently. I hear the third scream and open my eyes and see the two gorgoths standing a few feet from me. I push out the collected energy and wait.

Two large bolts of lightning strike the ground where the gorgoths are standing. The one closest to me starts smoking before it explodes. I put a magical shield around me as blood and guts fly in all directions, decorating the grass and nearby trees with gore. The other gorgoth just falls to the ground stunned. Liam runs over to me and stabs it while it's down. It lets out an earsplitting scream before disappearing like the others.

"Ryanne, are you okay?" he asks as he closes the distance between us. I drop the shield when he stops in front of me. His eyes move over my face and body looking for injuries, zeroing in on my leg.

"Yeah, I'm fine." I try to walk but can't get anywhere now that the adrenaline is gone. Blood is dripping down the leg that the gorgoth grabbed. Pain shoots through my body as I try to put pressure on it. I grimace and sit on the ground before looking around, expecting to see more beasts coming toward us. There are none; Liam and I are alone.

"I'm going to go and get Logan and then I'll wake you up. You may have sustained this injury in your physical body too."

Liam is a dream-walker. If a mage is having a nightmare, he will come and help them try and resolve whatever internal conflict they are having. I still don't understand how, but I can get injured in a dream and in my real body. I file that thought away for later as I feel the pull of my body being shaken in an attempt to wake me up. I close my eyes and fall backwards into nothingness.

COLTON

"SHOULD WE WAKE HER UP?" Logan turns toward me. "She's been out for a while."

I crouch in front of Ryanne and gently lift her head to place a pillow beneath her. She still doesn't move.

"No, she needs to sleep. She wasn't healed all the way. The wound closed, but she's still really weak," I tell him. Logan healed her stab wound, but it's obvious that she's still in pain. For crying out loud, she couldn't even get out of the car without help. She couldn't walk to the couch without help. She's not healing as quickly as she should be.

"I can't believe that you——" Logan starts but I interrupt him.

"Not now Logan. I still need to wrap my head around the whole situation." I look around the room. Everyone else is sitting around the kitchen table talking. I can't risk anyone overhearing. Not yet anyway. I glance down at her sleeping on the couch. Even sleeping, she has exhaustion written all over her face.

Out of the corner of my eye, I see Liam push away from the table and walk into the living room. He stops at the edge of the couch and looks down at Ryanne with a frown on his face. "I think something's going on with her," he says as he sits down beside her on the couch.

"Yeah, she was just stabbed and——" Logan starts, but Liam turns and starts shaking his head. Obviously he knows more than he's letting on.

"No, I think she's dreaming about something and needs help."

She seems to be sleeping peacefully to me. Her hair is falling onto her face. I reach forward and tuck the fallen curly strand behind her ear. A small sigh escapes her slightly open mouth when I touch her skin. My hand lingers against her skin for a few moments before I remember that there are others in the room with me. As quickly as I can, without being too obvious, I take my hand away.

"How can you tell?" Logan asks with a light tone. I know that he caught me, but I refuse to look over at him. He's going to give everything away.

"I just get this feeling when someone needs help. I think it has to do with…I just know. I'll be back in a minute." He closes his eyes and falls against the back of the couch in a sleep-like state.

"All he has to do is close his eyes and he can go into her dream?" Logan asks. "Can he do that whenever? What if she was dreaming about him?"

I clench my fists at his question. I hope she doesn't dream about him. Ever. I turn and look at him, trying to keep a placid expression. He is looking down at Ryanne, but when I move, he looks at me and smiles.

"Oh, this is going to be fun."

I OPEN MY EYES AND see Liam sitting in front of me with Colton and Logan standing behind him. I try to sit up, but wince when I feel the pain in my leg. At the sight of my grimace, Logan moves beside Liam and places his hands on the scratches, magically healing them. When he finishes healing the claw marks on my leg, he grabs onto my arms and pushes more magic into me, healing all the remaining injuries. I try pulling my arms away, but he tightens his grip, not letting go until I'm completely healed.

I blankly stare at him while he smiles and leans back, closing his eyes. Healing so many people recently has taken a lot of energy out of him. After the house exploded and the Gadramicks left, he helped heal everyone that needed it and I can definitely tell that he has overused his magic. He looks drained. His bright blue eyes lack their usual shine, and dark circles are under both of his eyes from exhaustion.

"I didn't want you to heal me, Logan."

"I know you didn't, Ryanne, but I don't like seeing you in pain and neither does anyone else. You could barely walk on your own and you've been sleeping for the last eight hours."

Eight hours? I turn toward the window and notice that it's indeed dark outside.

"Why didn't anyone wake me up?"

"Because you needed to sleep. Your body needed the rest, especially since you wouldn't let Logan heal you," Colton says.

"Logan's healed enough people lately, Colton. He didn't need to waste any more magic on me. I've used entirely too much of it to begin with." I angle toward Logan who is leaning back against the couch, eyes closed. I'm partially responsible for the constant use of his magic. He healed Colton, but I can tell that he isn't healing as fast as he usually does. "Logan, let me see your back."

"I'm fine, Ryanne," he tries to wave me off but doesn't seem to have enough energy to even do that.

"Logan, let me see your back," I demand as I scoot toward him. With a frustrated groan, he angles his back toward me and slowly lifts his shirt up. I gasp when I get a good look at the skin there. The cuts have scabbed over, but his tanned skin is covered in deep purple bruises and large red welts. It looks extremely painful. I find my back aching just looking at it. "Oh my gosh, Logan." He puts his shirt back on and turns back around. When he's facing me, I reach out and hit him on the chest.

"Ouch," Logan says, rubbing the spot I just hit. I know that I didn't hurt him. "What was that for?"

"You shouldn't have healed me, you big dummy. You need to save your magic!" I hear Colton scoff behind me. In response, I turn and glare at him. Liam shakes his head in amusement. I turn back to Logan who just shrugs at me. I really hate shrugging.

"Look at me, Ryanne. Since meeting you, I've healed you after you were kidnapped and tortured. You were also just stabbed. Believe me, what I'm going through right now is nothing compared to any of that." I just stare at him. I can feel Liam and Colton watching me. I have a feeling that I can help him. I really want to do something to help lessen his pain.

I wonder if…"Logan, can I try something?" I scoot closer to him. His eyes narrow suspiciously as I stop right beside him. I place my hands out and look up at him, waiting. His eyes move down at my hands and then back at me, questioning what I'm going to do. "Just take my hands." Not everything has to be so complicated.

Hesitantly, he grabs my outstretched hands, watching me warily. I close my eyes and concentrate on pulling small energy strands to the surface. When I feel their presence, I begin to push the vibrating magic toward my hands and create a small bridge between my hands and Logan's where the magic can travel. I hear him gasp, and his grip on my hands tightens. Concentrating harder, I let more flow into him. I'm not sure when to stop or how much is necessary for him to feel normal again.

After a few more seconds, I close the bridge between our hands and open my eyes at the same time that he does. "Did that work?" I ask. Instead of answering, he pulls me toward him and wraps his arms around me, burying his face into my neck. "I'll take that as a yes."

"Thank you," he whispers as he releases me from his embrace.

"What did she do?" Colton and Liam both move closer to us, confused as to what I had just done.

"She healed me." Logan's still staring at me in awe. I squirm under his gaze slightly and lean back against the couch.

"You're not hurting anymore? Your back is better?" I ask. With a nod, he turns around and lets me check his back. I lift his shirt and gasp when I see the smooth tanned skin. All the bruises and cuts that had previously marred him are gone.

Colton and Liam both look at me questioningly with raised eyebrows. "She can heal now too?"

"I didn't heal him necessarily. I gave him some of my magic so he could heal himself."

"That's amazing," Colton tells me. I wave off his compliment and look around the room. Besides the couch and TV, it is pretty bare. My eyes continue scanning the room before landing on the entryway to the kitchen. No one is in the room. Claire was always cooking something in the kitchen. If she wasn't reading a book, that is where you could find her.

Liam must have caught my look. "Ryanne, why don't I show you to your room?" I tear my eyes away from the kitchen, nod, and let him walk me upstairs. "You're sharing a room with Emma again," he tells me when we stop outside the bedroom door. I peek into the room and see Emma sitting on the bed, flipping through a magazine. I know that she's aware that we're standing outside the door.

Liam grabs my elbow as I'm about to enter the room and pulls me back into the hallway. Leaning against the wall, I look down at the floor avoiding his penetrating gray gaze.

"Ryanne, there was nothing you could have done. *Nothing.* Please stop blaming yourself," he lifts my chin until I am looking at him. I can hear someone walking up the stairs, but Liam is standing so close, looking down at me, that I can't see who is coming. I cross my arms across my chest. "Please." I can hear the desperation in his voice. I know that he doesn't like to see me this upset, but there's nothing I can do. I can give him all these promises and false hopes, but I don't know if I can keep them.

I can feel the tears coming again, but I blink them away. I hate how often I cry now. Exhaling, I respond, "I'll try, but you know how I am, Liam. I replay all the possible scenarios in my head over and over again, and always come to the conclusion that I could have done something else. Something more. Anything. I should have known."

"She knew what she was doing. More than the rest of us. She was doing what she knew was the right thing. We're all upset over her, but you can't take any of the blame."

"But—"

"No buts. You just can't. Okay?"

I will work on it, but I know that it will take time. Time heals all wounds right? I gaze up at Liam. He is very handsome. My eyes follow the jagged scar above this eyebrow until I meet his eyes. If a certain green-eyed boy wasn't always on my mind, I could see myself being happy with him. He is kind and considerate and I know that he cares about me. As if reading my thoughts, he gives me a small sad smile.

Tearing his eyes away from mine, Liam glances toward the stairs. He takes a small step back. I briefly see Colton walk past us and into the room directly across the hall. Liam turns back to me and says, "She wouldn't want you moping around upset over her. You know that. Now, go to bed. You still look tired." He gently pushes me into the room and leaves.

I walk over to the bed that Emma isn't occupying and sit down. Emma smiles sadly at me but doesn't say anything. I'm grateful for that because I don't really want to talk. Wrapping the covers around me, I turn and face the wall. More silent tears begin to fall from my eyes. Not wanting Emma to hear me cry, I stifle my sobs and let myself drift into a dreamless sleep.

CHAPTER
TWO

STRETCHING, I SIT UP IN bed and look around. The room is dark. Glancing to my right, I see Emma still asleep. Based on the color of the sky, it's early morning. I get out of bed and walk to the bathroom to take a quick shower. I grab a pair of white shorts and my black "Bazinga" *Big Bang Theory* t-shirt to change into.

All the doors in the hallway are closed as I walk out of the room which means that everyone is still asleep. I go through my bag and get out my iPod and find out that it's only 6:30 a.m. It will be a few more hours before everyone else wakes up. Grabbing my notebook, I go downstairs and sit down on the couch and open it up.

I have no idea what to draw.

I continue to stare down at the blank page. While listening to Sara Bareilles, I feel the couch dip beside me. "Morning," I say to Bragden without looking away from my notebook. Inspiration has to strike sooner or later.

"Good morning. What are you drawing?" I turn the notebook toward him, showing him the blank page. "Having trouble?"

"Yep, I've been sitting here for," I grab my iPod to check the time, "over half an hour and can't think of anything to draw."

"Draw something for me."

"Like what?"

"I don't know. You're the artist. Use this," he pokes my forehead and smiles at me. I look at him for a couple seconds, waiting for inspiration to strike and then I start drawing. When I think of the Kane family, Liam and Bragden, I think about the flame story that Liam told me once. I can feel Bragden watching me as I draw, but I don't stop.

I draw a bear claw. Bragden always reminded me of a bear and not just physically. He is the largest and most masculine of all of the guys I am around. Standing tall, he's prepared for battle. He's protective, brave, and determined, but he's also patient and kind-hearted. Inside the bear claw I draw flames similar to Liam's tattoo. When I finish, I turn the notebook around and let him look at it. He asks about the bear claw. Slightly blushing, I explain why he reminds me of a bear.

After my explanation, he continues to watch me. Without saying anything, he gets up and walks into the kitchen. Throwing open random drawers, he starts searching for something. "What are you doing?" He ignores my question and continues shuffling things through the drawers.

"Aha, found some." He walks back to the couch and hands me a pen and a permanent marker. "Draw it on me."

"What?" I stare at him incredulously.

"Draw that," he points to the claw, "on me. It would make a great tattoo."

Is he serious? When he waves the marker in front of me, I hesitantly reach out and take it from him. "Ok…where?"

He looks at me for a moment and then turns around, taking his shirt off. For the first time, I notice that he has a smaller necklace on similar to the one that Liam gave me. I make a mental note to ask him about that later. "Left shoulder."

I reach for my iPod, pause the song, and place it on the coffee table in front of me.

"How big?" I'm glad that he has his back to me, so he can't see me openly ogling his body. He is fit. *Extremely fit.* His skin is much tanner than Liam's. Liam is a little tanner than me, but considering how pale I am, that's not saying much. Bragden looks like he spends a lot of time outdoors. I may not be interested in him in that way, but I'm not blind.

"A little bigger than the drawing."

I move so that I am sitting up on my knees and put the pen on his skin. I lean forward, resting my arms on his back. "I'm going to draw it in pen first and then trace it in permanent marker, ok?"

I get the outline of the bear claw done when I hear the others start walking down the stairs. I'm in the drawing zone, so I don't look up to see who's there. My pen is tracing the outlines of the flames when Liam speaks up.

"What is she doing to you?"

"She's giving me a temporary tattoo," Bragden replies; his back shakes with his response.

"Don't move." He apologizes and chuckles. I stop drawing and lean so that he can see me glaring at him. "You wanted me to do this mister, but I can't draw if you keep moving," I try to sound stern but end up laughing as well. When he calms down, I return to the tattoo.

"What is she drawing?" asks Colton. I point to my notebook beside Bragden. Colton reaches out and grabs it to examine the drawing. "That's actually really cool." I finish drawing the flames, cap the pen, and reach for the permanent marker. I wave the permanent marker in front of Bragden, warning him. He laughs and promises not to move anymore.

I trace the outline and am about to draw and shade the flames when David and Emma walk into the living room. Emma looks at me and raises her eyebrows as her gaze shifts to Bragden. I move the permanent marker away from his skin and put the cap on, preparing for someone to talk. Who knows what will come out of either of their mouths. She whistles and starts fanning herself before sitting down in the chair. David looks at Bragden and smiles.

Sitting down in the chair beside Emma, he says, "Are you a parking ticket? Because you have *fine* written all over you." I lean forward and rest my head on Bragden's back. I don't want to laugh. I'm supposed to be mourning, but David has a way of cheering everyone up. I can feel Bragden laughing beneath me.

"That's the worse pick-up line ever dude. You'll have to do better than that," Bragden says, "if you want any of this." He motions to his body. I lose it.

"Okay, let me think," he pauses for a moment. David taps his chin and pretends to think. "Were you arrested earlier? Because I'm pretty sure it's illegal to look that good." I can tell that David is smiling as he speaks. I start giggling all over again.

"I think the only person those pick-up lines would work on is Ryanne. She's dying back there."

"No…" I shake my head and start laughing again. I lean back, "Oops, I just spit on your back." This causes everyone to laugh. I sit up on my knees again and use to the edge of my shirt to wipe off his back. Bragden leans back and looks at me smiling, "You okay?"

One last giggle escapes. "Turn back around. I'm almost done." I look at David and Emma, "Don't say anything for the next five minutes." Emma brings her hand up to her mouth and pretends to zip it. David just smiles at me. I get back to work tracing and shading the flames. The room is silent. I glance around once and see everyone watching me. I blush at their attention, but continue working.

Sitting back, I look at the drawing and glance over his shoulder to the notebook, comparing the two. They look exactly alike. "Ok, I think I'm done. You can go look at it."

He walks over to the bathroom, right outside of the kitchen, and examines the drawing in the mirror. I watch him, trying to judge his reaction. I mean, I did just draw on him with permanent marker. It'll take a while for that to wash off. Bragden stands at the mirror for a few more seconds before returning to his seat beside me. "It looks great. Thank you."

"No. Thank you." I look at him, hoping that he can see how thankful I actually am. He kept my mind busy for a little while; he kept my thoughts off of Claire.

A voice speaks in my ear. "Why is he shirtless?" I scream and jump off the couch. Losing my balance, I almost fall onto the coffee table, but Bragden reaches out and grabs me around the waist, pulling me back beside him.

"Why do you keep doing that?" I take deep breaths, trying to calm my frantically beating heart. Larkin just smiles arrogantly. Larkin has the ability to transport to any location he wants to. At one point, he was working for Dravin and helping the Gadramicks, but now he's helping us.

"How did you find us?" Colton asks, leaning against the edge of the couch. I glance over at him when I hear the harshness in his tone.

"I can sense her magic. She's got a lot of it."

"Can others sense it too?" I ask. "Is there a way to mask it?" I don't want to bring any more danger here.

"Only a few people can actually sense magic. And most wouldn't come toward someone with as much magic as you have. They'd go in the opposite direction. As for hiding it…sorry there's no way to hide it." I purse my lips and turn away from him. My magic was like a bright bulls-eye for all my enemies, constantly alerting them of my location.

"Is there a reason why you came here?" I can hear the annoyance in Colton's voice. I know that Colton doesn't like Larkin, but I'm not sure why. He's proven to everyone that he is trustworthy. In fact, he's helped us a lot recently. I glance over at Colton and see him glaring at Larkin. What is going on between those two? Larkin warned us about Dravin's attack earlier. He gave us time to gather people to help us; he saved our lives.

"I actually just wanted to make sure Ryanne was doing ok." I return my attention back to Larkin. He's looking down at me with concern. Hmm, that's a new expression for him.

"I'm doing better today if that's what you are asking."

Larkin eyes move away from mine and land on something behind me. When I see his smirk, I glance over my shoulder to see what he's looking at. Colton is the only thing there, but he is looking elsewhere. "That's good. Also, Dravin thinks that you were in the house when it exploded, so he won't bother you guys for some time." Larkin blinks out of the room.

"What are you all looking at?" asks Logan from the bottom of the stairs. Tom is standing behind him giving us the same confused expression. We all turn and look at them. Logan scans the room before he brings his attention back to Bragden and me. "What's going on here?"

I look down to see what he is referring to. Bragden still has his arm around my waist and I am still pressed into his side...his bare side. I blush at the same time as Bragden clears his throat and removes his arm. I scoot away from him as he reaches for his shirt.

"Nothing," we both mumble. I pick up the permanent marker and pen and walk back into the kitchen to put them into the drawer I saw Bragden get them from.

Tom walks into the kitchen behind me. "How are you holding up, kid?"

"I'm ok. I talked to Liam last night. He helped me feel a little better about the whole thing. It's just weird. I only knew her a couple of weeks, but I miss her. This kitchen feels really empty without her here. I keep expecting her to walk through those doors and tell us that she baked something." Tom comes over to me and gives me a small hug, kissing the top of my head; a very paternal gesture.

"I miss her too." I can hear the sadness in his voice. I look up at him right as he turns away and clears his throat, trying to hide his emotions.

"Tom, what'll happen to the bookstore?" Though I only went into the bookstore a couple times, it saddens me that others may no longer be able to go. There's no other bookstore in town. There was something special about the BlackMoon Bookstore, but I don't know how it'll run without Claire. She was the heart and soul of that place.

His eyes move away from the window above the sink, and he returns his attention to me. "I'm not sure, Ryanne. It'll be closed for the summer. After that…I don't know."

"Oh…" I don't know what to say. We all need Claire here. I walk over to Tom and give him a hug. Wrapping my arms around his waist, I rest my head on his chest. We take comfort in each other's embrace.

"Why don't you go join everyone?" he says after a few seconds. He doesn't want my comfort, so I slowly turn around and go back into the living room. I understand how he's feeling. When my mom died, I didn't want to talk with anyone. I just wanted to be left alone.

I realize now how wrong I was about that.

"Ryanne," he calls after me. I stop in the doorway and turn back around.

"Thank you," he whispers.

"For what?"

"The hug," he turns around and opens the fridge, searching for food. I whisper a reply back to him and head into the living room. Tom may not want comfort, but sometimes that's all you actually need.

"We should get rid of the piano and make that room our unofficial entertainment room," David suggests as I walk back into the room.

"There's a piano here?" I ask him as I sit down near Bragden again. Colton and Liam both glance at me strangely.

"Don't tell me you can play the piano too?" Emma says, sitting up.

"Well…I mean I haven't played in like a year. Jane didn't have a piano, so I don't know if I can *still* play."

"I have to see this." Colton stands up and grabs my wrist, pulling me from the couch and toward the stairs.

"Where are we going?"

"*You're* going to play for us."

"What? Like right now? In front of everyone?"

He drags me into a dark room. Releasing my wrist, he flips on the light switch.

A large ebony piano sits in the center of the room. My mouth hits the floor. Colton walks behind me and nudges me toward the piano seat. My legs move on their own accord. As I sit down, I turn toward him, "Do you realize that this is a Steinway grand piano?" I run my hand across the top, admiring how smooth it is.

"I don't know what that means."

"This piano is ridiculously expensive." I jump back from the seat when my mind finally catches up to me. "I can't play on that." I've never played on anything that nice before. The piano that I played on was an old wooden one that my mom inherited when Grandma passed away.

"Why not?" asks Liam.

"That piano is worth tens of thousands of dollars." I say pointing to it. Everyone just looks at me like I am crazy. I know my eyes are wide.

"Tens of thousands," I repeat. Are my words not being processed in their brains? Their expressions don't change. *Tens of thousands*. Why am I the only one that is worried about how much this costs? I can't be the only person here that understands the value of a dollar.

Colton rolls his eyes and pushes me back toward the piano. "Play something." I really do want to play it. However, I don't really want to embarrass myself if I mess up. It has been a long time since I've touched a piano, let alone tried to play anything.

"I don't know what to play," I say hoping to waste some time. They're going to make me play no matter what, but if I can prolong it for a little bit…

"Oh quit stalling, Ryanne. I want to hear you play," Emma whines. I place my hands on the cool keys and take a deep breath, preparing myself. I'll play a simple song first.

Facing everyone, I ask, "Can you not look at me? It's making me nervous. Turn around or something." Collectively, I hear frustrated sighs, but everyone listens and turns around. I take a deep breath and place my hands on the correct chords. I start slowly to make sure that I remember how to play the song and get adjusted to the weight of the keys. I close my eyes and let my fingers move across the keys, focusing only on the piano. Everything else is forgotten in that moment. It is just me and the piano.

COLTON

I ALMOST GROWL AT EMMA when she tells Ryanne to quit stalling. She looks over at me and smirks. Obviously Ryanne is nervous about playing in front of all of us. When she mentioned that she could play piano, I just had to hear it. It shouldn't surprise me that she could play though. I'm more surprised that she never mentioned it before.

She reaches up and pushes her long hair out of her face and looks down at the keys. I watch as she slowly places her small hands on the right keys. It looks like she is about to play, but instead she turns around and asks us if we can look away. I chuckle at the request, while everyone else groans. After everything that we've been through together, she still gets nervous and embarrassed around us.

I turn around and everyone follows. Ryanne exhales loudly, and then the notes start playing through the room. I try not to turn around like she asked, but after the first couple of seconds I can't help it.

I can't see her face, but she is moving with the music, her hands seeming to glide across the keys. I look around at Logan and Liam and see that they have similar expressions. She really can play. Emma walks over to me and puts a hand under my chin and pushes up, closing my open mouth. I blink a couple of times and smirk at her before walking toward the side of the piano. The music starts slowing and I expect her to stop playing, but she transitions into another song.

Her eyes are closed like I expected, with a calm countenance. Liam walks over and stands near me. Ryanne leans forward and clears her throat. Her long hair starts falling over her shoulders and shields her face from my view, so I can no longer see her expression. Under the notes of the piano, I can hear her humming along with the music, but I'm not prepared for what happens next.

She sings.

Emma gasps when Ryanne begins singing along with the music. "Did you know she could sing?" she whispers to me. I shake my head, not able to tear my eyes away from her.

Her voice is beautiful. She sounds so sad singing the song. The melody of the song flows through her. I can tell that Ryanne is releasing some of her emotions through this song. I have to force my legs to remain where they are, because I want to go over to her and comfort her in any way possible. I want to ease her pain and make the sadness go away. She starts moving more when the chorus comes; her voice becoming stronger and louder.

Such a big voice for such as small girl.

I WAIT UNTIL THE LAST note fades before I open my eyes again. A single tear falls down my cheek. I hear someone move behind me, and I tense. I forgot that I was playing in front of an audience. I'm afraid to see everyone's reactions. I quickly wipe the tear from my face. When I started playing, everyone was standing behind me. Now, they're all standing off to my side.

No one says anything.

"Was I really that bad?"

"Bad?" Logan says. "Holy crap girl."

I don't understand. "It's been a while since I've played. I wasn't really planning on singing, but I got caught up in the song."

"That was beautiful, Ryanne," says Colton. I look toward him and find his eyes focused on me. I blush under his gaze, but I can't look away. When he continues staring at me, my face reddens even further.

"What songs did you play?" Emma asks walking over to the piano breaking me out of my trance.

"Umm, the first one was called "River Flows In You" by Yiruma and the second one was "Breathe Again" by Sara Bareilles."

"Can you play anything else?" Colton asks as he leans across the top of the piano…still staring at me.

"Like what?"

"Anything." I know that most of the songs I listen to no one else will know. Oh, I know what to play. I smile up at him and then shift my eyes to everyone else.

"Ok, but only if you guys sing with me." They all agree and gather around the piano. I start playing "You Found Me" by The Fray. I look up when no one joins me in singing. They are all just staring at me. I glare at Emma, hoping that she will start singing with me. During the chorus, I hear another voice join mine. I look over and see Colton singing along with me. Our voices blend perfectly together. Everyone's heads whip between the two of us.

After the first bridge, I don't sing. I let Colton have his own solo. He has a great voice. Even though I don't need to, I look down at the piano keys to keep from staring at him. I join him again on the chorus. When the song finishes, I transition straight into "Apologize" by OneRepublic. This time everyone joins in. David obviously can't sing, but he makes it fun for everyone else because of his comical attempts.

When the song ends, I stand up and walk away from the piano. "That's enough for the day." I walk over and stand beside Colton. Everyone is still watching me. "What?"

"What else aren't you telling us?" Logan narrows his eyes at me but smiles.

When the room falls into silence, I hear a muffled sound. Listening harder, I hear my The Cab ringtone. "Is that my phone?" I walk out of room and back down the hallway to the bedroom. I hear the beep telling me that I have a missed call. In the last pocket I check, I find the phone. Jane's number flashes on my screen.

Redialing the number, I wait for her to pick up the phone. On the second ring, she answers. "Ryanne?"

"Hey Jane, I haven't heard from you in a while!"

"I know sweetie, I miss you! Oh my gosh. You haven't heard the good news yet have you?"

"What news?"

"Ross and I are getting married!"

"Really? Congratulations, I'm so happy for you!"

"Yeah, we've decided to have an early wedding. It's in two weeks!"

"Two weeks?" Why so soon?

"Yeah, I know you're working right now on your internship, but do you think you can get off that Saturday? I want you to be one of my bridesmaids. I know you can't really help out with any of the planning, but I want you to be a part of the ceremony." Internship? What internship? Claire or Tom must have made up a story for me.

"I can try. I'll have to talk to T…my boss and get back to you later. Is that okay?"

"Of course. Oh, and bring a date!" She hangs up. I stare down at the phone. Two weeks? I throw the phone down on the bed and walk out of the room. I hear voices downstairs, so that's where I go.

C O L T O N

WHEN RYANNE LEFT TO GO grab her cell phone, no one moved. We remained around the piano surprised at what just happened. Is there anything that girl can't do?

"Dude, since when can you sing too?" Emma leans against the piano, waiting for my answer.

"I can't really." I've never considered myself a good singer. Everyone can sing. Some people are just better than others. When she started singing "You Found Me," I couldn't help but join in. She looked so embarrassed when no one started singing with her.

"You can't? You two sounded perfect together. You could record that song and sell it. I mean Ryanne's like freaking Kelly Clarkson over there and you're like….well someone else who can sing," Emma says.

I ignore her comment and push myself off the piano and walk out of the room. I can hear their footsteps behind me, so I know they're following me. Passing by Ryanne's room, I see her pacing while on the phone. She doesn't seem in distress, so I continue downstairs. I sit down on the couch and wait for everyone to join. David and Emma sit together like they always do on the loveseat. Liam and Logan sit on the couch while Bragden takes the other chair in the room. Emma turns and smiles at me. I instantly recognize the look on her face and groan, waiting for whatever ridiculous comment is going to come out of her mouth.

"So, when are you going to tell my best friend that you're totally in love with her?"

My mouth basically falls to the ground. That wasn't blunt at all. "W-w-hat?"

"Ryanne may be oblivious, but the rest of us aren't. So. When. Are. You. Going. To. Tell. Her?"

"I don't…I'm not…" I look up and see Ryanne descending the stairs and stop talking. Well, I stop stuttering. Talk about perfect timing.

"This conversation isn't over," Emma loudly whispers.

"EVERYTHING OKAY?" COLTON ASKS WHEN I make it downstairs.

"Yeah, Jane's getting married and wants me to be a bridesmaid," I glance at him. He appears to be blushing. His cheeks are redder than usual. "Are you ok? Your face is red."

Emma starts laughing, and Colton glares at her. I look between the two of them. Logan, Liam, and Bragden are trying to hide their laughter.

When no one explains what just happened, I walk past everyone and into the kitchen to find Tom. "I'm on a summer internship?"

"What? Oh, yeah. Claire and I thought it was an easier explanation to why you wouldn't be with her at all this summer than you came into your powers and were being chased around by a crazy Gadramick. We didn't know all this would happen, but we thought it would be good for you to stay around and train. It turned out to be a good excuse." I nod, understanding the need for a cover-up. It'll keep Jane safer too.

"So, do you think that I could go to her wedding? It's two weeks from Saturday."

"I don't see why not. You'll have to bring one of the guys for protection though. I'd bring Liam."

"I figured as much. She said I had to bring a date anyway," I pause. "Wait, why Liam?"

"He hasn't told you?" I shake my head. Told me what? "Forget I said anything then."

What is going on? I look at Tom for a few more seconds, but he has returned his attention to the magazine in front of him. I walk back into the living room and plop down onto the couch between Colton and Liam. Turning towards Liam, I ask, "What aren't you telling me?"

"What do you mean?"

"Well, I mentioned that I had to bring a date to the wedding and Tom suggested you. When I asked him why, he said, 'He hasn't told you?'" I pause to gauge his reaction. His face remains expressionless. "So what haven't you told me?" He just looks at me. Then, his eyes move over me and land on Bragden, who nods, agreeing to whatever is silently spoken between them. What is going on?

Liam sighs and looks at me. "I'll explain everything tonight, okay?"

"Tonight? Like you'll visit me in my dream?"

"Yeah, think about the meadow where we met the second time before you go to bed. If I can't meet you there, I'll tell you in the morning." My stubbornness is telling me to argue with him and make him tell me now. I open my mouth to respond, when he says, "I promise."

"You know, I could just read your mind to see what it is." I won't do that, but it's still an option. They don't have to know that. "Why can't you just tell me right now?" I ask again.

"Please be patient, Ryanne." I fold my arms across my chest, frustrated that he won't tell me right now, but I agree.

"Everyone's always keeping something from me," I mumble and turn my attention back to the room. Logan glances over at Colton quickly, before bringing his attention back to the TV.

"What aren't *you* telling me?" I whip around and face Colton.

"What are you talking about?"

"I saw that look Logan just gave you. You're keeping something from me too."

"I'm not keeping anything from you Ryanne. I promise." He seems earnest enough. I can't detect a lie in his words. Logan's watching TV, not paying attention to our conversation; maybe I did jump the gun a little early on that accusation.

"Ok, I trust you, but I'm keeping an eye on you two," I point between Colton and Logan. They are up to something. I reach over Liam and attempt to grab my notebook, but can't reach it. It's not worth the effort of getting up, so I just lean back and face the TV. David and Emma are deciding on a movie to watch. Liam looks at me and laughs before reaching forward and grabbing my notebook and iPod off the table and handing it to me. I smile and thank him.

I put my headphones in and click shuffle. "All You Ever" by Hunter Hayes is the first song to play. The music starts, and I can no longer hear any of the voices around me. Flipping the page over in my notebook, I start sketching. I keep seeing this scene in my mind of a couple walking down an illuminated path in the rain. Standing beneath an umbrella, they are holding hands. A lamp post illuminates the area around them. Trees are located on either side of the trail. Puddles of water are sporadic on the ground. The outline of a city can be seen in the background.

I start swaying to the music as I shade the couple's silhouette. When the song ends, I briefly glance up before bringing my attention back to the notebook. My attention is quickly drawn back the room when I realize that everyone is looking at me.

"What?" I turn toward Liam, hoping that he will tell me why everyone is looking at me.

"You were singing." I feel my eyes widen.

"Like out loud?" I hear a bunch of chuckles. "I'm sorry. I didn't realize," I grab my iPod and turn the volume down, so I can tell next time whether or not I am singing.

"There's your answer, Colton," David says with a slight chuckle.

"Answer to what?"

"I wondered if you knew that you were singing out loud," he glances at me and smiles. My heartbeat increases under his attention. I curse at myself for reacting to just a simple look.

"I knew that I was probably humming, but I didn't think I was actually singing. Was I loud?"

"Not too loud."

"That's helpful," I roll my eyes. "I'll try to keep it down. Watch your movie." I click play and bring my attention back to my drawing, adding more details. I draw a design on the umbrella. Putting my pencil down, I push the notebook back and fully look at the picture.

Colton nudges my side with his elbow. I turn toward him. He's smiling at me again. I glance around the room and find everyone looking at me again.

"Shoot, I was singing again wasn't I?" David and Emma laugh, while everyone else nods. I point at Colton. "This is all your fault. You awoke the beast inside me. I was dormant until you made me play that piano and now all these songs keep spewing out of me."

"You just compared yourself to a volcano."

"To a really small volcano," I pinch my fingers together to show how small I am referring to. "Not like Mt. Vesuvius or anything. You'd all be in trouble if I was like Vesuvius. We'd have a disaster of Pompeii proportions."

Over everyone's laughter, I hear the sound of a gunshot. I look at the TV right as someone gets shot in the head. I jump and turn back to Colton. "You know, I can't unsee that." Another song comes on and I start singing again. I slap my hand over my mouth. "Oh my gosh, I need duct tape."

Colton grabs the hand that is covering my mouth. "No one can understand you if your hand is covering your mouth." He is smiling at me—his green eyes twinkling with amusement. My eyes glance down at his hand holding mine, before I look back up at him.

"I said, oh my gosh, I need duct tape," I repeat. To my delight, his smile widens. At that moment, I feel the familiar pull in my body, demanding my attention. "Catch me," I whisper as my body slumps forward.

CHAPTER
THREE

COLTON

I DON'T THINK I HEARD her right, until her body falls forward onto me. I pull her onto my lap so she doesn't fall off the couch.

"Ugh, she always has to ruin the moment," Emma says. "You know, Colton, a guy doesn't look at a girl like that unless he—"

"Don't finish that sentence, Emma," I tell her.

"I'm just saying. You've been watching her all night. I saw that smile you kept trying to hide." I wonder if Emma is like this to Ryanne, because if she is, I don't know how those two get along so well.

"She's having a vision, isn't she?" Liam asks.

"Well if she's not, we have something to worry about, because people shouldn't just pass out like that all the time," Emma retorts. "At least she was sitting down when it happened this time, and we don't have to worry about her hitting her head or something. I've seen you guys have some close calls when it comes to catching her."

I look down at my lap and cringe. I hate when she goes into her visions. She looks so lifeless. Her head is cocked to the side and her long hair is covering her face. There's always a possibility that she will come out of the vision bleeding or injured. I watch her until I see some movement that proves she is coming back to this time.

It isn't so subtle this time. She jumps up and off of me. "Larkin!" she yells and runs to the back of the house where all the weapons are kept for training. She's rushing around looking for something. Obviously, something is wrong. She comes back into the room carrying a large sword.

"Ryanne, what's going on?"

Instead of answering my question, she calls his name again. "LARKIN!" The desperation is obvious in her voice.

"Ryanne!" Liam yells. She turns and looks at him, but doesn't say anything. I start to walk toward her, when Larkin transports into the room.

"You called?" he smiles at her. I hate when he smiles at her like that—that smug arrogant smile that reveals way more than Ryanne thinks.

"Take me to Jane's," she steps closer to him.

"What?"

She hits him in the chest. "NOW!" He takes a step forward and wraps an arm around her waist, pulling her against his chest, and transports out of the room.

I continue to stare at the spot where she just was until my brain finally registers that she is gone. "What the hell just happened?" I yell as I turn back to the room.

Emma walks over to me. "Based on what just happened, I would assume that she had a vision that something dangerous and possibly life threatening was going to happen to Jane and/or Jane's fiancé, so she called Larkin. As we have seen, Larkin can transport to random locations and said Larkin is probably taking Ryanne to her house to save her guardian on some superhero mission."

"Emma, I think it would be best to not evoke a response out of him at this moment," Liam says while walking up to me and placing a hand on my shoulder. "Calm down, Colton. She'll be fine," he speaks through clenched teeth. I know it's hard on him too when she decides to play hero and not involve anyone in her plans.

"She just carried a sword out of here, Liam. A sword. She's not going skipping through a field of flowers. She's obviously going to fight something, and we've seen how well that has gone in the past!"

"She knows how to fight. She's not surrounded by anyone else. The chance of her risking her life for someone else is drastically reduced," says Logan. "And she has Larkin with her to help."

At the mention of Larkin's name, I feel the need to hit something. Liam and David both reach out to block me when they see the anger in my eyes. I'm reaching my dangerous point right now.

At the feel of their hands on my shoulders, I take a deep breath, but can't calm myself. "The last time she went into a fight with a sword, she got stabbed and I had to heal her!" I yell at no one in particular.

Ryanne is always doing this. She keeps putting herself into situations that end up with her coming back to me broken or on the verge of death. The room gets quiet after my outburst.

"What do you mean *you* healed her?" Emma asks, obviously confused.

I freeze. Throwing my head back, I close my eyes and exhale loudly. That didn't just happen. I didn't just say that. No one is supposed to know about that...not yet anyways. "Damn it." At the silence around the room, I open my eyes and face Logan. "Did I really just say that out loud?"

AS MY FEET HIT THE ground in front of Jane's, I am overcome with a feeling of dizziness and would have collapsed had Larkin not had a hold of me. "It's a little disorienting the first couple of times," he explains.

I don't care how many times it takes to get used to the feeling. There's something I have to do. I turn around and look around the yard for the man. When I see him step out of the trees, I take off toward him. Surprise is going to be my method of attack. Who would expect a 5'3" girl to come running toward them during the middle of the night?

My body collides with his and knocks us both to the ground. I push magic out and straddle him to keep him there. He is momentarily stunned before he starts to struggle out of my grip. I know I won't be able to keep him down for long.

"Ryanne, are you crazy?" Larkin reprimands me as he catches up to us. The man beneath me pushes against my magic and knocks me to the side. He turns around and punches Larkin in the jaw before returning his attention back to me. Larkin falls the ground, unmoving.

You can't count on a guy for anything.

I jump up and run toward him again. A few inches in front of him, I bring my foot up and kick him. I accidentally dropped the sword after the transport, so I need to figure out a way to injure this man enough to stop fighting.

When my foot connects with his chest, he stumbles backwards, but doesn't fall. He runs toward me again and I duck to avoid his outstretched arm. He moves quickly though and brings his other arm out and punches me in the side. I double over and gasp when a sharp pain shoots through my abdomen. I jump back before he is able to get another punch in. Larkin starts moving on the ground. I bring more magic into my limbs and attempt to kick the man. Again, he merely stumbles.

I back up when I see him grab the dagger from his belt. Larkin lifts his head and looks toward me and then to the dagger. He blinks once, and then without saying where he is going, he disappears. Did he really just leave me here? The man lunges for me, dagger pointed out. Attempting to avoid its sharpened blade, I jump to the side. The dagger just grazes my arm. I hiss when I feel the blood start dripping down my skin. He swings his other arm out and hits the same spot on my side, knocking me to the ground.

Larkin blinks back in front of me, sword raised. He stabs the man in the back. Cutting through all muscle and bone, the sword stops its forward movement and sticks out of his chest. Blood splatters onto me, and the man sputters and collapses. Larkin yanks the sword out and blinks away with the man's body. To where, I'm not sure.

A second later, I feel hands wrap around me, and I am transported back to the house.

Landing on my butt in the middle of the living room, I wince at the movement in my stomach. However, when I see Larkin standing over me, I jump up. "Why did you kill him?!" I yell at him.

"That's the thanks I get for saving your little butt?" he steps closer to me.

I reach out and hit him in the chest. "We could have questioned him."

"Ryanne, you're covered in blood!" Liam says.

"Most of it's not mine," I look down at my clothes. "Dang it, this was my favorite shirt." The blood splatters will never come out of my white shorts either. I bring my attention back to Larkin. "I need to know who he was working for, what he planned on doing, and what their next move is. We could have gotten a lot of answers out of him."

"Before or after you got stabbed again?" he steps closer to me again. I have to crane my neck to see his face. "You know who he was working for and you saw what he was going to do, otherwise you wouldn't have called me and asked for help."

"I can handle myself," I cross my arms over my chest and whimper at the pain that shoots through my body again. I know that everything Larkin said is true, but I don't like that Dravin is targeting those that I care about.

"Yeah, it sure looks like that. He punched you twice and probably broke a couple of your ribs." Larkin is getting angry at me. He's clenching his jaw, which I know is causing him pain. He reaches out and grazes the cut on my arm. He shows me his hand that's now covered in my blood. I ignore that.

"How would you know that? I wouldn't have gotten punched if you didn't get yourself knocked out right away. Some help you are!" I poke him in the chest. I know that taking my anger out on him isn't the right thing to do, but I need some outlet.

"Well, if you didn't just run and tackle a man three times your size, I wouldn't have had to jump in like that and wouldn't have gotten punched." He knows that I am just taking my anger out on him. I can tell by the look in his eyes. He is angry at me, but not that angry. He's trying to get a reaction out of me.

"Can they even hear us?" Emma asks.

"How else was I supposed to go about it then? Huh? I surprised him. It was working."

"Straddling a man may have worked in a different situation, but not one with orders to kill." Someone growls at his comment.

I take a step back, so I can see him better and quite frankly, my neck is starting to hurt. I take a deep breath to calm myself. "I'm sorry I yelled at you."

"Do you have a death wish? Because you only get so many close calls, Ryanne," he whispers to me, before turning toward the crowd still standing in the middle of the living room. "She needs healed."

"I'm fine. No need to heal me, Logan," I say, while glancing at Logan. Larkin reaches out and pokes me in the ribs. I hiss and jump back at the pain. "Was that necessary?" I ask him.

"You need healed." I take a step toward him to yell at him again when I feel arms wrap around my waist. I arch my back when my ribs snap back into their correct positions. A small gasp escapes when the brief pain shoots through me at the abrupt movement. There's a slight tickle on the surface of my arm. I glance down right as cut seals together and fades.

"You could have warned me first," I snap at Logan.

"With you, a surprise attack is easier," he smiles at me, which causes some of my anger to melt away. There's no reason for me to take my anger out on him.

"Larkin needs healed too," I smirk at Larkin when his eyes narrow at me.

Logan walks over to Larkin and heals his jaw. Then he turns back to me and asks, "What the heck just happened? Would you like to explain now?"

"Not really. I'm still mad at him," I point at Larkin as I start backing up. "And I want to go get all this dried blood off of me." I turn and start walking away. I glance behind me and see a lot of shocked expressions. "Have Larkin explain it," I yell as I make it to the top of the stairs.

I smile as I step into the bathroom. Their expressions were priceless. Larkin was knocked out for half of it, so that should be interesting. I undress and throw the clothes into the garbage can in the bathroom before turning the water on as hot as it will go. I stay in longer than I usually would have; I want to make sure all the blood, dirt, and sweat is off of me. I turn the water off when it starts to cool. I grab a towel and walk back into the room to find some clothes. Getting my "Dr. Sheldon Cooper for President" shirt and a pair of jean shorts from my drawers, I walk back into the bathroom to change. I scrunch my thick hair with a towel and walk back downstairs.

When I make it to the bottom of the stairs all conversation stops. Larkin is no longer in the room. I sit down on the couch in the spot I was in before I had the vision of the man killing Jane and Ross.

"Go on. Yell at me," I say, looking at everyone.

"You tackled a large man to the ground without a weapon?" Bragden asks incredulously.

"I dropped it when Larkin transported me there. I figured I might as well surprise him. I don't really think before I do stuff," I shrug. Colton scoffs beside me. When I look his way, I instantly tense. He's not looking at me, but I can tell from his tight posture that he's thinking about what happened. He is brooding and staring at the blank television screen. Oh dear. He's mad.

"Okay, so fill us in on what happened while Larkin was briefly out of it," Emma asks, leaning forward, waiting for my response.

"Well after I was knocked off of him, Larkin got punched. The man turned around, and I kicked him. Then he punched me. Then I kicked him again. Then he attempted to stab me, so I ducked. He punched, knocked me to the ground, and attempted to stab me again. Then, Larkin woke up, stabbed him, and splattered blood all over me. The end," I blankly stare at Emma.

She just smiles at my answer. "Short and simple. I like it. But couldn't you have told us what was going on before you disappeared with him? What would you have done if something happened to Larkin and he couldn't bring you back here?"

"I would have gone to Jane and tried to explain why I was covered in someone else's blood and had a couple of broken ribs."

"Can't you take this seriously?" Colton whispers to me.

I turn to face him and see how angry he actually is. I almost flinch away from him. "I am taking this seriously. It happened. I'm fine. There's nothing to worry about it."

"Nothing to worry about?" he angles himself more toward me. "Nothing to worry about!" he yells. This time I do flinch back and scoot more toward Liam. "Do you always have to be the hero? You could have died, and there wouldn't have been anyone there to save you!"

"I'm not trying to be the hero, Colton. I was given these visions for a reason. Me. You weren't given them. I was. I'm supposed to be able to help when it's needed. I saw Jane and Ross get murdered. Are you telling me that I was just supposed to sit here and do nothing? That I was supposed to let her be murdered when she doesn't know anything about this magic stuff!" I start yelling back at him. "I'm not going to stand here and watch more people die because of me!"

I can't experience another situation similar to Claire. I just can't.

"Ryanne," he opens and closes his mouth a couple of times, trying to gather his thoughts. "I understand why you had to go, but couldn't you have told us where you going? We were left here not knowing if we were ever going to see you again," he leans forward and tucks a curl behind my ear. "You may not care about your safety, but some of us do." His hand lingers at my ear for a moment, before he clears his throat and gets up and leaves the room.

My eyes follow him out of the room before I turn toward Liam, "What was that about?" Liam wraps an arm around my shoulder and pulls me toward him, but never answers the question. I scan the room.

No one can look me in the eyes.

CHAPTER
FOUR

I OPEN MY EYES IN the middle of the grassy field. I do love this place …when I'm not being attacked by anything. I sit up and look around, waiting for Liam to appear. I'm a little worried. What could be so important that he can't tell me in front of everyone?

"Ryanne."

I jump and look behind me to find Liam walking across the field in my direction. "When did you get here?" I ask.

"A couple of seconds ago," he says as he sits down on the ground next to me.

"Ok, so what's this big secret you're keeping?" I lean toward him, waiting and preparing myself for the worst. I can't think of anything that he would intentionally keep from me.

He sighs. "It's not necessarily a big secret. I just wasn't sure how you'd respond when you found out, so I thought this would be the best way to tell you." I lay down on my back and wait for him to continue. During his pause, I look up at the clouds. The soft white clouds move ever so slightly with the breeze. This place is so real. I turn my head towards him when he speaks again. "Do you remember when I told you the story about that pendant?"

"About how your mom made it?"

"Yeah, actually let me give you a little history lesson first. In my mage tribe, the Seasnáns, all the men are protectors. I am. Bragden is. When we reach puberty, our mothers will make a pendant for us signifying that we are now old enough and strong enough to begin our training to help and protect others. Each man only gets one, and he has to wear it every day. Every single day."

"What happens if you were to take it off?"

"All my strength will eventually be drained out of me. I'll gradually weaken. It doesn't happen quickly, but it'll happen. The pendant keeps everything connected together. Magic. Strength. Life."

"Oh my gosh, Liam." I grab onto the flame and start to take the pendent off when his hand stops me.

"You have to hear the rest of the story, Ryanne." There's more to the story? I let go of the necklace and give him my attention again. "As I mentioned, every male is given one pendent. It's said that the pendants are meant to be given to the one person that we are supposed to protect. Each man is given one person in life that he's meant to protect in some way. Apparently, you'll find a way to that person. Somehow you'll discover who you are going to protect.

"When you were stabbed in that dream, you would have been stabbed when you returned to your body. I had this feeling that you were the person I was meant to protect, so I gave you the pendant in the hopes that you wouldn't be injured when you returned. Considering you're still here, it must've worked; though, I honestly have no idea why. I'm supposed to protect you, Ryanne. You're the person that my pendant accepts. It's telling me that I have to remain by your side to protect you," he lets out a breathy laugh. "You're not making it easy for me either."

"So, you have to protect me…is that why I'm so comfortable around you?" I can feel tears start to rise in my eyes. For some reason, it really hurts knowing that the pendant is the only reason that Liam is my friend. I thought we shared something special.

"No, no. Ryanne, listen to me. That pendant doesn't affect you in any way. It doesn't affect your emotions or feelings. I'm your friend. That's why you're comfortable around me," he pauses and runs his hand through his hair. "I would have told you sooner if that was the case."

Ok, so the pendant doesn't affect me, but does it affect him? "Liam, what happens to you if I take the pendent off?"

"I'll die," he whispers. I shoot up and face him.

"What? Are you serious?"

"It wouldn't be instantaneous, but like I mentioned earlier, all my strength will be drained and I'll eventually die. I've heard it's very painful when someone refuses protection after the pendant has been given away. The pendants basically choose who they think are worthy of protection and mine chose you. I need to be able to protect you, Ryanne. I need you to trust me."

"This doesn't make you like my…" I stumble through my words.

"It doesn't mean that we are destined to be together, if that's what you're asking. I'm just meant to protect you at this point in your life. Because of the pendant, I can usually tell where you are. Sometimes I'll get this weird feeling if you need help or comforting," he explains. "Being around you gives me strength, which I'll need to protect you with. That means no more hero stunts, ok? I'm not sure any of us can take it anymore. You've scared us a lot recently."

"I'm not trying to, Liam. Danger just follows me around. I don't ask for it to come to me."

"I know. I know. Just next time you feel the need to go save someone, invite me, ok? I can help you. It's physically draining knowing that I'm supposed to help you, and you won't let me."

"If you told me earlier, I would have brought you. You're less annoying than Larkin." He chuckles at my comment. I watch him. I know that sounds weird, but it doesn't happen all too often with Liam. It's nice to see him smile and it actually reach his eyes. It's a good look for him. "I'll try to include you in my near-death experiences from now on."

"That's all I'm asking for. Now go get some sleep."

I WAKE UP THE NEXT morning, and Emma is already in the shower. Since I took a shower last night, I just grab my "Team Weasley" Harry Potter t-shirt and a pair of shorts and get dressed. Once I'm fully clothed, I knock on the bathroom door. Emma stops singing a Lady Gaga song.

"Yeah?"

"I'm coming in to brush my teeth. I'll make it quick!" I say as I open the door. Grabbing a washcloth off the counter, I wipe off the mirror. Because of Emma's shower, it's covered in steam. I gasp when I see my reflection. My hair is sticking up in every direction. I brush my teeth before I bother trying to fix my hair.

The water in the shower turns off, and Emma walks out with a towel wrapped around her body. She moves past me and heads into the room to get dressed, while I work on my hair. Ten minutes later and with no improvement, I give up. "Do you want to switch hair with me for a day?" I ask Emma.

"Of course," she laughs when she sees my expression. "Hmm, your hair is a little thicker today than it usually is." She grabs a couple of bobby pins and gets to work on my hair. She braids my bangs back and pins them down behind my ears. When she reaches for her straightener, I decide that I've had enough and run out of the room, before she turns back around. "Oh come on Ryanne, let me straighten your hair!" she calls after me as I run down the stairs and into the kitchen.

"What's up, buttercup?" Logan says with a smile at the same time that Emma runs into the room.

"You are such a spoil sport. First you refuse to dress somewhat girly, wearing all those nerd shirts with the weird sayings on them," she points to my Harry Potter shirt. "And now you won't let me do your hair or make-up." She puts her hands on her hips. "I don't know what to do with you." I walk around the table and sit down in the seat between Bragden and Liam.

"There's nothing wrong with how I dress, and what's the point in doing your hair and make-up when we always end up training and getting all sweaty and gross?" I pull my legs up onto the chair and wrap my arms around them. "And it's not like I'm trying to impress anyone. I don't really care about my appearance, Emma. Sorry to disappoint ya." My smirk turns into a full smile when I hear the guys laughing around me.

Emma turns toward David. "Do you see what I have to put up with on a daily basis?"

"Oh, I'm not that bad. No one has run screaming from me because I look *that* bad…yet."

"They haven't seen you when you first wake up," she looks around the table. "Her hair is literally this big," she tells them and puts her hands up to her head to show the size.

"I do not have an afro in the morning."

"Ok," she relents, "but it's still crazy."

"I'll give you that."

Tom comes into the room and grabs an apple off the counter. "Who all is going today?" David, Emma, Colton, and Liam all raise their hands.

"Going where?" I ask. They all made plans, but no one told me about them?

Tom looks over at Emma. "You didn't tell her?"

"Psh, if I told her earlier she would have locked herself in our room and pulled a bunch of magic around her so no one could touch her. So, no. I didn't tell her."

"What's going on?" I ask Liam. "Why would I have done that?"

"We're going shopping today," Emma replies. When I groan, she continues. "Well, you've destroyed like all of your clothes already, so you have to come with us. If you don't, I'll steal every article of clothing you have left while you're in the shower and hide them randomly throughout the house."

"I could just read your mind and find where you hid everything."

"I'll take all your bras and hide them in the guys' rooms." She crosses her arms over her chest and stares at me from across the table. The guys kept glancing between the two of us, waiting to see what will happen next.

She's challenging me? Shaking my head, I lean toward Liam. "She does realize who she's talking to, right?" David stands up and takes a couple steps away from Emma, knowing that I have something up my sleeve.

"Don't you dare, Ryanne!" I call my magic to me and concentrate on visualizing what I want to happen. I close my eyes and wait for her reaction—her scream when my magic hits her. When I hear her gasp, I open my eyes and smile. There is a small rain cloud directly above Emma, pouring water onto her. She is soaking wet and gaping at me in shock. Her blonde hair is plastered to her face, and her clothing sticks to her body. Everyone around the table starts laughing. Spitting water out of her mouth, she turns and glares at David. I call wind to me and blow it on Emma like a giant blow dryer. When I finish, her hair is a mess, but she is dry again.

"Now who has big hair?"

"Well played, but you're still going with us."

When the laughter dies down a little, I say, "Do you remember what happened the last time I was surrounded by a lot of strangers? I collapsed under the pressure. I can't block that many thoughts. It's too hard."

"That's why you'll focus on Colton the whole time. You can't read his thoughts, right?" Emma asks.

"No, but I'll still be able to hear everyone else." They'll be muted, but I'll still be able to hear them.

"You know what I'll buy for you if I have to go by myself."

I groan at the idea of Emma shopping for me. She'll buy every pink and frilly article of clothing out there as payback for what I just did. I can't let that happen. "Fine, but if I pass out, it's on you," I warn her.

"Yeah, yeah. Blame Emma. It's all her fault. No big deal. Now I have to go fix my hair," she mumbles as she turns around and leaves the room.

"Who's Weasley? And why are you on his team?" Bragden asks me.

I turn toward him, mouth hanging open, surprised at his question. Liam and Colton laugh at my reaction. "Who's Weasley?" I repeat his question.

He nods, so I turn toward Liam incredulously. "He doesn't know who Ron Weasley is?" Still laughing, he shakes his head. I turn back to Bragden, who is clearly confused at my reaction. "Muggle," I mumble to him, which causes the guys to laugh again. I definitely need to remedy his lack of Harry Potter knowledge and soon. What kind of mage doesn't know about the wizarding world of Harry Potter? I mean come on. We're the closest thing there is in real life to wizards.

Emma walks back into the room, hair fixed and purse in hand. "Ok, I'm ready. Let's go," she announces and then leaves again, heading outside. David gets up and follows her out. Liam and Colton push their chairs back from the table and stand, looking down at me. I just smile up at them and remain seated. I'm not going without a fight. Bragden and Logan laugh beside me, amused at how I'm acting.

"You're really going to make us force you to come?" Colton asks. I keep my eyes glued to the wall on the opposite side of their room and avoid their gazes. Liam just stands in the doorway, shaking his head at me. Seeing movement out of the corner of my eye, I put on the most innocent expression that I can muster. Colton walks toward me, so I move behind Bragden. When he gets closer, I push a shield of magic out, separating the two of us. Colton's smile widens as he looks over my shoulder. I turn to see what he is looking at when I feel an arm wrap around my waist and pull me toward the door.

"Shoot. That's not fair," I say as Liam pulls me out of the room. "Guys, I hate shopping." My voice comes out whiney, but I don't care. "Liam, let me go," I demand as he pulls me closer to the front door.

They're laughing at my feeble attempt to get away. When we make it out of the front door, I stop struggling, and Liam unwraps his arm from my waist. He shouldn't trust that I'll just listen to them. I walk a couple more steps before I turn around and try to run back into the house. I make it past Liam before Colton is able to stop me.

"I don't think so," he whispers to me as he guides me toward the vehicle.

"It was worth a try," I mumble as I get into the car. David is sitting in the driver's seat, waiting for everyone to get in. I follow Liam into the car and sit between him and Colton. When Colton closes the door, David starts the car, and we're off.

CHAPTER
FIVE

COLTON

SITTING IN A PARKING SPOT at the mall, I watch Ryanne as she tries to push as many thoughts as possible back into that 'mental box' of hers.

David turns around and looks at Liam and me. "I can't believe she tried to make a run for it. I've never met a girl who didn't like to shop before."

"She's not like most girls, David."

Emma unbuckles and turns around in her seat. "Wait 'til she finds out I'm taking her to Victoria's Secret," she says with an evil grin. "Teach her to use her magic on me," she scoffs and looks down at her.

Ryanne sits up. "I'm as good as I'm going to get. Let's get this over with." Emma jumps up and opens her car door. I get out and help Ryanne step out of the car. She grimaces at the mall. I laugh as we start walking toward the door. Liam grabs her wrist and pulls her along.

Standing just inside the doorway of the first store, Ryanne stumbles back into Liam. He steadies her as she closes her eyes, taking deep breaths. David and Liam both look concerned. We knew it would be difficult to be in such a public place like this, but I don't think any of us realized how difficult it would be for her. She slowly opens her eyes, "I'm good."

"Are you sure?" Liam looks down at her.

She arches her neck and looks up at him and says, "No, but I'm not going to get any better, so let's make this quick." Emma turns around and starts walking away. David takes one last look at Ryanne before following her. Liam keeps a hold of her wrist and slowly starts to walk. I stand slightly behind her just in case she is to fall.

After taking a couple of steps, she picks up her speed. She doesn't seem to be hurting anymore, so I'm assuming the voices aren't too loud. Emma stops and waits for the rest of us to catch up. "Where to first?" she asks. Ryanne just crosses her arms and scans the mall. A small smile forms on her face, so I look in that direction and watch an elderly couple walking hand in hand into the small bookstore. When Emma realizes that Ryanne isn't paying attention, she grabs her arm and starts pulling her toward a store. Ryanne turns around, sighs loudly, and lets Emma drag her.

An hour later, David, Liam, and I are standing outside a store, waiting while the girls shop. "She doesn't seem to be hurting too much," David says. "She obviously doesn't like to be here, but she's not complaining anymore."

"She's been blushing the whole time we've been here. She's definitely not enjoying herself." At that, Emma walks out carrying a bag, still dragging Ryanne behind her.

"She is the worst person to shop with. She won't look at anything."

"Everything in there was pink. Do I look like I wear pink?" She crosses her arms and then looks behind her, her blush darkening. I look past her and see a group of guys staring in our direction. Anger pulsates through me. They must have seen it on my face because they start walking away.

I move so I am standing behind her and scoot her between Liam and I. "Focus on me, Ryanne. Ignore everyone else."

She looks up toward me and I see the weariness in her expression. "I've been trying, but it feels like everyone is screaming at me." She closes her eyes and another look of concentration mars her pretty face.

I look up toward David and Emma, "We need to hurry up."

"Well, if she wouldn't make this so difficult, we could leave a lot quicker." Ryanne opens her eyes, and Emma starts pulling her toward another store. I laugh when I see the store Emma is walking toward. Ryanne looks up and stops dead in her tracks and starts shaking her head.

"Oh no. I don't think so." She starts to turn around, but Emma continues walking. Emma leans forward and puts all her weight into pulling Ryanne along. We stop and stand out of the way of the traffic and watch as Ryanne struggles against the determined Emma.

"I don't see this going well," Liam says with a laugh as Ryanne and Emma disappear into the store.

"Nope, not at all." A couple minutes later, Ryanne storms out of the store and grabs my arm, pulling me in the opposite direction, mumbling something about a stubborn girl and stupid pink stuff. I look behind me and see David and Liam laughing at me. I face forward right as Ryanne pulls me into Hot Topic.

She lets go of my arm and grabs a couple of random t-shirts. It looks like a couple Harry Potter, the Big Bang Theory, Mario Kart, and some comic book characters are in her stack of shirts. She walks over to me and hands them to me. "Here, can we go now?" A sales attendant who heard her, motions for us to follow him. I'm paying for the shirts when Emma walks into the store carrying a pink striped bag.

With an exaggerated groan, she says, "More t-shirts? For goodness sakes girl."

"I told you I wasn't going to wear anything pink and that I have no reason to dress up, so yes. More t-shirts." She sticks her tongue out at Emma. The man checking us out laughs at Ryanne's response to her and gives me *that* look. I smile at him and grab the bag with Ryanne's clothes. These girls are crazy, but there's nothing we would change about them. With the Hot Topic bag in one hand and Ryanne's fingers interlocked between mine in the other, we walk out of the store.

Emma turns to Ryanne. "Since I knew your size, I took the liberty of picking out some things for you. You're just going to have to deal with what I bought you from Victoria's Secret, since you refused to pick anything out yourself. Don't worry, there's nothing *pink*," Emma emphasizes the word pink. Then, she rolls her eyes and runs up to walk beside David. Ryanne continues walking, but glares at the back of Emma's head the rest of the time.

STANDING INSIDE DICK'S SPORTING GOODS, David, Liam, and Colton are looking for some clothes while Emma and I look for some extra work-out outfits. They remain close enough that they can keep an eye on us. "Colton's going to have a permanent scowl on his face if he keeps that up."

"Why is he scowling?" I glance across the store and do see that he has an upset expression on his face. Emma rolls her eyes for the millionth time today and ignores my question.

"Are you done?" She looks down at the clothes in my hand. I didn't look for much, but I nod anyway. I just want to leave the mall and go back to the house. David and Colton stop talking the closer we get to them.

They're hot. I wonder if they're with those guys. I look around for who's thinking that and find a sales attendant watching us.

"You guys done?" David asks us as Emma walks over to him, and he wraps an arm around her. *One down. That leaves the small one. A little on the short side but curvy. I can deal with that.* I cough in an attempt to hide my embarrassment. I can feel a blush rising again with each step he takes closer to us. Colton looks at me strangely as I look around for something to become suddenly interested in.

"Can I help you guys find anything?" the sales attendant asks when he stops in front of us. He looks around at all the guys, but stops at me. *Looks better up close. Hello.* I stare at the ground, waiting for him to leave.

Colton looks between me and the guy, before stepping forward and placing an arm around my shoulder and pulling me closer to him. "We're fine. Thanks." His words are polite, but his tone isn't. I watch his thoughts play out as realization hits him. *I knew she'd be taken. Time to go.*

"Well, if you need anything, don't be afraid to ask." He walks away, but keeps glancing over his shoulder at us. Colton doesn't move his arm until the guy is out of his sight.

"Can we leave soon? Please? I'm tired of hearing all these guys' thoughts and all the girls thinking I'm a lesbian because I'm surrounded by hot guys." They all laugh at the comment, but agree that it's time to leave.

As we're heading out, David spots a music store and asks if I'm ok to go in. One last stop is fine. Colton and Liam walk over to the rock section to flip through the CD's while David and Emma walk over to the movies. I walk to the back to look at the posters. I flip through a couple of boy bands, before I stop and look at a poster of the Beatles. I'm looking at that poster when I hear his thoughts again. *Ahh, there she is.*

I turn around and see the man entering the store. He's been following us all day. I'm sure it's him. Every time I turned around, I found him close by, appearing busy. When the image of him removing my clothes pops up in my mind, I gasp, turn around, and walk up to Colton. "Put your arm around me," I demand.

He listens without questioning me. He steps up behind me, creating a cage around me and the aisle of CDs in front of me. I pretend to be interested in the music selection in front of me. He continues to flip through the CDs, before he leans over and whispers in my ear. His breath against my skin gives me goose bumps.

"Not that I'm complaining, but what's this about?" When I see an image of myself lying in the man's bed, I turn around and bury my face in Colton's shoulder. His arm tightens around my waist, and I hear him tell Liam, "I think it's time to go. Go get David and Emma." He starts walking toward the exit, not releasing me from his hold. We get to the car and wait for the others to show up. I collapse in the seat, relieved that some of the weight from the thoughts is gone.

Emma closes her door, and David starts the car and pulls out before anyone questions me. "So what was that about, Ryanne?" She asks me. I lift my head from my lap and look at her.

"There was a man in there that kept following us. I'd spotted him a couple times today. His thoughts were…well let's just say they weren't PG rated, and it was starting to creep me out." Leaning forward again, I drop my head back onto my lap. My head is pounding. That was too much. There were too many people around…too many thoughts infiltrated my mind at once. It was too hard to control. I handled it pretty well all things considered, but my body is starting to react to my efforts. I close my eyes and try to tune out all the sounds around me.

I must have fallen asleep, because when I open my eyes again, I see the high beams of the ceiling in the living room.

"No, I already checked. She's fine. Her body is just tired from blocking everyone's thoughts all day. It takes a lot of energy to push all those thoughts into the back of her mind, so she can't hear them anymore," Logan says. I sit up and look around. Everyone is sitting in the kitchen.

I walk into the room and sit down beside Liam. "I told you I didn't like shopping," I say when everyone stares at me. Emma and David laugh at my response, but Liam and Colton don't react at all.

Logan walks over to me, places a hand on my shoulder, and closes his eyes. I can tell that he is checking to make sure that I am not experiencing any other side effects. "I'm fine, Logan." He heals my headache; a headache I wasn't aware I had until it was gone.

When he removes his hands, he looks angry. "That...that..." I know he saw what that man was thinking about me.

"Logan, don't. Please." Colton and Liam look at Logan, wanting to ask what is going on. I shake my head and silently plead with him. I know that if the guys find out what that man was thinking, they will overreact.

"Why didn't you say anything earlier?" he asks me. I glance around the room and see everyone watching us.

"Logan, please stop."

"You of all people know that some people will act on their thoughts, especially thoughts like that." Colton's jaw tightens. He starts clenching and unclenching his fists.

"Look, why don't we go and train?" I look over at Liam and smile, silently thanking him for the subject change. He winks at me. Colton jumps up from the table and leaves the room before anyone can say anything.

"Training sounds like a great idea," says David.

CHAPTER
SIX

COLTON

I GRAB A SWORD AND walk to the backyard. I am hoping that Bragden will spar with me today. I need to release some of this anger, and I know that he will fight me back. Sitting on the hardened grass, I try not to let my mind wander too much. I need to remain focused. I am stretching out my muscles when everyone walks out of the house. Since I'm alone, I don't have to suppress the groan that comes out when I see Ryanne smiling up at Liam, laughing at something he said. Her work-out outfits are way too tight for my liking. The fact that everyone can see her dressed like that...I want to push her behind my back and yell at anyone who tries to look at her.

Everyone walks over to where I am sitting and creates a circle, stretching. Ryanne is the most flexible one out of all of us. She sits down and reaches for her foot, resting her head on her knee. She then does the same on the other leg. She moves back a little and does the splits before moving forward, basically laying flat on the ground, stretching her legs and back.

"That's disturbing. No one should be able to do that," David says while attempting a similar move. David has trouble sitting Indian style, so stretching is almost comical with him.

She looks up and smiles at him. "You're just jealous." When she sees him, she starts laughing. "You really should try yoga, man." Her laugh is infectious. I can't help but smile with her. I look over and see Emma watching me. She smirks but doesn't say anything. I know that she'll try to start meddling, but I'm not ready to tell Ryanne yet. I'll have to talk with Emma later. She's not known for keeping secrets, and her sharing a room with Ryanne isn't going to make it any easier.

Her smile widens when I narrow my eyes at her. Ryanne glances between the two of us, wondering what is going on. Crap. She'll definitely ask about that later. She turns toward Liam and asks him to spar with her. He nods, and they walk to the opposite end of the yard. She doesn't spar with Emma anymore because they are too evenly matched. None of the opponents she's been up against so far have been similar to her size. I lean toward Emma when Ryanne is out of earshot. "Don't say anything to her."

"Why not? Come on, Colton. You know everything will be so much easier when you tell her."

"I'm not ready to tell her yet, and I know that she's not ready to hear it. Please don't say anything. Don't drop any hints and stop looking at me like that. She knows that something is going on. She already thinks I'm keeping things from her."

"Because you *are* keeping something from her. You're just lucky that she can't read your mind. If she reads it from my mind, it's not my fault," she gets up and walks over to David.

I look toward Bragden, and he nods at me, understanding my need to spar with someone who will fight back just as hard. We start sparring like normal. After the first couple of punches and kicks are thrown, we start to pick up the speed and intensity of the moves. Neither one of us can infuse magic into our hits like Ryanne can, but they still hurt. When she hits you, it hurts like hell. I'd been on the receiving end of some of the hits and they leave a nasty bruise if Logan doesn't heal them.

I glance over at Ryanne and see her sparring with Liam. He got a punch in on her shoulder, but she retaliated with a kick that knocked him to the ground. I would have laughed at that if Bragden didn't punch me in the gut. "You need to pay attention. She's fine. Liam's not going to hurt her."

"I know. I know." I duck one of his kicks. "It just bothers me that she always," I punch him in the shoulder and bring up my arm to block his arm, "takes everything so lightly. She doesn't care that she," I jump back, "is always putting herself in more danger than necessary." Bragden stops sparring with me and glances over at Ryanne.

"You know why she does it." I watch as they stop sparring, and Liam says something to her. She is breathing heavily but nods. When she turns her concentration towards the trees, a bunch of dead branches start coming toward her, and she creates a large pile in the center of the grass. I notice that David, Logan, and Emma have stopped what they are doing and are now watching to see what she is going to do as well. When the pile is big enough, she turns and looks at him, waiting for further instructions. He says something and points toward the house. She starts backing up. Liam takes a couple of steps to the side and nods at her.

"I WANT TO TRY SOMETHING new with you," Liam says after he stopped sparring with me.

"Ok, what is it?" I ask a little skeptically, while trying to calm my frantic breathing.

"I want to see if you are able to call magic to you while you are sparring. Not just into your limbs. Can you create a large pile of wood for me?" I nod and turn my attention to the forest in front of me. I close my eyes and push my magic out, picturing dead branches of wood creating a large pile in front of me.

"Now what?"

"Ok, now I want you to go stand near the house and get a running start. Halfway there, I want you to do some of those flip things that you can do."

I giggle at his expression. "Flip things?"

"You know what I mean. While you are flipping, I want to see if you can call magic to you and strike lightning into that pile of wood when you stop."

"Is that all?" He glares at me. "Ok. Flip. Concentrate. Strike. Got it."

I start to back up, getting closer to the house. I take a couple of deep breaths and concentrate on creating lightning. Liam takes a few steps back and nods at me. With one more intake of air, I start to run forward. After a couple of steps, I do a double full twist while visualizing lightning striking the wood. Flipping on grass is more difficult than doing it in a gym, since the ground is uneven and not spring loaded. I stop flipping halfway to the woodpile and push out the magic. I've only ever put a shield around myself before, but seeing the amount of magic going toward the wood, I use the last of my energy to create a large enough shield to protect everyone in the yard.

COLTON

I TURN TOWARD BRAGDEN AND ask, "What is she doing?"

"I'm sure we are about to find out." Running toward the wood, Ryanne jumps into the air and flips before twisting her body a couple of times. When she lands back on the ground, she turns around and doubles over. The large pile explodes; wood catapults in all directions. Bragden and I fall to the ground to avoid being hit when the wood seems to hit an invisible barrier. Bragden looks over at me confused. Shrugging because I have no idea what actually happened either. I look across the yard at Ryanne and see her standing there with her eyes closed, her face furrowed in concentration.

When all the pieces of wood stop raining down, Ryanne collapses. Bragden and I jump up and run toward her. Liam beats us to it since he is closer. Before Liam gets to her, she starts to move.

He helps her sit up. "Are you ok?"

She smiles up at Liam. Bragden and I make it over to her, right as she says, "It worked."

"What was that?" David asks when they reach her.

Logan pushes through everyone. "Are you hurt?"

She looks around at all of us, looking for something. "None of you got hit with any flying pieces of wood?" We all shake our heads. Liam removes his hand from her back. Pushing off the ground, she attempts to get up.

Logan stops her. "Maybe you should stay seated for a little bit." She brushes him off. Liam stands up and reaches a hand down to help her up. She takes it and sways as she stands.

"I didn't think that would work. I've never created a shield that big before. I didn't think I made it big enough to cover everyone." Her smile gets wider. A shield? She created a shield?

"You created a shield?" I ask.

"Is that why the wood just stopped moving toward us?" Emma asks with wide eyes.

"Yeah, I just pushed a lot of magic out right after the lightning. I pictured this wall between us and the wood. I did it once while I was in the dream world with Liam. I didn't know if it would work here, but I tried it anyway. I didn't want anyone getting hurt because of me."

"I'll admit, when I first thought of that, I thought it would take a couple of tries for it to work. I'm really impressed that you were able to do that on the first try," Liam says and then turns to everyone else. "I didn't tell her anything about a shield. I didn't know she could do that." I look toward Ryanne and notice her swaying. I take a couple of steps toward her.

"Ryanne, are you ok?" I touch her arm, trying to get her to look at me, but she is staring at the ground, blinking rapidly.

"I'm a little dizzy," she says right as her legs give out, and she collapses again. I reach out at the last second and catch her before she hits her head on the ground.

"Logan, can you tell me if she's in a vision or not?" I ask him.

"I'm not sure if I'll know if she's in a vision or not, but I can see if anything else is wrong with her." He crouches down next to us and puts his hands on both sides of her face and closes his eyes.

He shakes his head before he opens his eyes. "She's not in a vision." He looks down at her. "She just used too much magic. She would have been fine if she didn't put up such a large shield to protect us. Her body just couldn't handle pushing that much magic out yet." I look down at her and see her eyes are closed and mouth slightly open. I pick her up, cradling her against my chest.

"I think she's done training for now. I'll go put her in her bed." Tom is sitting in the kitchen when I walk in carrying Ryanne. He stands up when he sees her in my arms.

"What happened?"

"Logan or Liam will be able to explain when they finish cleaning up outside. I'm going to put her in her bed. I'll be back."

I walk past Tom and walk up the stairs. Entering Ryanne's room, I walk over to her bed, the one closest to the window, and carefully put Ryanne down on it. I take off her shoes and socks before pulling the comforter over her. Her head rolls to the side. I lean forward and place a small kiss on her forehead. One of these days, I'll get to do that when she is actually conscious and aware of me doing it.

One day, I hope.

Entering the kitchen, I find everyone sitting around the table. "So she passed out because she used too much magic?"

"Tom, do you think that if we continue working with her magic, she'll build up a resistance to it? So she can use it and not worry about passing out?" I ask after sitting down.

"I think that that's something that we should look into. She's pretty powerful, if she was able to strike a large pile of wood and then create a shield large enough to cover the whole yard..." he trails off. Tom has a small smile on his face. "She's pretty incredible, isn't she?"

Emma looks at me and grins evilly. I roll my head back and look at ceiling, waiting for her remark. "Colton sure thinks so." I groan. I reach over and lightly shove her out of her chair. She's pretty light for a tall girl. I can't help but laugh when I see her expression. She is completely shocked—eyes wide, mouth hanging open as she sits on the ground. Apparently everyone else finds it as funny as I do because there is a chorus of laughter throughout the room. Seeing her pointed glare, David reaches down to help her stand up.

Back on her feet, she points and me and says, "If I was Ryanne, you'd be soaking wet right now." Emma sits back down in her chair and crosses her arms. Though her posture is angry, I can see the smirk she is trying to hide.

"Liam, what did you tell her to do exactly?" Tom asks.

"I was just curious to see if she could concentrate enough to bring out any weather elements while doing something else. So I asked if she could do some of her flips and strike the wood with a lightning bolt. I figured that it might be beneficial in the future."

Tom nodded, "Yeah, it could be very useful. We know how she is. It was a very good idea."

"What was a good idea?" We all turn around and see Ryanne standing in the doorway, waiting for our response.

CHAPTER
SEVEN

"WHY ARE YOU AWAKE?" LOGAN asks. "You passed out. Your body needs to recuperate."

I shake him off. "I feel fine. Good as new." Everyone continues to stare at me. "What?" You'd think that I had grown a second head. I walk to Liam's chair and rest my arms across the top of the wooden back. Colton is directly across from Liam and watching my every move.

"Did you forget the part where you passed out because you used too much magic?" Colton pauses and points toward Logan. "You had to give Logan some of your magic when he used too much. How are you awake right now?"

"I don't know. I just woke up, and now I feel fine." They should know that my magic does some crazy things. I can't explain everything that happens to me. When they continue to watch me, I walk out of the kitchen and grab my notebook and iPod off of the coffee table in the living room. A vibrating sensation spreads through my limbs when I come into contact with the notebook. That's odd. Still feeling everyone's eyes on me, I shake off the feeling and return to the kitchen.

Tom pushes himself away from the table. "Here have my seat. I have to go do something anyway." He walks past me and out of the room. I slowly walk around and sit where he was. I put my notebook on the table and scoot the chair closer to the table. Clicking shuffle on my iPod, I pick up my pencil and start to draw. I have to draw this door. I don't know why. I had a dream about this doorway. Wide at the base, the top of the doorway meets at a point. Arabesque like designs are carved into its old wood exterior. A large black handle hangs low on the left.

I bite my lip to keep from singing along with the Katy Perry song. I can feel everyone's eyes on me as I draw, but for some reason, I can't stop. I need to draw this door. My pencil glides across the page creating intricate swirls and star like designs on the door. I add the last detail and sit back a little, looking at the drawing, when I feel someone tap my arm. I look up and see Colton watching me. I take my headphones out and face him, waiting for his question. "Yeah?"

"Why did you draw that?" His eyes flicker down to the door before meeting mine again.

"I don't know. I think I just had a dream about it earlier, so I..." I inhale and grab my stomach as an intense pain shoots through it. I lean forward and rest my head on the table, arms folded across my stomach. The pain is unbearable. I am on the verge of hyperventilating, when I feel myself start to fall.

COLTON

I WATCH AS RYANNE DOUBLES over, groaning in pain, and grabs her stomach. I look over at Logan and see him already walking toward her, preparing to heal her. What is going on? Her breathing increases. It seems like she can't get any air into her lungs. "What's wrong with her?" I ask Logan.

"I don't know," he replies honestly while placing a hand on her shoulder and closing his eyes. When his hand connects with her shoulder, she disappears. Logan stumbles forward when his hand is no longer resting on anything. Her chair scraps against the floor as Logan falls into it. "Where did she go?" I jump up from my seat at the same time as everyone else does. We're all staring at the empty chair she was just in.

"What happened to her?" I yell. "Where is she?"

Tom comes running into the room. "What's going on? Why are you yelling?"

"Ryanne disappeared…again. Only this time, she didn't have any help. She just disappeared," David says. "Poof."

"She promised me she wouldn't do anything irrational anymore," Liam says while pacing.

Emma is still staring at the chair that Ryanne was sitting in. "I don't think she meant to do anything this time. It's not like she yelled for Larkin or anything. The pain she was experiencing was real; you could see it on her face. I'd bet it had something to do with that," Emma says while pointing to the doorway she had drawn on the notebook page. I pick up the notebook and look at the doorway, but it doesn't look familiar to me.

"Why does it always have to be her? Last time we at least knew where she was going, this time…" I shake my head. I can't believe that she is gone, and we have no way of helping her or even finding her. What if something happens to her? I look toward Liam and see him leaning against the wall, eyes closed. He opens his eyes and hits the wall behind him, mumbling something. "Are you getting anything from her?"

"No. Nothing. She's not sleeping, so I can't try and go into her dream to see where she is. I'm not picking up anything from the pendant. I have no idea where she could be."

MY SCREAM IS SILENCED AS I land on a hard, dusty floor. Standing up quickly, I dust my clothing off and look around, assessing my surroundings. "Where am I?"

I'm standing in the middle of a dark and dreary hallway. Cement brick walls are the only thing I can see. Candles line the walls, casting shadows down the entire length of the corridor. The low hanging ceiling would have made any taller person feel claustrophobic. Squinting, I look down the hallway to the right. I can see a small door a ways in the distance. I feel a pull toward it. Similar to the pull I felt when searching for the library with David, I know that I am supposed to see what is on the opposite side of that door. My footsteps echo down the desolate hallway as I let my feet guide me in the direction of the mysterious door.

When the door is less than a foot away, I stop. This is the doorway that I'd just drawn in my notebook. I close the distance when I hear yelling echoing from the opposite side.

"She's not dead, is she?" a deep voice demands.

"Of course, she's dead. You saw the house blow up." I recognize that voice as Larkin's.

"I know she's not dead. No one else would have been able to get to Heratz." *Whack.* It sounds like someone got punched. "Are you helping her?" he yells. Dravin? Is that Dravin yelling at Larkin?

"No, I'd never go against you," Larkin says. His voice wavers a little at the end with fear. Larkin needs help.

"You're lying to me. Tell me where she is or you'll no longer be of any use for me."

"I don't know where she is." I look around for anything that I can use as a weapon and find…nothing. I guess my magic is going to have to work for now.

"Fine, then you leave me no choice…" Pushing some magic into my leg, I kick the door open, startling both guys. Dravin is standing over Larkin, who is hunched over on the ground, blood dripping from his nose.

I smile up at Dravin trying to fake confidence. "Looking for me?" I call my energy to me and thrust it toward him. I can't call enough in that short time though. He staggers back a little, but doesn't fall. Why does that never happen when I need it to? I run in front of Larkin, who is obviously injured.

Dravin charges toward me, fist raised, preparing to strike. I throw a shield up around Larkin and me. Dravin runs directly into my shield and bounces off. He growls in frustration before charging at it again—this time more forcefully. I feel it start to weaken with each of his attempts. I guess Logan and Colton are right; I do need more rest. I glance down at Larkin, who is trying to stand up, and ask, "Are you able to blink us out of here?"

"Give me a minute. It's harder to move two people and because I'm in pain, it's going to take more concentration," he breathily tells me.

Dravin charges into my shield. It weakens a little more. Two or three more attempts and he'll break through it. "I can't hold this up for much longer. He's too strong for me right now."

I can hear the fear in my voice as Dravin runs into my shield again. Larkin stands up, walks over to me, and wraps an arm around my waist. We are still in the room, and Dravin is still trying to break down my shield. I look up at him, while keeping my concentration, and see his eyes closed, grimacing while he tries to transport us. Dravin runs into the shield again. This time instead of bouncing off, he just stops. An evil grin slowly forms on his face, while he backs up further. Creating a sizable distance between him and the shield, he pauses for a second before running full speed toward it again. I scream and close my eyes, because I know this is it. I feel him break through my magical defense and head toward us.

My scream is cut short as my back slams into something hard and the wind is knocked out of my lungs. I cover my face as glass starts to fall around me. I'm back in the living room? I'm lying in the middle of the living room and the coffee table is turned on its side from me falling onto it. Glass shards are scattered all over the floor. I look over and find Larkin lying beside me, unmoving.

CHAPTER
EIGHT

COLTON

"SO WHAT ARE WE SUPPOSED to do?" Bragden asks. I am on the verge of panicking and can't sit still. During times like this, I pace. Walking back and forth gives me something to do so I'm not sitting...thinking the entire time. It's been twenty minutes, and Ryanne is still missing. How long will this go on? Where is that freaking door, and what does it lead to?

Tom walks over to me and places his hand on my shoulder. "There's nothing we can do. We just have to wait." Anger pulses through me. Wait? We just have to wait? I want to yell at someone, because no one seems to understand. I open my mouth to do so when a loud crash resonates from the living room. Everyone jumps up and prepares for an attack. I turn to see Ryanne rolling off the coffee table, knocking it on its side. She covers her face with her bare arms when glass starts to rain down from the impact. Larkin rolls into the entertainment center to her right. *Of course* she was with him.

"Ryanne?" Emma yells as I brush past her into the living room. She struggles to get up and starts crawling toward Larkin. She calls for Logan; her voice barely audible. Logan drops to his knees beside her, but Ryanne shakes her head and points toward Larkin, silently asking him to heal him first. Why is she so worried about him when she's bleeding profusely from her arms? She's not concerned about her safety at all.

Don't yell at her, Colton.

Don't do it.

"Where the heck did you go?" I demand.

Technically, I didn't yell.

She doesn't respond to my question; her eyes are still glued to Larkin as Logan heals him. Larkin stops cringing in pain, sits up, and looks across the room at Ryanne. Before Logan is done healing him, he moves toward her. I want to push Ryanne behind me and not let Larkin get any closer to her. It's because of him that she got hurt again. Crouching in front of her, he thanks her. What did she do? Why is he thanking her? Tom obviously is as impatient as I am because he asks the same question.

"She just saved me."

"I didn't really save you," she mumbles, blushing slightly at his attention. "I just interrupted Dravin before he could do anything."

"What? You were with Dravin?" I stare at her. Dravin. She'd been with the man who wants nothing more than to see her captured or killed. Now, Dravin knows for sure that she's still alive…I can feel my anger increasing, and I am starting to see red. Again. Tom places a hand on my shoulder, and what used to be a calming gesture has little effect on me now.

Ryanne is still sitting on the living room floor, wincing with every movement as blood drips down her arms. I close my eyes. I hate seeing her hurt. "Logan, please heal her. *Now.*" I take a deep breath, trying to control the anger inside me.

With my eyes closed, I hear the low rustling of clothing as Logan moves toward Ryanne. I open my eyes as he grabs both of Ryanne's hands and starts to heal her. Pieces of glass are pushed out of her arms and collect on the hardwood floor beneath her. My anger increases at each *tink* sound I hear as the glass is forced out of her small arms. He opens his eyes and looks at her with awe. Why does he always look at her with awe? She's putting herself in dangerous situations. Instead of letting go of her hands, he stands up and pulls her up with him. She sways a little on her feet with the movement, but thankfully doesn't collapse. He puts a hand on the small of her back and walks her to the couch. "Sit down."

"Can someone please explain everything to us?" Liam asks. I can tell he is having trouble controlling his anger as well. Liam's eyes are watching Ryanne as she sits on the couch. I glance over at her and see her mouth "sorry" to him. He nods at her, accepting her apology, and stands up. I can't accept everything as quickly as he just did—something in me won't let me. I'm not mad at her per say. I'm mad at the situation we're in. I walk over to the seat adjacent to her spot on the couch and sit down. I feel Emma's eyes on me as she tries to gauge my reaction. Meeting her eyes, I shake my head. I'm trying very hard to keep everything in right now. Giving me a small smile, she sits beside David and gives Ryanne her attention, waiting for her to explain what just happened.

Larkin speaks up first. "I'll give you the short version. Dravin caught me. When Heratz, the man who was sent to kill Jane and Ross, didn't come back, Dravin got suspicious. He started questioning me about you, Ryanne, and looking for any clues that you were still alive. Adam told him that before Colton knocked him unconscious during that battle, he thought that he saw me behind Thomas. Another guy confirmed that I was the one that killed Thomas with truth serum." He starts to pace the floor. "He cornered me and started asking whether or not Ryanne was actually dead because he couldn't get a read on her magic. He knew that since a body wasn't found in the rubble, you could still be alive."

He stops talking and looks back at Ryanne. "You shouldn't have come in there. I was barely able to transport you back here. He was so close to getting you again. It would have been worse this time, because he's no longer concerned about who you are staying with. It's you that he wants. No one else. How did you even get there to begin with?"

I turn and look at Ryanne, who's leaning against the back of the couch, trying to remain awake. She looks exhausted; she has dark circles under her eyes, and her normally pale skin is a lighter shade than usual. She is still wearing her work-out clothes from earlier, and they are a mess—covered in dirt, dust, and dried blood. Her long hair is tangled and falling out of its ponytail.

"I don't really know. I passed out from using too much magic earlier when we were training, and while out, I had this dream of a doorway. I woke up and realized that I had to draw it. I had to put it down on paper. I grabbed my notebook and went to the table and drew it. When I finished, I got this sharp pain in my stomach in the same spot that I was stabbed, and it grew in intensity until it became so bad that I couldn't breathe anymore.

"I don't really know what happened after. I closed my eyes waiting for the pain to stop, and the next thing I know, I'm sitting in a dusty hallway. I just started walking and came across the door—the same door that I drew. I heard Dravin yelling, and I knew that I had to do something." She looks toward Larkin and speaks to him directly. "I couldn't let you get killed because you were helping us. So, I just barged in, without a plan, and tried to act like I knew what I was doing."

She looks away from Larkin and glances around the room again. Seeing everyone's eyes on her, she looks down at the hands in her lap. "I wasn't strong enough to fight him, so I tried to put a shield up to separate us from him. But you weren't able to blink us out of there, and I was growing weaker each time he ran into the shield," she sighs and bites her bottom lip. "I honestly thought that I was done for—that we were done for. I didn't know what to do. I screamed when he got close, but then I landed in the living room."

My chest tightens at the thought of her in Dravin's hands again. I keep picturing what she looked like when Liam rescued her. Battered. Broken. Bloodied. She glances toward the coffee table, which is lying on its side with the glass top broken and grimaces before facing Tom. "Sorry about that."

"We're just happy that you're okay."

She looks back to Larkin. "I'm sorry you were almost killed because of me." Then, she brings her attention to Liam. "And I'm sorry I didn't take you with me." Without looking at anyone, she whispers, "I think I'm about to pass out aga..." she slumps over toward Liam without finishing her sentence.

He places an arm at the back of her head and shifts her so he can carry her upstairs. I follow her limp body until they are out of sight. I see Emma looking at me again. "Don't say anything."

"I wasn't going to this time." She reaches out and squeezes my hand before leaning back into David's arms. I look up and see that Larkin has stopped pacing. He is staring down at the broken coffee table.

"That girl...." he looks toward the ceiling and exhales loudly. "I've never met someone so adamant on putting herself in danger to protect others."

No one says anything right away. I turn toward the stairs and see Liam sitting on the bottom one with a solemn look on his face. I hadn't heard him come back down stairs. He doesn't like seeing Ryanne like that either, and I know it has to be eating him up that he wasn't able to help her.

Tom leans against the doorframe and crosses his arms before addressing everyone. "That's just what we need though." We all turn to look at him. "The prophecy says that a girl is supposed to end the war, which most likely means stopping Dravin. Do you think that would be someone who just stands by and lets others do everything for her? That relies on someone else for protection? No. We need someone with a backbone. We need someone who's strong, not for the sake of being strong, but for the sake of others. Her strength comes from her need to protect those she cares about. She needs all of us if she's going to do this.

"That girl is the most selfless person I've ever met. Sure, she tends to rush into dangerous situations without thinking, but she does it because she cares. She cares about every single one of you. That's what sets her apart from Dravin. Dravin does things for the sake of gaining more power. He doesn't care about others. He wants everything for himself. He wants control. Ryanne doesn't want any of that.

"She has saved all of our lives more than once. When she was kidnapped, she didn't reveal anything about us. It would have lessened the pain they inflicted on her, but she kept us a secret. She saved Claire from being stabbed." Larkin at least has the decency to look guilty. Tom continues, "She then just turned around and saved that same man tonight. She knocked all those arrows out of the way, so no one got hurt." Tom looks at me. "She knocked Adam away from you during the battle, so he didn't kill you. She even saved Jane. We all owe that girl.

"This isn't going to get any easier for her. She's going to have visions she doesn't want to see. She's going to be put in situations she doesn't want to be in. She's going to have to fight her hardest, and she'll get hurt." I glare at him. "Don't look at me like that, Colton. It's going to happen, but she needs all of us to be right beside her, helping her every step of the way. She needs to know that someone is rooting for her. She needs to know that she's doing the right thing. There's no point telling her not to do something, because she's stubborn and will do it anyway." Tom attempts to add a little humor to the situation. It works though; everyone laughs.

"Ryanne has been through so much in such a short time, but she's overcome all of it. She's got more power in her body than she knows what to do with. None of us know the extent of her magic. She keeps surprising us with it. She needs you guys to be there. Don't be so hard on her. She's got more pressure on her than any of us."

He finishes his speech and then leaves the room. The rest of us remain in our seats, silent. He is right. Ryanne's been through so much and hasn't let it affect her yet. She's much stronger than any of us are giving her credit for.

David speaks up first, "Who knew Tom could give speeches like that?"

I ROLL OVER AND SLOWLY sit up. Blinking away the sleep, I turn toward Emma's bed. It's empty. I reach down for my phone to check the time. It's 12:30 in the afternoon. Wow, I slept for a while. I get out of bed and get in the shower, letting the water rinse away all the dirt.

I grab my blue t-shirt with the Superman logo and a pair of shorts and get dressed. Everyone keeps telling me to me stop trying to be a superhero, so this shirt amuses me. I towel dry my hair and walk downstairs to search for everyone.

As I walk out of the room, I pause in the middle of the hallway. My chest tightens. There's something I need to do. Instead of going downstairs, I turn around and head past all the bedrooms. I stop when I walk past the room with the piano. I look both ways to make sure no one is in the hallway; then, I enter the room. I know that once I start playing, everyone will hear me. I didn't realize how much I missed playing until Colton forced me to play it the other night. Silently walking across the room, I sit down in front of the piano, place my hands on the keys, and start to play and sing "Get It Right" from Glee. I loved it when Rachel Berry sang it on the show. It resonated with me, and I knew that I had to learn how to play it.

Lately, it feels like everything I do ends up going wrong. No matter how hard I try, I don't know if I'll be able to do this, and I want so badly to be able to fulfill this. How many times will it take for me to get this right? How many mistakes can I make before I don't get any more second chances? If I can't even protect myself, how am I supposed to protect everyone else? Like the song said, "My best intentions keep making a mess of things. I just want to fix it somehow."

I take a deep breath and belt out the long note, not caring how loud I am anymore. I know that they aren't far from this room. They can hear me, and they are listening. I'm sure of it. I play the last note on the piano, but don't move from the seat. I wipe a single tear from my cheek as the low note echoes through the room. Outside of the door, I hear quiet footsteps running down the stairs.

With a small smile, I close the lid over the piano keys and stand up. I wait until I can't hear their footsteps anymore before I walk out of the room. No one looks at me when I walk downstairs and sit on the couch beside Colton. Seeing all their guilty expressions, I say, "I know you guys were outside of the room while I was playing."

"We've been down here for a while Ryanne," David says.

Seeing three young teens filming a webshow, I try to hold my smile in. "Watching iCarly reruns?"

He looks toward the TV and laughs. "That's not very believable, is it?"

"No, it's not." I bring my knees up to my chest and wrap my arms around them. Larkin is sitting on the ground, staring up at me. Squirming under his gaze, I ask, "What? What are you looking at?" He just shrugs and looks away from me. Everyone else is watching me as well. "Guys, stop staring at me. You know I hate that."

Logan walks over and crouches down in front of me, "How are you feeling?"

I groan. He's such a worry wart. "I'm fine. Would you like to make sure?" I ask jokingly and put my hands in front of him. He grabs my hands and closes his eyes. I look toward Colton, "I was kidding about that."

He opens his eyes and pats my leg, before standing back up. "She's good." I mumble an *I told you so* as he walks away. Being the childish girl I am, I also stick my tongue out at him.

"Ahh, she's back," David winks at me then continues flipping through channels. "Hey, is that the guy on some of your shirts, Ryanne?"

"Yes. I love this show!" He laughs at my excited response and puts the remote down. "You don't have to watch this if you don't want to."

Shaking his head with a smile on his face, David ignores me and continues watching the show. After a couple of minutes, I double over laughing. I can't breathe; I'm laughing so hard. Colton is laughing at how hard I am laughing.

Larkin is smiling at me, amused at my response, and asks if I'm all right. He watches me for a few seconds after I nod before he looks away.

Everyone is watching me. I can't help it. "Bazinga." I start giggling all over again. A few seconds later, I take a deep breath and calm myself down, "I'm good now."

When I stop laughing, Tom places a plate on my lap. I look down at the sandwich and turn around and look at him. "What's this for?"

"You missed dinner last night, breakfast this morning, and lunch. You need to eat something, Ryanne." I nod and thank him.

"No need to thank me. We should thank you."

That's an odd statement. I lean toward Colton. "What does he mean by that?" He smiles at me, but shakes his head. Everyone glances at each other, but no one answers my question. "Fine, be like that you bunch of secret keepers." I take a bite of my sandwich and watch the show. "If I really wanted to know, I could just read your minds."

"So Ryanne, are you able to train today?" Liam asks me, changing the topic.

I put a finger up and quickly swallow the food in my mouth, "Yeah, just no more giant shields."

"Okay," he laughs. "We'll work more with your magic though."

"I want to blow something up. I like doing that." Everyone laughs at me. I put on the most deadpan expression that I can muster, "I'm serious."

"We know. That's why it was funny," David says.

I pick up my plate and walk into the kitchen to clean it and put it away. The sink is full of dirty dishes. For a few moments, I just stare down at the stainless steel in front of me. Claire always had the dishes clean and the sink spotless. Turning the water on, I grab the soap and get to work. Someone has to do it.

I am scrubbing the dishes when someone bumps into me. I look up and see Larkin standing beside me waving a towel. "I'll dry." I pass the plate to him and let him dry while I grab another.

"Look Ryanne, I wanted to thank you again for showing up when you did. I don't know how you did it, but thank you."

"I don't know how I did it either," I laugh and hand him another plate. "You don't have to thank me, Larkin. You've helped us a lot lately. I should be thanking you. Last time you helped me, I yelled at you."

"Let's call it even then."

"Sounds good to me."

CHAPTER
NINE

COLTON

I AM TRAINING WITH LOGAN today, but I can't get into it. "Dude, what's gotten into you lately?" I glance over at Ryanne, who is working with Larkin again. It's been a few weeks since Ryanne rescued him and since then, he's been hanging around her more often and helping her train with her magic. "He's just helping her."

"I know. It's just....Ugh, I don't know." Larkin steps closer to Ryanne and whispers something in her ear. She laughs and shoves him away. "I don't like him." They've been spending a lot of time together. Larkin watches Ryanne just like Liam does. Emma says that it's just his way of showing his gratitude for what she did for him, but I don't like it. She's always with Larkin or Liam. I trust Liam, but I don't fully trust Larkin yet. There's just something about him...

Logan stops trying to punch me. "You've got it bad."

"I keep telling him that!" Emma yells over to us.

I turn to Logan again. "How does she do that? She's not even near us." Emma stops sparring with David and walks over to us. "Look, Larkin's flirty, but he's harmless. She's not into him like that," she winks at me and turns her attention back towards Ryanne.

The wind picks up, so we know Ryanne is concentrating on doing something. Her ponytail is whipping around her. Dead branches are collecting into a pile at the end of the yard again. We collectively take a couple steps closer, trying to hear what Larkin is telling her. Tom is standing on the porch, watching the scene play out as well. He's been watching over our training sessions lately, trying to see if there is anything he can do to help Ryanne out with her magic training.

"If you start to feel weak at any time, stop. I'll make sure to catch you. Don't push your limits, Ryanne."

"He'll catch her?" I ask Liam as we get a little closer. "What are they doing?"

"You'll see."

Ryanne backs up to the house again. "Is she really going to try that again?" I glance between Ryanne and Liam. Is he really going to let her do that again? Liam shakes his head, not taking his eyes off of her. I watch as she closes her eyes and concentrates. The wind picks up even more.

"Are you ready?" Larkin asks her. She zeroes in on the wood and nods. Turning toward us, he says, "You may want to step back a little." We all take a couple steps back as Ryanne runs forward. Lifting her hands above her head, she does a couple back-flips and twists her body mid-air. Instead of landing back on the ground, she shoots upward into the air, squealing as she goes higher. Hovering above the ground, she turns around and faces the pile of wood. "Don't push it, Ryanne," he warns.

Emma gasps behind me as we watch Ryanne float about ten feet in the air. She slowly brings her hands above her head and thrusts them forward, shooting magic toward the pile of wood. The pile explodes.

We duck to avoid the flying pieces, but like the other day, an invisible barrier blocks any advances.

"Ok, let go of the shield," Larkin tells her once the wood stops flying toward us.

"I don't know how to get down," she yells. The wind is still picking up. "I'm afraid of heights!"

"Pull in the energy. Grab onto the strands and slowly reel them back in." Larkin takes a step toward her, arms outstretched as a precaution. She concentrates on the energy. You can always tell when she is concentrating. Her nose crinkles up in this adorable way.

"It's not working!" She is starting to panic. She rises a couple more feet in the air.

"Concentrate, Ryanne."

Nothing happens for a few moments. We're all silent as we watch her. *Come on, Ryanne. You can do this.* I push my encouraging thoughts toward her. I know that she can't read my mind, but as I think those words over and over again, she slowly begins to float toward the ground. Larkin reaches out and grabs her around the waist when she is less than a foot in the air and helps pull her the rest of the way down.

With her eyes still closed, she asks, "Am I back on the ground?"

"Your feet are firmly planted on the ground," Larkin tells her through his laugh.

Ryanne opens one eye and looks down at her feet. With a relieved sigh, she opens both eyes. "Short people are not meant to be that high up. I'm low to the ground for a reason."

Logan walks up to her, "How do you feel?"

"I feel good. I'm not dizzy. I didn't push out as much magic toward the wood, and my shield wasn't as big this time because you weren't on the opposite side of the yard. Yeah, I'm good." She grins knowing that she's slowly strengthening her magic.

I smile just because she is so happy. She glances at me, and her smile widens before she looks away. Is she blushing?

"I think that's enough for today!" Tom yells from the porch.

I HATE WHEN HE LOOKS at me like that. He doesn't even know what it does to me. He looks at me like I am something special, and I can't help but smile back at him when gives me that look. His green eyes twinkle as he smiles down at me, and I find myself losing focus on everything around me. Yeah, I just said his eyes twinkled. How dorky am I? Now, I'm talking to myself. Get it together, Ryanne. Looking down at the grass, I can feel a blush coming on. I'm so glad that no one can actually read my mind.

Tom mentioned that we'd trained enough for today, so I start walking toward the door. Oh wait! I turn around. "I forgot to clean up the yard." Colton grabs my elbow as he walks past me and pulls me toward the door. "I need to pick up all the wood!" Instead of letting me go, he laughs and continues pulling me. His deep laugh almost causes me to stumble. Get a grip girl! Once inside the house, Tom hands me a water bottle. "That was an impressive trick you just did."

I start giggling. "Magic trick," I glance around the room. "I'm a mage-ician." David is the only one who laughs with me. At everyone else's strange expressions, I stop laughing. "Fine, you guys are lame." Turning toward Tom, I tell him what everyone else already knows. "I didn't like that. I'm afraid of heights, and I thought that I was stuck up there. I was about to have a panic attack."

Tom chuckles and pats me on the back, "Well, it's good to know what you can do. You never know when you'll have to use it."

"True, but I won't like doing that if I ever have to. Well, I'm going to go change. I'll be back in a minute." I start to walk away, but Emma runs up to me.

"I'll come with you." She turns around and winks at someone. I thought it was David, but he's talking with Logan.

"Who are you winking at?" I ask her. Colton is looking over at Tom while Liam and Larkin are talking. No one is looking at us.

"No one. Come on."

"You winked at someone."

"My eye twitched." She starts dragging me out of the room. What is she keeping from me? I could read her mind...No, she must have a reason for not telling me. I trust Emma—if I should know, she'd tell me. Once inside the room, I grab one of the few shirts I stole from Liam and a pair of yoga shorts. Emma changes into a black camisole and running shorts.

"Oh come on, Ryanne." I walk out of the room, ignoring her comment. While walking down the stairs, she yells, "At least tie up the shirt a little, it looks like you aren't wearing any shorts. It's way too big on you." Emma runs up behind me and tries to tie the shirt back. I turn around and slap her hand away which makes her try harder.

Getting into a girly slap fight, I say, "Emma, it's my pajamas. I really don't care what it looks like or how it fits."

She stops and crosses her arms across her chest. "Well you should care more."

"Well, I don't. You should just accept that I'm not gonna change."

"Ugh, you stubborn little girl."

"You tell her, Ryanne!" David says and sticks a hand out for a high-five. I smack his hand as I pass him and sit down on the couch next to Colton again.

"Hey, you're supposed to be on my side," Emma pouts while sitting down in his lap.

"I pick the winning side, honey."

I look around the room and notice that Larkin isn't sitting with us. "Where's Larkin?"

"He's picking up something for you," Tom answers from the kitchen.

"Something for me?" He has my attention now.

"I wouldn't get too excited, dear," he laughs. "I got a call from Jane earlier saying that she shipped the dress she wants you to wear to the wedding on Saturday. Larkin's going to get it since I gave her a fake address."

"Oh," I turn back around. "I'm scared now." They laugh at my reaction. "It's not funny. She's like Emma. She's going to get back at me for all those times I refused to wear 'decent' clothing."

Larkin blinks into the room, holding a medium sized box. "I don't want to open that," I turn back around and face the TV. I know Jane's style, so I'm not sure I want to see what is in that box.

Emma jumps out of the chair, takes the box from Larkin, walks into the kitchen, and places in on the table. "I'll open it for you." She grabs a knife and cuts the tape on the outside of the box. I groan and walk into the kitchen as she starts pulling the dress out of the box.

"Oh dear Lord. She's getting back at me for prom."

"Oh my gosh. This is so pretty. I'll go for you!" Emma squeals in delight while holding the dress up to her.

"Please do."

Colton walks into the room and places his right hand on my shoulder. I look up right when he asks, "What happened at prom?"

"I didn't go. She didn't like that. She was all like, 'it's your senior prom, you have to go,' blah blah blah. But one, I don't dance and two, I hate shopping."

The dress is midnight blue, floor length, and strapless with a sweetheart neckline and pleated surplice bodice. A matching belt with a fabric flower adorns the natural waist. It flows down with a full pleated skirt. The dress is pretty but not something I would pick out for myself...since I wouldn't have picked out anything. I lean over the box and see another small rectangular box that most likely holds the shoes Jane wants me to wear. I reach in and take out the shoes. I'm sure my mouth drops to the floor. There's no way. The metallic glitter peep toe pumps match the dress perfectly. However, they are four inches in height.

"I'll never be able to walk in these. Is she trying to kill me?" I hold the shoes up and away from me as if they were some sort of infectious disease. Emma squeals again and grabs the shoes.

"What size are those? I want to borrow them." She looks at the shoes, "Shoot, they're a 7.5. That's too small."

There's a note at the bottom of the box:

Ryanne,

When you get this dress, make sure to hang it up. It'll get rid of any wrinkles it got from sitting in a box. Also, you HAVE to wear this dress and those shoes. Don't try to get out of this. You only have to wear it for a couple of hours. You'll survive. Please wear that gorgeous hair of yours down, possibly curled. You can wear any jewelry you want. See? I can compromise. Don't forget your date! Try to arrive a little early, so I can run through everything with you. Excited to see you!

—Jane

P.S. I only plan on getting married once, so please don't be stubborn and wear the dress. You'll look great.

"Dang it, she knows me too well." Emma grabs the note from my hand and reads it.

"I'm totally doing your hair and make-up. No ifs, ands, or buts about it." Emma runs out of the room smiling with the dress and shoes.

I turn toward Liam, "Do you think Jane will notice if Emma goes in my place?"

Liam wraps an arm around my shoulder and pulls me toward him. "Probably," he laughs. "You'll only have to wear it for a couple of hours. Then you can come back here and change into an over-sized t-shirt and athletic shorts. I'm sure you can manage."

"You've obviously never walked in heels before."

CHAPTER
TEN

I WAKE UP EARLY SATURDAY morning and take a shower. Dressing in my usual jeans and a t-shirt, I walk downstairs and see Colton and Liam sitting at the table, talking quietly.

"Hey guys," I say when I enter the kitchen.

"Good morning. You ready for today?" Liam asks. I scowl at him and walk to the fridge to get a cold bottle of water.

"What are you going to wear?" I ask Liam as I shut the fridge. Liam isn't one to worry about appearances either. I'd never seen him in anything but black or a slight variation of gray. I'm curious to see what he'll look like dressed up.

"I guess you'll find out in four hours' time."

"Four hours? That's plenty of time to get ready."

"Ryanne!" Emma yells my name from upstairs. I cringe at the sound.

I jump up and walk behind the guys' chairs. "Hide me." At that moment, Emma runs into the room. "Get over here. We are on limited time!"

"We have plenty of time."

"Have you seen your hair, girl? We don't have *enough* time!" She walks around the chair and grabs my wrist. I turn around to the guys and mouth 'help me' before Emma pulls me out of the room. I can hear their laughter as we ascend the stairs. Emma drags me into our bathroom. In the middle of the floor is a small chair. Stopping in the doorway, she points to it. "Sit down." I groan, but listen. There's no point arguing with her today—especially not when she's in one of these moods. Emma can be just as stubborn as me. "I'm going to straighten your hair and then re-curl it."

"Is that really necessary? Can't we leave my hair the way it is." You'd think I just told her that I ran over a kitten based on her expression. I decide from then on to keep my mouth closed and let her 'fix me up' as she would say.

Two hours later, my hair is done and covered with plenty of hairspray. Apparently my hair is difficult to straighten. Who would have guessed? With the amount of hairspray in my hair, I'm surprised that my hair isn't stiff; though, I do make a mental note to stay away from open flames. Emma starts to work on my makeup. I close my eyes as she applies eyeliner and eye shadow to my eyelids. I'm not allowed to look at myself until she is completely finished and has given me her stamp of approval.

When I feel the brush leave my eye, I open my eyes and look up at her. With a satisfied grin, she walks to our small closet to grab the dress. "Don't turn around!"

I don't want to endure the wrath of Emma, so I stay seated. She comes back into the room, carrying the dress, pumps, and a strapless bra. "Get changed, but don't you dare turn around. I want to see your reaction when you see yourself for the first time. I'll be right here if you need any help."

The dress fits perfectly. I've slimmed down a little this summer from all the training I've done, so I'm not sure how Jane knew what size to get. I call Emma back into the room to help me zip the back. I step into the shoes and gain a whole four inches in height. So, this is what taller people see. I'm still shorter than her but closer than I usually am. She steps back and smiles, "You look great. One sec, let me go get you some earrings."

I wait in the bathroom, just staring at the shower. I can hear Emma shuffling through her jewelry box. She walks back into the room and hands me a pair of small dangly diamond earrings. I take out the silver studs I usually wear and put in her earrings. I am expecting them to be heavy, but they are surprisingly light.

"Can I turn around now?" She nods, and I slowly turn around. I'm not sure what I was expecting, but what I see is not it.

My hair is curled in large barrel waves, hanging down to the middle of my back. Emma has only curled the ends of my hair, so it gets more voluminous as it goes down. She added some glitter spray to the ends of the waves, which makes my hair sparkle whenever I move.

The dress fits my body perfectly, highlighting my curves and small waistline. Its low back and sweetheart neckline show more skin than I'm used to, but it still remains tasteful. My eyes are outlined with black eyeliner, and the mascara adds twice as much length to my dark lashes. The dark make-up brings out the green in my eyes, making them look brighter. My lips glisten from the light pink gloss Emma applied. Liam's necklace hangs low, hitting against my stomach when I move. Jane will hate it. I smile thinking about how she will react. She did tell me that I could wear whatever jewelry I wanted. After learning about what it would do to Liam, there is no way I will take it off.

I actually feel somewhat pretty and satisfied with my reflection. "Thank you, Emma."

"You like it?" Her eyes widen as she waits for my response. I know that she worked really hard to make me look more suitable for the wedding.

"You did a great job."

"Yay, time to go downstairs. Liam is already waiting."

COLTON

"HOW HARD DO YOU THINK Emma's fighting her up there?" I turn and ask Liam. Liam is dressed in black dress pants and a white button down shirt. He keeps buttoning and unbuttoning the cuffed sleeves. "Relax, man."

"I don't know why I'm so nervous," he laughs and looks around the room for anything to distract himself with. I smile at his reaction. I'd be doing the same thing if I was going in his place. I wish I was the one taking her, but out of all the guys here, I trust Liam the most—especially when it comes to Ryanne's safety. I know he'll protect her with his life.

"Ryanne, you will get your skinny butt downstairs right now!" Emma yells from upstairs. I glance over at Liam and see him laughing. I knew Ryanne wouldn't come without a fight.

"Is everyone downstairs waiting?" she asks.

"Yes." Emma is starting to get frustrated, and it doesn't usually turn out well for her when she goes against Ryanne.

"Then, I'm more comfortable in here where no one can see me."

Emma and Ryanne are moving around upstairs. Liam breaks a smile at the amount of shuffling sounds that comes from the girls' room.

Emma storms out of the room and down the stairs, mumbling. "She has to be the most stubborn girl…" She stops in front of Liam and me. "She used a shield against me. Can you believe that?" She looks between

Liam and Larkin. "Well, don't you two look spiffy. I approve." Turning back toward Larkin she asks, "Can you go get her, and force her to come down here."

"She won't like that," he says and starts smiling. "Sure." He transports out of the room.

"You guys are in for a treat." Emma turns toward Liam and me with a huge grin on her face. "If only she would let me help her every day."

"Oh no you don't," Ryanne says loudly from upstairs. Suddenly, Larkin appears again, holding a very shocked Ryanne against him. She sways a little against his chest when he lands. "I really hate when you do that. I would have gotten away if I wasn't wearing these death traps on my feet." Normally, I would have laughed at how angry she is, but I can't pick my mouth up fast enough. Thankfully, she is staring at the ground and avoiding eye-contact with anyone.

I let myself fully soak in her appearance. The dress hugs her body like a second skin until it hits her waist and flows outward. Her arms are crossed across her chest, which isn't helping my staring any. The dark blue color of the dress contrasts with her pale skin tone. A small slit begins right above the knee and travels down to the floor. A small toned leg peaks out the side. It isn't meant to be sexy, but on her it is. Because she is looking down, her hair is covering her face. The long dark hair falls against her skin in large waves. It looks like Emma has added some glitter to the ends, which gleams whenever she moves her head.

Emma walks over and elbows me in the stomach. I stop gaping at Ryanne and forcefully pull my eyes away from her. She is glaring at me with wide eyes, silently demanding me to say something. I rack my brain for something to say, but all I get are incoherent, stuttering thoughts.

"Wow," is all Liam can say. It appears that he is having as much trouble with words as I am.

"You look beautiful, Ryanne," her name comes out really breathy. Crap, could I be any more obvious? She glances up at our comments, and I have to fight really hard to keep my mouth shut this time. Emma has lined her large eyes with dark eye-liner making them appear even larger and more luminous. Her normally hazel eyes have large specks of green in them, similar to mine. Her gaze meets mine, and her blush deepens, but she doesn't look away this time.

The moment is short lived when we hear the sound of a camera click. Emma is standing there with her cell phone pointed toward us and a large smile splayed across her face. "I couldn't help it. You two looked too cute." I roll my eyes and look back toward Ryanne, but she is looking at Liam.

With a huge grin, she looks him up and down and says, "You clean up nice."

"Th-thank you." I laugh at his stutter, which results in a glare from him.

"Let me get one picture of the two of you together," Emma says, pointing between Liam and Ryanne. When Ryanne groans, she continues, "It's only one picture. It won't kill you."

"You don't know that for sure," she mumbles as she steps closer to Liam.

He wraps an arm around her small waist while she places a hand on his chest. It takes every bit of strength I have to not growl at how close they're standing. Where did this possessiveness come from? Posing for the picture, her leg peeks out of the slit. I have trouble dragging my eyes away from the exposed skin. I see her in shorts every day, but there is just something about that dress…

I clear my throat and walk over to the couch. David is shaking his head at my reaction, but I can see the amusement in his eyes. For the first time, Ryanne notices that Larkin is also dressed up. "You're coming too?"

"Yep, I'm crashing the wedding. Someone has to keep an eye on the both of you, while Liam is just focusing on you."

"Oh."

"Okay, come here." Ryanne looks up at him, confused. With an exaggerated sigh, he explains, "I'm going to take you to the church and make sure you find Jane and then I'm coming back here for Liam." She walks over to him, and he wraps his arms around her waist and disappears.

"Holy crap, I'm so screwed," Liam says while running his hand through his long hair.

"I'm good. I know." Emma is really proud of herself.

"Did you have to be that good?" Liam asks. "I'm going to have to fight off every guy there."

"Especially the drunk ones," adds Logan. "Hopefully there won't be too many people there, and she can block their thoughts since she won't be able focus on Colton."

Emma looks toward me. "You're so lucky she's oblivious to everything around her because you were staring at her like you wanted to rip her dress off and mmhmm mhmm mmhmm——" David covers Emma's mouth so she can't finish her sentence. I glare at Emma; I can tell that she is smiling under David's large hand.

"Thank you," I say to my brother. He nods at me but continues laughing.

Larkin transports back into the room, laughing. "Jane is just like you, Emma. The first thing she said when she saw Ryanne was 'Of course, you wore that necklace.' *Then* she complimented her on how she looked." He walks over to the couch. "You're in trouble, Liam. All of Ross's groomsmen have already taken an interest in Ryanne."

Of course they have. I clench my fists. She's only been there a couple minutes and already attracted the attention of all the males in the building. I really wish I was the one going. The image of her burying her face into my shirt when she read the mind of that man in the mall keeps running through my mind. The whole ordeal with Adam is so fresh in her mind that she gets scared whenever she hears something like that. Most men don't censor their thoughts which freaks Ryanne out. Liam must have known what I was thinking. He pats me on the shoulder, "I'll watch out for her." I thank him and watch as Larkin transports him to the wedding. I run a hand through my hair and start pacing.

"I don't think we really thought this through all the way."

CHAPTER
ELEVEN

PAUSING BRIEFLY IN THE DOORWAY, I push back all the thoughts. There aren't that many people back here, so it's not too difficult. Larkin warned me to be extra careful with the thoughts tonight. If I concentrate too hard on pushing them back, I'll wear out much quicker. Tonight is one night that I don't want to pass out. I want to be here for Jane.

"Where is your date?" she asks me as I enter the room she's using to get ready before the ceremony. Before answering, I glance over my shoulder and see all the guys' eyes on me as I pass. What are they staring at? I give my attention to Jane in front of me. My grin is instantaneous; she looks beautiful. She is wearing a large A-line gown with a halter neckline. The top portion is simple, but as the dress lengthens, the beaded lace becomes more prominent. Two-dimensional flowers on the lace are an exact replica of the three-dimensional flower on my dress. Her hair is done in an extravagant up-do with small spiral curls framing her face. A large chapel train follows her as she walks.

"He's here somewhere; I wanted to see you first. You look amazing!" She runs over to me and gives me a hug.

"I'm so glad you could make it; it's been too long, Ryanne. You look beautiful. Thank you for wearing the dress." She bends down and lifts the dress a little to see if I was wearing the shoes she gave me. She smiles when she realizes that I listened to her.

"You have very little faith in me," I tell her.

Rolling her eyes, she hands me a small bouquet of pale yellow flowers. "You'll walk in after Mindy and before Amy." I turn, and both Mindy and Amy wave at me. "After the ceremony, we're going to take some pictures, so be ready for that. You won't have to give a speech or anything at the reception; don't worry about that. I know how you are with public speaking. I think that's about it. Please try and enjoy yourself tonight." I nod, give her another hug, and follow Mindy and Amy out of the room. The wedding is going to start in fifteen minutes, and we need to get into our positions for the ceremony.

The doors of the church open, and Mindy walks out. I wait until Amy taps on my shoulder and then I follow her. Ross and his groomsmen are already waiting at the end of the aisle. Bouquet against my chest, I concentrate on not tripping as I walk. Ross smiles at me when I walk past him. I wink back at him and get in line behind Mindy. I turn around and see Amy halfway to us. I look around the seats looking for Liam, but can't find him. An organ sounds behind me, and everyone stands up and faces the back of the church. Jane is standing there, arm linked with her father, but her attention is on Ross. When she sees him, her smile widens. Jane looks beautiful, so it is no surprise that Ross has the same expression.

As Ross says his vows, I let my mind wander. Will I ever get a chance to have this? A wedding? I don't even know if I'll make it out of this situation alive. I feel tears well up in my eyes because of how beautiful the ceremony is and because I'm unsure if I'll ever have a chance to experience what Jane and Ross have. It's too dangerous. I look out at the crowd again and finally find Liam sitting in the middle, toward the back. He smiles sadly at me, knowing what I'm thinking. Liam has this uncanny ability of knowing what is on my mind. He knows how to comfort me in situations like this.

After the ceremony, I'm forced to endure an endless amount of pictures. The photographer makes me stand here, smile like this, pose like that, etc. It is exhausting. I don't know how models do this. Toward the end, I'm sure my smile looked more like a grimace.

At the reception, I have to sit up at the center table with Jane and Ross and the rest of the bridal party. Liam is sitting off in the corner, politely talking to the couple beside him. During the meal, we keep making eye contact and giving small smiles. Mindy leans over to me, "Is that your date?" I follow her line of sight and see her looking at Liam. I nod.

"He's hot." I glance at Mindy. She looks younger than I originally thought. Though probably in her mid-twenties, she shouldn't be ogling Liam. Granted, Liam does appear older than he actually is. That's a mage quality apparently.

After the father daughter dance, Jane drags me out to the dance floor. "You have to dance. Where is your date?"

I'm not sure. I try to look over everyone, but even with heels on, I'm still on the shorter side. A slow song starts to play through the speakers. My eyes continue to bounce around the dance floor looking for Liam. Ross moves through the dance floor and grabs Jane around the waist, twirling her into his arms. She laughs lightly as they start moving around the dance floor and away from me. I smile and look toward the table where Liam was previously sitting, but it's empty. I stand awkwardly by myself on the dance floor while couples move around me. Where's Liam?

I'm about to walk back to my chair when I feel a tap on my shoulder and turn around to find Liam standing there, smiling down at me. "May I have this dance?"

Relief floods though me, and I smile at him. "You may."

I step closer to him as he wraps his arms around my waist. Because of the heels, I am only about six inches shorter than him now and am able to wrap my arms around his neck. We dance in silence for a while before he leans down and whispers in my ear, "Is something wrong? You seemed a little upset during the ceremony."

"I'm fine. I was just thinking," I pause and glance around the room. Everyone seems really happy. I wish that I could be that carefree. I've already been through so much that I don't know if it'll be possible to be like that again. Liam waits for me to continue. "I was just thinking about how I might not ever get to experience this myself." I glance up at him and see him watching me. "Despite the appearance I put out, I want all of this. I want to find love, and I want to get married. I want to walk down the aisle in some ridiculous dress and be blissfully happy. But I don't think that's going to be possible." I lean forward and rest my head against his shoulder. He tightens his grip around me. Jane's watching me from across the room with a smile. I try to smile back at her. I look past Jane and see Larkin standing in the corner, watching the room.

"You can't think like that, Ryanne," Liam rests his chin on top of my head. "You never know when you'll find love. Look at David and Emma. They found each other under strange circumstances, and you already know that they are going to get married. Your time will come."

"How do you know that?" I whisper.

"Because you're Ryanne freaking Arden." I chuckle at his expression. "I know you, Ryanne. I know how you think. Don't close your heart because you're afraid. You may have already met the one you're meant to be with. You never know. Let everything play out like it should. You have so many people that care for you and will protect you. You're not going anywhere any time soon. I promise."

I let his words sink in. I *do* do that. I run away from my emotions. I shut myself out for fear of getting hurt. I just don't think I can handle opening myself up like that and getting hurt. The song ends, but neither of us moves. Thankfully the next song is also a slow song.

"Do you think I can do this, Liam?"

"Do what?"

"Everything. All this magic stuff. I'm afraid of letting everyone down."

"Ryanne, look at me." I lift my head off of his shoulder and look into his gray eyes. "No matter what happens, you're not letting anyone down. We're here for you. I have complete faith in you, and I know that everyone else does too. You're way stronger than you give yourself credit for, and you'll be surprised at what you can do when you accept that yourself. You need to see what everyone else sees."

I open my mouth to respond when I feel someone tap my shoulder. Jane's standing behind me with a large smile on her face as her eyes dance between Liam and me. I hadn't realized that the music had stopped.

"Oh, hey Jane." She continues glancing between Liam and me. Light bulb moment! "Oh, Jane, this is Liam. Liam this is Jane."

"It's very nice to meet you, Liam." She looks at me with wide eyes and an even wider grin. Without even reading her thoughts, I know that she is silently commenting on Liam's attractiveness.

Liam unwraps an arm from around my waist and reaches out to shake Jane's hand. "It's very nice to meet you too. Congratulations on getting married. It was a beautiful ceremony."

"Thank you. I hope you guys are having a good time." She looks around and sighs. I look in the direction she's looking in and see her mother scowling at her. "Apparently, I'm not spending enough time talking with my relatives who flew a long ways to be here. I've got to 'socialize' with everyone else now," she pouts. Putting on a fake smile, she turns back to Liam and me, "Have fun!" I watch as she walks away.

"She reminds me of Emma."

"Yeah, I never realized how similar they are until today." A faster song starts to play, and I start to walk off the dance floor, but Liam stops me.

"I don't think so, Ryanne. I know you can dance. You need to have some fun every once in a while." I stop in front of him and stare at him blankly, unmoving. Laughing, he walks toward me and places his hands on my hips, coercing me into moving. I bite my lip as I watch Liam dance in front of me. He gives me one of his rare smiles as he continues to move me. Considering how ridiculous I feel, I relent.

I relax and move with the music, forgetting all my worries for a short period of time. I close my eyes and let the rhythm of the song move me. Surprisingly, Liam can dance. I would have never pegged him as a dancer before. I can feel his body behind me moving with the music, but I don't open my eyes. Arms lifted above my head, I dance along with the song. I can feel other people watching us, but for the first time I don't care. Like Liam said, I need to have some fun.

After a few songs, I feel someone tap my shoulder. "As much as I enjoy watching you guys, I think it's a good time to get going," Larkin says. "Some people are starting to get antsy." I stop dancing and try to catch my breath. Small beads of sweat form on my forehead.

"Ugh, it's hot in here," I glance around looking for Jane. "I'll go tell Jane we're leaving. Be right back." I spot her standing in the corner. I make my way over there.

Halfway there, someone jumps in front of me. "Hellllllo there, pretty laaady," a drunken man slurs. Before I have time to think, he grabs me and pulls me against his chest. For a drunk guy, he's pretty fast. I push against his chest, trying to move away from him, but his grip is strong. I could use my magic, but that is only as a last resort. I don't really want to cause a scene, and I can't risk exposure.

"Let her go," Liam's deep voice demands behind me.

"She'sssmine," his speech runs together as his grip around my waist tightens. Liam reaches forward and grabs the hand that's on my back and twists the man's arm to the side. Not hard enough to break any bones, but enough to cause discomfort. He curses and lets go of me, pushing me back into Liam's chest.

Because of the heels my balance is already off, so the sudden movement causes me to slam into Liam. Liam steadies me and glares at the man as he walks away. "I say it's definitely time to go," he says to me.

I thank Liam for catching me and slowly step away from him. I walk the rest of the way to Jane, keeping an eye on my surroundings. A couple guys watch me as I pass, but no one tries to confront me again. I tighten the mental barrier I have up. The loud music makes it easier to tune out the voices around me. When I get over to her, she stops talking to an older woman and turns toward me. "Hey Jane. Sorry for interrupting, but I'm going to head out. I...I have to work tomorrow."

"Oh..." A disappointed look crosses her face. "I'm so glad you could make it. I haven't seen you all summer!"

"I know. I'm sorry about that. I've just been really busy."

"I understand. Keep in touch, okay? I miss you!" She hugs me. "And keep a hold of that boy. I like him."

"I'll do what I can," laughing, I turn around and start walking away. "Let's go," I say to Liam and Larkin. We exit the building, and Larkin guides us to the side.

"I'm going to bring Ryanne back first. I'll be back for you in a minute." Larkin grabs me around the waist and blinks me back to the house.

COLTON

"WHAT'S TAKING THEM SO LONG?" I ask to no one in particular. Ryanne, Liam, and Larkin have been gone for a while. Who knows what could be going on right now.

"They're at a wedding. The ceremony and the reception are usually a couple of hours long. They're fine. Quit worrying," Logan answers.

"They've been gone for over four hours now."

"Which means that they'll be back soon," Emma says, while turning toward me. "You're not upset because she went with Liam instead of you, are you?"

"No, it's not that. I just—" I stop when I see movement beside me. Larkin transports into the room holding Ryanne around the waist. She stumbles back into him from the impact. He steadies her then transports out of the room again.

"I really don't like his power. It makes me dizzy."

"Did you have fun?" Emma asks her. Instead of answering, Ryanne takes off her heels. She pouts once she is back to her normal height. I can't help my laughter. She looks so cute.

"Gosh, I'm so short." I hear a few more laughs around me, but I don't take my eyes away from Ryanne. She steps over my legs and sits beside me on the couch. "Yeah, I did have fun actually. I'm glad I went." She tries to hide a small smile. She purses her lips, deep in her thoughts. Ugh, she doesn't know how crazy that drives me. I wonder what they would taste like…feel like against mine. "I'm actually going to go take a shower," she says. I shake my head, trying to clear my thoughts. I can't have thoughts like that right now.

"Ugh, you're going to ruin your hair and make-up," Emma whines.

"You have pictures for a reason," Ryanne calls as she walks upstairs. She has to hold the dress up, so she doesn't trip up the stairs. I follow her up until she is out of my line of sight.

"That girl is impossible." She shakes her head, right as Larkin and Liam appear in the room. Liam, like Ryanne, is sweating with his sleeves pushed up to his elbows.

"Where's Ryanne?" he asks.

"Taking a shower. Ruining all my hard work," Emma turns and leans toward Liam, practically falling out of the chair in the process. "I have two things I want to say to you. First, you should dress up like that all the time. It totally works for you, especially when you're all sweaty, and I can see your tattoo through your shirt. Secondly, spill. What happened? Ryanne won't tell me anything, so I need you to tell me. Spill all the juicy stuff and don't leave anything out."

"Nothing really happened. We ate. We danced. We left." Larkin scoffs beside Liam. I glance over at him. Did something happen? Is Liam not telling us something?

"Ooooh, Larkin, tell me what happened?"

"Nothing really happened...per say. They were just dancing extremely close. You couldn't fit a piece of paper between the two of them and then when the music picked up...all male eyes were on her. I even had trouble looking away." I clench my jaw, preventing myself from saying anything. "And then there was the drunk guy."

"It wasn't like that, Larkin. She was upset."

I face him, "Upset? Why was she upset?" If someone did something to her... "Drunk guy?"

"Nothing happened with the drunk guy. I took care of it," Liam exhales loudly and looks up at the ceiling. I can hear the sound of water running upstairs, so we know that Ryanne is still in the shower. "I shouldn't really be saying any of this...She's got herself convinced that she's not meant for a 'happily ever after.' I think she still believes she's not going to make it out of this whole ordeal alive. She admitted to me that she wants a wedding. She wants love. She wants to go wedding dress shopping," he looks at Emma. "I thought you'd like to hear that." He pauses, before whispering, "She's afraid of letting everyone down."

"Afraid of letting everyone down?" I ask. That's insane. Nothing she could do would make us feel let down.

"I'm just telling you what she told me. And for the dancing…yes, I made her dance with me. She's a teenager. Sure she's eighteen, but she's barely lived. She didn't even go to her high school prom. She needed to have some fun. She needed to forget about everything that's going on and live a little," he stops talking and runs his hand through his hair.

"I don't know why, but I know what's going on in that head of hers. She doesn't have any confidence. She thinks people only focus on her flaws and her faults. She doesn't see what the rest of us see. Ryanne walks into a room, and everyone watches her. I've seen it from all of you. I admit even I do it. So obviously dancing is going to bring more attention to her. She doesn't know that she's beautiful, which automatically makes her more attractive to everyone. She was *happy* tonight—happy in a way that I don't think I've ever seen from her," Liam pushes himself off the couch and walks upstairs.

"That's twice we've gotten speeches about Ryanne lately," Emma says.

CHAPTER TWELVE

I LOOK AT THE CLOCK: 11:30 p.m. You'd think after dancing all night that I'd be tired, but I feel more energized than usual. I look at my reflection in the mirror and feel a little disappointed. I am back to normal. The beautiful Ryanne is gone. All that is left is little ol' me. I hang my wet towel up and walk out into the room. Emma is rummaging through her drawers looking for something to wear.

"So how was the wedding? And please don't give me the 'I had fun' line. I want details."

I walk over and grab my notebook and pen. As I open it to a blank page, Emma walks into the bathroom and changes into her pajamas. "It was great actually. Jane looked amazing." I give Emma details on Jane's dress as I begin sketching it. I describe how Ross was really nervous before the ceremony and the look on his face when Jane walked down the aisle. I want someone to look at me like that; like I am the most special and important person in the world. I give her all the details on the food, the music, and the dancing. I tell her about my conversations with Liam. Everything.

"Ryanne...I had no idea." She's looking at me with a mixture of sadness and determination. Determination for what, I'm not sure.

I like having moments like this with Emma. It is nice to have some girl time—to have someone to talk to about everything. I like the understanding and concerned Emma, but I love the loud and blunt Emma more. She is able to take a bad situation and make everyone smile. During these times, we all need that.

"It's nothing really. My mind just wandered for a minute. I can't think about the future. I have to live in the here and now." As Emma continues to watch me, I close my notebook. Pushing myself off of the bed, I start to walk out of the room and expect Emma to follow me, but she doesn't. I stop in the middle of the hallway and turn around. What is she doing? Walking back into the room, I find her staring at the floor in the exact same spot.

"You ok, Emma?" I ask.

She blinks repeatedly and looks at me, as if seeing me for the first time. What just happened? "Oh, yeah, sorry. Just thinking." She laughs and starts walking downstairs. "See what being around you does to me? Emma thinking? Preposterous." I laugh but look at her closer. Nothing seems wrong. She just seems a little out of sorts.

"Are you sure you're ok?"

"When did you turn into the worrier?" she asks me. "Usually everyone is worried about you."

"You thinking has us all confused," I tell her. "Don't do that any-more." With a laugh, she bumps her shoulder into mine as we enter the living room.

All the guys are seated on the couch or on the floor, watching a movie. I walk into the kitchen and grab a water bottle out of the fridge before returning to the room. I stop behind the couch and look to see which movie they are watching. I gasp when I see Robert Downey Jr. assembling his Iron Man suit. I am a sucker for superhero movies. Liam and Colton both turn around and look up at me smiling, obviously amused at my reaction.

I jump over the back of the couch and plop down beside them. Laughing, they move to the side a little to give me more room. I lean forward and throw my notebook on the new coffee table. I don't know when Tom had time to buy new furniture. I lean back against the back of the couch. Colton's arm, which is resting on the back, moves forward onto my shoulders. I lean into his side but don't look at him. I still don't know anything about his situation with Natasha, but after my last confrontation with her, I know I don't want to find out anytime soon.

I refuse to acknowledge the tingly feeling that spreads through me while his fingers unknowingly trace patterns into my arm. It takes everything in me not to glance down at my arm and watch his hand move across my skin. If I draw attention to it, he'll stop, and I don't want that. I peek over and see Emma watching us with a sincere smile on her face. She isn't grinning obnoxiously trying to embarrass me, which is out of sorts for her. She's up to something...

The movie ends, but no one moves. "Ryanne, is that a mustache on your shirt?" I look at my shirt to see what David is talking about before looking back at him.

"Yes. Yes it is." I nod but keep my expression blank. He raises an eyebrow at me, silently asking me why I have a shirt with a mustache on it. With a shrug, I say, "Mustaches are cool."

"Since when?"

"Since forever. All the cool guys have a mustache." I turn around and look at everyone in the room. Not a single one of them has a mustache. It's a shame, really. I mumble an apology before turning back toward David.

"Name one cool guy with a mustache," challenges David.

"Umm, Charlie Chaplin and Clark Gable had mustaches. There's two for ya," I pause and think about more men who have or had mustaches. "Oh, Tom Selleck has one." David is looking at me like I'm crazy. Well, I'll give him crazy. "Mario and Luigi. The Pringles guy. Papa Smurf. Captain Hook. Jafar. Gepetto. Yosemite Sam." I pause trying to think of any more. "Mr. Potato Head!"

David, Colton, and Liam all start laughing. No one can say anything through their laughter. "I told you so." I lean back against Colton. He is still shaking with laughter. To my right, Logan, Bragden, and Larkin are all laughing at my response. Emma just shakes her head at me because she was expecting that. She seems to be the only person that understands how truly strange I really am.

David picks up the television remote and starts flipping through the channels, quietly laughing still. "You're pretty cool, Ryanne," he says with his eyes glued to the television screen.

"It's about time someone realizes it," I mumble. David smiles at me, while Colton and Liam chuckle again. Without realizing it, I move closer to Colton and snuggle against his chest, making myself comfortable. My eyes are starting to feel heavy. I want to keep them open, but my body refuses to listen as I drift to sleep.

COLTON

I LOOK DOWN AND WATCH Ryanne sleep against my chest. Her dark eyelashes fan across her cheekbones. I reach down and gently pull on a spiraled ringlet and watch as it bounces back into place. When she lets her hair air-dry, it's very curly. I honestly like her curly hair better. It's unruly and incredibly attractive on her because she just doesn't care. Ryanne is naturally beautiful, without all the make-up and the hair products that Emma keeps trying to get her to wear. I'm glad that Ryanne is adamant on that issue.

"If only she could see how you're looking at her right now," Emma whispers to me. When I look at her, I see the sincerity in her eyes. What's going on? Emma always has a completely blunt and ridiculous comment to say about my feelings toward Ryanne. I narrow my eyes at Emma and find David also giving her a confused look. Neither of us knows what is going on. Slowly, I ask, "What are you doing Emma?"

"Nothing. I was just talking to Ryanne earlier today, when she got out of the shower. She basically told me the same thing that Liam said," Emma glances over to Liam. "It was then that I realized how young she actually is. I mean, she's only a year younger than me but has to deal with so much more. I wouldn't be able to do it like she is." Ryanne starts moving, but she's still asleep. She does look so much younger when she is sleeping. Her facial expressions are smooth and peaceful. She doesn't look worried or determined. I look toward Liam. Understanding what I'm asking of him, he leans back and closes his eyes.

"She's just dreaming," he says a few seconds later. "Nothing bad is happening. It's a normal dream." It's always good to check. She's woken up with numerous injuries from the dreams she goes into. None of us know how she constantly is able to transport into a dream. Like a lot of things Ryanne can do, it's inexplicable. Liam can usually tell when something is wrong, but it never hurts to be completely positive.

"I think I'm going to go put her in her bed," I shift her in my lap, so I can carry her upstairs. Emma gets off the couch and kisses David goodnight.

"I'll join you. I'm pretty tired myself."

THE NEXT MORNING, I WAKE up early and get dressed in my usual dark jeans and a black fitted t-shirt. I walk into the hallway and stop short when I hear her voice. There isn't a piano accompanying it. The hall is empty and quiet, so I know everyone else is still sleeping. I slowly walk down the stairs, trying not to make any noise. I don't want to disturb whatever she's doing.

The living room is empty, but I can hear water running in the kitchen. As I get closer, I can suddenly hear the music playing quietly. I stop in the doorway and watch. Ryanne is standing over the sink, washing the dishes. Her iPod is placed into a docking station to her left. A man's voice is coming out of the speakers. Ryanne is singing along with the country music, slightly dancing. The song is more upbeat than any of the songs I've heard her sing before.

I cross my arms and lean against the doorframe. She would hate that I caught her singing and dancing to the music and didn't alert her when I first came into the room. I watch as her tiny frame moves with the music. She doesn't look like your typical mage. Most of us are large. We're born to be prepared to fight and defend ourselves and others. The majority of the women are at least 5'10," but Ryanne is a good seven inches shorter than that. She is almost a full foot shorter than me. Her small stature makes her looks so breakable compared to the rest of us and despite the muscle she has gained from training, she still looks fragile. She brings out all the protective genes in us; especially Liam and me.

The song transitions from the country song to one I recognized: "Under Control" by Parachute. She starts singing and moving along with this song as well. I can see the bubbles rising in the sink. Ever since Claire…died, Ryanne has taken up the cleaning duties. We try to help her, but like Claire, she usually refuses any help. I feel a twinge in my chest when I think about Claire. I really do miss her. I barely remember life before Claire took David and me in.

"I told you. And she wasn't even singing last night," Liam whispers as he walks past me and into the kitchen. He opens the fridge and grabs a bottle of Gatorade. He quietly closes it and comes back to me. Ryanne still doesn't know that we are in the room. She places the wet plate onto a towel and reaches for another dirty plate. I walk forward and grab some of the wet plates and dry them, before giving them to Liam to put away.

She goes to put the next plate on the towel, but I take it out of her hand before she can. I smile down at her as she realizes that we are here. She abruptly stops singing and freezes, but the music continues in the background. Her large hazel eyes widen, and her cheeks redden with her blush. She gets embarrassed so easily. I can't help the laugh that forms when I see how embarrassed she is at being caught.

"How long have you guys been standing there?" she quietly asks.

"Long enough." I can hear the amusement in Liam's voice when he answers her question. She groans and reaches for another plate. I continue drying and handing the dry dishes to Liam. She moves so her hair falls across her face, blocking it from me. Since her hair is so long, it is almost sitting in the dirty, soapy water.

"Your hair is going to get all wet," I tell her. She mumbles something about not caring, but a couple seconds later she flips it over her shoulder.

Another song comes on, and I recognize the singer. Ryanne loves Sara Bareilles and listens to her music often. She knows how to play most of her songs on the piano. She starts to hum the song but can't hold it in anymore. When the chorus comes, she starts to sing again. I look to Liam and roll my eyes. She can't stay mad at us for long. She finishes washing the dishes and dries her hands off before turning to us.

"I didn't wake either of you did I? I was trying to be quiet this morning…but obviously I wasn't." A slight blush rises onto her cheeks for a second time this morning.

"Nope. I was already awake," I reply at the same time that Liam said, "You didn't wake anyone up." She nods, looking somewhat relieved. She always worries about everyone else. I glance down at what she is wearing and smile when I read her t-shirt. She is wearing an "I'm with a Muggle" shirt with an arrow pointing to the right. She has the strangest shirts ever, but they completely show her personality.

She must have seen me look at it because she says, "I'm hoping Bragden stands right here." Waving her hands over the area to her right, she continues, "I mean, who doesn't know who Ron Weasley is?" she mumbles as she walks out of the room.

"Hope you're up to date on your movie references, otherwise you're screwed," Liam whispers as he follows Ryanne out of the room.

Liam is sitting on the couch, and Ryanne is lying on the ground on her stomach with her notebook in front of her. She pushed the coffee table against the wall, and with a pencil between her teeth, she stares down at the paper in front of her, thinking.

"You do realize that the entire couch is free for you to sit on?" I ask.

Her eyes don't leave the paper, but she takes the pencil from her mouth. "You do realize that Liam is sitting on the couch, so it's not entirely free anymore, don't you?" she says. I move around her and sit down on the couch, watching as Ryanne slides her pencil across the page. It looks like she is drawing a bird cage. Inside the cage is a small detailed bird. The door of the bird cage is hanging open. Cursive writing wraps around the exterior of the cage. I lean closer a little to see what she wrote: *If you love something, set it free.*

David, Emma, Bragden, and Logan all come down the stairs. David and Emma are laughing and Bragden and Logan are talking. All the guys go into the kitchen to find something to eat for breakfast, while Emma sits down in the chair.

"Do the guys have cooties or something, Ryanne?" She doesn't say anything but continues to add details to the drawing. That always happens; she gets so into something that she forgets about her surroundings.

She stops drawing and looks back a little. She sighs and then looks up at Emma, who is also watching her. "Did you say something?"

Emma shakes her head, "Nope. I didn't say anything." Ryanne obviously doesn't catch the sarcasm because she nods and gets up. She leaves her notebook on the floor and walks past us into the kitchen. She grabs a water bottle out of the fridge and takes a sip. Placing the bottle on the table, she stands next to Bragden. David starts laughing before Ryanne even says anything. Bragden looks as confused as ever.

All of the sudden, Ryanne stops smiling and whispers something. Bragden reaches out and catches her before she falls to the ground.

CHAPTER
THIRTEEN

THE ROOM IS BRIGHT. TOO bright. The lighting makes it hard to keep my eyes open to see where I am. The smell of harsh cleaning products permeates the air. My head is throbbing as I try to sit up. I feel like someone hit me in the head with a brick. Black spots invade my vision as I try to stand. When the room starts spinning, I lean back against the wall trying to regain my equilibrium. What the heck just happened? Reaching up, I feel my head, wincing as I hit a sore spot.

How did I get here? What's going on? I lean forward and try to clear the fog in my head. I can't remember anything. When the spinning stops and only the headache remains, I straighten up and look around the room. Nothing. There's nothing in here; just bare, bright white tiled walls. It looks like a holding cell.

A holding cell!

Oh my gosh, am I back at Dravin's compound? A single door is centralized in the wall in front of me. I slowly walk to it and find it locked. I struggle against it, but it remains shut.

Why can't I remember anything? I start to pace the room. Someone locked me in this room. The last thing I remember is training with Liam and Larkin in the backyard. What happened after that? I am still wearing my training outfit, so whatever happened must have happened shortly after that. I try to call my magic to me, but nothing happens. This is starting to feel eerily similar to the last time I was captured.

The door across the room opens, and Adam walks in with a small smirk on his face, looking as arrogant as ever. I push myself up against the wall as he slowly walks toward me, trying to look confident. I'm not afraid of him…I can't be. He stops a foot away from me and stares, but doesn't make a move to do anything. I see four other men enter the room after him, two on either side of me.

"Adam, move." Dravin demands as he enters the room, followed by three other men, all struggling to contain someone. The man's hair is falling down in his face, but I instantly recognize who it is. When he lifts his head and his green eyes connect with mine, I start to run toward him. Two guys grab my arms and pull me back. Adam stands off to the side, watching everything play out. Colton looks tired and weak. I'm positive that he put up a fight against the men containing him. The darkness under his eye from being punched and dried blood under his nose are indicators of that.

"Ryanne, we've been in this situation before. Obviously, it didn't work out so well the first time, so we've evolved in the way we collect information," Dravin informs me. "I think you'll find this way much more effective."

I stop struggling against the two men and listen to what he's saying. This may be the only way we'll get out of here alive.

"Now that I have your attention, I want to inform you that we found a way to extract the magic from a mage. So, once we find out the extent of your powers, I can take your magic from you and let you live…if you

cooperate. Or, you can refuse to tell me anything, and your little friend here will experience a little of what you went through last time. What will it be?"

I look toward Colton. He's shaking his head, demanding me to remain quiet. I can't let anything happen to him, but I don't want Dravin to have my magic. He will use it for his personal gain only. He wants power and control and doesn't care about the consequences of his actions.

"Fine. If that's how it's going to be." Colton hisses in pain and falls to the ground, holding his head. I recognize what is happening to him. Dravin is making him see his worst experience in his mind. He is making him relive it. I start to fight against the men holding me. I get loose and kick the man in the jaw to my right. He falls to the ground unconscious. I turn around and punch the other man in the stomach. He doesn't fall but staggers back a little. I then kick him in his groin, and he doubles over in pain. Another man comes for me, and I kick him in the chest, knocking his head against the hard wall. He slumps to the ground, unmoving. Adam comes over and grabs me around the waist, forcefully pulling me against him.

"I'll tell you! I'LL TELL YOU!" I scream at Dravin. "Stop hurting him!" I whimper against Adam's hold. Dravin turns away from Colton, but doesn't lessen his magic, and smiles at me.

"That was pretty impressive. You just took out three of my best men without the use of any magic. There may be a use for you once all this is over after all."

Bringing a small dagger from the band around his waist, Dravin crouches beside Colton. Stabbing the dagger into Colton's side, he glances over his shoulder to gauge my reaction before yanking it out of his body. I cry out as deep red blood starts oozing out of the wound. I fight against Adam, but he just tightens his grip on my stomach. I can't *breathe against his hold. Dravin stands up and cleans his dagger on his pants and walks toward me.*

"Do you know what I made him see?" he asks me. I don't take my eyes away from Colton. "I made him see his worst fear. Do you know what that was?" He's still watching the scene play out in his mind, oblivious to his fatal wound. I need to get to him, but Adam's hold on me is too strong. "His worst fear was watching you be killed in front of him when he couldn't do anything to help you." Dravin starts laughing. "Which is kind of ironic because now you have to watch him die, while you can do nothing to save him."

I watch Colton as he stops writhing. He never opens his eyes. A large pool of blood is forming on the ground beneath him. Dravin and his men start to leave the room, but Adam and his death grip on me still remain.

Stopping in the doorway, Dravin turns and addresses me, "Next time, I'd give up the information I need. You still have other friends I could find." With that, he leaves the room and the grip around my waist disappears. I scramble away from Adam and run toward Colton. I roll him onto his back and check for a pulse, a heartbeat, anything.

Nothing.

Colton is dead.

COLTON

"THIS IS THE LONGEST SHE'S ever been in a vision." I'm starting to get a little worried. What is she seeing?

Bragden is holding Ryanne's limp body back against his. He is supporting her weight, while keeping her upright. Liam is staring at Ryanne with the same worried look we all have. He is unconsciously rubbing his upper arm. I open my mouth to ask him about it when I hear Ryanne gasp.

We all turn toward her and can instantly tell something is wrong. She starts blinking rapidly. I can do nothing but watch as sadness and anger bleed onto her face before she collapses to the ground. Bragden tries to catch her before she falls, but she hits the ground and starts sobbing, curling herself into a small ball.

Liam and I start to walk toward her. I stop back a little way and let Liam crouch down beside her, "Ryanne, what did you see?" Placing a hand on her back, Ryanne's cries quiet a little, but they don't stop. After a couple seconds, she stands up and looks around the room; her eyes land on Larkin.

"Take me to Dravin." Larkin's eyes widen as her statement sinks in. What did she see that would make her want to go to Dravin? Larkin shakes his head, refusing to listen to her. "I need you to do this for me, Larkin. Take me to Dravin." Her voice is pleading with him, desperate for someone to take her away from here. Tears are streaming down her face.

No one says anything. The room is tense and silent. Larkin walks over to Ryanne. He better not be considering her demand. She will not be going back to Dravin's compound. He slowly shakes his head at her again. She stares up at him for a couple seconds, possibly waiting for him to change his mind. Her bottom lip starts quivering. She turns around to run out of the room, but I block her. She runs straight into me. I wrap my arms around her small frame and hug her to me.

Her body tenses momentarily, before she hugs me back and starts sobbing again. I look over her head toward Liam, wondering if he has any idea what is going on. He is rubbing his arm again. He follows my eyes down to his arm. A confused look crosses his face before he says, "Colton check her arms and stomach for bruises."

Ryanne starts shaking her head and tries to get away from me. I lean down and slowly brush her sleeve back. I hear everyone behind me gasp at the sight. She stops struggling when I see the deep purple bruises on her arm in the outline of a hand. I reach down and slowly lift the bottom hem of her shirt to see her stomach. I hiss when I see the even darker bruises forming against her pale skin.

I look back into her eyes and see the tears silently running down her face. I step forward and place my hands on either side of her face, wiping off the tears. She closes her eyes and leans into me. "What happened?" I whisper. I want to help end the pain she is experiencing, both physically and emotionally. I need to be able to do something to help her. Her eyes snap open when Logan starts walking toward her. She steps away from me and starts walking backwards.

"Please don't. I don't want you to see that," she says quietly. Her whole body is shaking. Logan reaches out and gently grabs her small arm and closes his eyes. I watch as Logan's face transforms from one of concentration, to one of anger, then to sadness. He opens his eyes and looks at her with that same reaction, before turning to me. I am about to ask what he saw, when Ryanne collapses to the ground again, violently shaking.

"Step back," Liam says as he runs toward her. "She's losing control of her magic."

She cries out as a loud clap of thunder shakes the house. We all take a step backwards. "How can we help her?" I ask Liam frantically. I've never seen her not in control. It upsets me that she has seen something that's causing her to react like that.

"I don't know!" he shouts. I've never seen Liam like this either. He is always so collected—never showing any emotions except around Ryanne. He looks down at her and then glances at Bragden. Bragden nods, agreeing to whatever Liam silently told him. "I have to knock her out. I'm going to go into her subconscious."

He reaches out and touches her back. He winces as his hand connects, but he doesn't move away. Closing his eyes, he goes into Ryanne's mind. I wasn't aware that he could do that. I watch Ryanne on the ground; she's still shaking as she tries to regain control. Liam's face scrunches together, and he places his other hand on her as well. This isn't going to work. Ryanne's still whimpering. More thunder rumbles outside. Liam pushes himself onto his knees and applies more pressure to her back. A couple seconds later, she goes limp under his hands. He breathes in deeply before staggering backwards. His hands are red as if he held them over an open flame.

"Ouch, she's stronger than I thought." Logan walks over to heal him. None of us move.

When Logan finishes healing him, Liam bends down and picks Ryanne up off the ground. He sets her down on the couch. I can see the tension in his back as he crouches in front of her. Liam's just as upset over all of this as the rest of us. Liam and Ryanne have a unique connection, and it bothers him when he's unable to help her in these situations. Ryanne's head rolls to the side, and her hair falls across her face. Gently, he reaches forward and brushes it away and turns toward Logan. "Which one of us was it?"

"What are you talking about," I ask him.

"Ryanne wouldn't act like that unless she saw something happen to one of us. She was shaken up when she saw herself get stabbed, but this…this was different. She saw something happen to someone in this room." Liam turns back toward Logan, waiting on his response. Logan walks into the living room and sits down in the chair closest to Ryanne's head. I sit down on the couch near her feet. David and Emma walk over to their chair. Larkin, Bragden, and Liam all remain standing. Waiting.

"Colton," he finally says. "She saw Colton die."

I just stare at Logan, while everyone turns and looks at me. Me? I look down at Ryanne unconscious on the couch, beside me. "She reacted like that because she saw me die?"

"Dravin killed you. Right in front of her. You told her not to tell him anything, so she didn't and you were killed because of it."

Emma shakes her head, "Please start from the beginning. What exactly happened?"

Logan explains everything. He made sure not to leave out any details. "It was horrible," he shakes his head and looks at me. "I never want to hear her scream like that again. I'll never be able to get that sound out of my mind," he leans forward and rests his head in his hands. "She took on five guys, without any magic to try and save you, but it was too late. You were...dead."

"What happened after that? After Adam released her?" Emma asks. I tense at his name. I never want that guy near her again. It makes me incredibly mad that he is still able to hurt her when he isn't around us.

"Dravin told her that she should have given him the information he wanted. He threatened to find the rest of us if she didn't tell him soon."

"You could tell her now," Emma suggests to me.

"No," Liam, Logan, and I all shoot down Emma's idea. We aren't trying to be rude, but I can't tell her now. This is definitely not the time for that.

"She would definitely find a way to give herself to Dravin if I told her," I explain. I can't believe that she would lose control like that; it frightens me that she will react that violently over something happening to any one of us. It was just a vision. I look over at Logan and see him pretty shaken up as well. He keeps running his hand through his short hair, taking deep breaths.

"I would react similarly if I had the vision. Especially after some of the stuff she's seen. It's one thing to be told what happened, but to actually see it…" Logan shakes his head. "I've seen almost everything she's been through but to actually feel it and experience it…I can't imagine," he isn't talking to anyone in particular. Ryanne groans and grabs her head. We all quiet. I know that she's blocking our thoughts, well blocking everyone else's thoughts.

She sits up slowly but doesn't look at anyone. She leans forward and rests her head on to her knees, letting her hair create a curtain around her.

"Did I hurt anyone?" she quietly asks.

"No."

She shakes her head again. "I don't know what happened. All of the sudden, I couldn't keep it all down anymore. I was trying to fight it, but it wouldn't go away. I couldn't control it. I was so afraid that I was going to hurt someone." She still won't look at any of us. "Logan told you, didn't he?"

"Ryanne, can I talk to you? Alone…" I ask. She doesn't move. I move over and grab her wrist, gently pulling her off the couch. She complies and follows me out of the room.

CHAPTER
FOURTEEN

"LOOK, I'M SORRY I REACTED that way. I'm just tired of seeing everyone get hurt. I'm tired of these visions. I only see death. It's so hard." I tell him as we enter his room. He lets go of my wrist and turns around to shut the door.

"Ryanne, you can't do that." I'm not sure what he is referring to. The fact that I lost control of my magic? I didn't mean for that to happen. I tried really hard to fight it. When I don't respond, he continues, "You can't ask Larkin to take you to Dravin. You can't give yourself to him. No matter what happens from here on out, you can't surrender yourself to him."

"I can't watch that vision play out, Colton. I can't watch anyone else die because of me. I can't." He's standing a couple feet away from me, leaning against the closed door. He closes his eyes and leans his head back until he hits the wooden surface.

Exhaling loudly, he says, "I don't care if that vision plays out, Ryanne. You can't tell Dravin anything that he can use to hurt you. Do you know what it would do to us if something were to happen to you?"

"If something were to happen to me? To me? I don't have anyone besides you guys. You have a brother, Colton. You have an Uncle. You have a family! They love you and would be mad at me if I didn't do something, anything, to stop that vision. You have more people that care for you than I do. They'd be more upset if something were to happen to you than to me. People would only be upset because I'm the prophecy girl. If I wasn't, you wouldn't even know me! We wouldn't be in this situation. Everything that has happened is entirely my fault! I need to put an end to all of this."

"You don't need to do anything. No one would be mad at you if something happened to me. You're *our* family! You have us. All of us— Liam, David, Emma, Logan, Bragden, Tom, even Larkin—we care about you, Ryanne."

"I'd be mad at myself. Don't you understand that? I don't care what happens to me!"

"You need to start caring!" He is yelling now. "You need to care about what happens to yourself. We all need you. You're the only one that can help us get out of this situation." I flinch as if he'd slapped me.

"So that's all I am? A way out of this situation?" He starts to refute my comment, but I interrupt him. "Because I already know that. I'm just a pawn. The easy way for all of this to end is to remove myself from the equation."

Taking a deep breath to calm down, Colton pushes away from the door and steps in my direction. "We can change the vision," he says softly.

"What if we can't?" He stops right in front of me. I look at the collar of his shirt not meeting his eyes. I can't think straight when I look into his eyes. "What if nothing can change it? What then? I can't watch that vision play out in real life, Colton. I can't watch you die." He wraps his arms around me and pulls me against him.

"The future can always be changed," he pauses to collect his thoughts. "The future is affected by the course you are on now and the actions you make while on that course. The past is the only thing set in stone, and change is the only thing constant in life. You can't think about how to change it; just let it happen naturally. Everything will work out in the end."

"You can't ask me to endure watching you die while I do nothing. I couldn't take it."

"I watched you die, Ryanne, right in front of me," he whispers. I finally lean back and look up at him. His green gaze meets mine. "I wanted to walk right out into that fight and hurt every single person I came across because of what happened to you. But I didn't. I stayed with you." There is something more to that, and I am going to ask him about it, but I stop when I see the look he is giving me.

He searches my eyes for something before his eyes land on my mouth. "Colton," I whisper. My heartbeat starts racing—the racing it does whenever he looks at me, but this is different. Standing so close to him, I can feel his heartbeat increase as well. Does Colton have feelings for me too? His eyes return to mine. He tucks a strand of hair behind my ear. His hand lingers there for a moment before slowly moving to the back of my neck. My legs must have a mind of their own because I find myself moving closer to him. He looks back at me one more time before leaning in. I close my eyes and wait.

His lips gently brush against mine at first. I'd never been kissed before, but already I feel like jello. With his lips pressed firmly against mine, my knees start to become wobbly. I need to steady myself. I slide my arms up his hard chest and stand up on my tip-toes to wrap them around his neck. His arm tightens around my waist, pulling me closer against him. I tentatively open my mouth and brush my tongue against his lip. It feels like a million tiny volts of electricity are running through me. An unfamiliar heat spreads through me as I press myself closer to him. He groans and moves his hand from my neck and fists it into my hair.

The kiss becomes more urgent. I push against him harder. The butterflies in my stomach are now fluttering uncontrollably. My feet leave the ground as he lifts me up, so I am closer to his height. Our mouths move in synchronized movements. I gasp when his tongue meets mine. The hand around my waist bunches into my shirt. His hand brushes against the bare skin on my back, sending goosebumps up and down my arms. I run my hand through Colton's hair, enjoying the way it falls through my fingers. He lowers me back to the ground, slowly kissing me still.

He pulls back; his lips lingering in front of mine. He kisses me once more before pulling away again. I keep my eyes closed, waiting for my mind to process what just happened. Colton just kissed me…? When I no longer feel his breath hitting my cheek, I open my eyes and find a green pair watching me. Colton is trying to hide a smile. I bite my lip, trying to savor the taste of him, and smile up at him. He takes a small step back and runs a hand through his hair, taming the mess I made.

"I-I…" he starts.

"Colton," I begin but stop when something flashes before my eyes. It appeared and left so quickly that I'm not sure what I actually saw. I try to start the sentence a second time, but a blinding pain shoots through my head. I wince and gently place a hand on my temple.

Colton moves toward me again. "What's wrong?"

I shake my head. I'm pretty sure this is nothing to worry about. "Nothing. I'm sorry, I just got a headache. I think I'm going to go lay down."

COLTON

I WATCH AS RYANNE BRUSHES past me and walks into her room, closing the door behind her. If she didn't wince and grab her head, I would have thought that was an excuse to get away from me. I can still taste her against my lips; feel her pressed against me. Is there anything I can do to help? She probably just needs to rest. A lot has happened to her recently. I hear Emma laughing downstairs, so I slowly turn away and walk back to the living room.

The room gets quiet when I enter it. All conversations stop. I sit down on the couch. Everyone is watching me. Thankfully the only people in the room are David, Emma, Liam, and Logan. My brain finally catches up with me. What did I just do? I groan and cover my face.

"Ooooh, now you have to tell me. I was going to wait until you were ready to talk, but after that reaction I need to know what happened right now," Emma says excitedly. "Did she yell at you? Hit you? Did she call you some inappropriate name? I've never heard her cuss before...tell me what happened or my thoughts will not be as PG rated as they are right now. Do you want me to say everything else that I think could have happened?"

"I kissed her." Why the hell did I kiss her? What is wrong with me? When Ryanne said that I wouldn't know her if she wasn't the prophecy girl...I wanted to tell her everything. I wanted to tell her how wrong she was—to show her.

"You kissed the kissing virgin?" asks Emma. I glare at her, while David laughs. I glance toward the window. The sky is darkening. Is Ryanne doing that? "Was she any good?"

If she didn't tell us that she'd never kissed anyone before, I wouldn't have believed it. Ryanne could kiss. There is no denying that.

I push away from the couch and start pacing behind it. "I shouldn't have done that. I just couldn't help myself. The way she looked at me….Ugh, I'm supposed to be distancing myself from her, trying to make it easier in case something were to happen to me, but no. I just *had* to kiss her!" I punch the wall. I don't want to bring myself closer to her. I'm already too close. I need to protect her, not complicate things. She will already do reckless things in order to save everyone else.

Emma walks in front of me and puts a hand out to stop me. I stop pacing and give her my attention. She is a lot taller than Ryanne, so I don't have to look down. "Don't regret what you did, Colton," she moves so that she is standing directly in front of me. "Ryanne would have acted out whether or not you kissed her. You remember what she did for you when you were fighting Adam. It's just who she is. She's always had feelings for you, Colton. At least, since I've met her. I promised her I wouldn't tell you that, but you're too stupid to realize it on your own."

"What?" Ryanne has feelings for me? I thought back…I make her blush easily, but she blushes for everyone.

"Yeah, she told me about how she met you in the bookstore. About the gazebo. About the times you tried to kiss her before. You should have seen her when she caught you kissing Natasha…I wanted to hit you for doing that to her." Emma takes a step toward me. I didn't realize how close Emma and Ryanne were. I didn't know that Ryanne would tell her everything. Wait…

"She saw that?"

"Yeah, she did. Liam knows." I look over at Liam and find him nodding.

"She was crushed," he says.

"I was so mad at you for not realizing it then, and then your stupid girlfriend kept telling Ryanne all this crap about how she'd never be good enough for you, so she gave you space. Ever since Natasha, Ryanne's been trying to move on from you because she thought she wasn't good enough. She compared herself to Natasha and thought that you'd never be interested in her after that. But I see how she looks at you when you aren't looking, and I see how you look at her. Don't you dare go and break her heart again, Colton. If you do, you'll have a very mad best friend to deal with, got it?"

Ryanne's too good for me, not the other way around. However, I understand where Emma is coming from; I want to keep her safe too. Emma wants to keep Ryanne safe from me though. She is afraid I am going to hurt her. I'm not sure that I won't end up doing that. I lean back against the wall and think about what Emma just told me.

"Where is Ryanne now?" Liam asks.

"Her room. After…wards, she winced and grabbed her head. She went to lie down because she had a headache." Emma heads upstairs to go check on her.

"Even Emma is protective of Ryanne. Who knew?" I mumble.

"I did. You should hear how she talks about her."

"Guys, something's not right," Liam says. I turn and look at him. He looks worried.

"With Ryanne?" I ask. Emma runs down the stairs and thrusts Ryanne's notebook at me.

"Have you seen this door before?"

"Umm…." I look at the drawing. It looks like a normal door—one that could belong to any house. It isn't as detailed at her other drawing.

"Ryanne's missing! Have you seen the door?" Emma yells. Liam winces and grabs his leg. Ryanne is hurt somewhere.

"I think it could be Jane's. I'm not sure though."

"Larkin!" Emma screams. Larkin appears in the room. Emma throws the notebook at him.

"Go there. Find Ryanne. Colton thinks it's Jane's house."

CHAPTER
FIFTEEN

I FINISH DRAWING THE DOOR when I feel myself being thrown backwards. I close my eyes because the transportation is always easier when I don't try and watch. When I keep my eyes open, it feels like my body is being pulled in all different directions, slowly ripping apart. I land on my stomach in the grass. "Ouch." I wince and jump up, moving toward the bushes, waiting for something to happen. I wouldn't have been transported here if I wasn't needed.

I stay down, unnoticed, until the three men get closer to me. I notice the knives two of them are carrying. I glance at my empty hands. Why do I never think to bring a weapon with me? Well, this could get interesting.

I jump out of the bushes and run toward them, calling magic to me. I do a double full twist like I did during training with Liam and visualized lightning striking the man with the larger knife in his hand. All men stop when they see me flipping toward them. When my momentum stops, I hit the man with my magic. He flies backwards and slams into a large tree in the distance. I turn back toward the other two men and instantly start fighting.

I'm not sure how I am doing it or how my body knows exactly what to do, but somehow I haven't been stabbed yet, which is an accomplishment for me. Despite my lack of a weapon and the fact that it's two large men against a small girl, it's a pretty even fight. I can feel the bruises forming on my shoulders and arms from where I am hit, but all things considered, I'll take a few bruises. I duck as the man with a knife swings it around, attempting to slice me. Instead, he hits the other man. He falls to the ground, grasping at his chest. I bring my leg up and kick the injured man. He falls to the ground, spitting up blood. I turn my attention back to the other man. However, my attention is a little too late. I cry out as he plants the knife into my left thigh. When dark blood starts spilling out of the wound and running down my leg, he jerks the knife out and smiles down at me. I call more magic and thrust it toward the man as I fall to the ground. He staggers backwards but doesn't fall.

I stand up and balance myself onto my right leg. I gather up more energy and thrust it toward him again as he starts to walk toward me. I am slowly losing energy. When my magic connects with him this time, he is sent flying backwards like the first man. "Larkin," I try yelling, but my voice isn't as loud as I want it to be.

I look down at my leg and see the steady stream of blood cascading down the entire length of my leg. "Larkin," I call again, even quieter than the first.

I fall to the ground and cry out in pain at the movement. I try to crawl away but can't move my left leg at all. I feel hands wrap around my waist, pulling me into a standing position. I scream and start to fight until I look around and see Liam and Colton staring at me.

"Logan," Larkin yells. He turns toward Liam and Colton. "I have to go clean up the yard. I'll be right back." When Larkin lets go of me, I fall to the ground, no longer able to support my weight. I shriek when my left leg hits the floor. I roll onto my back and grab my leg, trying to hold back the tears that threaten to spill.

"Holy sh..." Colton starts, but Logan runs into the room and interrupts him.

"What's going on?" His eyes widen when he sees me lying on the floor, blood oozing out of my leg.

He drops to the floor beside me, closes his eyes, and concentrates on healing me. I close my eyes as the room begins to spin around me. I'm seeing doubles of everything, and the lights are too bright. The pain in my leg starts to dissipate, and a dull pain replaces it. "For some reason, I can't heal it all the way. I've stopped the bleeding though."

I sit up and try to stand but can't move my left leg very well. Logan helps me stand. I grab onto his arms and let him pull me up. Liam hands me a wet towel. I hop over to the wall and lean against it. Bending over, I clean my leg of the dried blood and avoid everyone's penetrating gazes.

I am still dizzy and out of breath from fighting, but I manage to speak. "You should see the other guys," I say when everyone continues to stare at me.

"Guys? There was more than one?" Colton yells. I knew he would be upset when he found out that I wasn't in my room, but it wasn't my fault.

"There were three actually. I took care of it."

Liam slowly walks over to me. "You promised me you'd stop going on these crazy missions of yours alone."

"I didn't mean to. I was in Colton's room when this image flashed across my mind, and I got a really bad headache, so I went back to my room. I had to draw something. I grabbed my notebook, and my hand just drew Jane's door and the next thing I know I'm sitting in her front yard, hiding in the bushes, waiting for something to happen." I don't mean to keep scaring him like this. I can't control everything that happens to me.

Larkin blinks back into the room. "You destroyed two trees in their front yard. It's going to be obvious that something happened there."

"What was I supposed to do?" I try not to grimace as I stand up straight, balancing my weight on my right leg. "I didn't have a weapon, while two of them had knives. My magic was all I could use."

Logan turns toward everyone, "Get off her case. She can't control when that happens. She did pretty well, all things considered." *Finally*, someone who understands.

"All things considered?" Colton steps forward. "She comes back here screaming and bleeding profusely, and you think she did pretty well?"

I push myself off the wall and take a step toward him. "I went against three large men and didn't get myself killed! I got injured, but that's nothing new." He growls at me. I flinch back but stay where I am.

"You shouldn't be going anywhere that's going to get you injured!"

"I can't help it. You said earlier that you need me to help you all get out of this situation. Well I'm doing my best to make sure that nothing happens to you guys! I can't always control everything."

He lowers his voice, "You know that's not what I meant."

"It doesn't matter what you meant. You still said it. I'm doing my best here, Colton." He needs to understand that I am trying really hard not to get myself killed. I'm just doing what has to be done. "I don't know much about the magic that's in me, but when I see something, I know I have to do something to help. I can't always control when or how it happens, but I see this stuff for a reason. I don't want to be thrown into these dangerous situations any more than the next guy, but for some reason, I am. For some reason, it has to be me." I turn around and look at Liam, "For some reason, I'm supposed to go alone." I take a small breath; I'm starting to feel really tired. "I can't drag you guys down with me."

Colton walks the last couple of steps toward me. He places a finger under my chin and tilts my face up, so I'm looking at him. Though I try not to, I glance at his lips for a split second, and I know he catches it.

"I can't handle watching you die again, Ryanne. I won't survive this time," he lets go of me and walks upstairs.

My eyes follow him as he walks away, but I don't say anything. There's nothing to say. Doesn't he know that I don't want to get killed either? I flinch at the sound of a door being slammed. Everyone else in the room just stares at me, waiting for my reaction. The throbbing in my left leg pursues and my eye lids start to close again.

"Liam, can you take me to my room? I'm not feeling well." Liam walks over to me, and I wrap my arms around his neck as he cradles me against his chest. The hall begins to spin as Liam carries me up the stairs. The colors around me blur into a vortex of nothingness, and I lose my battle to stay awake. I close my eyes and am surrounded by darkness yet again.

COLTON

I SLAM MY DOOR. I haven't done that since I was a kid and my parents yelled at me because I refused to clean the kitchen after I threw food at David. Now that I think about it, David and I always got in trouble for throwing food...why did we do that? I got grounded and thought that everyone hated me, so I ran up to my room and slammed my door. I realize how childish slamming my door just now was, but I couldn't help it.

I didn't mean to yell at her, I'm just so tired of her coming back to me covered in blood. I keep seeing her small body crumpled on the kitchen floor, blood pouring out of the large wound in her stomach after Thomas stabbed her. Every time she disappears, that flashes across my mind. I watched as she coughed up blood. I watched as she took her last breath. I watched as her eyes rolled back into her head, and her body went limp. As the life drained out of her eyes, I watched. I can't watch that happen again.

I just can't.

Someone starts knocking on my door. Emma's probably going to start yelling at me again. I don't mean to be such a jerk to her all the time. It's just very frustrating that she feels like she has to do all this stuff alone. We all want to help her. We're all standing here beside her, offering to help her, yet she won't accept it.

I open the door and instead of Emma, I come face to face with Liam.

"Did you really have to yell at her?" he asks me. "You know that she can't control that." I think I'd rather have Emma yell at me. At least I know what to expect with her. Liam's still a mystery to me.

"I know. I know. It's just so frustrating knowing that I can't do anything. That I can't help her."

"I understand that. I do. I feel every injury she gets. Obviously not as bad though. My skin just gets really itchy. I'm supposed to protect her, but I can't," he pauses briefly before continuing. "That girl that you can't help just passed out in my arms as I carried her to her room, while you were up here brooding. She needs you, Colton. Don't push her away right now. You can only push someone so far before they stop coming back. Even Ryanne has a limit."

"I'm not pushing her away. It's just that every time I see her come back with another injury, I picture what she looked like after Thomas stabbed her. The image is ingrained in my mind." I grab the back of my neck and look toward the ceiling. "It freaks me out that it could happen again. I won't be able to do anything the next time."

"You can't think like that. She needs someone to help her. She needs that to be you."

"She won't let me," my anger is slowly building. "I've tried to help her, but she won't let me."

"You're not trying hard enough, Colton. You just get mad at her when she does something wrong. When she wakes up, you need to go talk to her."

Liam walks out of the room, leaving me alone with my thoughts. How can I help Ryanne when she is always doing things on her own? How am I supposed to help her when she won't accept any? The only thing I am good at is fighting. It's what I've been trained to do my whole life. Tom worked with us every day when David and I were younger. As we got older, he stopped coming around as often, and David and I started training together.

I remember the day when David came into his power. We were training in the attic at Aunt Claire's house, when we went to grab our swords. David's came to him, while I had to walk over to get mine from the wall. David was so excited, and even though that was only two years ago, he started jumping around like a kid who got his favorite toy for Christmas. He'd just turned eighteen and was as giddy as a child. Eighteen is the age that most mages get their powers, but some don't get theirs until their mid-twenties. That is the situation for Bragden, Emma, and me.

Bragden is the oldest one of us. Being twenty-two, he should be coming into his powers soon. With Emma, at nineteen, and me, at eighteen, we still have time. Granted, I am going to be nineteen in a week but still. Who knows when it is going to happen for either of us? It could be tomorrow. It could be in a few months. We could still have years to go.

I walk out of my room and cross the hall. Ryanne and Emma's room is directly across from mine. Emma is sitting on her bed, flipping through a magazine while Ryanne is asleep in her bed with the white comforter pulled up to her chin. Her long curly hair is fanned across her pillow. I briefly wonder what it would look like against my green pillowcase. Shoot, Colton. Distance. Now, is not the time for *that*.

"Is she alright?" I ask Emma as I lean against the bed post at the end of Ryanne's bed.

"For now. When she wakes up? I'm not sure. She's been through a lot in the past couple of hours." Emma's also mad at me…not the loud anger she usually displays. I've never seen Emma like this before. Ryanne soundlessly rolls onto her side and places her hands under her cheek. She looks so serene. "Logan said she'd probably fall asleep from exhaustion."

"Emma, I'm not trying to hurt her. I'm trying to protect her. It's just sometimes the two correlate."

"I know you're not purposely trying to," Emma turns and looks at Ryanne too. She sighs loudly and looks back at me. Her blue eyes are more open than I've seen before. "Ryanne's not as strong as she wants everyone to believe. She's tough, but she's not indestructible. She does have limits, and she has been pushed toward them a lot lately. She's straddling the line right now, and she needs us to help pull her back."

I glance back over at her bed. Ryanne is on her side still with lips slightly apart, breathing quietly. Her hair is slowly sweeping forward, sliding across her shoulders. The covers have fallen, so I can see her t-shirt covered shoulder. She looks so peaceful now, but I know that when she wakes up, that countenance will change. She'll be the strong, determined girl she feels she needs to be.

"Look, I don't know if you've noticed, but Ryanne's changing. She used to wake up in the morning and come downstairs and join everyone, smiling, happy, and slightly overwhelmed. Now, she wakes up first, goes downstairs and does the dishes. The first thing she does in the morning is the dishes, Colton. Then, she finds her iPod. She listens to music and draws. Barely talking to anyone. She's stopped watching movies with us. She trains, Colton. That's the only time I see her act like she used to. Training makes her feel like she's doing something right. Besides the wedding, I haven't seen her actually smile in a while; the smile never reaches her eyes. She does what she has to to make sure that we don't notice anything. Liam and I have noticed little changes in her. Nothing major yet, but it's coming. She's freaking out about what is going on with her, and everyone keeps getting upset with her over things she can't control."

Why am I the one that's getting this speech all the time?

CHAPTER
SIXTEEN

RUNNING THROUGH THE DARKENED FOREST, I try not to trip on the uneven ground. Small, low-lying branches of the trees move and try to grab me as I rush past them; their leaves sway in the wind creating eerie whispers that echo from all directions. My skin is scarred from tree limbs jagged ends, but I push forward. I can't stop running. I can't slow down. I can't be caught.

Not again.

The footsteps behind me get louder as the man chasing me starts to close the distance between us. The darkness of the night mirrors the atmosphere of the forest. Everything in here is against me. I can't think, breathe, or move without someone or something trying to kill me.

A root of a large tree in front of me rises, trying to trip me or at the very least slow my momentum. I jump over the raised root and make a sharp turn to the left. Not sticking in one direction may help me lose the man following me.

I glance over my shoulder and watch as he also makes a sharp turn. Ducking another moving branch, I cry out as its sharpened edge slices through my arm. Deep red bloods start flowing down my skin, but there's nothing I can do right now. I have to keep moving.

"You can't keep running from me," Dravin's voice echoes through the dark forest. I can't tell where the voice is coming from, but my fear causes me to run faster. Jumping over another root, I turn to the right. I can hear water flowing in a nearby river ahead.

"I'll always find you," his voice rides the wind to my right. Suppressing my feared cry, I run in the opposite direction of the sound. The footsteps behind me are still following my every movement. My chances of losing him are slim to none. I know that the man chasing me isn't Dravin, but he is near—watching everything play out like a sick game.

"No one is safe." I feel his breath on the back of my neck. I scream and seeing the water in front of me, I run toward it. Maybe the man behind me can't swim. It's worth a shot. Trying to keep my momentum, I run into the river. The rapid water pushes against my side, trying to pull me under. Again, everything is against me.

A large hand wraps around my arm and jerks me backwards. I whip around and attempt to fight off whoever grabbed me. The sudden movement and the intensity of the water causes me to lose my footing. I scream as my feet are lifted up off of the rocky bottom and I fall into the cold, dark water. The stranger's grip around my arm disappears; my body is pulled by the current down the river.

Gasping for air, I try to keep my head above the surface. The water is flowing too rapidly for me to swim to the other side. I should have noticed that before I ran into the river, but I was too focused on getting away. This seemed like my only chance of losing him, and I did lose him, but at what cost? Spotting a floating tree trunk off to the side, I stop struggling and let the water move me in that direction. If I could just grab onto it, I could use it to stay afloat.

I collect a breath of air before the current pulls me under. I can't see anything through the darkness. I push my arms upward to try and reach the surface, but I don't know which direction it is in. I can't panic; that won't help anything. The cold water sends chills through my body, slowing everything down. I can't move my limbs as quickly as I could mere seconds ago.

Out of sheer luck, I break the surface. Sputtering, I spit water out of my mouth and search around for that tree trunk again. Yes! It's within an arm's reach now. My muscles protest as I try to swim towards it. Hypothermia is already setting in. My arms wrapped around the wood, but its water logged surface snaps in half and I go under again. I don't have time to catch my breath. With my lungs filling with water, I struggle to reach the surface. My arms and legs are moving in all direction, but I'm still pulled deeper into the freezing water.

Disoriented and growing weaker with every second, my need to fight wanes. My body can't push anymore. Deep laughter echoes around me as I sink further into the darkness. The chilled water freezes my muscles in their current positions. The water pushes me from all directions: up, down, left, right. I can't fight. My lungs protest for air, but I have no way to get any. I swallow more water.

Dravin's won.

With that thought, I close my eyes and wait for Death to come to me. He's near. I can feel his presence around me. It's not harsh and domineering like Dravin's. Death is…misunderstood. In this instance, I don't fear it. At this moment, I welcome it. My lungs reach their limit and my body starts shutting down. I'm no longer in control. My eyes snap open as an unearthly gray light spirals through the water towards my frozen hand. Slender, ashen colored fingers extend from a closed fist and point at me. The hand, covered in tattered black cloth, grabs onto my wrist and pulls me down further. I can't fight Death's grip.

I gave it my all. There was nothing else I could do. Dravin was just stronger. It's that simple.

A scorching pain spreads through my stomach and Death halts his momentum. Though underwater, everything around me becomes clear again. I open my mouth to scream as the pain shoots through my body. Death's grip disappears and by some invisible force, I'm pulled upward. Small bubbles float around me as I fly to the surface.

Heat continues to spread through my body, and the second I break the surface, all the water from my lungs disappear, but the pain remains. My eyes close as I start coughing, trying to steady my furiously beating heart. Fighting the current, whoever has a grip on me, pulls me out of the water and onto the grass.

With my back on the dry ground, the grip around me leaves. Since I'm still weak, I can't sit up. I roll over to thank whoever helped me, but find the area empty. Out of the corner of my eye, I see a woman running back into the forest—long blond hair falling down her back.

"Claire?" I whisper as another coughing fit seizes my body.

I WAKE UP WITH A start. "Claire," I call out, but quiet when I don't see any trees around me. I'm back in my bedroom. That was just a dream, right? My heart is beating crazily in my chest, but I don't feel like I just about drowned…A dream. That was definitely just a dream. Claire died in that explosion; there's no way that she could have pulled me out of the water, right?

I glance around the room, toward the window. Not much sunlight is streaming in which lets me know that it's early. Emma is still sleeping soundlessly in her bed. As quietly as I can, I walk towards the bathroom to take a shower.

While lathering the shampoo into my hair, I start to think about everything that has happened recently. Everything was great at the wedding. I had fun. *Real* fun for once. The music spoke to me in ways nothing has for a while. I forgot about the situation we are in and just danced with Liam. Then we came back, and everything has gone downhill from there. I wish I had Hermione's Time-Turner for times like this.

I saw that horrible vision of Colton dying in front of me. He saw me die before, so shouldn't he understand how hard it would be for me to witness that for real? He doesn't seem to understand that I'll do anything to make sure that vision never plays out. If we ever get captured by Dravin, I'll tell him everything. I don't care if he takes my powers. I don't care if he has all my magic. I can't let that vision play out.

Then yesterday, he kissed me. Colton. Kissed. Me. My first kiss. He acted weird afterwards, so he probably regrets doing that, but I can still feel him holding me. The taste of him against my lips; the way his hair felt as I ran my fingers through it. I can remember it all. That is a good thing because it will probably never happen again. It can't happen again. I need to protect Colton, and if people find out about my feelings for him, they'll use him against me just like that vision showed.

I turn the hot water off and step out of the shower. Today is an air-dry type of hair day. Curls all the way, I guess. Afterwards, I get dressed in a plain white v-neck t-shirt and a pair of jean shorts. I don't feel like wearing any of my signature graphic tees. Yes…it's one of those days.

As I head downstairs, I realize that I'm not the only one awake. Larkin is sitting on the couch staring at the black TV screen. He looks up at the stairs when he hears me coming down.

"How are you feeling?" he asks me.

Instead of going into the kitchen to do the dishes, I plop down on the couch beside him. I lean my head against his shoulder and think about the question. How am I feeling? I don't have an answer. I am alive still, which I guess is a good thing. But am I really living? I don't know. I feel like no matter what I do someone ends up upset or hurt. Mentally and emotionally, I'm not doing well. Physically? I've been better. "I don't know," I answer honestly.

"I'm sorry I didn't come sooner yesterday," Larkin whispers to me, patting me on my knee.

"You came at the right time, Larkin. Can you do something for me?"

I can see the hesitance in his eyes, but in the end his curiosity wins. "What?"

"Can you keep an eye on Jane and Ross? That's twice that they've almost been attacked. I can't protect them all the time from here, and I'm scared that something is going to happen to them."

I don't know what he expected me to say, but based on his reaction, that wasn't it. Slowly, he nods. "I can watch them. But my main goal is keeping you safe right now. I can't promise anything." I know that that's as good of an answer as I'm going to get. I sit back on the couch and lean into Larkin's side. Yes, Larkin's annoying sometimes, but I completely trust him. He's done nothing but proved himself worthy of it.

On the coffee table in front of me is my notebook. I'm not sure how it got there, but I reach over and grab it. Flipping to the back, I frown when I see the amount of blank pages I have left. I'll have to go get another one soon. Putting in my iPod headphones, I click shuffle. Sara Bareilles starts playing. I've been listening to her a lot lately, but her songs speak to me.

I draw a spider web—a large detailed spider web. Dew drops cling to each silky stand. In the top left corner, I draw a gruesome looking black spider with many eyes. It looks feral...hungry. In the bottom corner, is a small bug. A bug struggling to get away but can't because it's tangled in the web. I feel like the tiny captured bug. Dravin is getting closer to capturing me again, and there is nothing I can do to get away.

I am stuck in a web watching and waiting for my enemy to come and finish me.

When I finally look way from the drawing, the room is full. Colton is sitting off to the side, not looking at me. Tom is sitting in the kitchen. Everyone else is in their usual locations. I take out my headphones, place my notebook back on the coffee table, and walk into the kitchen to talk with Tom. "Good morning, Ryanne," he says with a smile as I sit across from him.

"Morning, Tom." I'm not sure if Logan told him about the vision I had. "Can I ask you something?" He puts his magazine down and nods at me, so I continue. "Is it possible…to extract magic from someone?"

"Is this about the vision you had?"

"Yeah, Dravin said that he found a way to extract magic from a person. I'm just curious if you think he was telling the truth or if he was just trying to scare me."

"I've never heard of it happening before, but a lot has happened recently that I've never heard of prior to this. I think it would be difficult for him to extract magic from a mage, but I don't necessarily think that it would be impossible. You might be a different story. See, mages are born with magic basically imbedded in them because of our ancestors. You're a different story because no one in your family was ever a mage."

I can hear people entering the room behind me, but I only pay attention to Tom. "So you think it'd be easier for someone to extract magic from me because I wasn't born into a mage family?"

"Possibly. Like I said earlier, I've never heard of it happening before. You're one of a kind, Ryanne. I do know that if he got a hold of the amount of magic you have, he'd be unstoppable."

"Inconceivable!" David yells.

"You keep using that word. I do not think it means what you think it means," I say and turn toward David, waiting for his response.

"Dang it," he says.

"If you're going to use a movie quote, make it a little more challenging than The Princess Bride."

"You're killin me smalls!"

"The Sandlot," I turn my attention back toward Tom. I hear David mumble behind me. "Thanks, Tom." I stand up and walk back into the living room. "Boy, do I hate being right all the time," I call over my shoulder.

"JURASSIC PARK!" David yells. I turn around and smile at him before returning back to my previous position on the couch.

So there goes my plan of letting Dravin just have my magic. I can't give him any more power than he already has. We're having enough difficulty fighting him off as it is. We don't need him to be any more powerful. I'd originally thought that giving up my magic would save everyone, but I know that Dravin won't use it for good, so that wouldn't work. I'll have to find something else to do.

Soon after, everyone comes back into the living room too. I sit on the opposite end of the couch than I usually do. Liam takes the spot beside me. Colton sits in his usual spot. Bragden sits on the ground in front of me. Larkin stays in the kitchen with Tom.

I ask Bragden to get my iPod off the coffee table, since he is sitting in front of it. When he reaches forward, the back of his tank top moves a little, and I swear I see something on his skin. He hands me the iPod and turns back around to face the TV. David and Emma are already looking for a movie to watch.

Leaning forward, I move his shirt to the side a little and see the black marks I briefly saw earlier. Moving the shirt over a little more, I gasp at what I see on his skin. He still has the bear claw that I drew on his shoulder. It's as dark as it was when I first drew it.

"How is that still there?" I lightly trace the outline with my finger. "Shouldn't it have washed off by now?" I tear my eyes away from the drawing and look at him. He is smiling widely at me. "What?"

"Do you remember when you guys went out shopping?" Of course I remember that day. "Well, while you guys were out. Larkin took me to the closest tattoo parlor and I made it permanent."

"That's a tattoo?"

"Yep, I liked it so much that I wanted it to be inked into my skin." I look back down at the tattoo. It does look good on him.

"Really?" I smile widely at him. That's awesome. I know that he didn't get it for me, but it still feels good that he liked my drawing so much that he got a tattoo of it.

COLTON

RYANNE LEANS FORWARD AND KISSES Bragden on the cheek. Just a simple peck on the cheek and a freaking surge of jealousy shoots through me. I groan and lean back against the back of the couch. I know that David and Emma hear me, but it doesn't look like anyone else did. Ryanne is obviously ignoring me, but why? She's acting normal around everyone else, but she won't even look my way. She's sitting on the opposite side of the couch instead of beside me where she usually is.

I glance over at her as she flips through songs on her iPod. Her lips purse as she tries to find a song to listen to. I'd kissed other girls before, but none felt like that. I didn't think about their kiss for much longer afterwards. I wasn't frustrated with those girls as much as I am with Ryanne. What does she want from me?

I can hear the beat of the music coming from her headphones. I turn toward Emma, "Did you talk to her this morning?"

"No. She woke up before me. Have *you* talked to her yet?"

"Not yet. I came down here to talk to her this morning and she was talking with Larkin." I turn toward Larkin, hoping that he will tell us what they were talking about. "And she appears to be ignoring me right now."

"She asked me if I could watch out for Jane because of the attacks against her. She's worried about her."

Ryanne's music starts to quiet, so we stop talking. Another song starts, but no one says anything. I draw my eyes from the TV screen one more time and look at her. She is staring down at the floor, biting her lip.

"Liam, is she okay?" Since Ryanne isn't going to talk to me, I'll have to settle for finding things out from a second source. He glances over at her. She takes a headphone out and turns toward him. I can see the unshed tears in her eyes.

"What's going on, Ryanne?" Liam asks her. She doesn't say anything to him. She looks down at her iPod, and then after a couple of seconds, she hands it to him.

"Listen to this song." Once he has the headphones in, she walks upstairs. I watch Liam, trying to decipher his reaction to the song. Without saying a word, he hands me the iPod. I listen to the song and frown as I listen to the lyrics.

The sadness in the voice of the lead singer and the grim resonance of the lyrics pierce through me. Is this really how she feels? The song stops, and I pull the headphones out and turn the iPod off. I need to talk to Ryanne. She's worse than she's letting on. I stand up to go get her when she bounces back down the stairs, fully dressed in work-out clothes, pulling her hair into a ponytail.

"What are you doing? We're not training until later," asks Liam.

"I'm going for a run." She grabs her tennis shoes and sits down on the last stair, quickly tying the laces.

"Not on your own," I tell her.

"Then someone can come with me. I don't care, but I'm going on a run."

Before I can say anything, Bragden volunteers. "I'll go. I'm already ready." Bragden is always wearing a training outfit. He says it's easier than having to change twice a day. Ryanne brushes past everyone and walks out the front door. She begins stretching in the driveway as she waits for Bragden.

"I hate running," Bragden mumbles as he follows her outside.

CHAPTER
SEVENTEEN

ABOUT EIGHT MINUTES INTO THE run, I start to hear Bragden breathing heavily behind me. We've only gone a mile, and he is having trouble keeping up. How is he that well-built if he can't run a single mile? I stop running and walk back to where he's standing on the side of the road.

"How do you have so much energy?"

"I don't. I'm just frustrated. I needed to get out of that house for a while. I needed to be away from everyone. Running seemed like a good idea; I haven't run in forever." I pause and wait for Bragden to catch his breath, so we can continue.

"I'm good. Let's go." I slow my pace a little to keep up with him, but after a couple of minutes, he starts to breathe heavily again.

"Larkin," I call out.

Larkin blinks in beside Bragden and looks between the two of us, looking for danger. I shake my head at him. "Can you see if Liam can run with me? I think Bragden is dying."

"Yeah, I'll be right back," Larkin disappears.

Bragden nods his head, "That was a good idea. I definitely wouldn't have made it back to the house."

We wait a couple minutes before Larkin appears again with Liam at his side. Liam looks between Bragden and me and smiles when he sees how winded his brother is. Larkin puts a hand on Bragden's shoulder, and they disappear.

"How far out are we?" Liam asks.

"A little over a mile. I need to run further though," I start to run again while Liam stays where he is. "Please try to keep up," I yell over my shoulder at him. Liam snaps out of it and runs after me. Unlike his brother, he is able to run a good distance before tiring.

I am enjoying the way my muscles feel being strained like this. This is different from training. During our training, I use all my muscles, but I haven't pushed myself like this before. I like how my heart rate increases, and it becomes harder to breathe. Strange as that sounds, it makes me push harder. I like hearing the sound of my footsteps echoing off the hard ground. I like how the sun feels against my skin, and how the wind feels against my face. If I could, I would just stay out here forever.

"Ryanne...can I ask you something?" Liam asks while running beside me. I am more comfortable running with Liam. He matches me with athletic ability.

"Sure..." I reply, without breaking my strides.

"Is it really that bad? Like that song?"

"I don't know," I take a deep breath, so I can continue running while I talk. "It's just frustrating knowing that so many people depend on me. I don't know what to do." Inhale. Exhale. "I feel like I'm being pulled in all these different directions, and I know that I have to keep on fighting, but sometimes I don't want to. I feel like everyone knows what needs to be done but me. I'm so lost." I stop running to try and catch my breath.

Liam stops and joins me, but doesn't say anything. That's one of the things I love about Liam. He knows when to say something and when I just need to talk everything out. Nothing he could say would make me feel any better, but it feels good to just tell someone—to finally get it off my chest. He lets me catch my breath, before turning to me and smiling.

"I'll race you back."

"That's three miles."

"I know." He takes off, leaving me behind. He knows I can't turn down a challenge. I start to follow him, keeping an even pace, but he remains in the lead the entire way. When I see the house up the road, I start to pick up my pace. Since Liam ran faster the entire way, he is starting to tire. I kept a much slower pace so I could use my last burst of energy at the end. I speed past him and run up the driveway. With a smile, I look over my shoulder at him and stick my tongue out as I open the door to the house and patiently wait for him to enter.

"You won that one…I'll give you that," Liam says when he enters the house. At least I'm not the only one having trouble breathing. Liam is just as out of breath as I am. I slowly walk into the kitchen to grab a bottle of water out of the fridge and bring one back for Liam. He thanks me and gulps down half of it right away.

"I see you lasted longer than I did," Bragden says.

Liam takes a deep breath and turns toward his brother. "She beat me. She ran a whole extra mile, and she beat me."

Emma walks into the room followed by David, Colton, and Logan. "How long did you run for? Based on how heavy you two are breathing and the amount of sweat dripping off of Liam's head, I'm assuming you went pretty far."

"About six miles. We raced back the last three," I walk over to the couch and lean against the back end. "Are you going to train?" I ask to no one in particular.

"Yeah, but you should rest," Logan suggests.

I take another sip of water. "No, I need to continue working with my magic. I don't want to lose control like I did the other day." I glance over at Larkin to see if he will train with me. He nods at me and gestures for me to follow him outside.

COLTON

"SO, RYANNE SEEMS A LITTLE better." I glance over and watch as Larkin tells her something. Ryanne will listen and then attempt to do whatever he asked. Usually she can accomplish it, but from where I am standing, I can tell she is getting frustrated at this task. She has her hands outstretched in front of her, facing each other, with her eyes closed. Her face is scrunched up in that expression she gets when she's concentrating really hard on something. I watch as a translucent blue ball begins to form between her hands.

"I think she just needed to take a step back from everything and take a slight breather. She would have continued running if I hadn't challenged her to run back. She can't turn down a challenge," Liam says.

At a closer look, the object forming between her hands looks like a ball of water. She takes a couple steps backward, and with a mischievous smile on her face, she turns to Larkin.

"No...don't do it!" Larkin yells. Ryanne throws the ball of water toward Larkin when he turns to run away. He tries to duck, but it hits him in the middle of his face. She laughs and spins around to run in the opposite direction. He shakes his head, but I can see his shoulders moving from his laughter. He transports right behind her and grabs her around the stomach. She screams as he starts tickling her. Despite the fact that I still don't like Larkin, I'm glad that someone is able to make her laugh.

Tom calls for us from the porch, telling us that we should finish up soon. I look toward him and see him smiling slightly at the sight of Ryanne. Everyone stops sparring and starts making their way inside. I get inside first, followed my Liam; Ryanne and Larkin enter last. Emma starts cracking up when she sees Larkin, who's standing in the middle of the kitchen with water dripping off of him.

"You think this is funny?" Emma tries to stop laughing, but can't manage it. Larkin transports behind her and hugs her, effectively getting her wet. She screams and tries to squirm away from him but only manages to get herself wetter. Ryanne walks past everyone and goes upstairs. Larkin lets go of Emma and takes a step back.

Emma puts her hands on her hips and pouts at Larkin. He blows her a kiss and transports out of the room when he sees the look that David is giving him.

"I really need a power that can go against those two. They are always picking on me." She leaves the room and heads upstairs. The stairs creak under her feet as she ascends.

Tom, who is standing near the sink, looking out the window, turns to us. "Ryanne seems better."

Liam shrugs, "I think she just needs to do something. She needs to release some anger in non-magical ways. She could have continued running earlier, but in a way, I made her turn around. She doesn't like sitting around here doing nothing. That may have been fine before, but a lot has happened recently."

"That's understandable. I never understood how you guys could just sit around and watch movies all day anyway." David and I laugh. That is an old argument with Tom. He is always telling us that watching a movie every now and then is fine, but every day? He thinks we are crazy.

The doorbell rings. Tom answers the door and comes back with three large pizza boxes. "One's cheese for Ryanne and Emma. The other two are for everyone else. Dig in."

CHAPTER
EIGHTEEN

I AM WAITING IN THE bedroom for Emma to finish her shower. I don't want to go downstairs by myself. I know that everyone is worried about me, but I feel fine now. The run today really helped. I feel more energized than I have in a long time. Emma comes out of the bathroom dressed and drying her hair with a towel. I've rubbed off on her a little. She doesn't spend much time on her hair anymore.

"So Ryanne...you and Colton...?" She crawls onto my bed and stares at me, expectantly. I knew that she would ask me about him eventually. She's knows more than she's letting on. It's only a matter of time before she tells me. Emma's not very good with secrets.

"There's not a Colton and me."

"And why not?"

"Because...I don't know. I can't let there be. I need to keep him safe. That vision was horrible, Emma. I can't let it play out."

"What about what he wants?" Emma asks me. "I know about the kiss."

"How do you know about that?"

"Colton told me."

"He told you?"

"Why didn't you tell me?"

Why would he tell everyone about that? Did he think it was bad? "Nevermind. He doesn't want to be with me, Emma. He wants to keep me safe. He needs me to help make sure everyone makes it out of this alive."

"Ryanne..."

"I can't let anything happen between us. I need to focus on changing the vision. I can't put you all into any more danger. That kiss shouldn't have happened, and I have to make sure it doesn't happen again."

I get off the bed and start to go downstairs. "Can you at least tell me if it was good?"

I stop in the hallway and glance down the stairs. I can hear the guys' voices but can't see anyone which means that they are in the kitchen. "It was amazing," I whisper honestly while I turn and walk down to the kitchen.

Everyone is in the kitchen, eating pizza when Emma and I walk in. There is a box placed off to the side for Emma and me. I grab a piece, and Emma grabs two. I sit between Liam and Larkin.

"This will be more fun with you, Ryanne," Emma starts giggling. "Oh, get your head out of the gutter. Elevator Shenanigans: Part II. The Speed Round," Logan says.

"Did you just come up with that title?" I ask him.

"Yes, thought of it literally a second before I said it out loud. Pretty good, I know," he smiles at me. "Okay, the first person to say umm loses. Since this is a speed round, you can't take long pauses to think either."

"Are we just saying funny things to do in an elevator?"

"Yep. I'll go first." Logan is awesome. He knows that if I sit silently for any length of time, I'll get lost in my thoughts. He's trying to keep me distracted. "Shave."

"Do yoga."

"Start a sing-along."

"Enforce a group hug."

"Meow."

"Challenge people to duels." We go back and forth like this for five full minutes, neither one of us giving up. Everyone is watching us in fascination. Our answers start to get more and more random. Logan and I are trying to get the other to laugh, which would be considered a pause between answers.

"Tell everyone that comes into the elevator that this is your first time flying," I say.

"Announce that you're not wearing any underwear."

"Put your ear up against the walls, and pretend that you can hear voices."

"Yell 'you're fired!' to every person that enters the elevator."

"Every time someone leaves, say 'Live long and prosper.'"

"Nice," David mutters.

"Ask everyone what floor they need and push the wrong button," Logan says.

"Place a square on the floor with tape and yell "Get out of my space!" to every person that touches the tape." Oh my gosh, this is getting hard.

"Start stripping."

"Stand holding the door open, and say that you're waiting for a friend. After a while, move out of the way and let the doors close. Turn to the side, where no one is standing and say, *Hey friend. How are you today?*" Logan smiles at the suggestion but continues.

Goodness gracious, Logan. Take a breath or something.

"Do the hokey-pokey."

"Pull out a couple of Barbie dolls from your purse and walk up to a man, holding a Ken doll. Ask him to be your Ken. If he refuses, take the heads off all the dolls and throw them at him while screaming, 'I'm a Barbie girl, in a Barbie world.' And then walk out of the elevator crying dramatically." Logan just stares at me. Long pause. "Ha!" I jump up and point at him. "I win!" His smile widens.

"I can't believe you thought of that," David says. I plop back down in the chair and pretend that I am wiping sweat off my forehead.

"That went on for a long time."

"Yeah, it went on for seven minutes and twenty-one seconds," Larkin says while waving his phone. "I timed it."

"That actually happened to me when I was younger. I had a crush on the little boy who lived next door to me, and I asked him to play Ken, but he said no because it was a stupid girl toy. So, I took the head off the doll and threw it at him. It hit him in the middle of the forehead. I ran away crying, and that afternoon his mom came over to my house and made me apologize to him because I left a bruise on the middle of his head. I made the song part up though."

"Did you really?"

"Yeah, my mom was cracking up when they left. It was hilarious. She gave me ice cream for making a little boy cry," I smile as I remember my mom. Thinking about her doesn't make me upset anymore. Now, I cherish the memories I have with her. She made me who I am today, and I wouldn't be here if it weren't for her.

"Ryanne?"

I blink rapidly. I turn toward the sound of the voice and notice everyone staring at me again. My cheeks instantly redden. "Huh?"

Emma laughs. "I knew you weren't listening. I asked if you were done eating."

I look down at my plate. I've barely eaten the piece of pizza, but I'm not really hungry. "Yeah, I'm done."

"Ryanne, at least eat that pizza. You ran six miles earlier. You need to eat something," demands Liam.

"Yes, mom," I pick up the cold pizza and take a small bite out of it. I slowly chew it, trying not to make a face as I swallow. I hate cold pizza, but the microwave is on the other side of the kitchen, and I really don't want to get up. *Laziness at its finest.*

Colton reaches across the table and grabs my plate. Shaking his head, he places the plate in the microwave. Leaning against the counter, he crosses his arms and looks at me, smirking. "Was that so hard?"

"Well, it's a lot easier if someone else does it for you." I mumble a thank you when he places the newly heated plate in front of me. His hand brushes against my shoulder as he walks out of kitchen and into the living room to sit with Logan and Bragden.

"That doesn't look like a guy who doesn't want you," Emma whispers loudly to me.

I finish eating the pizza. "I'm not having this conversation right now, Emma."

Liam turns to me, "What is she talking about?"

"Ryanne has herself convinced that——" Emma starts.

"Emma, stop!" I say to her. She pauses before turning back to Liam. All the heads in the living room whip around and look at us. She's not going to stop?

I don't want to do this…

"She's convinced that Co——" I call my magic to me and make it rain above her again. She jumps up and shrieks.

"I just took a shower, Ryanne!"

"I don't tell you this stuff so you can tell it to everyone else," I say to her. "Some things I say need to stay just between us."

"Ugh, ok. I understand. I forgive you for making it rain on me...*again*. Now, I'm going to go change into some dry clothes." She stomps up the stairs dramatically and loudly closes our bedroom door.

I pick up my plate and put it in the sink. I'll do the dishes in the morning. I walk into the living room and sit down on the couch, avoiding everyone's eyes because I know they're on me.

"So...Ryanne...what was that about?" Logan asks.

"Nothing." Believable answer, Ryanne. That's the way to make them stop asking questions.

"You don't make it rain on someone over nothing."

"People should start doing that more often then, so it doesn't look as suspicious when I do it." No one says anything after that. Emma comes downstairs a couple minutes later in dry clothing though her hair is still a little wet.

She smiles at me as if to say that she isn't mad. I smirk at her and rest my head on Liam's shoulder and watch the movie with everyone. Liam moves his arm and wraps it around me. I curl into his side, taking comfort in him, and glance over at Colton. I know that I shouldn't, but I can't help myself. He's staring at the screen, but his body seems very tense, and his jaw is tight. He keeps clenching and unclenching his hands. I open my mouth to ask him what is wrong when someone's thoughts enter my mind.

So tired. So hungry. I sit up and look around. *It's dark. I hate the dark.*

"Ryanne, what are you doing?" Liam asks me as I get up. I open the front door and stand on the porch. Whoever is thinking these thoughts has to be nearby. The cold night air brushes against my exposed skin, but I don't see or hear anything. I walk back inside. *So tired. Scared.* If it's not out front...I walk toward the backdoor. I know what everyone must be thinking: Ryanne's finally lost it.

I step on the small deck and look around. *Oh, someone's coming. Should I be scared?*

"You don't have to be scared. I won't hurt you."

"Who are you talking to?" Emma asks.

"I don't know. I can hear someone's thoughts." I whip around when I hear something move behind me. *She doesn't look scary.*

"You just walked outside after hearing someone's thoughts?" Colton asks me.

"Something about these thoughts are different." I continue looking around. *They're so big.*

Big? That means that whatever is thinking this is small. I get down on my hands and knees and look on the deck floor. The only hiding place is the small lawn chair in the right corner. I crawl over there and look under the chair and find a pair of reflective blue eyes looking at me. *She sees me.*

"Hey. I won't hurt you. Can you come out here?" I coo. I tap the deck flooring trying to get this animal to come toward me. "It's not dark inside."

"What the heck is going on?" Emma states. I ignore her and continue to talk to whoever or whatever is underneath the chair. *What if they hurt me?*

"No one here is going to hurt you. I promise." Meow. The animal under the chair is obviously a cat. I push myself up onto my knees. "Is anyone allergic to cats?" Everyone shakes their heads. I bend back down. "Here kitty kitty kitty."

"She can read a cat's mind too?" David asks with disbelief lacing his words.

The cat under the chair starts to move toward me, slowly. It doesn't know whether or not it should trust me. In the end, its desire to get out of the darkness and find some food wins. When the cat gets close enough to me, I reach out and pick it up. It's much smaller than I thought it would be. "It's ok. We're going to help you."

Carrying the cat, I walk past everyone and into the kitchen. I carefully hold onto it in one arm and search through the cabinets. Giving up, I turn around, "Does anyone know what to feed a cat?"

I like chicken.

I glance down at the cat and then back to everyone else. "She…are you a girl?" *Yes.* "She said that she likes chicken."

Liam walks over to the fridge and gets out some chicken. He starts cooking it for me. I can always count on him while everyone else believes I'm crazy.

"You can read her thoughts?" Colton asks me.

"Apparently, otherwise I think I'm losing it."

I glance down at the cat in my arms and realize that she isn't even old enough to be considered a cat. I place her on the ground and see how small she actually is. She's no larger than my hand. *So many people.* I sit down on the ground next to her.

"It's a little overwhelming at first. I'm Ryanne," I tell the kitten. I point to Liam, who is making the food. "That's Liam," I introduce him and then go on to point to everyone else stating their names. Each person gives a small wave to her before I move onto the next person.

I can't remember all that.

"It's ok. You'll remember them sooner or later. I'll help you." It's so bizarre that I am having a conversation with a kitten. It was even weirder how human she sounds. Her thoughts sound slightly different—I can't place my finger on what specifically is off though. Liam places a small bowl of chicken in front of her. She walks toward it; her little paws taking small tentative steps. She stops at the edge of the bowl and sniffs the food before taking the first bite. *Yummy.*

Liam reaches out to help me get off the ground. I gladly accept his outstretched hand and let him pull me up. She stops eating and looks at me. *Tell him I said thank you.*

"She said thank you." I walk to the sink and fill another bowl with some water and place it on the ground next to her.

"You're very welcome." He accepts the weirdness of this whole situation and goes along with it. I lean back against Liam's chest. I glance over and find everyone else watching the kitten on the kitchen floor. I wait until she is done eating before I ask her a couple of questions. She sits back and licks her lips before twitching her nose. Aww, she's so stinkin' cute.

"Do you have a name?" *No.*

"Do you have a home? An owner?" *No.*

"Do you remember how you got to our porch?"

A scene starts to play out. I see a woman with curly black hair dropping a box of kittens on the side of the road. A woman driving a minivan stops and looks down into the box. She gasps and grabs the box when she sees the kittens and takes them to the animal shelter. All the kittens in the box end up getting adopted. A little girl with long, straight blond hair presses her nose up to her cage and exclaims, "Mommy, mommy, I want that one!"

"She's not old enough for a pet!" a man yells.

"Give her a chance to prove it to you," a kinder voice says. I see a large man walking toward her and picking her up. Opening the back door, he throws her onto the back porch and into the chilled evening air. She's been walking around ever since then—taking food out of trashcans and sleeping under patio furniture.

"Oh my gosh, that's so sad." I look up at David, Colton, and Logan, "Do you think that Tom would mind if we took care of her? She doesn't have anywhere else to go."

CHAPTER NINETEEN

COLTON

RYANNE'S TALKING TO A CAT. A cat. A. Freaking. Cat. How is that possible? Don't they think on a different wavelength or something? Logan leaves to go talk to Tom about the cat while the rest of us remain in the kitchen. Ryanne is crouched on the ground, talking with the cat...the cat.

Liam just accepted the fact that she could read her thoughts, but I still can't wrap my mind around the fact that she is talking to an animal, and it's communicating back.

"Can you read other animal's thoughts?" I ask her.

"I don't think so. I've never noticed any before today." She's still staring at the cat, a slow smile forming on her face. "She's special apparently." There's no way I'll let Tom take that cat away from her now.

The cat is running between Ryanne's legs. She giggles and follows the cat's every movement. Logan comes back into the room with Tom and looks down at the cat.

"You can really talk with that cat?" He seems genuinely shocked.

"She's a kitten," she clarifies before continuing, "and yes, I can read her thoughts."

"Amazing."

"Let me guess, you've never heard of this before?" I ask. Tom shakes his head but continues watching Ryanne interact with the *kitten*.

Ryanne looks up at Tom, "Do you think she can stay here?"

"Is anyone looking for her? Does she have a home?"

"No, her previous owner threw her out."

Tom rubs his chin but must have seen the look on Ryanne's face as well because he smiles at her. "I don't see why not. Someone will have to go to the store tomorrow and get some things for her. Not you Ryanne, that didn't go too well last time…"

Thank you, Tom. I don't want Ryanne going out in public either, especially if there is going to be a lot of people involved. I am prepared to argue with her when she nods, surprising us all.

"I'll go. I've had a cat before," Emma volunteers.

Larkin steps up next, "I'll take her. It'll be quicker that way."

Tom nods, agreeing with the plan. "You guys do that in the morning. Has she gotten any food or water?"

"Yeah, Liam fed her, and I got her some water," answers Ryanne. She looks up at me, smiling—the smile actually reaching her eyes. Wow, she's beautiful. I knew that before, but it still hits me like a ton of bricks when she looks at me like that. My lungs constrict, denying any oxygen from reaching them. I notice that Ryanne's appears to be holding her breath as well. It's good to know that I'm not the only one affected. If only I could tell her…

She breaks eye contact and looks down, her cheeks reddening in the process.

Tom pats me on the shoulder as he leaves the room. Apparently, he caught our exchange. Ever since I kissed Ryanne, she's avoided being alone with me. In fact, she avoided me completely for a little while. It's nice to see a smile from her directed at me.

Ryanne stands up and walks out of the kitchen. She giggles as the kitten follows her footsteps. Since meeting her, that's turned into one of my favorite sounds.

I walk over to the couch and sit down in my usual spot. She's taken to sitting on the opposite end of the couch with Liam beside her.

"Ryanne, you have your first pet." She looks at me, still smiling, but slightly confused. "You can cross that off your list." I watch the realization seep into her expression.

"I can't believe you remembered that." If only she knew that I remember everything she tells me. I just shrug and look toward Emma. She is shaking her head at Ryanne. Emma knows something that I don't.

"So, does she have a name?" Liam asks her.

"Not yet," she laughs again. "She said that the daughter of her last owner used to call her fluffy, but she's not fluffy." She looks back at the kitten, "Do you mind if we try to rename you?"

Emma instantly starts saying names, "Cookie, Cream, Cotton, Lily, Kitty Purry. That's what Katy Perry's cat is named. Snowflake, Bitsy, Didi, Miss Meowington III, Foxy, Elmo, Kiwi, Emma II, Lola..."

Olive. Olive? Where did that come from?

Ryanne laughs at each suggestion that Emma makes but keeps shaking her head. The kitten doesn't like any of those names.

"Olive?" I quietly say. Emma keeps going.

"Oh, wait. She likes Olive," Ryanne turns around and looks at me. "You just named her."

"Why didn't I think of Olive? Oh yeah because it's a food, not a name," Emma mumbles.

"You said Kiwi. Last time I checked, that was also a food," Ryanne points out.

Emma stares at her blankly. "So," she finally says.

Ryanne looks toward Olive. "No. This is Liam," she points toward Liam and then toward me, "Colton named you." Olive must have said something because Ryanne blushes a little, "I know."

TWO HOURS LATER, BOTH RYANNE and Emma are sleeping. Emma is curled into David's side while Ryanne is leaning against the armrest of the couch with Olive asleep in her lap. I am glad that she isn't leaning against Liam, but her position doesn't look very comfortable. I miss her sitting next to me; she'd always fall asleep curled into my side. Once the movie is over, David lifts Emma and carries her upstairs. It looks more difficult to carry Emma than Ryanne because of how tall Emma is.

Larkin blinks out of the room. Logan and Liam stand up at the same time. Liam looks toward me and then glances toward Ryanne. I nod. I'll take her upstairs.

I crouch down in front of Ryanne, who's sleeping soundlessly, and pet Olive on her head. She slowly opens her eyes and looks at me. "I have to carry Ryanne upstairs." Olive stretches, yawns, and then hops off of Ryanne's lap. "You can follow me. I'm sure Ryanne won't mind if you sleep in her room."

I lift her into my arms, still amazed by how light she is, and carry her up to her room. Emma is lightly snoring in the bed closest to the door. I try to be quiet as I walk to the other bed in the room. I glance behind me and see Olive following. I put Ryanne down on the bed and pull the covers up. Reaching down, I pick up Olive and place her next to Ryanne.

"Goodnight, you two," I whisper as I close the door and exit the room.

I WAKE UP THE NEXT morning and roll over. *Ouch.* I jump up. What was that? Oh my gosh, I just rolled on top of Olive. "I'm sorry. I didn't know you were there."

She yawns and stretches. *It's ok.*

"I'm going to take a shower. You stay here, ok?" When she nods her little white head, I jump out of bed and skip into the bathroom. I get in and out of the shower as quickly as possible. I throw on my Batman t-shirt and black shorts. I feel like I should be going on some top-secret mission right now since I'm wearing all black. Can mages be spies? I feel like they would be awesome at that job. I run a towel through my long hair and walk back into my room. Emma is still asleep, so I quietly pick up Olive and leave the room. When she starts squirming in my arms, I place her on the ground. I understand the height issue.

Colton and Liam are quietly talking in the living room. Their conversation stops when I start walking down the stairs. They're up to something. "Morning," I say as I walk past them to go to the kitchen to do the dishes.

Olive follows me into the kitchen. She stops under the table and looks up. *This looks fun.* She starts running between the legs of the chairs in circles. Crazy kitten. I fill one side of the sink with soapy water and spread a towel over the counter on the left side.

I grab the first plate and start scrubbing, trying to get off all remnants of previous meals. I immerse the plate in the water. Up to my elbows in soapy water, I wash. I hear footsteps behind me as someone walks into the kitchen. Before turning, I instantly know who it is. I can smell Colton's outdoorsy cologne. "Here, I'll help you."

I neither look at him nor do I say anything, but I scoot over to let him help me. His arm keeps brushing against mine every time he reaches for another plate. I try to ignore the butterflies in my stomach and the erratic beat of my heart as he stands so close to me, enveloping me with his smell. The kiss we shared the other night keeps running through my mind. I wish I was a normal teenage girl. I want that relationship. I want to have someone want me as much I want him, but I can't have that. I can't risk someone's life like that. I have to find a way to change that vision.

"Ryanne, can we talk about the other night?" Colton whispers into my ear, giving me goosebumps, as he puts a plate on the towel.

"There's nothing to talk about," I say as I dunk another dirty plate under the soapy water.

"That wasn't nothing. I know you felt it too."

I don't want to have this conversation. I don't say anything right away, but as I continue to feel his eyes on me, I stop with the plate I am washing and turn toward him. "I can't afford to let myself feel something, Colton."

"Is this about the vision?" He turns toward me, mimicking my stance. Now that he is looking at me, I have to arch my head up to see him.

"I can't risk losing you," I whisper and turn back to the sink. I can't think straight when he looks at me. "Because someone wants to use you against me."

I can feel him staring at me, but I try to become busy with the dishes. I didn't realize that I've been washing the same plate over and over again until Colton takes it out of my hands. I go to reach for another one, but the counter is empty. Dang it. Colton grabs my shoulders and turns me so that I am facing him—so that we are standing only a couple inches apart. I can hear the water droplets dripping from my soapy arms hitting the floor. On their own accord, my eyes move up and meet his.

"Can you at least answer a question for me?" I tense, waiting for his question. He looks down at me, searching my eyes. "Do you have any feelings for me? At all?"

How could he think that I don't? I didn't think that I was that good at hiding my emotions. I stare into his mesmerizing green eyes. His feelings for me are obvious in this moment. My gaze lowers from his eyes down to his lips—his soft, sensual, full lips. I want nothing more than to lean forward and kiss him again. I know that he caught me staring at his mouth because his breathing increases. I look away and take a step back while slowly nodding. "Yes," I whisper.

Colton moves forward to close the distance I just created between us. He reaches forward and tucks a curled strand of my hair behind my ear. I look into his wide, expressive eyes as he says, "Then, I'll wait, Ryanne. I'll wait for you."

CHAPTER
TWENTY

EMMA AND LARKIN BLINK BACK into the living room, holding a couple of bags. I didn't even realize that they had left. Emma looks at Colton and me and smiles. I can feel another blush rising. Goodness, do I have an off button? I shake my head and take a step away from Colton. There is nothing going on. There can't be. Her wide smile turns into a frown. I don't understand why though. She knows my feelings on this issue, so she shouldn't have been surprised. I look past Emma and Larkin and see everyone else sitting in the living room. When did they get there, and what did they hear?

Reaching into a bag, Emma brings out a can of cat food. I watch as Olive stops running in circles and bounces toward the bowl when Emma places the food on the ground. I brush past Colton, avoiding eye contact, and walk into the living room. Sitting down on the couch, I lean against the armrest and grab my notebook off the coffee table.

"What's wrong?" Liam asks me when he sees my frown.

"Nothing's really wrong. I just realized that I'm on my last page," I flip over the page to show him.

"Well then, we'll have to get you another one soon."

Nodding, I pull the pen that I keep in the metal spirals out and place it onto the page. I wait until an image flashes in front of my eyes and then I start drawing. My pen sweeps across the page, and I draw a snake. I'm not really sure why, but I draw it anyway. A king cobra to be more specific. Such a beautiful creature yet deadly when provoked.

Why are you drawing that? Olive is sitting on the armrest beside me watching me draw. I shrug, "I don't really know. Usually I just draw the first thing that comes to mind."

"I still can't believe that she can talk to the cat," Bragden says while leaning toward Logan.

My name is Olive, you big oaf, not cat. Get it right. Giggling, I cover my face with me notebook, trying to stifle the laughter. When I bring the notebook down, I see everyone watching me—some smiling, others confused. I turn toward Bragden and tell him what Olive just said, oaf and all.

"My apologies, Olive. Please forgive me." I see the slight hint of a smile in Bragden's response. *Hmph, that's more like it.* Oh goodness, I'm going to like Olive.

I look past her, and my eyes land on Larkin. He's standing in the corner against the wall, looking distracted. What's going on with him? I turn to ask him when something in the room beeps. Larkin looks down at his wrist and sighs. He starts to walk toward the couch while he keeps his eyes down. He places a hand on my shoulder. "I need you to come with me for a moment." Without waiting for a reply, he transports us out of the room.

COLTON

SHE'S STARING AT HIM AGAIN. Every time I look at her, her eyes are on Larkin. Larkin is always involved. Studying him, I can tell that he's up to something. He seems really distracted—fidgeting with his watch and casting nervous glances around the room. A beep sounds, and Larkin starts walking toward us.

He places a hand on Ryanne's shoulder and says, "I need you to come with me for a moment." Liam and I jump up when they disappear. Ryanne's notebook falls onto the floor. Liam closes his eyes, rolls his head back, and groans.

"Seriously? He couldn't have told us where they were going? What they were doing?" I yell.

"Why does he keep doing that?" Liam's voice sounds strained like he is trying to control his anger.

Emma walks over to me and places her hand on my arm. "Don't worry. Ryanne trusts him, and I know he cares about her. He won't hurt her. She saved his life." Her attempt to calm me doesn't work. I hate that she openly trusts him like that. He used to work for Dravin for crying out loud. He was there when she was tortured! Doesn't anyone else remember that?

I move past Emma and start pacing behind the couch. The only thing that will calm me is Ryanne coming back. I'll refrain from yelling and taking my anger out on anyone in this room but only for so long. If she doesn't show back up soon, I can't promise anything.

WE LAND IN THE THICK of a forest. There is nothing around us. Why would he take us here? I turn around to face him and see him looking around, turning in circles. He stops and faces the area to my right.

Grabbing my wrist, he starts dragging me after him. "Larkin, what's going on? Where are we?"

"I need you to see something. Well, I need you to confirm something before I tell everyone else."

"Why couldn't you have told me that before we left instead of surprising me like that? You know that everyone is going to be mad at you."

"They'll be angrier if this is true...I didn't want anyone to come after us. It's not safe out here. I had to transport us to this location because it won't set off the sensors. Dravin won't know that we are here."

"You're taking me toward Dravin's compound?" Is he insane? When Colton and Liam find out where I am, they are going to freak out.

"You won't be seen. You're safe with me. If anything happens, I'll transport us away."

I stop asking questions and just follow him. I can't get back without his help anyway. I can't afford to talk. It's distracting, and I have to focus to remain on two feet. We aren't on any trail. I have to dodge low hanging limbs, uprooted trees, large branches and twigs, and pointed roots. Larkin tries to help me as much as possible, but since the ground is wet, I also have to find the correct footing. Low branches keep getting caught in my hair and hitting my exposed skin, scratching my face, arms, and legs.

Finally we get into a small clearing. Larkin slowly creeps to the edge and crouches down behind a row of thick bushes. He motions for me to do the same. Crouching down beside him, I can see through a small opening between the bushes. Dravin's compound is right in front of me...well part of it. I can only see one of the building's exits since most of it is covered by trees. Nothing happens for the first couple of minutes. Larkin is watching the door, so I know that something is supposed to happen soon. I'm about to ask him what is going on, when I hear a noise. I peek between the bushes. The door to the compound is opening up.

My mouth drops to the floor when I see who walks outside with Adam.

COLTON

"WHERE THE HELL IS SHE?" I can't take this much longer. I need to know. "It's been over an hour." Everyone is starting to get antsy. Emma is rocking back and forth in her chair, staring off into space. David is sitting beside her, rubbing her back, but not looking at anything in particular. Liam is tense. Very tense. However, he doesn't seem to be in any discomfort. Bragden is standing near his brother, not really knowing what to do. I look at Liam, "Can you get anything from her?"

"She's not hurt. That's about all I know." That's a good thing, but the thought doesn't console me at all. I understand what Liam is going through...in a way. He gave her that pendant because he's chosen to protect her. He's supposed to fight beside her, ensuring her safety. However, nothing can be simple with Ryanne. She's always going or getting taken to places and not telling us where she's going. We're left in the dark, worrying about her.

The wait is agonizing. It feels like something is squeezing my lungs, making it difficult to breathe. This always happens when she disappears, and there's nothing we can do. In this situation, there is no way to find her. Larkin could have told us where he was taking her—what he was doing. He should have told us something!

I'm about to take my anger out on some poor inanimate object when they transport back into the room. *Gah*, took them long enough. Larkin lets go of her hand when they land on the ground. Ryanne is standing in front of him, mouth open and eyes wide. Her clothes are damp, and her hair is much curlier than it was before they left. She has random twigs and leaves stuck to her. She would have looked adorable if it wasn't for the expression on her face and her skin. Her smooth skin is marred with small scratches.

Something is wrong.

"Do you know her?" Larkin asks her, waiting for confirmation.

"Are you freaking kidding me?" Ryanne yells. Yep, something is definitely wrong. "Are you serious?" Ryanne doesn't yell, so when she does you know it's serious. I look at everyone else in the room. No one has any clue what is going on. She lets out a small laugh and runs a hand through her hair. She pulls out a small twig. Normally, I would have laughed at the confused look on her face, but I can see the fear in her eyes. "If I didn't already have enough people that wanted me dead..." her voice trails off.

"Ryanne, what's going on?" I ask her.

Instead of answering me, she turns back to Larkin. "Are you sure she's working with him?"

Larkin reaches out and pulls a leaf out of Ryanne's hair. "Yeah, I just wanted confirmation before I told everyone else." Told everyone what? What was going on?

Ryanne walks backwards and leans against the back of the couch, crossing her arms across her chest. "It's her," she says.

"Would someone *please* explain what's going on?" Emma asks. Ryanne doesn't move, so Larkin starts to explain.

"I got news from a source of mine inside Dravin's compound of some new recruits. There was one name that I recognized, but I'd never met her before, so I needed someone to confirm her identity for me. So, I brought Ryanne to the forest outside the compound. We had to walk for a while to avoid setting off any of the sensors that Dravin has located randomly in the forest. We watched as this recruit exited the building with Adam, and Ryanne claims that it's the same girl."

"Who?" I ask.

Ryanne looks up at me and whispers, "Natasha."

CHAPTER
TWENTY-ONE

"WHAT?" DAVID AND COLTON BOTH jump up.

"Natasha is working with Dravin and Adam?" Emma asks. "The same girl that trashed our room? The one that you shot against the wall and then she tried to kill you? The one that I tackled to the ground?"

"That's the one," I whisper. I walk past everyone and start going up the stairs.

"Where are you going?" Colton asks me.

"I need to go on a run again. Liam?" He nods and walks upstairs after me to get ready. I grab a pair of athletic running shorts and a fitted black tank top. My shoes are downstairs, so I put on a pair of socks and head back down. Liam is already downstairs waiting for me.

"Why would she do that? I know she doesn't like Ryanne or me but to you, Colton?" Emma asks. I try to ignore the twist in my stomach whenever I'm reminded of Colton's previous relationship with Natasha. It actually hurts to think about them together. She's gorgeous, so I understand the physical aspect, but she's horrible. Colton can do way better than that girl.

He doesn't respond to Emma's question. Does he still have feelings for her? I can tell by his tense posture and tight jaw that he is fuming. Colton has two types of anger. This silent kind is the worse. I'd much rather he yell it out than keep it bottled up like this.

I grab my shoes and sit down on the bottom stair to tie them. I know Colton is watching me, but I focus only on tying my shoes. I need to get out of this house before I say something about Natasha that will anger Colton and David more than they already are. I walk over to Emma and ask for a hair tie. I always forget about pulling my hair up before exercising.

"Are you sure it is her?" she asks as she hands me the elastic from her wrist.

"Tall, blonde, and gorgeous?" I pause, "Yes, it was definitely her."

"Could it have been Natalie?" Colton asks.

"It was Natasha, Colton," I tell him while grabbing Liam's arm and walking outside to stretch, leaving everyone in the living room. I quickly throw my hair into a pony tail and start stretching. I can tell that Liam is watching me, but right now I don't want to talk to anyone. I just want to go for a run. With a sigh, he starts stretching too.

I walk down to the end of the driveway and take off running. I know that Liam is following close behind. I push myself harder than necessary, but I really need this. I need to clear my head.

Natasha is working with Dravin—with Adam. I know that she doesn't like me. I heard *everything* she told me. My whole life people picked on me, even before Adam. However, senior year it got worse. Adam and Lily made sure to make my life a living hell. No one would talk to me in school. No one wanted to be around me. I ate in the library to avoid everyone's stares and whispers. I can only take so much.

I tried to give Colton space because I thought he was interested in getting back together with Natasha. She cornered me in the hallway one day and told me that I was never going to be good enough for Colton. She said, "No one would want you for you. They want to be with the girl from the prophecy. Not you. Don't flatter yourself with thinking that any of these people would be interested in you if you didn't have all that magic." I never told anyone what she said, not even Emma.

I continue running. By this time, we are miles away from the house. I can't stop—just like I can't stop everything that is going on in my life. I don't get a rewind button here. That's reserved for Hollywood. I can't go back to a time before all this stuff happened. In all honestly, despite everything, I don't know if I want a rewind. I just want to take out certain elements of my life. I want to be given the chance to live a normal life like everyone else.

But that'll never happen.

Adrenaline rushes through me, so I push harder—enjoying the way the muscles in my legs feel with the movement. When I started running, it was sunny, but because of how mad and angry I am, it is getting cloudy. Dark clouds are battling the sunlight and winning. The wind starts picking up, but I don't stop. The rhythmic beat of shoes behind me tells me that Liam is still behind me. I push even harder. I wish that I could run away from my problems like that. I wish that I could run away from Dravin. From Adam. From Natasha.

My lungs are on fire. I stop and put my hands on top of my head, trying to catch my breath. When Liam catches up to me, he asks, "Do you want to talk about it now?"

I shake my head right as the first couple drops of rain begin to fall. I know that I am causing this weather fluctuation, but I can't stop it now. I sit down on the ground and pull out the pony tail, letting the wind blow my hair around my face. I pull my knees up to my chest and rest my head against them. Small drops of water land on my skin and run down my arm. When I catch my breath enough to talk, I look up at Liam. He is seated beside me on the grass. "Why does it have to be me?"

He doesn't even pause to think about his answer. "Because you're the only one strong enough. You're the only one that doesn't look at it as just having magic. You don't want to use it for yourself. You see it as a way for protection—a way to protect others. You're strong enough mentally and emotionally, as well as physically. You have the biggest heart I've ever seen in anyone. You have all the qualities to be a leader, but you don't want to lead. You don't want power; you want a life. And you're willing to do what needs to be done to get that. You're the only one that can do this, Ryanne."

The rain transitions into a steady downpour. I don't even care that I'm getting soaked by my own magic. "Are you guys only with me because I'm the prophecy girl?"

Liam looks at me with his mouth hanging open; his grey eyes as wide as saucers. I've never seen him react like this before. He seems genuinely shocked. "Why would you think that?"

"Natasha told me that once."

"Ryanne, I gave you that pendant before I knew you were the girl from the prophecy. And I can guarantee you that no one in that house looks at you like that."

"Now I have to worry about Dravin, Adam, and Natasha. Dravin wants my magic. Adam wants…." I shiver. "Natasha wants me dead because she thinks I took Colton from her. So I have to deal with a mad man who craves power, a sexually frustrated teen, and Colton's crazy ex-girlfriend. All who would like nothing more than to watch me crash and burn. Everyone wants to watch me fail."

"Ryanne, if you believe in yourself, you can accomplish anything. *Anything*. I know how cliché that sounds, but it's true. Those people are just flickers in the flames. Someday the flame will burn bright again." Liam has to shout over the rain for me to hear him. I look over at him and see that he means every word he said.

Instead of replying, I yell for Larkin.

Larkin transports beside me. He gives me an annoyed look when he realizes how hard it is raining. "Can you take Liam and me back to the house? It would take a while to run all the way back, and I don't think I'll make it."

Larkin nods and extends a hand to help me stand up. I let him pull me up and wrap an arm around my waist to bring me back to the house. It's easier for both of us that way because it helps me keep my balance when we land back in the house.

COLTON

"NATASHA'S WORKING FOR DRAVIN? CONNER just helped us fight him…something's not right." David is pacing the living room, thinking out loud. It's been a while since Liam and Ryanne left. My eyes are drawn to the window, and this time I see the sun's light being swarmed by clouds. Ryanne's obviously upset.

"I never liked that girl. I knew that she would do something when you kicked her out of the house after she used her power on Ryanne. I didn't think she would join Dravin's side, especially after Ryanne told her what happened when she was captured," Emma says. She is trying to get David to stop pacing. Neither one of us are taking this well. We grew up with Natasha.

"Was she with her sister? Where was Natalie?" I ask Larkin.

"Natalie wasn't a recruit. I think that we should find a way to talk with Natasha—see why she decided to help him. I can understand why Dravin would want to use her. Her magic is a powerful weapon."

I knew it would not turn out well when I saw Natasha standing in the kitchen with her twin sister. I was glad to see Conner, but I ended things with Natasha. I knew that nothing was ever going to come from it. I didn't share her feelings and thought it would be better to end things than drag them out further. It's an understatement to say that she didn't take it very well. She yelled, fought me, threw things, etc. When I walked into the kitchen and saw how Natasha was glaring at Ryanne, I knew that I wasn't doing a very good job at keeping my feelings to myself. Ryanne is oblivious, but that doesn't mean everyone else is.

Larkin looks up toward the ceiling. I glance up but don't see anything worth looking at. "Ryanne's calling. I'll be back." He transports out of the room. They've been out for almost an hour. Ryanne probably ran six or seven miles. I don't know how that girl does it. Despite the positive change in her attitude, she's still pushing herself too hard. A minute later, Larkin transports back into the room holding a very wet Ryanne. He lets go of her waist and disappears again.

Why is she soaking wet? Her hair is stuck to her face in loose ringlets. Small drops of water cling to her eyelashes; the lights overhead reflects off of them each time she blinks. Water droplets drip off her skin and pool onto the floor below her. Her already tight work-out clothes cling to her slim curvy body. I try really hard to not make it obvious that I am checking her out, but I can't. She is so…

"What happened to you?" Logan's voice interrupts my thoughts.

"It rained," she mumbles and starts shivering. I walk into the laundry room, grab a clean towel, and hand it to her. She thanks me and wraps it around her shoulders. Larkin blinks back into the room with Liam. Both, wet. "Sorry guys," she looks down at the floor, slightly embarrassed, which lets us know that she's responsible for the rain. She is more upset than she is letting on. She looks up and looks straight at me. I can't decipher the expression on her face. Clearing her throat, she announces that she is going to go take a shower and change. Liam and Larkin both leave to do the same.

Ryanne's been trying to control her magic lately. She is past the point where she causes unexplainable storms. Usually only one or two elements are manifested. The fact that it is pouring outside, proves how upset she really is. I want to know what is bothering her. I know this is more than just Natasha.

Larkin and Liam both come back downstairs in clean dry clothes. I look toward Liam to see if he will explain what is going on. He shakes his head choosing not to share what Ryanne is upset about. Dang it. How am I supposed to help her if she won't tell me? Olive runs over and jumps into my lap. I reach down and start petting her. She starts purring, so I'm assuming that she likes it. I've never had a cat before. It would be easier if I could read her mind like Ry.

Larkin shrugs and sits down on the ground. "I don't know. I transported to her and got drenched. She was like seven miles out."

"She can run. I couldn't keep up with her. It also helped that she's angry, frustrated, upset, scared..." Liam tells us. "Just pretend that nothing's changed," he whispers to us as Ryanne descends the stairs. She sits down on the opposite end of the couch and reaches for her notebook. Frowning, she places it back on the coffee table. She is out of pages. I'll have to go buy her a new one tomorrow.

Lying down on her back, she closes her eyes. "I pushed myself too hard," she says. "I'm so tired," she yawns once and almost instantly falls asleep.

CHAPTER
TWENTY-TWO

"HELLO, DARLING."

My eyes snap open and I instantly tense when I hear his voice. Slowly turning around, I find Dravin leaning against the doorway...of this room. I've never been in this room before. This isn't a containment room like the cell I was in last time I was at Dravin's compound. This room is smaller than that. There's a small window located to my right. All I see outside of it is greenery. A small brown couch takes up the entire length of the opposite wall. Besides that, there is no other furniture in here. "How did I get here?"

"Well, you were thinking about me before you fell asleep, so I pulled you here. Granted your body is still at your house, so your little friends won't know what's going on." He pushes off of the doorframe and takes a couple steps toward me. I step back until I am pressed against the hard wall.

"What are you going to do to me?" He stops walking and stares down at me. Dang, all mages are incredibly tall. He towers over me just like everyone else.

"Is Larkin with you?" That's the last question I was expecting. "Is he blocking your trace? It's very strong right now." He takes another step toward me. Is he blocking my trace? What's my trace exactly? Larkin said that he couldn't block my magic.

"Why do you want to know where Larkin is?"

"Larkin was my best man before he betrayed me," he growls the last part of the sentence. He's very angry that Larkin is now helping us. There's no way I'm going to tell him any information about him. I keep my mouth closed. Looking at him defiantly, I put my chin out, attempting to show him that he doesn't scare me. However, inside I'm trembling.

"Why are you doing this, Dravin?"

"Because I need more power. I need your power. Once I find a way to take it, you can believe me I will. Those with power have control. I'm tired of working alongside those measly humans. They know nothing about us, and we are immensely more powerful than them. Even the mages who have no magic yet are more powerful. It's time they realize that."

"Why do you have to hurt people for control?" I ask. "Can't you just take the resources you already have and use it for good?"

"Where's the fun in that, love? Being bad is so much more fun." He smirks at me and before I know what is happening, he grabs my chin and pulls me toward him; his mouth suddenly hard on mine. I scream against him and bring my left knee up. I am aiming for his crotch, but my knee connects with his stomach instead. He breaks away from me. I then bring that leg up and kick him against the chest. He staggers backwards, shocked. "So, you've been training, I see," he grins evilly and slowly walks toward me again. I feel the dull pain of the impending headache as his eyes narrow in concentration.

I grab my head and fall to the ground as the pain intensifies. I cry out as the pain gets even worse. I don't see any images this time, just feel the blinding pain. My knees curl under me as I start gasping for air. A sharp pain hits me in the stomach. My body is thrown to the side from the kick.

The pain in my head lessens to the point that I become conscious of my surroundings again. I see Dravin standing over me. "You've gotten stronger, but you're still nothing compared to me." I gasp as I try to sit up. When I'm standing again, Dravin walks toward me, "I'll never stop looking for you, so you better hope that nothing happens to Larkin." He punches me in the jaw, sending me flying backwards. My head cracks into the hard wall. I'm out before I hit the ground.

COLTON

I AM WATCHING RYANNE AS she sleeps on the couch. I keep glancing over at Liam to make sure he isn't acting strange or in pain. Whenever she falls asleep, I'm always worried that something is going to happen to her.

"What did you do to Natasha? You must have done something really bad to make her want to join Dravin." Emma just had to bring it up again. We'd gone a full ten minutes without anyone saying anything.

"I didn't do anything to her."

"Did you have sex with her and then dump her? I'd be angry if that happened to me," Emma says.

"I didn't have sex with her, Emma—not that it's any of your business. I did break up with her though."

"Hmm, I'm just trying to figure out why so many people are trying to hurt Ryanne. I mean look at her. Does that look like the face of some ruthless killer?" Right as Emma says that, Ryanne gasps and rolls off the couch. She lands on the floor with a thud. Pushing herself up, she grabs her side, along her ribs, and hisses. I jump up when I see the giant red mark on her jaw.

"What happened?"

"Where's Logan?" she whimpers. She must be in a lot of pain if she is asking for Logan. I yell for Logan and walk toward her. She tries to stand but cries out and falls back to the ground. She removes her hand from her side and grabs her head. Where's Logan?

He runs straight to her side and places his hands on her back. She is still making pained noises. His face furrows in concentration as he heals her. She gasps and arches her back. The slight pop of bones moving back into place sounds from her body. She quiets beneath his touch and stills. He takes a step back, and I can tell that whatever he saw made him extremely mad.

Ryanne pushes herself off the ground and slowly stands up. She turns around and walks straight toward Logan. "Please don't say anything," she reaches out and grabs his arm, trying to make him look at her.

"Logan, what happened?" I demand. I need to know what Ryanne doesn't want us to know. Logan looks like he needs to punch something. Heck, I want to punch something, and I don't even know what happened to her specifically.

"*Please.*" She's pleading with him now. Logan looks down at her and shakes his head. She sighs and leans her head against his chest. He wraps an arm around her and looks over her to me.

"Dravin," whispers Logan. Ryanne tenses against Logan and for good reason. She knows how angry I am at him for what he did to her last time.

"It's not that bad," Ryanne says—her voice muffled against Logan's chest.

"Not that bad? You woke up and fell off the couch crying out in pain!" She turns around and looks at me. She looks fine now, but that's only because Logan healed her. If Logan wasn't a healer, she'd be in a lot of pain.

"I've had worse. I just wasn't expecting that to happen."

"What happened exactly?" Liam asks. He's angry too, but calmer than I am. "I didn't feel anything."

"I don't know. I fell asleep and then all the sudden Dravin was talking to me. I kicked him, so he got mad and retaliated. Nothing really," she shrugs and walks back to the couch. Olive runs over and sits down in her lap. Ryanne starts absentmindedly petting her.

"Ryanne," says Logan, "more than that happened."

"Yeah, but we don't have to tell everyone what actually happened." I can't help it. I growl at her. What happened that she doesn't want everyone to know? "He was just giving me a warning."

"Logan, what happened?" I try to sound calmer than I feel. I know that I'm really not fooling anyone. Ryanne drops her head into her hands as Logan starts explaining.

"He cornered her and started asking about Larkin." Logan looks toward Larkin who is standing in the corner, looking worried. "He wanted to know where you were; if you were helping her. He said something about needing more power. He wants Ryanne's power because with power comes control. She asked if he would ever consider using his resources for good. Dravin said that being bad was more fun and then he——"

Logan stops talking and looks at Ryanne. She's staring at him with wide eyes and shaking her head. "He kissed her."

"He what?" Ryanne winces as I yell. I glare down at her. She stands up and starts walking toward me.

"I took care of myself, Colton. I'm not the same girl that Adam attacked a year ago in the park. I'm able to defend myself now." I look down at her. I know that she can defend herself, but I hate that these guys are always able to find a way to hurt her. I hate knowing that someone else had their lips on hers. Her soft supple kissable lips that are parted and right in front of me... I know that she didn't kiss him back, but I am still angry anyway.

"She did fight back, Colton." I don't take my eyes from Ryanne, who is staring back at me. This waiting thing is going to be very difficult.

"What happened next?" I say without looking away. I am asking Logan because I know that Ryanne will leave out details. She blinks and steps away from me, but remains close. Logan explains everything, not leaving out any details about her injuries. She places a hand on my crossed arms to try and calm me. I actually do feel calmer when she touches me. I'm still angry, but glad that she's here safe and not stuck with that man.

"It was just a warning to me. He wanted to prove that he's stronger than me; that he still has ways to get to me. Granted, I didn't use any magic against him, so I don't know how he knows that he's *so* much stronger than me," Ryanne says, hand still on my arm. I'm trying not to look down at my arm, because I know she'll remove her hand and step away if she sees my glance. However, she does the opposite of that. She takes a step closer, so she's basically pressed up against me and whispers, "We need Larkin's help, so stop glaring at him like he's the bad guy." I hadn't realized that I was doing that. Sighing in frustration, I look away from him.

"Why didn't you defend yourself with magic?" David asks her. Darn David. She takes a step back and turns toward him, removing her hand. It takes all my will power to suppress a sad groan.

"I don't want Dravin to find out what I can do with my magic. In the vision of...in the vision I had, he said that once he found out the extent of my powers he could extract all of it. I didn't want to give him any information about my magic." I know that the vision she is referring to is the one where she saw Dravin kill me. Ryanne looks away from my brother and glances back up at me. "Do you think you and Liam can help train me again? Without magic?" She glances between the two of us. Without looking at Liam, I agree. I'd probably agree with anything she asked me to do…to an extent. Especially if it's accompanied by that breathtaking smile she just gave me.

CHAPTER
TWENTY-THREE

WHEN I DON'T INFUSE MAGIC into my limbs, fighting is a lot harder. David and Colton had trained me previously, but apparently I've gotten lazy because of my magic. I'm not hitting as hard as I thought I was. It seems like while everyone gets stronger, I stay fixated at the same strength level. On top of that, since the guys know that I can do gymnastics stunts, it's hard to surprise them. I have to work really hard to even get a staggering hit in. I'm knocked flat on my butt more times than I can count.

Two hours later, I am lying on my back with Liam and Colton sitting on either side of me, breathing heavily. "That was not fun." Placing my arms over my eyes, I block out the sunlight. The sun is setting, disappearing behind the trees, casting small shadows across the yard. The warm and cool colors merge together as the darkness pushes forward. Colton and Liam both stand up. Colton puts a hand out to help me stand up. "No thanks. I'm good down here." Laughing, he reaches down and grabs my arms. Without my help, he lifts me off the ground and sets me down. Playfully, he pushes me toward the back door of the house.

I smile over my shoulder at him. "Gosh, no need to be pushy." I hear him laugh as I skip into the house. Shortly afterwards, everyone joins us in the kitchen. Larkin grabs a bottle of water and sits down at the kitchen table. He opens his mouth to speak but stops.

I jump up on the counter and take small sips of my water. Colton walks over and stands beside me. He's still slightly taller than me. Not fair. "I think that we should find a way to bring Natasha here and question her. Find out why she joined Dravin's side," Larkin finally says.

I start choking on the water I was swallowing. Colton reaches behind me and starts hitting me on the back. "You want to bring her here?" I manage to get out after a few seconds.

"I have a friend that's still in Dravin's compound. He says that he can get her outside. I've already discussed a location to meet with him. I'll sneak up on them and put a blindfold on her so she can't see anything about the house. We don't want to give her any clues to our location. I don't think you, Ryanne, should be around when we question her though; just to be on the safe side."

I don't want to be around anyway. It makes me so mad that she would just blindly accept whatever Dravin told her. I told her everything that happened to me when I was captured by Dravin, and she still went over to his side. "When are you going to do this?" I jump down from the counter, waiting for his reply.

"I'm meeting with Kyril in five minutes."

So soon? "I'll be sure to make myself scarce at that time." I lean against the counter and try to keep a placid expression. I know that Liam and Colton are watching me trying to determine how upset I am about this development. They don't need to know how bothered I am by Natasha's presence. I finish my bottle of water and put it in our recycling bin when Larkin's watch beeps. He looks toward me, silently telling me that it is time.

"I'm going to go take a shower. I need one after that training exercise anyway." *I'll keep you company.* Olive tells me as she follows me upstairs.

Entering the bedroom, I smile down at her and place her onto my bed. "Stay here, I'll be quick." I jump into the shower and wash the sweat off my body and out of my hair. I lather the floral smelling shampoo through my hair and rinse it out. After shampooing and conditioning, I get out of the shower. I don't want to leave Olive alone for too long. I get dressed in a large grey cut off sweatshirt and black yoga shorts. I push the sweatshirt to the side, revealing my left shoulder. Since I have time, I decide to blow dry my hair. When I blow dry my hair, it is straighter than when I let it air dry—still a wavy mess but less curly.

I set the blow dryer down and start to walk back into the bedroom when my chest tightens. I stop and lean against the door frame, trying to coax air into my lungs.

Ryanne, what's wrong?

I open my mouth to respond, but I can't get anything out. I gasp as the air is pushed further out of my lungs, and I stumble to the ground. If I can make it to the stairs…

I try to make it to the bedroom door, but can only go halfway. Olive jumps off the bed and runs toward me. I lose sight of her as the room around me starts spinning. I've experienced this once before and already know who is responsible. I black out.

COLTON

LARKIN TRANSPORTS BACK INTO THE room holding a very surprised, but not scared Natasha. A large black blindfold is covering her eyes. "Ahh, now I see what's going on. Well, not technically, but you know," she waves him off and then straightens up. "Hello, Colty," she coos at me.

I take a small step toward her. Liam places a hand on my shoulder and pulls me back. I've never wanted to hit a girl before, but she's now the first one on my list. "Why Natasha?"

"Why?" She has the audacity to laugh. "Why? Because everyone that was at the battle talked about how great she was. The girl got herself stabbed! How is that great? I came over here that day to see if we had a chance of getting back together, and I see you with her. I saw the way you were looking at her. It was obvious that you had feelings for her. She's nothing compared to me, Colton. She can't give you what I can."

"Jealousy? That's why she did this?" Emma whispers to David.

"Don't talk bad about her, Natasha. You have no idea what she's going through," David says, the anger obvious in his voice. He pulls Emma to his side—to protect her and to keep him calm.

"See, she's got you all wrapped around her tiny little finger," Natasha points, but since she can't see us, she isn't pointing at anything. "That girl is nothing special. She got lucky and has a lot of magic, but one girl can't stop everything that's going on. It's better that you guys realize it now and join the winning side."

"Ryanne told you everything that happened with Adam and Dravin, and you still went to their side. Why?" Liam asks.

"Dravin's kind. He wouldn't do something unless it was totally necessary. She has information; he needs it. Adam told me all about their little sexscapades."

"Sexscapades!" I yell at her. Liam is fully holding me back at this point. Olive runs into the kitchen and prances around my feet. I ignore her and turn back to Natasha. "Adam lied to you."

"Who cares? At least now I get a chance to get revenge for what she did to me! She took away any chance I had with you!"

"I took that away, Natasha, not Ryanne! I didn't and still don't ever want to get back together with you." Liam gasps behind me and loosens his grip. He falls to his knees, grabbing his chest.

"I understand that now," she says as her smile grows. "Oh, and there's one thing about me you should know: my power's evolved. I no longer need to be in the same room as someone to asphyxiate them. You might want to go check on your little girlfriend upstairs. She's probably unconscious by now…if she's not dead."

Larkin transports Natasha out of the room. Logan and I run out of the kitchen and bound up the stairs, taking them two at a time. I slam the door open in Ryanne's room and rush in. She is lying on the ground on her side with one arm is over her head, the other is across her stomach. I run over to her body and roll her onto her back. Placing an ear on her chest, I listen for a heartbeat. *Thump….thump.* It is faint but still beating. Logan falls to the ground beside me, hands outstretched and already trying to heal her.

Emma, David, and Bragden all run into the room. Liam stumbles in a couple seconds later, still having difficulty breathing. Larkin transports into the bedroom and looks at her. "Is she going to be fine?"

"I don't know. She's still alive but barely. Logan's trying to heal her." I glance down at Ryanne, willing her to respond to Logan. I need her here. She still hasn't moved. I look at Logan, and he's still concentrating. Something isn't right.

I look over her body looking for anything obviously wrong.

"She not breathing, Logan!" I say. My panic levels are starting to rise. What if Logan can't heal her? Logan opens his eyes and shakes his head.

"Move out of the way." I move backwards and let Logan move to where I was previously sitting. I don't want to leave her side, but Logan knows what needs to be done; I don't. My feet move me so that I'm standing near Liam and Emma. She already has silent tears streaming down her face and Liam looks…horrible.

Kneeling near Ryanne's head, Logan places a hand on her forehead and two fingers under her chin and tilts her head back. Leaning down, he moves his ear over her mouth and confirms that she isn't breathing. Taking a deep breath, Logan bends down, pinches her nose closed, and places his mouth on hers, expelling the breath into her. He continues to do this, only pausing to breathe himself. When nothing happens, I fall to my knees. I crawl over to her limp body and grab onto her hand.

Ryanne, don't you dare leave me! I need you here. Quit being stubborn, and come back to me!

Logan continues to do mouth-to-mouth resuscitation. She's unresponsive. I've watched her die once; I can't watch it again. I realize now how much I hate the idea of her not being in my life. She is stubborn, sarcastic, impulsive, and infuriating at times, but I love all that about her. I love her…I love her. She makes things interesting, and I can't imagine not seeing her smile again. Not watching as she yells at me or hearing her laugh at something I say. Not being able to make her blush so easily. Not seeing her…

Emma is sobbing now. David is trying to console her, but it isn't working. I stare down at Ryanne waiting for any sign of life. Anything that will tell me that everything will be all right. After an agonizing amount of time, Logan exclaims, "She's breathing!"

I tighten my grip on her hand. He stops mouth-to-mouth and goes back to healing her magically. After a couple of seconds, Ryanne gasps and opens her eyes. Rolling to the side closest to me, she begins coughing violently. I reach out and rub her back, trying to help calm her. She tries to push herself off the ground, but her arms are too shaky. Logan and I help her move into a seated position.

Blinking rapidly, she stares ahead, not looking at any of us. Her breathing is still abnormal. Taking a few deep breaths, she tries to steady her breathing rate. She coughs one last time before looking over at me. "Your ex-girlfriend's not very nice."

I choke on a laugh and pull her to me. That's the first thing she says after she almost dies? Typical Ryanne. She hugs me back. Resting my chin on her head, I look over her to Logan. He looks exhausted, but at least he's smiling.

I can't contain the single tear that escapes and starts to run down my cheek. Ryanne pulls back and looks up at me; her eyes zoning in on the tear. She slowly leans forward and kisses my cheek where the tear is. Pulling back, she looks me in the eyes. "Don't shed a tear over me, Colton," she pushes herself off the ground and smoothes her clothing.

"You almost died, Ryanne."

"I'm too stubborn for death," she says before walking out of the room, not saying anything to those standing against the wall.

I stand up and stare at the door Ryanne had just walked out of. "She's going to be the death of me."

CHAPTER
TWENTY-FOUR

AS I WALK DOWNSTAIRS, I try to steady my frantically beating heart. I am scared. Natasha almost killed me without even being near me. I needed to get out of the room before my emotions got the better half of me. I don't want anyone to see how freaked out I am by this new development. Thunder rolls outside. My steps stumble on the stairs when the house shakes. That's not what I was going for when I thought about hiding my feelings.

I walk over to the window and notice the storm clouds rolling in. I take a deep breath and try to calm myself. The storm clouds lighten and transform into rain clouds. At the moment, that's the best that I can do. I know everyone is standing behind me. I turn around, arms crossed across my chest, and try to smile at them. I'm not fooling anyone.

Colton looks torn. Liam looks hurt. Emma's face is tear-streaked. David keeps glancing between Emma and I. Bragden and Larkin look upset, and Logan looks exhausted. I walk toward Logan and grab his hands, linking ours together. Palms touching palms, I close my eyes and call my magic to me. When I feel it push to the surface, I move it to my hands. The magic feels like silk caressing my skin. It's a pleasant feeling that I'm glad can benefit someone else as well. Logan sighs as my magic connects with his. I open my eyes and watch as the exhaustion leaves him. When he looks better, I stop the flow of magic and step away from him. In my own way, I am the healer of the healer. I smile at him as he gives me a one armed hug.

"Thank you, Logan," I whisper.

"You scared us," Logan says. "You weren't responding to my magic and then you stopped breathing." I stopped breathing? I feel my eyes widen; I didn't know it was that bad. That explains why Emma was crying, and Colton was shaken up. "I had to perform mouth-to-mouth resuscitation, and you were still unresponsive for a while." I step forward and wrap my arms around Logan's waist. He wraps his other arm around me and holds on tightly. "I thought we had lost you. Again."

"You can't get rid of me that easily," I try joking about it. I don't like talking about how close to death I've come recently. One of these times, no one is going to be able to bring me back. I'll be gone. For good.

"Ryanne…"

What's a sexscapade?

"What?" I ask Olive, taking a small step away from Logan.

The blonde lady said Adam told her about your sexscapades.

"What?!" I look at Liam and Colton. "My sexscapades?" I can't control the anger in my voice. Liam and Colton's facial expressions transform to ones of shock. Colton and David both curse and look down at Olive. I bend down and pick up Olive. "What does she mean, my sexscapades?" I'm staring at Colton, waiting for him to explain.

"Adam told Natasha that you had…" Colton starts but can't finish. He looks at Liam and David to see if anyone else can explain. I can see and hear Colton's anger when he is speaking about Adam.

"He said we had sex," I say it as a statement. Adam is spreading more rumors about me. I flinch as a loud clap of thunder shakes the house. I need to remain calm. I am getting really fed up with Adam. I take a deep breath and look back at Colton.

"What else did she say?" Colton just stares at me. "Would you rather I read someone's mind?"

It's Emma who speaks first. "She says she's doing it to get back at you for taking Colton, though you didn't. Dravin's kind. Adam's great. Sexscapades. And that her power's evolved which we've obviously figured out. Now, you're caught up."

Short and simple.

I nod and walk over to the couch. I already knew that she didn't like me because she thought I was interested in Colton. Granted, I was...still am, but I didn't let anyone know that. I didn't try to take Colton from her, that's why I stopped talking to Colton. Now, I know that Colton actually does have feelings for me. This incident is just another reason for me to not start a relationship with him. I don't need Natasha to take her anger towards me out on the others. Thunder rolls again. It isn't as loud this time, but it is longer.

"I'm sorry for bringing her here, Ryanne."

"There's nothing to be sorry for, Larkin. Don't apologize. We needed to know exactly what was going on, and now we do."

THEY'RE STILL WATCHING ME. I just want to turn and yell at all of them that I'm fine. *Almost.* Like all the other times, I put on a fake countenance. It's been a couple hours since Natasha tried to kill me again. I've calmed down, but inside I'm still freaking out. Everyone seems to be out to get me. Dravin can pull me in through my dreams, Adam's in my nightmares, Natasha's...Natasha's just a....

"Penny for your thoughts?" Colton sits down next to me on the couch.

I don't want Colton to know what I am actually thinking about, so I say the first thing that pops into my mind. "Why isn't combobulated a word?" That's a pretty good question actually. I should get a cookie for thinking of that under pressure.

"What?"

"How do we become discombobulated if combobulated isn't a word to begin with?" I turn and look at him, watching as his concerned expression turns to one of amusement.

"That's a very good question," he nods and smiles at me. I can tell by the distant look in his eyes that he is still thinking. I laugh and lean over toward him. He moves his arm and wraps it around me, pulling me into his side. I probably shouldn't have allowed that to happen, but my mind and my heart aren't really on friendly terms anymore. If I am going to momentarily forget my rules, I might as well do it fully. I scoot closer to him, placing my arm across his chest. Emma smiles at me from the chair she's sitting in with David. I close my eyes and let myself drift to sleep, feeling safe for the first time in a long time.

COLTON

I KNOW THAT THIS WON'T happen again, for a while at least, so I let myself enjoy it while it lasts. Tomorrow, Ryanne will go back to sitting on the opposite side of the couch, talking to me only when others are around and avoiding being alone with me. I tighten my grip around her. In her sleep, she snuggles closer to me—a breathy sigh escaping from her slightly open mouth.

"When are you going to tell her, Colton?"

"I honestly don't know, Emma. I've thought about telling her so many times, but something just doesn't feel right. And I told her that I'd wait until she was ready. She's still worried about the vision. She won't let herself get any closer to me. I can understand it, but it's frustrating. I can't tell her if she's adamant on distancing herself."

"I get that. Both perspectives actually. I'm just worried about her. Seeing her lying on our bedroom floor earlier, not breathing, while Logan tried to revive her the ol' fashion way...I don't know, it made everything so much more real. I was so scared that she was actually gone." Emma's blue eyes are glistening as more tears threaten to fall again.

I just nod because I don't know what else to say. I need to get away from everyone's watchful eyes right now. I place an arm under Ryanne's legs and slowly pick her up, cradling her against my chest. I walk up the stairs and open her door, pausing in the doorway. Hours ago, she was lying on this floor, unresponsive. Not breathing and barely clinging to life. I push the thoughts out of my mind and walk over to her bed. I've done this same thing so many nights before, but something feels different tonight. Laying her down in her bed, I pull the covers around her and kiss her forehead, enveloping myself in her floral scent. I don't know what she uses, but she always smells like springtime.

I start to step away when something brushes against my leg. Olive is jumping at the bottom of the bed, wanting up. Bending down, I pick up the little white fur ball and place her on the bed near Ryanne's head. "Goodnight you two," I whisper. Turning around, I slowly walk out the door, pulling it shut behind me. I don't know how late everyone is going to be up and don't want them to wake her up. She's been working hard lately and needs all the sleep she can get.

I walk into my room, frustrated at how this day turned out. It was going so well until Natasha. Training with Ryanne earlier had been more fun than I was expecting. She gets angry when someone's able to defeat her. She's cute when she's angry, so of course Liam and I had to push her harder. Walking into the kitchen, I could tell that Larkin wanted to say something but was having trouble. What he said was not what any of us were expecting. Bringing Natasha, especially after what happened last time, was asking for trouble; however, we all wanted to know why she decided to join Dravin. Why she went to the dark side—I don't see Dravin as the cookie type. I freeze in the doorway. Wow, that was totally a Ryanne comment. She's rubbing off on me.

Running into Ryanne's room and finding her lying on the ground, not breathing…I almost lost her again. She looked so lifeless. I couldn't even pretend she was asleep because even in your sleep you move. On the verge of death, you don't move at all. I should have realized that something was wrong when Liam started acting weird, but we all thought that Natasha couldn't use her power from that much of a distance. We thought we were the only ones in danger.

Pulling my shirt over my head and changing into a pair of flannel pajama pants, I walk to the bathroom. I have to stop thinking about it. She's alive and asleep in the room across the hall. Natasha didn't kill her. With shaking hands, I turn the cold water on and splash it onto my face. I need to get a grip. Closing my eyes, I grasp onto the edge of the sink, taking deep breaths. What is going on with me?

Standing over the sink, with water dripping off my face, I try to push the images of Ryanne's beaten, bloodied, and almost dead body out of my mind. I don't know when she became so important to me, but losing her scares me more than anything. Grabbing a clean towel, I dry my face. This has to stop. We need to take more precautions when it comes to her safety. If she's annoyed with how much attention we give her now, she has another thing coming. Standing up straight, I remove the towel from my face and look into the mirror. What the hell? What's going on?

I reach my hand out and gasp when I see right through it. Glancing back at the mirror I am standing in front of, I see the shower door behind me.

Holy crap, I'm invisible.

CHAPTER
TWENTY-FIVE

COLTON

OKAY, I CAN DO THIS. *Become visible.* Staring at the mirror, I can still see the shower behind me. How the heck do I become visible again? I've been standing here for ten minutes, trying to reverse this invisibility without luck. Why don't these powers come with an instruction manual?

I slowly walk down the hallway to Tom's room. Empty. Dang, I don't want to go downstairs like this. Taking small steps, I try to be as quiet as possible. Wait. What am I doing? No one can see me, so why am I walking like I am about to be caught doing something I shouldn't be? Running down the stairs, I see Emma sitting in the chair. She looks at the stairs and a look of confusion crosses her face. I'd be confused too if I heard someone running down the stairs but didn't see anything. Everyone is seated in the living room still. I walk past them and into the kitchen where Tom is.

"You've got to help me," I say to him. His head jerks in my direction but to him there is nothing there. He stands up and looks around the kitchen. "Tom, I'm right here." I reach out and touch his shoulder. He jumps back and hits one of the chairs at the table, knocking it to the ground with a loud bang. David, Emma, and Logan all rush into the kitchen to see what is wrong.

"Colton?" Tom whispers.

"Yes, I need your help."

Emma gasps and takes a step backwards when she hears my voice. "Where are you?" She is looking all around the kitchen, but considering the fact that I am invisible, she won't find anything. I walk to her and place both arms on her shoulders, showing her that I'm right in front of her.

"I'm right here."

At my touch, Emma screams. Slowly reaching a hand out, she waves it into the space in front of her. When she hits my chest, she gasps again. "Holy crap, Colton, you're invisible."

"I realize that. I can't figure out how to reverse it." I let go of her shoulders and turn back around, facing Tom. "Tom, can you help me?"

He shakes his head and opens his mouth. He's obviously as shocked as everyone else. "I don't know. There has to be a trigger or something that sets it off. What were you thinking about before you became invisible?"

Emma takes a step forward and slams into my back. "Ouch dude, hold something so we know where you are."

"Sorry," I reach forward and grab an apple from the fruit basket on the counter. After a couple of seconds, the apple becomes invisible as well.

"That's so awesome," Emma says.

"Colton, focus. What were you thinking about?" Tom says, walking in the general direction I'm standing. He is looking at the area to my right. Close enough. I put the apple down and think back to what I was doing when I became invisible.

"Umm…I don't…Oh. I remember." I was thinking about Ryanne. I was thinking about what happened earlier today. Despite wanting to push those images out of my mind, I think about them again. Nothing happens. I am still invisible. "It's not working."

Larkin, Liam, and Bragden walk into the kitchen to see what all the commotion is about. "What's going on?"

"Colton's invisible," Logan explains.

"Seriously?" asks Liam.

"Yeah, I'm right here," I start waving my arms back and forth but stop when I realize how stupid this is.

"Let's see. Colton, are you listening?"

"Yep."

"Think of the opposite of what you were thinking about earlier. If it was sad, think about something happy and vise versa." Instead of picturing Ryanne hurt, I think about the times she's laughed. I think about training earlier when she smiled and skipped into the house. I think about the way her hair looks when she sits outside and it blows around her. The scene of her singing The Fray while playing the piano pops into my mind. When I saw the embarrassment in her expression, I just had to join her. I couldn't stop staring at her because she was so surprised when our voices melted together.

"It's working. Keep it up."

I think about when I quoted One Direction lyrics to her, and she fell over laughing. I picture the way her eyes light up when she's smiling. I remember when she was singing and dancing in the kitchen, not knowing that someone was watching her. I see her cheeks turning a deep shade of red as I easily make her blush and the total embarrassment on her face when everyone saw her wearing her bridesmaid's dress, despite how beautiful she looked.

My skin feels like it is vibrating. I feel like I'm sitting in a giant massage chair. It feels weird, but familiar, like I am supposed to know this feeling. I wonder if this is what everyone else feels when they use their magic.

"It worked. We can see you." I glance down and am finally able to see myself again. I've waited for so long to get my power and my power is invisibility. I don't know whether to be ecstatic or disappointed.

Now I know how Ryanne feels when it comes to attention; only hers is basically twenty-four-seven. Emma whistles and glances down at my chest. I'm still shirtless. Quirking an eyebrow at her, I ask, "Like what you see?"

She smiles at me and makes a show of fanning herself. David growls and lightly elbows her. Laughing, she reaches up and kisses him on the cheek. "You're still my favorite," she turns around and skips out the room. David glares at me for a couple more seconds before following her.

Tom turns to me and asks, "What's the trigger?"

I start to walk out of the kitchen. I'm actually starting to feel tired— the events of the day are starting to weigh down on me. Do I really want to share that with everyone? They already know everything else, so I guess it can't hurt anything. Before leaving the room, I whisper, "Ryanne."

THROWING ON MY JACK SPARROW t-shirt and a pair of jean shorts, I skip downstairs. I woke up in a really good mood this morning. I'm not sure why, but I'll take it. Maybe it's because I actually woke up for another morning. All this almost dying stuff is starting to make me appreciate life. Who knew?

Everyone is already downstairs by the time I make it down. Didn't I use to be the early riser? I walk past everyone and into the kitchen. I put food and water into Olive's bowls and turn to the sink to do the dishes. Once all the dishes are clean, I dry my hands off and turn to put them all away. Emma walks into the kitchen. "Here, let me help you. I know how much trouble you have reaching the top shelf."

I put a hand on my chest and with mock gratefulness, I reply, "Oh my gosh, Emma. That's so kind of you! Thank you so much for your help. I'm eternally grateful." She laughs but grabs some of the dishes. We finish putting them away and walk back into the living room. Everyone is staring at Colton.

What is everyone looking at? "What's going on? Why are you staring at Colton like you expect him to grow a second head?" I ask as I walk over to the other side of the couch and sit beside Liam.

Emma sits down on David's lap. "Colton came into his power last night."

"Really? What is it?" I turn and look at him. He is already watching me. With a small smile, I watch as he disappears. Gasping, I sit up straight and look around the room. No one else is surprised that he just vanished. "Where'd he go? Can he transport like Larkin?" Larkin shakes his head. "Then where'd he go?"

Right as I ask that question something pulls all my hair off of my shoulders. I scream and jump up, slamming into a barrier. Though I can't see anything in front of me, I can hear Colton laughing. Everyone else in the room starts laughing as well. "I'm invisible, Ryanne." Colton whispers in my ear. I shiver as his breath hits my ear. I can't even see him, and he still makes me react like that.

He materializes right in front of me—standing so close, I have to crane my neck further than usual to see him. "That wasn't very nice. Simply telling me would have sufficed."

"Where's the fun in that?" He moves away from me and sits back down on the couch with a large smile on his face. I cross my arms and return to my seat as well. Liam pats my knee, still laughing.

"It always has to be fun with you guys. Let's scare the crap out of Ryanne. Let's tickle her until she cries. Let's come up with all the short jokes possible. Ha Ha. I'm surrounded by a bunch of comedians," I mumble and lean against the armrest, ignoring everyone's laughter at my rant. "So Colton, are you excited about it?" I ask him. He rubs the back of his neck, thinking.

"I don't know yet."

"You don't know? I think it's an awesome power. Think about all the stuff you can do."

"Don't you dare come into our room when we're in the shower or changing! I may not have a power yet, but I can still kick your butt," Emma says.

Colton scoffs at the butt kicking comment. "I wouldn't do that. I'm not Larkin."

"Hey. I did that once. Two times tops. And it's not like she was naked or anything. She had a bra on," Larkin tries defending himself, but only gets glares. I can feel a blush rising. A topic change is in order.

"Just think about it, Colton. During a fight, you can go invisible and go all ninja on everyone," I say. "Oh! You'd always win at hide and seek!"

He laughs at me. I love it when I am able to make him laugh. His melodic laugh always makes me smile. "I like the way you look at things, Ryanne." He looks over at me, still smiling. Be cool, Ryanne. I'm sure I am grinning like a crazy person. "I just hope it comes in handy, and someone can benefit from it."

"There will come a moment when you will have a chance to show it. To do the right thing," David says, but he isn't looking at Colton. He is smiling at me, waiting.

"I love those moments. I like to wave at them as they pass by." I grin at him. "Oh, David you'll really have to do better than that. Do you think I'm wearing this shirt just because I like Johnny Depp?" I pause. "Actually, I do love Johnny Depp, but I like the movies almost as much."

"One of these days I'm going to stump you."

"I look forward to it."

TRAINING TODAY IS JUST AS brutal as it was yesterday. Liam and Colton are definitely not taking it easy on me because they know that my enemies won't either. I am getting stronger, but it's going to take a lot more training for me to be able to take on more than one person without magic. The good thing is, because of my size, people don't expect me to be able to fight back at all. They see a tiny girl—an easy target. That's one thing I have working to my advantage.

Colton reaches out and swings an arm toward my head. Instead of ducking, I bend backwards and do a back bend. When my hands connect with the ground, I kick my feet up and hit him in the chest. He staggers back, but quickly recovers. Jumping up, I turn and face him again, waiting for his move. He smiles at me and then disappears. I quickly scan the area around me, looking for any signs of movement.

A foot connects with my stomach, knocking me to the ground, flat on my back. The wind is knocked out of me from the fall. Liam stands off to the side, laughing. I feel a slight pressure against my hips and something pins my arms to the ground. I start struggling as Colton reappears above me with a huge smile splayed across his face. "That's not fair. If I can't use my magic, you can't use yours!"

"When did we make those rules?" I struggle against him again, but stop when I realize that I'm trapped. He has me pinned to the ground. If that's how he wants to play...

"What are you going to do to me now that you have me here?" I bat my eyelashes at him and bite my lip. His smile falters a little, and his grip loosens, giving me the advantage I need. I pull my knee up and connect with his oh so sensitive area—the one way a girl can get the upper hand in any situation. He grunts in pain and moves off of me. With a smile, I hit him with a blast of magic that sends him flying a few feet away before landing with a thud on his back.

Liam falls to the ground laughing. Everyone else has stopped sparring and is watching us. I slowly walk over to Colton, "Two can play that game." All the guys are laughing, and Emma is jumping up and down, clapping. With that, I turn around and walk past everyone into the house.

CHAPTER
TWENTY-SIX

I GRAB A WATER BOTTLE and sit down at the kitchen table, waiting for everyone to join me inside. When the door opens and everyone comes in, I can't help but giggle at the way they are looking at me. Emma looks really proud, while everyone else is amused. When I see Colton walk in last with a grimace on his face, I smile innocently at him. "What's wrong?"

He just glares at me, "Not cool." Liam is trying very hard to contain his laughter.

"You should know that if you're not going to play fair, then I won't either."

"Noted," he grabs a water bottle and sits down at the table, still brooding. I can't help but smile at his reaction. He's so cute when he is upset. Emma walks past me and gives me a high five.

Entering the kitchen, Tom stops when he sees the look on Colton's face. "What's wrong with him?"

"Ryanne just beat him at his own game," David says and goes on to explain what happened. Liam cuts in a couple times since he was closer and knows everything that was said. Before the end, Tom is laughing along with everyone else. While David is talking, I glance over at Colton. He's struggling to contain his smile as well. It's good to know that he's not really mad at me.

"I'm going to go change. I'll be back in a minute." I walk upstairs and into my room, locking the door in the process. I grab my Jack Sparrow shirt and shorts from the bed and quickly change. Running a brush and some leave in conditioner through my hair, I try to tame my curly mess. When I feel decent again, I open the door and slowly walk out.

Halfway down the hallway, someone grabs me around the waist. I scream, but when the fingers start moving, my scream transitions into giggles. "Say it." I shake my head and continue trying to get away. I double over laughing. The tickling continues, and my stomach starts to hurt from laughing so hard. "Mercy!" I yell through the laughter.

Colton lets go of me. Spinning around, I call magic to me and make it rain above him. Through the rain, I can see the outline of his body. I start laughing and run down the stairs. Once in the kitchen, I run behind Liam and wait for Colton to come into the room. Colton walks into the kitchen, fully visible and soaking wet. I'm not the only one who laughs at the sight of him standing there with water dripping off him.

"Oh, it's on, little one. It's on," Colton says from the doorway. I peek around Liam's shoulder and smile at him. He shakes his head, but I can hear the amusement in his voice.

David looks between the two of us, "This is going to be funny."

I KEEP AN EYE ON Colton all night. I just know that he will try to retaliate sooner or later. I'm hoping for sooner rather than later. The later it gets, the more likely I am to forget. He's sitting on the opposite end of the couch with a small smile on his face. What is he thinking about? He's up to something.

Suddenly, his smile disappears and he stands up and walks over to me. My eyes follow him warily. Stopping in front of me, he sticks his hand out. "Can I try something?" I stare at his outstretched hand suspiciously. Is this a trick? "I promise that I'm not going to do anything. I just have an idea and want to see if it will work."

I slowly grab onto his hand, still cautious of his motives. He laces our fingers together. Closing his eyes, he appears to be concentrating. Colton disappears, but keeps a hold of my hand.

"Colton, what are you doing?" My arm starts to vibrate. I look down and see that my hand is starting to disappear. First my hand goes and then my arm. It's like someone is taking a giant eraser and erasing me. I gasp. I can see through my arm. Colton pulls me up so that I am standing. I feel something wrap around my waist, and I am pulled against his invisible chest. My entire body starts to vibrate. I look down and watch as I completely disappear. "Oh my gosh, I'm invisible!"

I can't see Colton, but I can feel him. I am still pressed up against his chest. It's a good thing that I'm invisible because I'm pretty sure that I'm blushing. "It worked," he sounds surprised.

"This is so awesome. I wonder what else you can do," I whisper to him.

"They could totally be making out right now, and we wouldn't know," Emma says. I turn to glare at her.

Colton's chest rumbles with his laugh. "You know she can't see you right?" he tells me.

"How did you know I was glaring at her?" I whisper to him. "Can you see me?" He just laughs, but doesn't answer my question. "How do you become un-invisible?" I ask Colton. Colton steps away from me but keeps a hold of my hand. Slowly, I feel his grip leave my hand. I'm visible again. "That feels so weird."

A couple seconds later, Colton materializes. Liam looks up at him. "That could actually be a really helpful power. If you ever need to get out of a sticky situation, you could just become invisible. It'd make getting away easier."

Speaking of helpful power, I start to feel the pull of mine. Before I can tell anyone, I fall into another vision.

COLTON

IT MAKES SENSE. MY INVISIBILITY would be incredibly helpful in battle as a way to go about things unseen. If I am around, which I will be, I can help Ryanne get away from Dravin or Adam. I can do more than just fight now.

I am looking over at Liam, when I notice Ryanne starting to sway. She's still standing very close to me. I look at her right as she collapses. I reach out to stop her from hitting the ground, but end up falling with her. I cushion her fall, so she doesn't land straight on the hard floor. "A little warning would have been nice."

"I don't think she really had one. She was smiling one second and then...well she collapsed," Emma says.

I glance down at Ryanne. Her small body is lying across my lap. Her neck is lying over my arm at a very unusual angle. I shift her so she is in a more comfortable position. Liam's watching Ryanne, waiting for a sign that something is wrong. He isn't displaying any signs of discomfort, so Ryanne must be seeing the scene play out instead of being in the vision. The room is silent as we wait for her to come back.

What is she seeing? How will she react when she comes back? I've seen her laugh, cry, get angry, become stunned, demand to be taken to

Dravin, etc. We've seen it all. What would it be this time? I hate when she sees visions that upset her—especially the last one where she lost control of her magic. Please, don't let her have to go through that again.

Her head rolls to the side, and she sighs. She's going to be alert in a couple more seconds. On cue, three seconds later she opens her eyes and looks around. "Shoot," she jumps off me and starts running. Jumping over the arm chair, she flies toward the stairs. Using the banister to propel herself forward, she runs up, taking the stairs two at a time. Once we get over the initial surprise, we all spring into action. Liam and I run after her first. I make it up the stairs and follow her into Tom's room. She never stops running. Jumping, she tackles someone to the ground. I hear a female scream and then someone starts coughing.

Entering the room, I find Tom on his hands and knees coughing violently, and Ryanne on the floor with a very angry Natasha. I go over to help her, but can't. I run straight into an invisible barrier. Damn it, Ryanne put up a shield. She can't fight and keep up the shield for long. I understand that she's trying to protect us, but we don't need it right now. She's the one that needs help. The others come into the room and start pushing against the shield as well.

Ryanne jumps up and flips backwards right as Natasha runs toward her. I can tell Natasha is trying to asphyxiate her, but she isn't affected. She must have a shield around her too. She drops to the ground and swings her leg out, knocking Natasha to the ground. It doesn't look like Natasha is trained as well as Ryanne. She rolls to the side and gets back up. Natasha runs toward her and jump kicks her in the stomach. Ryanne flies backward, slamming into the bathroom door.

We all gasp. That looks like it hurt. I beat against the shield harder. I can't stand watching her get hurt like this knowing that I can help. Jumping up, she closes her eyes. Natasha starts to move toward her. Liam and I start pounding against the shield even harder. Someone behind me is yelling, but I'm not listening. My eyes are fixed on the stubborn girl in front of me.

The atmosphere in the room starts to change. I can tell that Ryanne is calling magic to her. Her hair starts flying around her like she's surrounded by fans. She thrusts her arms forward, and her magic connects with Natasha, sending her flying into the back wall. Hitting Tom's dresser, she knocks off all the belongings on top and falls to the ground where she remains. She groans, but doesn't get back up.

Ryanne falls to the ground and finally the shield falls down. Larkin runs over to Natasha and places a hand on her unconscious body and transports her out of the room. I rush over to Ryanne, who is panting on the ground. "She was...she was...going to kill...Tom. I had to...to stop her." She slumps back into me. Logan crouches down and tries to heal her before she passes out. Ryanne sighs as the magic heals her physical injuries from the fighting, but a couple seconds later her head falls to the side as she starts losing her battle to stay awake. Logan can't do anything about the exhaustion from using too much magic at once.

I bend down and push the hair out of her face. She arches her chin up and looks at me, "I'm sorry about the shield." Any words that I intended to say get stuck in my throat when I see the dark circles under her hazel eyes. Going limp in my arms, Ryanne passes out. Yet again.

Ten minutes later, we're all sitting in the living room in silence. No one really knows what to say. I just put Ryanne in her bed. She's still out and probably will be for a while. Tom seems to be in shock. He hasn't said anything since Ryanne tackled Natasha. He just keeps opening and closing his mouth.

"She saved me." We turn our attention to Tom. "She attacked Natasha...to save me." He starts shaking his head and pushes his fingers through his hair as he stares down at the floor. "She put a shield up and tried to fight on top of that."

"No matter how stupid it is, we've kind of stopped questioning what she does. She does what she thinks is right," explains Liam.

Logan speaks next. "I'm sorry for saying this Colton, but she seems to be doing a pretty good job. I mean, she's able to deflect these attacks with little to no help."

"Just think about how many of her injuries could have been prevented if she had help," I rebut. I'm starting to understand why she does what she does and why she feels like she needs to do it, but that still doesn't mean I like it.

Tom is still shaking his head. "I just can't believe that Natasha would try to kill me. I've known her since she was child."

"Natasha's just following Dravin's orders, and like Claire, Dravin knows that your death will cause Ryanne pain and she'll act out."

"I don't ever want to experience that again. I don't know how Ryanne has gone through it twice. It was horrible. It felt like the life was being drained out of me. I could see everything in color and then all the color faded away; I only saw black and white. Life and death."

"Like everyone keeps saying, she's tough. There's no other explanation," Larkin says.

"She saved me," Tom whispers again. I don't think his mind has fully processed what happened tonight.

"She's saving us all."

CHAPTER
TWENTY-SEVEN

"LIAM." I LOOK AROUND WAITING. Nothing. "Liam." I can do this all day…or night. I'm not sure what it is right now. "Liam. Liam. Liam." Come on, I'm starting to annoy myself. "Liam. Liam. Liam. Liam."

"Quit saying my name." I look behind me and see Liam walking into the clearing, dressed in all black with a smile on his face. My eyes follow him as he sits down beside me. "You called?"

"Took you long enough." He doesn't respond to me, just continues staring. "Ugh, fine. I don't really know why I called you here. I passed out, didn't I?"

"Yes."

That's it? That's all he can give me? Some company he is.

"How mad is everyone?" I bite my lip and anticipate his response. If they are mad, I have a lot of apologizing to do when I wake up.

"They're not mad. Well not very mad."

"What? That's not possible. They're always mad when I do something by myself. *You* are usually mad."

With a sigh, Liam lies down on his back. Turning his head toward me, he says, "Speaking for myself, I understand why you did it. It would have been more difficult to take on Natasha if you were trying to keep a shield around everyone while they were moving. We just don't like seeing you get hurt. Having to just watch and not be able to do anything is really hard."

"I didn't want her to use her power on anyone. Believe me, it's not a fun experience."

"I get it. You don't have to explain yourself to me." I lie down on my back and look at the sky too. "Colton may be another story."

I grimace and ask, "Is he really mad?"

"He's trying not to be. He keeps going invisible," Liam chuckles and continues. "Negative emotions make his magic stronger."

"So, do you think that when I wake up he'll be fine? He won't start yelling at me again? That's really annoying."

"No, I think you'll be fine." That's a good thing. I hate when he is upset with me. "He doesn't like being mad at you any more than you do. You just know the right buttons to push to elicit that response."

"It's one of my powers. I should come with a warning. Warning: May Push Buttons," I laugh. "I should get that made into a t-shirt."

"You're going to be a handful for someone. You know that, right?"

"Of course I am, and I take pride in that." We descend into a comfortable silence. I glance over at Liam once. He's staring up at the sky watching the clouds. How is this place so real if it is only a dream? "Liam, how do we always end up in this field?"

"Your subconscious picks it. It's probably because you feel safe here." That makes sense. I do feel safer here. I've never been attacked by gorgoths or any weird dragon things.

"Why don't gorgoths appear here?"

"I'm not sure why you get attacked by so many gorgoths. They only appear in mage's dreams, but it usually only happens once. Twice at most. In a way, they're sort of a training exercise for dream-walkers. I think that maybe being around me has caused you to see them more often; I'm not really sure."

"But why do they always try to kill me?"

"I don't know, Ryanne. I don't know." I start to feel the pull. Consciousness is trying to capture me again.

"I think I'm starting to wake up. I feel like I'm being pulled in another direction."

"I don't think you're waking up. You're probably moving onto another stage of sleep."

"How long do you think I'll be out?"

"For a couple more hours at least. I'll see you in the morning, Ryanne."

WITH A YAWN AND A stretch, I slowly open my eyes and look around. Considering the amount of light streaming in from the window, it is probably mid-morning or early afternoon. Olive is sitting on the bed next to me. "Morning Olive."

Morning. Feeling better?

Rubbing my eyes, trying to get rid of any evidence of sleep, I mumble, "Yeah. I feel better." And I do feel better; I'm just a little tired still. Hopefully, a shower can fix that.

When the water turns cold, I turn the handle all the way over and step out of the shower. I don't feel much more awake than I did earlier, but that's going to have to be good enough for now. As quickly as I can, I get dressed and head back into the bedroom.

"You didn't have to stay with me. I'm sure you're pretty hungry right now." I pick Olive up off of the bed.

Wanted to stay.

I hug Olive to me and walk downstairs. Everyone stops to look at me as I pass them on my way into the kitchen. Filling up Olive's bowls, I put her down on the floor and walk back into the living room. Stepping over Colton and Liam's legs, I plop down on the end of the couch. "Sup." I make a popping sound on the "p" at the end of the word.

Colton laughs and shakes his head in amusement. Everyone else just smiles at me. "How are you feeling?" asks Liam.

"I feel fine."

"You look tired," Logan says. I turn and glare at him. Of course he has to mention that.

"I'm not. However, if I close my eyes for an extended period of time, I'm just blinking *very* slowly—not sleeping."

"I'll make sure to not scare you while you are blinking…slowly," Colton says. He has that mischievous smile again, and I instantly push taking a nap out of my mind. I don't trust him when he smiles like that.

"That would just be mean."

"Who said I was nice?" His grin widens. I continue to watch him. His smile falters a little when I don't look away. I forget that we are in a room full of people until I hear Emma start laughing.

"Good point," I lean back in my chair, but not before I throw a secretive smile toward him. His smile falters more when he sees my expression.

Try to decipher that, Colton.

"WHAT ARE YOU THINKING ABOUT, Ryanne?" I stop staring out the window and look at the person who sat down next to me. I meet a pair of brown eyes watching me with curiosity. David has a seriousness in his expression that I don't see too often with him. He tries to keep everything on the comedic side which, in most of the situations we're in, helps a lot. I glance behind us and see everyone else laughing, sitting around the kitchen table.

"I was thinking about how I miss hiking through the woods." Pulling my knees under me, I turn toward him. "Do you guys ever regret helping me that day?"

"Not one bit," he says without even thinking about my question. "Why?"

"I don't know. I just feel like you guys have all had to give up so much in order to help me. Don't you miss being able to go out and not worry about being attacked? You all have basically left your previous lives to be here."

"Ryanne, you've brought us all together. We're all here because we want to be, not because we're being forced. And the worrying about an attack does kind of suck, but we've all been trained and knew what we were getting into beforehand. You couldn't get rid of us even if you wanted to." David leans over and bumps me with his shoulder. "Keep your chin up. Someday there will be happiness again."

"Thanks," I stand up and start walking toward the kitchen to join everyone, "and that's from Robin Hood."

"Dang it. I thought I made that up," David says following me into the kitchen.

"You may be good, but you're not that good, David."

COLTON

SITTING AT THE KITCHEN TABLE, I turn and look at everyone. We're an odd bunch. For the circumstances we're in, I can't imagine myself being surrounded by anyone else. These mages have become my family these past few weeks. I glance into the living room and see David sitting beside Ryanne on the couch. Based on their expressions, it seems like they are having a serious conversation which is weird for David. David usually resorts to comedy in serious situations.

"Larkin, do you think you can take me to the store later?" I ask.

"For what?"

When I see Ryanne stand up, I just shake my head at him. "Just can you?"

"Sure, I guess," he says while giving me a strange look. Larkin knows that I'm not his biggest fan, so I understand the expression.

"You may be good, but you're not that good, David," Ryanne teases. David just glares at her, but I can see the amusement and challenge hidden beneath.

"You're telling me," Emma mumbles and then smiles innocently at David. Ryanne sits down in the chair across from me and laughs at Emma's comment. David sits down in the chair next to Emma and playfully pushes her.

Laughing, Emma gets up and grabs the iPod docking station and brings it to the table. "Ryanne, do you have your iPod with you?"

"It's on the coffee table. I'll go get it," Ryanne pushes her chair back from the table and walks into the living room. Coming back into the room, she hands it to Emma. Emma starts scrolling through Ryanne's playlists, looking for something to play. She keeps looking over the iPod and giving Ryanne these weird looks.

"Do you know the words for "Grow Up" by Cher Lloyd?" Emma asks her.

"Yeah, she's a little more pop than I usually sing, but I know the words. Why?"

"You're going to sing it with me. I'll do the rap-like parts."

Ryanne's eyes bulge. "You want me to sing right here?"

"Yes, you've sung in front of us before so don't try to get out of this." Emma plugs in the iPod and turns the volume up. A pop song starts playing, and Ryanne sings along with it. She isn't singing as loudly as we know she can. Judging by the red tint to her cheeks, it's obvious that she is embarrassed. When the rap section starts, Emma jumps straight into it. Holy crap, Emma can rap. We all stare at Emma while the music continues. Ryanne is supposed to be singing, but she is staring at Emma as well. Even David is surprised.

"You can rap? Since when?" Ryanne demands.

"Since forever. Now, sing," Emma says, but the song is almost over. "Ugh, fine, we'll do this one. Same situation. You sing. I'll do the rap parts." Ryanne participates this time. Both girls get into the song. This is the most animated I've seen Ryanne recently. Emma is always happy, so we are used to seeing her like this. Emma jumps up during the middle of the song and pulls Ryanne up. Ryanne refuses to at first but then starts dancing along with the song. She runs over and pulls Liam out of his chair. Singing, she starts dancing in front of him. He laughs and shakes his head but dances with her. Emma does the same with David. Bragden, Logan, Larkin, and I just watch the scene play out.

I totally understand the wedding dance situation now. Acting carefree makes her beauty shine through. It's taking all my will-power not to jump up and make her stop dancing. I don't like all the other guys watching her like that. When the song ends, she starts laughing, but stops dancing. She walks back to the chair across from me and sits down. I smile at her. She bites her lip, but smiles back. A couple seconds later, she diverts her gaze.

Ah, there is the blush again.

Twenty minutes later, Ryanne is sitting on the kitchen counter. Emma is still dancing, though not like earlier. It is nice to see everyone acting like normal teenagers for once—well those of us who are teens. I'm leaning against the island in the middle of the kitchen when the song "Run" by Matt Nathanson ft. Jennifer Nettles came on. I quietly sing along with the song. I don't have the best singing voice, but I'm not that bad. I sang the first chorus by myself. When it comes time for the Jennifer Nettles part, I am prepared to sing it as well but am shocked when I hear Ryanne start to sing. I look up at her and find her watching me. The room quiets. Her beautiful voice fills the room as she sings out. We sing the next line together. I forget that there are other people in the room. My focus is completely on Ryanne.

Neither one of us moves, but we continue singing. I take a deep breath and sing out the next part. I watch as Ryanne mimics what I do. She can hold her notes longer than I can. She continues to hold out a note, while I sing. I'm amazed by how well our voices blend together. I've sung with her before, but this feels different, more intimate. The music fades and we are left with silence. Neither one of us move. She continues to stare at me, and I can't look away either. The next song starts to play, but the room remains quiet.

Ryanne tears her eyes from mine and looks at those around us. Her face turns every shade of red possible. She hops down from the counter, and with her head down, she silently walks out of the kitchen. I hear her footsteps go up the stairs. When I stop staring at the spot on the counter where she was just sitting, I realize all eyes are now on me.

"This waiting thing is getting more and more difficult," I mumble before walking out of the room as well.

CHAPTER
TWENTY-EIGHT

I KNOW THAT I SHOULDN'T have started singing with Colton, but I couldn't help it. I saw him staring down at the counter, singing quietly, and I wanted him to sing louder. I love his singing voice. I remember when he made me play the piano and how well our voices sounded together. I wanted to experience that again, and it was great while it lasted, but it is making things difficult. I like Colton so much. It hurts being around him all the time, but not actually able to be with him. I don't know what to do anymore.

I look down at my clock and see that it is getting late. I'd slept through the whole morning, so it is already night time. To avoid going back downstairs, I decide to just go to bed. I am already tired; it wouldn't be surprising if I fall asleep. I change into a pair of athletic shorts and a black cami and brush my teeth. Emma comes into the room with Olive following her. "Are you ok? You left the kitchen pretty quickly."

Spitting the last bit of toothpaste out, I wipe my face off and turn the bathroom light off. Getting into bed, I reply, "Yeah, I'm fine. Just tired. I'm going to go to bed." Emma places Olive onto the bed with me. With a sigh, she walks out of the room and turns the lights off.

Are you really ok?

"No, but I will be. Don't worry, Olive. Goodnight."

Goodnight, Ryanne.

Closing my eyes, I let myself drift into sleep.

"Long time no see." Tensing at his voice, I slowly turn around and see Adam staring at me in a very lustful way. I shiver and take a step back. Hitting the wall, I freeze. How the heck do I keep getting into these situations?

"How did I get here?"

"I pulled you here. You're not the only one with magic."

"What is this exactly?"

"This is a dream, of course."

"Oh." I need to keep this conversation going, but I don't know what to ask.

"I'm sure you're wondering why I brought you here."

"I'm pretty sure I already know, but please enlighten me." He smirks and begins walking toward me.

"I heard about your little visit with Dravin." Adam crosses his arms and stops a couple feet in front of me. "Now, he's mad. If you don't want anything to happen to your friends, I think you should tell me your location. We just need you. Your friends will be left alone."

"Why should I believe you? You've done nothing to make me trust you."

"Smart girl. You can't trust me, but if something happens to your friends because of your stupidity, everyone will blame you."

"You called me smart and stupid in the same sentence."

Ignoring my comment, he asks, "Where are you?" He takes another step toward me. I take a step forward, meeting him. He's not going to intimidate me that easily. I'm no longer a scared little girl.

"Currently, I'm in a dream that you dragged me into." He smirks and while looking down at me, I notice the look in his eyes change. I take a step back; I recognize that look. He had the same look when he attacked me in the cell. He takes a step forward and slams me into the back wall. Hitting my head, I wince but don't cry out.

"You will tell me where you are!" He is seething. Pupils dilated, nostrils flared—he is a walking billboard for intimidation. I try to punch him, but he grabs my hands and pins them above my head against the wall. Stepping on my feet so I can't move, he leans forward and whispers in my ear, "Feel familiar?" He's referring to the first time in the park. I don't know how to get out of this situation. Considering I can't read his mind, I'm pretty sure I can't use any magic here.

"Why are you doing this, Adam? Why me?"

"You mean in the beginning? Because of Colton. He got everything. When I found out that he was interested in you, I had to prove that he can't have everything he wants. It worked out perfectly. Until he found out that you had magic. If I found you first…well we'd be in a different situation. Though I'd want it to be similar to the one we're in right now. The fact that you turned out to be a mage was just an interesting turn of events. "

"What? You forcing yourself on me?"

"I'm not forcing myself on you. Do you see me doing anything?"

"That's bull crap, Adam, and you know it. You're holding me against my will."

"You got yourself into this position."

"I wouldn't be in this position if you didn't bring me here!"

He leans forward, and his lips brush against mine. I freeze. "Tell me where you are, and I'll let you go." I spit in his face. If I can't fight back,

I might as well make him angry enough. If he's angry, he won't think about what he's doing. He'll just react. On cue, he reaches out and slaps me with the hand that's not pinning my wrists to the wall.

My head jerks to the side. The slap stings so bad that I feel tears welling up in my eyes. With a hiss, I blink rapidly, making the tears disappear. "That's the best you can do?"

"I've not even started."

He lifts his leg and knees me in the stomach. It friggin' hurts, but it gives me the advantage I need. When I double over, his grip on my hands loosen. Pulling my hands out of his reach, I thrust my palm up and break his nose. Blood squirts onto me while he yells and moves away. Saying a bunch of obscenities, he rushes forward and swings his leg out and kicks me in the shoulder, knocking me into the wall. My head connects with concrete, and I slump to the ground.

The room around me starts spinning. I am too dizzy to try and get back up. Walking over to me with predator like finesse, Adam steps onto my hand and deliberately applies more pressure, crushing the small bones with a piercing snap. I cry out as the pain shoots up my arm.

Crouching down, Adam whispers in my ear. "Don't mess with me. You'll never win." Because I am losing consciousness, he can't keep me in this dream. I needed him to attack me so I can get out of here.

I smile up at him and whisper, "I already did."

GASPING, I BOLT UP IN bed and then quietly cry out in pain when my body starts aching everywhere. I glance to my right and see Emma sleeping. My cry didn't wake her up; Olive, on the other hand, sits up when I move.

Something wrong?

"I'll be right back," I whisper. I try to keep my voice steady; I don't want her to worry. Closing her little blue eyes, she snuggles against my pillow and falls asleep once more.

Getting out of bed proves to be extremely painful. Each movement causes pain to shoot through my entire body. My head aches from hitting the hard wall, my cheek is swollen from being slapped, my hand is broken, and my stomach aches from the punches. Thankfully, my legs are fine, so once I am able to get out of bed, I am able to get out of the room.

Opening the door, I peek down the hallway. It's empty, and the coast is clear. Colton's door is closed, and the lights are off. Thankfully, he won't see me tonight. I don't really want to hear him freak out again. I walk down to Logan's room and lightly knock. Logan opens the door and gasps when he sees my appearance. I must look as bad as I feel. "Can I come in?"

"What the hell happened to you?" Logan whispers loudly. Moving out of the way, he lets me come into the room. Liam and Colton are sitting on the ground and both of them jump up when they see me.

"Shoot," I turn around and point to Logan. "Why didn't you tell me that they were in here?"

"You didn't ask."

"What happened to you, Ryanne?" asks Liam. I look toward Colton. Oh dear, he's livid. I open my mouth to talk, but the room starts spinning. I can't tell where the ground is as the dizziness takes over. A pair of arms wrap around me as I sway backwards.

Knowing that they are Logan's, I ask for him to heal me as more black spots start to cloud my vision. Logan sits down on the ground, taking me with him. My head slumps back against his chest as I feel the early stages of the healing begin. A numbing sensation moves through my body lingering on the obvious injuries. I gasp when I feel the bones in my hand mend back together. A hiss echoes through the room at the sound of my discomfort. I'm not sure which guy it came from. A tingling sensation sweeps through my stomach and moves upwards toward my head. The swelling on my cheek decreases, and the dizziness and the headache go away.

I feel Logan tense behind me when he is done healing. I turn around and look at him. He has his angry face on. In my mind, I picture Mr. Potato Head pulling out his angry eyes. "I provoked him on purpose, Logan. It was the only way I knew how to get out of there."

"Logan, what happened?" Colton demands.

"It wasn't as bad as it looked!" I turn around and point to Colton, "See, I'm all better."

"All better? Are you serious? You come in here looking like someone used you as a punching bag."

"Well, someone kind of did. That's what I was trying to get Adam to do."

"Adam?" Colton and Liam both yell.

I jump up and run over to them. "Shhhhh. Can you please be quiet? I don't want to wake anyone else up. The less people that know, the better."

"Did he…" Colton starts.

"No, I spit in his face before he could do anything." The corner of Colton's mouth moves up slightly. I see the smile that he is trying so hard to hide. He is still angry, but not as much as earlier.

"What did he want?"

"My location," I say. "Dravin's mad because I didn't give him any information last time, so it was Adam's turn to try and get information from me."

Colton reaches down and lightly swipes his thumb across my cheekbone. "You have blood on your face."

I take a step back. I don't like the tingly feeling that I get when he touches me. Well if I'm being honest with myself, I do like it. A little too much. Logan's room is set up exactly like mine, so I walk over to his bathroom and splash water onto my face, cleaning away all of the blood. "It's not mine," I call out. "I broke Adam's nose."

"Really?"

Drying my face off, I walk back into the room. "I do know how to defend myself. I just have to improvise when I'm pressed up against a wall with my feet being stepped on and arms pinned above my head. So, I provoked him. When someone's angry, they just react. They don't think."

"You purposely tried to get him to attack you?" Colton asks.

"Yes."

"You're crazy," Colton says. I can tell that he is no longer angry. I think finding out that I broke Adam's nose put him in a slightly better mood. At least I didn't just let him brutally beat me.

"Thank you," I sit down on the floor and lean back against the wall. "Do you think they'll ever stop? I don't remember the last time I had a normal dream." Colton walks across the room and sits down next to me against the wall.

"Can I suggest something?" asks Logan as he gets comfortable on the floor a few feet in front of us.

"Sure. Suggest away."

"I think you should try sleeping with Liam."

"Huh?" I say, right as Liam says, "What?" and Colton lets out a "Hell no."

"Wait a second. I don't mean it like that. I mean, I think that she should go to sleep with Liam. Just sleep. I think that if he touches her while she's sleeping they won't be able to get to her. It's just a suggestion." Colton starts shaking his head, so Logan goes on, "Would you rather she keep getting attacked in her sleep?"

"Well, no, but——" Logan interrupts him, but I stop listening to their conversation. My eyelids are starting to feel heavy. Curling into a ball, I lie down on my side and rest my head in Colton's lap.

With a yawn, I say, "Wake me up when a decision is made."

COLTON

UGH, I'M NOT READY TO be awake. Squeezing my eyes shut, I try to fall back asleep. My back aches like I've been sitting in the same position for a long time. Leaning back, I hit something hard. Oww, I open my eyes and look around. Logan is on his stomach, sleeping with his head on his arms across the room. To my right, Liam is asleep on his back. My leg is numb; I start to move it when I hear a small breathy groan. Ryanne is sleeping on my leg…why? When I see her, the previous night's events come back to me. She was attacked by Adam again.

My whole body is stiff and sore, but I don't have it in me to wake her up. I lean my head back and close my eyes again. "I knew it. She gets to have all the fun," Emma says as she enters Logan's room. Hearing voices, Logan jerks awake and sits up.

"Ugh, it's too early. Go away."

"Did you guys have a party without me last night?" Emma asks. She sits down on the floor next to Logan and looks around expectantly.

"Ryanne got attacked by Adam last night. I healed her. She fell asleep in here," Logan says while popping his back. Liam groans and sits up as well.

"Oh, why didn't she wake me up? She got you guys…"

"She didn't want to wake anyone up. She only wanted to find Logan, but Liam and I were already in here," I try to speak quietly, but loud enough for Emma to hear me.

"She wasn't attacked again was she?" I glance down at her. Her hair has fallen over her face, hiding her features. Brushing her hair aside, I don't see any injuries. She has lines from the fabric of my pants on her face, but other than that, she seems fine.

"I don't think so." Ryanne stretches her legs out and yawns. Despite her petite stature, in those shorts her legs seem to go on forever. I know that Emma catches me staring, but I'm past the point where I care.

Ryanne pushes herself up off of my leg and grabs her face, "Oww." With her hand still covering the part of her face that was resting against my leg, she turns to me with sleepy eyes and mumbles, "Your leg is not very comfy." I look away as she stretches her back and arms. I see the guys do the same. We're not blind, and Ryanne is showing a lot of skin. Emma laughs at our reactions which Ryanne doesn't hear or chooses to ignore. "Oh my gosh, I totally had a dream last night."

"Really? What happened?" Emma asks.

Ryanne sits Indian style on the ground and starts to tell us about her dream. "I was at a mall, and suddenly everyone started to go crazy. I went over to find what the commotion was about and saw all these people lining up to see Christian Bale. You know me; I love the Batman films. However, I thought it was fake, so I didn't get in line. I stood off to the side and laughed at a kid, who was literally in tears. Someone placed a hand on my shoulder and asked if I knew who that kid was.

"I said no and turned around to find Christian Bale smiling at me. Well, of course, I fainted when I saw him. When I woke up and saw him still standing over me, I turned around and threw up on his insanely cute bodyguard. He bent down to help me stand back up, and the last thing I remember is the crying kid yelling, "She knows Batman." And then I woke up."

"That's what you dreamed about?" I try not to laugh, but that is the weirdest dream I've ever heard of.

"Yeah, and it was freaking awesome. You know besides the throwing up on the bodyguard part."

"You're a strange girl, Ryanne," David says from the doorway.

"Never claimed to be anything else." She stands up and walks over to him, "Be who you are and say what you feel because those who mind don't matter, and those who matter don't mind." At the confused expression on David's face, Ryanne laughs and leaves the room.

"It's not from a movie, big guy. Dr. Seuss said it!"

"Dang, how does she do that?"

"I'm awesome!" she yells from down the hallway. I start laughing. Even David laughs at that. Pushing myself off the ground, I walk past everyone and out of the room to take a shower and get dressed. Hopefully the hot water from the shower will relax my stiff muscles.

"HAPPY BIRTHDAY!" EMMA SHOUTS AT me as I come into the living room. I stop short and look around the room. Nothing is out of the ordinary. She runs over to me and gives me a hug. "Why didn't you tell anyone that it was your birthday? We could have done something."

"Because I didn't want anyone to know." I glare at David. He's the one that probably told everyone.

David says, "Oops," but I can tell that he doesn't mean it. Because of the short notice, they didn't have time to plan anything. We have bigger things to worry about right now than a birthday.

Larkin is sitting at the table. "Can you take me the store now?"

"Sure," he stands up and walks over to me.

"What are you going to the store for?" I just shake my head. I don't have to keep it a secret, but knowing that it'll kill Emma to not know, I decide to leave her in the dark. With a smile, I wave at her as Larkin transports us out of the kitchen.

CHAPTER
TWENTY-NINE

I'M HUMMING "IT GIRL" BY Jason Derulo as I skip down the stairs. I feel so much better after the shower. I decide to wear my Avengers t-shirt and jean shorts today. I've been on a superhero kick recently.

Entering the kitchen, I go over to the food bowl and fill it for Olive. *Thanks.* She starts eating, and I walk over to the sink to do the dishes. Emma comes over and starts to help me. I keep humming because the song won't get out of my head. When the last plate is put away, I turn around and see all the guys sitting at the table, eating. Dirtying more dishes. Emma and I groan, but don't say anything. Boys gotta eat, I guess.

I glance around the table and see a couple empty seats. "Where are Larkin and Colton?" I sit down in the chair next to Liam.

"Colton needed to go to the store," David says through a mouthful of cereal.

"Please swallow before talking. No one needs to see that," Emma chastises him. He smiles at her—a big toothy food covered grin. I can't help but laugh at her disgusted expression.

"What did he need to go to the store for?"

"He wouldn't tell us," Emma doesn't like to be left out of the loop. By her pout, you'd think that someone just took away her favorite toy.

"Hopefully, a birthday present," David mumbles.

"A birthday present for who?" David's eyes widen, but he doesn't answer me. Everyone is looking down at their food. "Whose birthday is it?"

"No one's."

"It's Colton's birthday, isn't it?" I ask. Liam and David just nod. Logan and Bragden keep their attention on their cereal.

"Are we going to do anything? Why didn't he want me to know?"

"It's not just you. He didn't want anyone to know, but I kind of spilled the beans," says David.

"Are we going to do anything?"

"There's not a whole lot we can do…" Liam replies.

"There's always something we can do…" I think about it. What could we do that didn't involve leaving the house? "We could make him a cake at least."

"Ha, I can barely make toast, and you want me to bake a cake?" Bragden says. I don't doubt him. He doesn't seem like he'd be a baker.

"Well, Emma and I could bake a cake. I'm sure we have enough ingredients here." I walk into the pantry and start gathering the supplies. There isn't a box of cake mix. That'd be too easy. We'll have to make this from scratch.

Placing everything on the counter, Emma and I start to organize all the dry ingredients into a pile. We'll need them first.

"How do you know how to make a cake from scratch?" Emma asks when I start to measure out all the ingredients.

"I used to bake with my mom on weekends. I'm really surprised I wasn't a fat child," I smile as I remember baking with my mom. We'd always make a mess and have to spend more time cleaning than baking. "For some reason, I remember the measurements…or at least I think I do." When I have all the dry ingredients measured out, I turn to Emma, "Can you mix all those in a large mixing bowl?"

"You got it Rachel Ray."

"Rachel Ray is a chef, not a baker," I inform Emma.

"Same difference."

"Not really."

"Hey Logan," I call to him. "Is it possible for a mage to get fat?" I don't think I've ever met a mage who was fat. They've all been big, but that was because of their muscles. I glance over at Bragden. He's the largest mage I've ever met, but there's not a single ounce of fat on him. I've never been on a specific diet before, but I used to consider how many calories I was consuming. Now, I just eat whatever is available.

"Not really," he tells me. "You can gain a few pounds, but the magic in our bodies keeps us healthy. It heals anything that's not supposed to be there."

"Is that why I don't have to take any of my iron pills anymore?" I haven't really thought about that much. Before I came into my powers, I was anemic. I had to take iron pills every morning.

"Yeah, your body recognized that your irons levels were low, and they basically fixed that. We're meant to be fighters, so the magic keeps our bodies in optimal conditions."

Emma walks over to my iPod and turns some music on. With a laugh, I return my attention back to the ingredients in front of me. I start mixing the milk and vegetable oil together, and when Emma is finished with the dry ingredients, we combine the two. Adding in the butter and vanilla extract, we search for a mixer. I give it to Emma and start spraying the pans.

She turns on the mixer before placing it fully in the bowl, and cake batter flies all over us. She screams and jumps back, dropping the mixer into the bowl. Cake batter continues to splatter everywhere. I rush over and turn off the mixer. I slowly turn toward Emma with my mouth hanging open.

She covers her mouth with her hands and starts cracking up. We're both covered in cake batter.

Emma walks over and grabs a handful of flour and throws it at me. I turn at the last minute, so it only covers my hair and clothes. I gasp and stare at her with wide eyes. Did she really just do that? I grab a handful and throw it at her, but she doesn't duck soon enough. It hits her in the middle of her face. Staring at me with a white powdered face, she huffs, sending flour everywhere.

All the guys at the table start cracking up. We glare at them, but don't do anything. It *is* pretty funny. I walk over to the cake batter and decide to mix it. Emma obviously hasn't used an electric mixer before. I add the eggs and continue beating it for a few minutes. While I am doing this, I give Emma instructions on how to make the chocolate icing.

I finish pouring the batter into the pan, when I hear Emma exclaim, "Oh my gosh, this is heavenly," she says while eating a spoonful of chocolate icing.

"Hey, save some for the cake." She sticks her tongue out at me and continues eating. I place the cake in the oven and turn around and assess the room. We created a very large mess. I turn back to Emma and start laughing all over again. "It Girl" plays through the speakers. Emma jumps up and rushes over to me, dancing. I refuse at first, but this song has been stuck in my head all morning, so I join in.

Might as well have some fun.

COLTON

LARKIN TRANSPORTS ME BACK INTO my room. I place the bag on my bed and walk out. From upstairs, I can hear music playing in the kitchen. I think I can even hear Ryanne singing along with it. I walk down the stairs and into the kitchen and freeze.

Are my eyes deceiving me?

Ryanne and Emma are in the middle of the kitchen, singing and dancing along with "It Girl" by Jason Derulo. The most shocking thing is the state the girls are in. They're a mess. Liam, Logan, Bragden, and David are all sitting at the table, watching them and laughing.

I look back at the girls. Ryanne has flour and something else stuck in her hair. Her dark hair now has a whitish tint. Emma has flour caked to her face and chocolate on her nose, but neither girl seems to care. Their outfits are covered in what looks like cake batter. Emma sticks her hand into a bowl and wipes chocolate on Ryanne's face. She screams and retaliates with more flour. I lean against the doorframe to watch. Larkin walks into the kitchen and instantly starts cracking up.

Both girls stop and look our way. Their eyes widen when they see us. Ryanne tries to hold her laughter in, but she falls to the ground laughing. Emma stares down at her silently for a few seconds before she starts laughing again. She walks over and sprinkles sugar on Ryanne, who is still on the floor. Ryanne snorts from laughing so hard which makes everyone laugh. She gets up and walks over to me.

Hitting me on the chest, she says, "Why didn't you tell me it was your birthday!" She has to yell in order to be heard over the music. Emma turns the volume down.

I act like that hurt. Instead of answering her question, I grab the end of her hair. "Do you know you have flour in your hair?"

She crosses her hands over her chest and looks up at me. "Emma doesn't know how to use a mixer." I let go of her hair and look over her head toward Emma.

She has an evil grin on her face, and with silent steps, she makes her way across the kitchen. Moving her arm back, Emma throws something in our direction. Ryanne ducks at the last second, and I'm hit in the chest with whatever Emma just threw. I look down. Egg yolk is dripping down my shirt.

Emma's eyes widen. "How did you know I was going to do that? You weren't even looking at me!"

"Well, I'm kinda psychic. I have a fifth sense. It's like I have ESPN or something." Ryanne stands up and smiles over at David. I'm guessing that was from a movie, since it makes absolutely no sense what-so-ever.

Emma jumps up and points at David. "Mean Girls!" Clapping, she continues, "I got one!"

"That and I saw Colton look at you, so I figured you were going to do something," she shrugs. "I ducked." Staring at my shirt, she says, "Which I'm glad I did. Egg is not my color."

"I think you'd look pretty good in it," I tell her as I reach forward and hug her to me.

She screams and tries squirming away, but the damage is already done. I let go of her, and she takes a couple steps backwards. Egg is stuck in the ends of her hair and plastered to the front of her shirt. She gapes at me, before turning around and grabbing a handful of flour. I try to turn around, but run straight into an invisible barrier. "That's not fair." My eyes are glued to her as she slowly walks closer to me, an evil grin on her beautiful, cake-covered face.

"I thought we already established that I don't fight fair," she says as she stops right in front of me. She brings the handful of flour up to her face and slowly blows it onto my face. I close my eyes and wait for the flour attack to stop. Then, she runs backwards and hides behind Emma, giggling.

If that's how things are going to be...I think about Ryanne last night when she came into the room after Adam's attack. My anger turns me invisible. I hear Ryanne mutter "Oh shoot" as she darts across the room and stands behind Bragden. Grabbing onto the wooden back of his chair, she whispers, "Do you know where he is?" I walk toward the island, trying to not make a noise.

"He's invisible, Ryanne. If you can't see him, neither can I," Bragden says. He starts shaking his head, chuckling at her question. Liam's watching her, laughing. It is nice to see Ryanne finally happy, not worrying about something. She keeps looking around the room, searching for any signs of movement. I wait until she looks away. The bowl of chocolate icing on the island beckons me forward. Walking over to the bowl, I place my hand inside and wait until the handful of icing disappears. I know that Emma sees it because she smiles in my general direction. She takes a couple steps back and leans against the counter. I take the handful and rub my hands together, smearing the chocolate between both hands.

"I really don't like his power," Ryanne mumbles. She is still looking around the room. I stop right behind her and lean down, slowly wrapping my arms around her, without actually touching her, I say, "Boo," and grab both sides of her face with my chocolate covered hands. She screams and I jump back and become visible again.

Bragden and Liam bang their hands against the table and start laughing. Ryanne turns around and glares at me, mouth hanging open. Even a mess, she looks adorable. She takes a handful of icing and wipes it across the front of my shirt. I grab her arms and wipe the rest of the chocolate down them.

"What the heck is going on?" Ryanne freezes, and I tense up. Everyone stops laughing, and we all slowly turn toward the doorway. Tom is standing there—his eyes scanning the mess in the kitchen.

Emma replies, "We're baking a cake."

Ryanne makes a weird noise, and I glance down at her. She's struggling to hold in a laugh. I know that Tom sees it too, because his anger lessens. It's really hard to remain mad around her. Ryanne turns around, leans against my chest, and starts giggling. I wrap an arm around her back and start laughing as well. I glance over at Tom and see him crack a smile. There's no way he can be mad at something Ryanne is involved in. He still hasn't gotten over the fact that she saved his life.

"Just make sure you clean everything up," Tom says as he begins to back up. Ryanne is still laughing, and Emma is trying not to smile. All the guys at the table are attempting to hold back their laughter as well. Tom looks at Ryanne once more before turning and leaving the room. I swear I can hear his laugh as he goes up the stairs.

Beep. Beep. Beep.

The oven behind me starts beeping. Ryanne pushes away from me and grabs a pot holder and reaches into the oven to pull out a cake. She places the cake on top of the oven and turns it off. Leaning back against the counter, she looks around the room and grimaces.

"We really made a mess in here," she glances over at Emma. "This is all your fault. I think you should clean it all up."

"Ha, I don't think so. You're going to help me," she points at Ryanne and then glares up at me. "I don't care if it is your birthday; you're going to help too."

I throw my hands up in surrender, "Yes, mom."

We get to work cleaning up. Bragden, Logan, Liam, and Larkin all help too. Liam and Logan take every opportunity to wipe something else on Ryanne. I've never seen her smile so much. I can't help it. I don't care if anyone sees me. I keep glancing over at her. She's watching me as well. Instead of ignoring me, she smiles back. Even covered in almost every ingredient required to bake a cake, she is beautiful.

"Go get cleaned up, we'll finish this," David says. He looks between Ryanne, Emma, and me.

"You guys didn't even make this mess," Ryanne argues and continues cleaning.

Larkin reaches over and grabs her hand and transports her upstairs. I could hear her yelling at him in her room. I laugh and stand up. I reach down and help Emma up. "Thank you!" she calls over her shoulder to the guys cleaning as we head up the stairs.

CHAPTER
THIRTY

STUPID LARKIN AND HIS STUPID power. I don't want to make the guys clean up a mess that they didn't even make. It should have just been Emma and me cleaning it. We're the ones that made it. It's Colton's birthday; he shouldn't have had to clean anything up. Walking into the bathroom, I flip on the light switch and finally see my reflection. Oh my gosh, I look ridiculous. I have flour and cake batter stuck in my hair, chocolate handprints on my face and arms, and just about everything else on my clothes.

Emma walks into the room right as I am about to undress. "I'm just grabbing some clothes; I'm going to go shower in David's room."

"You've got a little something on your nose."

Emma reaches up and wipes off some of the icing. "Better?" she asks with a wide grin.

"Much," she laughs as she heads out of the room.

I undress and get into the shower. The water going down the drain turns a lovely shade of brown for the first couple of seconds as I wash the chocolate icing off. After washing all the flour out of my hair, I jump out and get dressed. Wearing my black v-neck "One Fish, Two Fish, Red Fish, Blue Fish" Dr. Seuss shirt and a pair white shorts splatter painted with violet and navy blue paint, I run a towel through my hair and walk downstairs. Colton is already down there, but Emma isn't. I walk over to the end of the couch and lean against the armrest.

"Do you know how difficult it is to get dried icing and cake batter out of your hair?" I look around at everyone. They are staring at me with small smiles. "No. I don't think so. Well let me tell you, it's extremely difficult. I had to shampoo my hair twice and douse my ends with conditioner before it all came out."

Emma comes downstairs and sits on the loveseat with David. "Well that was fun. Next time, avoid the hair please." She looks around. I point at her. "What?"

"I already told them how difficult it was to get everything out of my hair." Sitting back, I glance up at the TV and see Legalos shooting an arrow. I gasp and start watching. Liam laughs at me. "I've got a tiny little crush on Aragorn." I pinch my fingers together to show how small I am talking about.

"Which one is Aragorn?" Emma asks me. I wait until they show him. "Oooh, I can understand the crush."

Thirty minutes later, my eyes are drawn to the coffee table. Sitting on its shiny surface, placed next to my old notebook, is a black book. I reach out and pick it up. Its black exterior has a magnetic tab closure and slightly rounded corners. I open it up and gawk at the large white pages inside. It's a sketchbook; an expensive sketchbook. The page binding allows the artist to easily use both pages since there aren't any metal spirals separating the two. The thick pages are suitable for all types of mediums. I'd always wanted to buy myself a real sketchbook like this, but since I'm cheap, I never could get myself to spend the extra money.

Why is this sitting there? Whose is it? I look up, and my eyes are instantly drawn to Colton. He's watching me with a small smile on his face. *Of course.* I should have known that he would go out and buy me something like this. He knew that I was out of pages in my notebook.

I crawl over Liam's lap and hit Colton in the chest with the hard sketchbook. "You stupid head. You don't buy other people stuff on your birthday!"

"I told you so," Larkin says from across the room.

"How do you know I got it for you? How do you know it wasn't someone else?" he asks. I am still basically in Liam's lap. I scoot myself off of him and glare at Colton.

"Because you're the only one who would do it! How much did it cost you? I'll pay you back."

"No you won't," he crosses his arms across his chest and turns toward me. "I won't accept any money from you."

"How much was it?" I demand.

"Nope." I hit him with the sketchbook again. "Ouch, stop doing that."

I hit him one more time. "Don't tell me what to do." I lean back and look at the TV again.

Colton leans down and whispers in my ear, "A simple thank you would suffice." Butterflies erupt in my stomach when I feel his breath against my ear. His amazing smelling cologne floods my nostrils, so I hit him again and move back to my original seat. I mumble a thank-you and put the sketchbook back on the coffee table. Colton is rubbing his chest where I'd hit him, but is smiling a little which means that he's not mad at my reaction.

"A handful, I tell ya," Liam whispers to me.

Pulling my knees up to my chest, I wrap my arms around my legs and turn toward Liam, "I don't think anyone will be able to handle me,"

I laugh and lean down against his shoulder, "It'll be a good challenge though."

"That it will be."

"WHERE ARE YOU TAKING ME? This isn't pay back for hitting you earlier today, is it? Because you're supposed to hit the birthday person the same amount of times as their age; so, technically, I still have…like fifteen more to go."

"Just keep your eyes closed," Colton says to me as he pulls me somewhere. We've decided that we aren't going to train today. We're allowed to have one day off. "Trust me." This is kind of exciting—not knowing what is going to happen, but I don't like blindly walking. I just hope this isn't one of his pay-back moments.

"When can I open my eyes?" I trip over something on the ground, and Colton reaches out to steady me. He grabs my other hand and slowly pulls me forward again.

"I'll let you know," he continues pulling me forward, warning me if there is anything in my way. I keep my eyes closed the entire time, ignoring the temptation to peek. I start humming to pass the time.

"Are you humming the alphabet?"

"Yep. Don't be hatin'."

"Wouldn't dream of it." I can hear the amusement in his voice. I can imagine him giving me the *Ryanne is silly* look and shaking his head.

Colton suddenly stops moving. I take a step forward and smack into his chest. "Whoa there," he says with a laugh.

"You could have warned me you were going to stop," I mumble as I take in my surroundings. I can hear birds chirping above me. It sounds like we are in a forest—the wind is rustling the leaves together creating a symphony of noise. "Okay, you can open your eyes now."

I open my eyes and look up at Colton, who's staring down at me, waiting for my reaction. I look around and gasp in delight. I was right. I am standing in the middle of a small trail in the forest. Tall, leafy trees surround us. Random spruce and pine trees are growing among the tall birch, maple, and oaks. Their branches start high up on the trunk, creating a canopy-like structure around us. The fading sunlight filters down through the leaves, creating shadows and spots of light all around.

I smile up at Colton. "This is beautiful." I love being in the forest. There's just something comforting about it.

"You told me once that you used to go into the woods to think and draw—that you felt relaxed here. I thought you'd been through enough lately, you could use a little relaxing…" he seems nervous. He keeps rubbing the back of his neck and looking around us. I walk over to him and wrap my arms around his waist. I can't believe that he remembered that. That seems like so long ago.

"Thank you," I let go and walk around him. "Can we go further?"

"Yeah, but I think you should put a shield around us just in case." I nod and am about to push my magic out when a swarm of monarch butterflies take flight from a nearby bush and surround us. The shield is forgotten momentarily as I watch the orange and black wings flutter around me. I glance up at Colton and see that he's just as mesmerized by the event as I am. Tilting my head back, I watch as they get smaller the higher they go.

A few butterflies linger nearby. I raise my hand towards one of the ones hovering in the air between Colton and me. The butterfly lands on my hand.

My eyes flicker up to Colton who also has a butterfly in his hand. A quizzical expression crosses his face briefly before a small smile takes over.

"My mom used to tell me that butterflies were the presence of those who have left us," I whisper to him while watching the butterfly crawl over my hand. "A reminder that no one is really gone. That they're always watching us."

"Claire used to have a butterfly garden," he tells me. My eyes leave the butterfly and watch him as he speaks. "She would spend hours in it, taking care of the plants and just watching the butterflies fly around. You could tell that she loved it in there."

"What happened to it?" I ask him.

Colton looks away from the butterfly and down at me. "She decided that she loved the bookstore more," he says. At the same time, both of our butterflies fly out of our hands and fly in the direction that the others went in. "Still want to go further?"

I nod and push my magic out around us, creating a shield. If there's anyone else in the forest, they won't detect us.

"Shield's up," I tell him and start walking. He follows behind me. For the next hour we just walk and talk. I find out that his favorite color is green. He played basketball in high school, which I didn't know. I never went to any games. He likes rock music and has always wanted to learn how to play guitar. He had a golden retriever when he was younger named Scooby after his favorite cartoon, Scooby-Doo. He wants to travel the world when he's older. After talking about himself for a while, he turns the questions on me.

I find myself opening up to him. I tell him about how I used to go up on the roof of my house just to watch the stars all night. I tell him about my love for traveling too. I've always wanted to travel to Puzzlewood in the Forest of Dean. I love anything with chocolate and peanut butter, so Reese's are basically the best things ever. I tell him about my mom. I've never really opened up about her before. I tell him about how much I miss her; how I miss having a mother like figure, and how upset I was when Claire died because in a way she filled that void.

We come across an old bench on the trail. It doesn't look sturdy enough to sit on. To prove me wrong, Colton stands on top of it and jumps up and down. "If it can hold my weight, it can definitely hold yours," he sits down and motions for me to sit down next to him.

After I sit down, neither one of us speaks for a while. I just look around, admiring the environment. I love being surrounded by greenery. The forest is always full of life. The plants. The animals. The atmosphere. Everything is alive in some way or another, and everything is connected. My fingers move across the old wooden surface. Feeling an indentation in the wood, I look down. Someone carved the initials A.F. into the seat of the bench. I move over the curvature of the letters, wondering how he or she stumbled upon this area.

I close my eyes and let the slight breeze blow around me. My hair blows across my shoulders, giving me the chills. With the sun going down, I am starting to get cold. Colton must have seen my goosebumps because he takes off his light jacket and wraps it around my shoulders.

I smile and thank him. Turning toward him, I ask, "Colton, what happened to your parents?" At my question, his body instantly tenses. I scoot closer to him and place my hand on his forearm, "You don't have to tell me." I really don't want to upset him. I'm just curious. He never talks about them. Colton looks down at my hand on his arm before his green eyes connect with mine. I can see his inner conflict in his gaze. I know how difficult it is to finally open up to someone after so long.

"No, no. It's fine." He looks out at the trees and starts talking. "Scott and Lynelle Wagner," Colton says their names. My eyes are glued to him as he talks. I can't look away.

"My parents were high school sweethearts. They met when they were sixteen. He was the football quarterback, and she was head cheerleader. Cliché, I know. They got married when they turned twenty and had David shortly after that. A year and half later, I came along. For a while, we were that perfectly happy family.

"One night when I was eight years old, we were walking through the trails behind our house, and these men attacked us. My dad's power was the strongest. He could control air while my mom could control emotions. My mom was focused on keeping us calm while my dad attempted to fight them off. They were both trained, but so were the men. My dad fell first. He was trying to fight the men off, while my mom tried to get us away. He was stabbed in the stomach and then one of the men broke his neck." I can feel the tears welling up in my eyes. Colton is blinking more often, trying to keep his own at bay.

"My mom pushed us back and tried to protect us. She ran up to the men and fought with all she had. She was only one person; she couldn't take on four men of that size. They stabbed her through the stomach and laughed as she died. David and I were frozen with fear. We didn't know what to do or where to go. We were stuck. The men came over to us and said, "The end is near." They knocked us out, but let us live. We were supposed to be a warning. The men were both mages, rebels so to say, who ended up working for Dravin later on."

A couple tears start to fall. I instantly want to make his pain go away. I scoot toward to him and hug him. "I'm so sorry, Colton." He wraps his arm around me and pulls me closer.

"It happened a long time ago," he says, but I can hear the sadness behind his words. I reach my left hand up and lightly brush his tears away. I can feel his eyes on me, but I focus on the tears falling from his emerald green eyes. My heart starts rapidly beating with each tear I wipe away, and it becomes harder to breathe. I notice him reacting similarly. I move so I am sitting up on my knees and face him.

Leaning forward, I place a small kiss on his jaw. When I hear his breathy groan, I move to the right and kiss his jaw again. The stubble on his cheek scratches against my smooth skin, but it spurs me on. The arm around my waist tightens.

"Ryanne…" I lean up and kiss the area right next to his mouth. The edge of my lips touches the edge of his mouth. Colton freezes and turns toward me slightly. Ah, I can't fight it anymore. What happens in the forest stays in the forest, right? I am leaning forward to kiss his lips when I hear a twig snap. I freeze and look to the left. The light echo of voices resonates through the forest. We both tense at the sound. Who would be in here besides us?

Colton goes invisible beside me. I can still feel his arm around me, so I know he hasn't moved. The hem of my shirt rises slightly. The cool night air brushes against my exposed skin as Colton wraps his arm around my waist. Skin-to-skin contact makes his power work faster. I hear shuffling beside me as he stands and pulls me back against his chest.

Colton starts pulling me backwards when the two figures finally emerge from the trees. I glance down and let out a sigh of relief when I only see the grass below me. Colton's invisibility is cloaking me too. I open my mouth and would have said something, had Colton not placed his hand over my mouth, silencing me. I don't know how he knew, but I'm glad he did. I strengthen the shield around us and let him pull me backwards.

"We'll find them. I know they're close," Natasha says while sitting down on the bench we were on literally seconds ago.

"We better. Dravin's getting angrier as each day passes, and there's nothing," Adam says while sitting next to her. "Despite what Dravin says, that girl is strong. She's not just going to come to us. We have to lure her." Colton starts walking backwards again. "Now that she's banging Colton, he's the obvious choice for it." I start struggling against

Colton's grip. That freaking…guy. He has no idea what he's talking about.

"Ryanne, stop," Colton whispers to me.

"Let me take your mind off of everything," Natasha says. She moves so that she is straddling his lap. She leans forward and starts kissing his neck. When we hear the sound of a twig snapping again, we all freeze. I don't know which one of us stepped on it, but we both tense, preparing for the worst.

Adam and Natasha both turn and look in our direction. Colton and I remain frozen mid-step. I hold my breath and wait for them to look away. After a few agonizing seconds, Natasha shrugs. "It was probably just an animal," she says and leans forward kissing Adam's neck again. Adam leans his head back giving her access, but continues to stare in our direction. Finally, he turns away and gives his attention back to Natasha.

Letting out a silent breath of relief, Colton starts pulling me back, faster this time. Once we are far enough away, he lets go of my stomach but laces his fingers through mine and starts running back to the house. Because of the recent running I've been doing, I'm able to keep up with him. It's dark by the time we make it out of the forest. Bounding up the stairs leading to the deck, Colton runs straight for the back, not stopping until the door is open. He pulls me through the doorway then closes and locks the door behind him.

Everyone is sitting at the kitchen table, looking at the back door. "Colton, we're still invisible." He lets go of my hand, and I become visible. I bend down and take a couple deep breaths. How did they find us? They'll find us within the next couple of days at this rate. A couple seconds later, Colton appears next to me. Emma's eyes widen as she looks us over. Her eyes and most of the guys' eyes land on my stomach. I look down and see a couple inches of exposed skin on my abdomen from where my shirt had risen up. I quickly reach down and fix it. I can feel the blush rising onto my cheeks.

"So what happened?" Emma asks slowly. I walk over and sit in the empty seat next to Bragden and slam my head against the table. My windblown hair falls forward blocking my face from everyone. I am still wearing Colton's jacket, but I don't feel like giving it back just yet. I lift my head up and bang my head lightly on the table a couple more times before I angrily exhale. I hear the sound of a chair being drawn back, so I'm assuming Colton just sat down too.

"We just can't catch a break," I mumble against the wooden surface of the table.

"We saw Adam and Natasha in the forest. They're looking for Ryanne." Bragden reaches over and rubs my back. There must be something I can do to prevent them from finding us.

I wonder if…I push away from the table. "I'll be right back."

I walk out of the room and run up the stairs into Tom's room. "Hey, Ryanne," Tom looks up from his book. His smile falls when he looks at me. I must have that crazy determined look in my eyes that Emma says I get when I'm angry or upset.

"Do you know the enchantment that Claire used to put around the house?" I ask him.

"Yes, but it takes a lot of magic to complete it."

"Let me try it. We just saw Adam and Natasha in the forest. They're getting closer to the house, and I can't let that vision play out, Tom. I can't watch someone else die because of me again."

Tom stares down at me. He doesn't want me to do this; I can see that in his eyes. When his features soften and he sighs, I know that I won. "Ok, you can try it. I have to go get it from the house though. Let me go get Larkin," Tom says while getting off of the bed. He walks past me and heads downstairs. Following after him, I think about what I just asked him. I'm planning on performing an enchantment that takes a lot of power. Apparently, I have more magic in me than the others, but do

I have enough to accomplish this? I don't know. I pass out if I use too much. It'll most likely happen if I attempt this. The guys definitely aren't going to like this.

"Larkin, I need you to take me to the house."

I enter the kitchen after Tom and I see everyone look between the two of us. Larkin stands up and walks over to Tom. Without asking any questions, he transports him to the house.

"What is he going to get?" David asks me.

"The enchantment that Claire used to put on the house." David and Colton both jump up and glare at me. Totally called that reaction.

"You want to try that spell?" David asks.

"Do you have a better idea?"

"You can't ask us to let you—" Colton starts.

"I'm not asking, Colton. I have to do something. If I pass out, at least I can say I tried it." I flinch and wait for him to start yelling at me. Instead, he clenches his fist and disappears. Where'd he go?

"That happens. It's ok," Liam assures me. I turn back to where Colton was standing previously.

"If I don't at least try something that vision could play out, Colton. Would you want to re-watch what you told me about earlier?" I pause though already know the answer. "No, you wouldn't. I've already seen you die in a vision; I can't watch it play out in real life too. I can't. I have to try something."

Even if it's the last thing I do, I have to do something.

CHAPTER

THIRTY-ONE

COLTON

DEEP BREATHS. CONCENTRATE. I REMEMBER how things were an hour ago in the forest. She told me things I know she's never told anyone else, and I did the same. I'd never talked about my parents' deaths before. David and I never talked about it. We got over the initial surprise and filed everything away to never mention it again. Claire tried to get us to talk about it when she came to take care of us, but we never opened up. When she asked earlier about them, I realized that I wanted to tell someone. I needed to get it out, and there was no else I wanted to share it with than her.

I've thought about that night so many times, but never cried. I didn't even cry when it happened because mom was trying to keep us calm. Afterwards, I just felt numb. So, I don't know why I actually shed a few tears today. The way she was looking at me when I was telling the story....I don't even know...she opened a door that I had kept locked for so long.

The way she looked up at me when she saw my tears was so full of trust and...love. I know that she feels the same way I do. That moment confirmed it for me. When she leaned forward and kissed my jaw, I thought I was going to lose it. It never felt like this with anyone else. Everything inside me was on fire and felt like it was trying to find a way out of my body. My stomach was churning, and my heart was beating a mile a minute and increased with each movement she took toward me. She was going to kiss me. Ryanne was going to kiss me. She was going to cross that invisible line she'd put between us because of the vision. Then Adam and Natasha had to come and ruin everything. My ex-girlfriend and...

Focus Colton. I need to think about positive things if I want to become visible again, not this. Everyone is staring at the area I was at before I went invisible. Closing my eyes, I picture Ryanne and me in the forest earlier. I was walking forward, trying to make sure the path was clear enough for her to walk since the girl literally trips over her own two feet, when she giggled and ran to the right. I didn't like her diverting from the trail.

She stopped next to a fallen tree trunk that was resting against the stump and climbed up onto it.

"Are you sure that's safe?" I asked her as she balanced herself on the edge.

"Nope," she mumbled as she slowly walked to the other side, arms outstretched on both sides for balance. "Seems sturdy enough," she looked over at me and smiled.

"What are you going to do?" I didn't like the look on her face. That was the expression she gives me when she is going to do something that she knows I won't like, but is going to do it anyway. Because she *has* to keep things interesting apparently.

When she turned around so the length of the log was behind her, I knew what she was going to do. She put her hands into the air and took a breath. "Ryanne, I don't think that's a good idea." She grinned at me once more before leaning her body forward a little. Taking another deep breath, she jumped backwards and flipped once and then went into another flip, this time her hands didn't come down on the wood. She landed and extended her arms up and smiled down at me.

"Ha, just like a balance beam." I walked over to the edge of the log and extended a hand to help her get down. She looked down at my hand and quirked an eyebrow at me. Jumping down herself, she smiled up at me and said, "I don't need any help, but thank you." Walking past me, she went back to the trail and headed further into the woods

I turned around and watched as she left. Smiling over her shoulder, she stopped and shouted, "You coming, slow poke? You got the long legs. Keep up mister."

I feel the invisibility slowly start to fade. I think about when I came back this morning and saw Ryanne and Emma covered in food, while singing and dancing. The smiles on both of their faces were infectious. Even Tom couldn't stay mad at them when he saw the mess.

I look down and see that I am completely visible again. I sit back down in the chair and look straight at Ryanne. "Look, I don't like this, but I understand why you want to do it." Ryanne's large hazel eyes widen as she takes in what I just said.

"You're not going to yell at me and tell me that it's a stupid decision? I could get hurt yada, yada, yada?" she asks in a shocked tone. No one was expecting me to comply so quickly.

"Nope."

"Huh," she sits back in the chair and crosses her arms. She is staring at me, but I don't think she is actually looking at me. She's here, but I can tell that her mind is somewhere else. She's still wearing my jacket which looks incredibly good on her. The sleeves are way too long, so she has to push them up often and the bottom completely covers her shorts, only revealing a long length of leg. She jumps when Larkin transports in behind her with Tom. Tom hands her a piece of paper. She grabs it and reads through it.

"What do I have to do with this?" she turns around in her chair and looks up at Tom, waiting for his instructions.

Tom crouches down until he's eyelevel with her. "I'm not sure exactly. Claire was the only one that was able to do this enchantment. I just know that while you're reading it, you have to push your magic outward. You'll know if the enchantment is complete. Claire said it felt like everything snapped together."

"So just read and push. Got it."

Why is it always Ryanne? Why does she always have to do this stuff? The rest of us can't control our magic like that. I can feel the magic running through me, but I can't grasp it and control it like Ryanne can. It is a part of me, firmly connected to my inner being. I understand that in this instance, she's literally the only one of us that can do this, but I still don't like it.

"Do I have to read it more than once?" she asks.

"I don't know. You'll be able to tell."

She bites her lip and looks back down at the paper. Standing up, she says, "Ok, let's do this."

We all stand up, "Right now?" I ask her. I knew that she would want to do this soon, but I didn't think it would be tonight.

"There's no better time than the present," she says while walking into the living room. She stops and stands in the open area beside the couch. She turns and looks at Emma, "I feel like I'm in an episode of Charmed. Blessed be."

"We just need another girl around her, and we could be the Charmed ones," she replies.

"Can I be Piper?" Ryanne asks. "She can blow stuff up and I like making things magically explode. I wonder if I can freeze things…"

"Only if I get to be Paige. She married Henry and he was just adorable," Emma says.

I'm not the only one glancing between Emma and Ryanne, confused at their Charmed conversation. "Don't you want to sit down on something?" I ask, while stopping beside her.

Shaking her head, she replies, "No, it's easier to call my magic to me if I'm standing…I think. I really haven't experimented yet, but I feel like I should be standing." She glances back at me, "Just stand behind me in case this takes too much magic." She's asking me to catch her if she passes out from exhaustion. Because she could pass out from exhaustion. Again. Seeing the determination in her eyes though, I can't say no. Agreeing to her, I move so that I'm standing behind her.

"If anything goes wrong and I can't control the magic, please knock me out, ok?" she asks Liam. He instantly shakes his head, refusing to do that. I know that he doesn't like having to do that to anyone, especially her. "*Please.*" He looks away, but slowly nods. Like me, he can't say no to something like that. If it comes to it, he knows that he'll have to do it.

Everyone takes a step back, except for me. Ryanne takes a deep breath and starts reading from the paper. I can feel her magic filling the air around us.

Magic come forth, I call you to me,
Protect our home from danger so evil cannot see
Hide the lines through an invisible veil
So those who happen upon will believe they failed
Protect our home from those with eyes
Who only seek for our demise.

I call you to me during this time of need
To protect those within from anger and greed
Protect our home from danger so evil cannot see.

Ryanne's voice quiets as she starts to repeat the enchantment. The more she reads, the more her magic fills the air. I look over her and see everyone watching in wonder. We can feel the magic emanating from her. It feels like electrified silk skimming over our skin as it moves through the house. I look up toward the ceiling and gasp. Floating lights are twinkling above us. It looks like thousands of tiny fireflies have swarmed our home.

The tiny lights are floating down the halls and up the stairs, filling in every available location. Hovering near the doors and windows, they brighten. I never saw any lights when Claire performed the enchantment. I tear my eyes away from the lights and back to Ryanne. She is still saying the enchantment over and over again, her body slightly swaying. I wrap my arms around her as she falls back into me. Her eyes are closed, but her mouth is moving. Though she isn't saying it out loud, she is still thinking of the enchantment. I look up over at Tom to see if he knows what to do. It feels like she is vibrating in my arms because she's still pushing magic out. Tom shakes his head, silently telling me that she isn't done yet.

She goes through the enchantment one more time. When she finishes with the last line, she falls limp in my arms. The magic stops pouring out of her. I catch her as she starts falling, but a second later, she gasps and is able to support herself. Taking a step away from me, she looks around. "Did it work?" I want to reach forward and pull her back to me, but I refrain.

"You're awake?" Logan asks.

"Yeah. Did the enchantment work?" She gives him a confused look out of the corner of her eyes as she walks over to the window and looks out. "How do I know if it worked?"

Tom is still staring at her in awe. "I'm pretty sure it worked." She smiles and hands him back the paper with the enchantment on it. Sitting down on the couch, she leans back and closes her eyes. Despite not passing out, she looks pretty tired. She sighs loudly and says, "Stop looking at me like that."

"Do you know what you just did?" Liam asks.

"The enchantment?"

"You just did one of the most difficult ones there is…and you didn't pass out like you usually do when you use too much magic. You had complete control of your magic."

"Isn't that a good thing?" she asks.

"Yes."

"Then why are you guys looking at me like I just told you I was leaving the shire and taking an afternoon stroll to Mordor?" Leave it to Ryanne to throw in a movie reference. "Do I need to make it rain all up in here to snap you all out of it?"

Emma snorts and sits down in the chair. "Heck no. I hate it when you do that."

I DON'T UNDERSTAND THE BIG deal. Claire used to put this enchantment up. Why was it different when I do it? After I soaked Larkin, everyone realized that I was serious and quickly sat down and pretended like everything was hunky-dory. I can feel them all watching me. I don't know how they were expecting me to react, but this apparently wasn't it. Olive, who is sitting on my lap, meows. *They're watching.* "I know."

"Stop," I mumble. "Please stop."

"Stop what?" Bragden asks innocently.

"You're all watching me like you expect me to sprout claws and scratch your faces off. I'm not Wolverine. What's going on?"

"How are you awake? Even Claire had to rest afterwards and she'd been using magic for much longer than you have," David says.

Oh, I get it.

"I don't know. This was different. When I make a shield, I have to use a lot of magic and energy to make sure it stays in place. The larger the shield, the more magic I have to use, which is why I tend to pass out from using too much. For that enchantment, I wasn't the one using the magic. I was pushing the magic out of me and making sure it extended across the house. I wasn't using it, and I think that is why I don't feel very tired now. The extra magic that I pushed out flew back into me once I was done, which was why I fell backwards." I glance over at Colton and nod to him, thanking him for catching me…again. "I wasn't using the same type of magic that I use when I tend to pass out."

"I think the thing that shocks us the most is that you have enough magic to push out like that. We don't have that," Tom speaks up. "We can't push our magic out. At least for me, my magic is connected to me. It's imbedded inside me. It's extremely rare to be able to push it out like that, especially to that magnitude."

"Oh." Pushing out magic is easier for me than actually using it.

"The fact that you can easily push that much out is amazing. We could actually see your magic around you. We watched it move throughout the house. I've never seen anything like it before."

"You should have seen your aura," Larkin says.

"My aura?" What is he talking about?

"Yeah, I can see auras. You knew that," Larkin smiles at me. *Light bulb moment.*

"Oh, I totally forgot about that. You don't talk about it much."

"No, I don't really. It's only useful when I first meet people. I get a sense on whether they're good, bad, truthful, lying, you know—the general information. When you were saying that enchantment, your aura literally started glowing. That's why I kept staring at you. Like Tom said, I've never seen anything like it before."

I nod and bite my lip. "I think I liked it better when you guys were trying to discretely watch me. I don't like hearing about how different I am from everyone else."

"Ryanne—" Colton starts, but I don't really want to hear any more. I'm not trying to be rude, but it's still a lot to take in. Everyone is always saying how different I am from all the other mages. I'm just Ryanne. Not some amazing mage they keep saying I am.

"I'm actually starting to get tired; I think I'll go to bed. Good night." I walk around the couch and up the stairs as quickly as I can before anyone can say anything else.

I'm just me.

Why don't they understand that?

CHAPTER
THIRTY-TWO

I CRAWL INTO BED WITHOUT changing out of my clothes. I don't have the energy to do that. I'm not tired from using magic like everyone thinks. I am tired of always being afraid. Afraid of what the future may bring. I am afraid that one of these mornings I am going to wake up and find everything changed for the worse. That everything I've done has been for nothing. I am afraid of Dravin and Adam and what they're capable of doing to me.

Olive didn't come upstairs with me. I hope Emma remembers to bring her in. Closing my eyes, I feel the pull again. Crap. I try to open my eyes, to fight back, but it doesn't work. I go under.

"You're not just a beauty, are ya? You've got some brains in that pretty little head of yours." I groan and turn around.

"What do you want, Adam?"

"You were in the woods today. I know it."

"What woods are you talking about?" I fake confusion.

"I could feel your magic. It wasn't as strong as it usually is, but I could still feel it around me. You're close."

Leaning back against the wall, I cross my arms. "That depends on where you are, doesn't it?"

"Don't play games with me, Ryanne. Where are you?"

"Why the *heck* would I tell you that? So Dravin won't be mad at you? So you can get back on his good side? I don't think so, Buster. You'll have to do better than that."

"Oh, believe me, you won't like my better," Adam says while taking a step toward me.

"Does Natasha know you keep bringing me here?"

"Why? Are you jealous of Natasha?"

"Ha. Ha. That's really funny. You're a real jokester."

"Wouldn't Colton be a little jealous of you meeting me here?" Adam walks over to me. His hand brushes against my thigh as he grabs the bottom of Colton's jacket that I happen to still be wearing and glances down at me.

"I'm not meeting you anywhere. You're forcing me to be here."

"Good point. Let's stop this meaningless conversation and get back to the important issue: your location." Adam takes another step closer. I keep my arms crossed. I don't want to end up in the same predicament I was in last time. "You can either tell me or we can do this the hard way."

"What's the hard way? I like a challenge." I smirk at him, "I see you fixed your nose." Taking a final step, he stops directly in front of me. I have to arch my chin up to see him. What's up with all mages being so freaking tall?

"You won't like this one." Instead of waiting for him to do something, I bring my knee up and hit him in the stomach. Turning around, I gain momentum and kick him again in the chest. He staggers backwards. A look of shock crosses his face before he quickly recovers. Gaining his footing, he hisses at me and charges.

I duck away from his punch and swing my left leg out and hit him in the shins. He howls but brings his foot out and kicks me in the stomach. This movement is so forceful that I lose my balance and fall to the ground. I scoot backwards and do a back somersault and jump back, despite the pain. He reaches forward and punches me on the shoulder, knocking me into the wall behind me. I cry out when I collide with the hard cement surface. Moving to the left, I try to catch my breath before I face Adam again. He's hurt as well, so he's not moving as quickly as he usually does.

I regain my footing and glare at him. I'm in pain, but this isn't over yet. I recover and prepare for another attack. Adam runs for me again, so I jump forward and perform a Karate Kid worthy move. Twisting mid-air, I extend my leg and kick him in the chest. He flies backwards, but doesn't stay down nearly long enough. Getting back up, he rushes forward and slams me into the wall. He isn't even trying to do any specific moves; he just wants me to stop fighting. Hitting my head, I fall to the ground as the room spins around me. While stuck on the ground, Adam straddles me and pins my arms above my head again. "I thought you liked a challenge?"

I close my eyes and wait for the room to stop spinning. When I finally open my eyes, I come face to face with him. "You call that a challenge?" With a smile, I bring my knee up and hit him in the crotch. He groans. Twisting so he is beneath me, I say, "Don't underestimate me," I punch him in the jaw with enough strength to knock him out.

"Aaaahhh." Ouch, that hurt my hand. I start shaking my hand trying to make the pain go away. I get off of Adam and look around. I thought knocking him out would wake me up.

I close my eyes and concentrate on going back. I feel a pull similar to transporting with Larkin and then I open my eyes.

It's pitch black.

Yes! I'm back in my room. I look over toward Emma and find her asleep in her bed again. Without waking Olive, who's curled into a small ball at the end of my bed, I push myself up into a seated position trying to ignore the pain radiating from my body. Pushing back the jacket, I look down at my shoulder. A large blackish blue bruise the size of Adam's fist has formed there. I lift the hem of my shirt and see another bruise forming there. My head starts pounding from being pushed into the wall; I definitely need Logan to heal me.

Slowly getting out of bed, I walk out of my room and tip-toe down the hall toward Logan's. Stopping in front of his room, I lean an ear on the smooth surface of his door trying to hear if anyone else is inside. The door flies open, and I stumble into someone's chest. I arch my head up and look at a very surprised Logan. "Ahh, don't scare me like that."

"Can I help you with something?" Logan smiles down at me. I straighten myself up and peek into his room.

Seeing Liam and Colton sitting on his floor again, I say, "Uh, never mind. I'll see you in the morning." I try to turn away, but Logan places a hand on my shoulder to stop me. I try really hard not to cry out, but a small hiss escapes. Logan pulls me into the room and closes the door.

He reaches over and moves the jacket to the side to see the skin underneath the fabric. When he sees the large bruise, he looks back at me. "Adam?" Liam and Colton stand up when they see the black mark on my pale skin.

"No, I fell out of bed. I'm pretty clumsy. Goodnight." I try to leave the room again, but Logan reaches around and blocks my exit.

"Ryanne, come here," Logan says. I turn around briefly and see two very angry guys standing there. I slowly walk toward Logan and let him heal me. When he is done, he cracks a smile.

"See, it's not as bad as it looks! I knocked him out this time."

"Why can't I tell when you go into those dreams with him? I don't even feel your injuries afterwards," Liam asks. I have no idea how he can feel my injuries sometimes and not other times.

"So, you knocked him out?" Colton says. I sit down on the ground similar to what I did the other night. Colton sits down beside me. Logan goes on to explain everything that happened. Liam reaches out and high-fives me when he hears what I did to Adam.

"Those training things are helping a little. It still hurts like none other to punch someone without any magic, but I'm getting used to it."

"You shouldn't have to get used to it," Colton says to me.

"Well, until I find a way to keep Adam from pulling me into those stupid dreams, I'm going to have to get used it." I look up at him, "I can handle myself."

He wraps an arm around me and pulls me closer. "I know that," he tells me. I let him move me. It's getting harder to fight this attraction to him. I lean my head against his chest and close my eyes. I know that we are still in Logan's room. Someone will take me back to my room later. I let his rhythmic breathing lull me to sleep.

C O L T O N

"IS SHE ASLEEP?" LOGAN ASKS. I glance down at Ryanne—she definitely looks asleep. Her breathing is slow and steady, and her hair is falling across her face while her arms are limp against me.

"Yeah, I think so."

"What are we going to do about this Adam situation?"

"I don't know. It just angers me how easily he can get to her. He's always been able to get to her. He's always there to hurt her." I rehash what she told David and me when Adam delivered a pizza to our house at the beginning of the summer. Logan knows the gist of the situation, but doesn't know everything. A girl should never have to go through that, and no one should have to experience it multiple times.

"I'll never understand how someone can do something like that," Logan says. He is watching Ryanne, and I know Liam is too. Liam is upset because the past two nights he hasn't been able to sense that she was hurting.

"I want to know why it started. Because it started before she came into her powers," Liam says from the corner of the room.

"I actually know why it started…" Logan says very quietly. Liam and I both turn our attention to him. He knows, and he hasn't told us? "You're not going to like it."

"Why?"

"Adam told Ryanne that he attacked her to get back at you. He said that you got everything. When he found out that you were interested in her, he set out to prove that you can't always get what you want. He spread those rumors about her, and you believed them. He said that it worked out perfectly…until she came into her magic. Then Ryanne spit in his face." I don't realize that I am squeezing her until I hear her groan and feel her moving. I loosen my grip around her shoulders, and she sighs and snuggles closer to me.

I'm the reason she was attacked by Adam? I'm the reason that her senior year was ruined by those rumors? It was because of me. This all needs to end. Adam needs to be stopped. He can't keep this up for long.

"When did he tell her that?"

"Last night." He told her yesterday? Ryanne knew the reason that Adam attacked her was because of me, and she hung out with me all day? She attacked me this morning with cake and then joked and laughed with me in the forest. She almost kissed me after finding that out. Even now, she's in here, sleeping against my chest. She isn't mad at me because of what happened…why?

"She doesn't blame you, Colton," Liam says.

"How do you know?"

"Because that's just what Adam told her. Adam's not known for being truthful. Honestly, it doesn't matter to her why he did it. She wants to move on and forget about it, but there's always something reminding her. She didn't even know you when it happened, but she does know you now. There's no way she could blame you. Adam acted alone, motive or not. *He* is the only one that hurt her."

"He's right," I tense as Ryanne mumbles into my shirt. She lifts her head from my chest and looks at me through sleep laden eyes, "I don't blame you at all." Yawning, she reaches up and rubs her eyes. She pushes herself into an upright position. When she starts to lean forward, I reach out to steady her. She is so tired. I laugh and pull her back against me. "Adam's a jerk, Colton." With one last yawn, she closes her eyes and falls back asleep.

Logan and Liam start cracking up. They try to remain quiet enough to not wake her up again. "You should listen to her," Logan says, "because if you don't, she'll soak you, throw cake batter at you, or kick you in the crotch again."

Liam starts laughing all over again. "Oh man, that was hilarious."

Hilarious isn't a word I would use to describe it. Granted, I did get a laugh once I thought about it, but it wasn't *that* funny. "Yeah, you wouldn't say that if it happened to you."

"I remain on her good side for a reason," Liam throws his hands up in surrender.

"Good choice," I mumble to him.

"WHAT'S A GIRL GOT TO do to get in on this party?" Emma asks. I open my eyes and look toward the doorway.

"Get attacked in your sleep by someone," Logan mumbles from the floor. He is lying on his stomach, his face literally in the carpet. I bring my right arm up and rub my eyes, trying to rub my sleepiness away. Based on the amount of sunlight streaming in from the windows, it is mid-morning. When I look up, I realize that I am in a different position than I remember falling asleep in last night. I'm lying on my back, looking up at the ceiling. I don't know how I got here. I lift my head up and find Ryanne curled up in a ball, lying with her head on my stomach, still asleep. I look across the room and see Liam, asleep against the wall.

"Adam got to her again?" The sadness and anger in Emma's expression is palpable.

"Yeah, she defended herself well this time. She knocked him out and was able to pull herself out of it when he was unconscious."

"Wait, are Adam and Dravin only able to get to her when she's alone?" Emma asks and looks between us.

"I don't know…" Liam says. I didn't know he was awake.

"Have either of them contacted her when she's with you guys?"

"No…I don't think so," I say.

Ryanne stretches her legs out and rolls over so she is lying on her back. "Why is my pillow moving?" she mumbles and glares at me.

"Sorry," I say, while trying to hide my smile. She reaches up to push her hair off her face, but the sleeve of my jacket hits her face first. She screams and then starts laughing.

Rolling off my stomach, she lays on her side as she tries to calm her laughter. I can't help but join in on the laughter. "The sleeve scared me. I thought a spider fell on my face or something. Why are your arms so long anyway?" She pushes the sleeves up and sits up, still laughing. "I don't think my brain works properly when I'm tired."

She pulls her knees up and leans her head against them. I sit up and look over at Logan and Emma. They are still laughing. I see a small cloud forming over them, and little droplets of water start to fall. It shuts Emma up pretty quickly. Ryanne giggles but remains sitting with her head on her knees.

"What happened to the sweet little morning girl?" Emma asks. Ryanne doesn't reply to her. She's gotten pretty quiet. Emma crawls over to her and pokes her in the side. She gasps and jumps backwards into me.

"Goodness gracious. You almost gave me a heart attack." She scoots forward a little and shakes her head at everyone. "You're all impossible. I'm going to go take a shower." She gets up and jumps over Logan, who is sitting in the doorway, and leaves the room.

Emma turns to me, "I don't think you'll get your jacket back any time soon."

"That's fine. It looks better on her anyway."

CHAPTER
THIRTY - THREE

AFTER GETTING DRESSED IN MY Team Edward…Scissorhands t-shirt and a pair of black shorts, I mosey on downstairs. For some reason, I'm still incredibly tired. Fighting off Adam and Dravin at night is starting to take a toll on me. I feed Olive and sit down at the table with everyone else.

I scoot my chair really close to Liam and rest my head on his shoulder. "You ok?"

"Peachy," I say with a yawn.

"You know there's a thing called sleep…maybe you should try to get some," Larkin suggests.

"Wow, I never thought of that. Thank you, Captain Obvious," I say with my eyes closed. If I don't move, I'll probably fall asleep right here.

"You're welcome. It's what I'm here for." I glance over at Larkin. He's giving me his arrogant smile. I've noticed that Larkin has about three different smiles. One, his *I'm awesome and I know it* smile. The second one being the *you're crazy, and I don't know you* smile. The last one being a genuine smile that was reserved for a select few people. He doesn't use that last smile often. He has an image to uphold after all.

"You know what?" I tell him.

"What?" He flashes the you're crazy smile.

"You—" I start but stop when my head starts pounding. I gasp and grab my head as the pain intensifies.

"Ryanne, what's wrong?" Colton asks standing up.

"Not again. Not again," I start crying and fall out of my chair. I scream as the pain intensifies even more. I can't focus on anything. I can't hear anyone talking to me, though I know that they are freaking out. The image of my mother's death starts flashing through my mind again.

This time, when the images go away, it doesn't stop. New images start to form. Dravin is standing over me while Gadramicks hold onto Colton, Liam, Emma, and David. We are standing in the backyard. He smiles down at me and says, "You could have stopped this." Men walk up to all of them and simultaneously slit their throats. They all fall to the ground, blood gurgling out of their mouths as they slowly die. I scream and try to run over to them, but Dravin grabs me and makes me watch.

Deep red blood slides down their throats and pools into the fabric of their shirts. Emma is the first one to stop moving. Tears are streaming down my face as I watch my family die in the yard. The men holding Liam, Colton, and David let go of their bodies so all three of them drop to the ground. Colton's eyes remain open as he stares in my direction and takes his last breath. The last thing I see are his green eyes piercing mine as blood continues to flow onto the grass beneath him.

The images dissipate into darkness, and the pain starts to fade. I whimper as someone tries to help me up. I push away from them and scoot myself into the corner. I curl my knees up and put my head on them. I start sobbing. Dravin knows where I am and wants to show me what he will do if I don't bring myself to him. I've received the message loud and clear. Someone reaches out and tries to comfort me. I flinch away from their touch. I need to get away. I jump up and try to run out of the room, when someone grabs me and pulls me into their embrace. I tense until I get a whiff of the familiar cologne. Leaning into his chest, I let out the rest of my tears. This can't be happening. I can't let that happen. I push away from Colton and look for Larkin.

"*Please.*"

Without elaborating, he knows what I'm asking. He shakes his head, refusing my plea. I bite my lip to try and stop the tears that threaten to fall again. "Dravin?" Colton asks me.

"He doesn't know where we are exactly, but he knows I'm close. He…he…" I hiccup. I can't think about that. I need to do something. I need…I don't even know. Everyone is still watching me. My eyes land on Liam. His breathing is labored. I slowly walk over to him and hug him.

"I'm sorry you had to experience that," I tell him. He wraps his arms around me and rests his chin on my head. "Did you see the images too?" I quietly ask him.

"No, I just felt the pain. Though, I'm sure it wasn't as bad as what you felt."

"Ryanne, what images did you see?" Larkin asks me. I tense and turn toward him, shaking my head. I can't tell anyone.

"Just the car crash," I lie.

"There's more to it than that," Larkin says and takes a step toward me.

"How would you know?"

"Your aura. It darkens when you lie." It's like I have a light up sign above me alerting him to my every move.

"Ryanne," he repeats my name again.

"It was just a warning. I'll figure everything out," I try to walk out of the room, but Larkin grabs my upper arm and pulls me back.

"You're not going to give yourself to Dravin. No matter what, you can't do that." He is scared that I'm going do something stupid. I yank my arm out of his grip and walk out of the room. I can't promise that I won't do that. I don't know what I am going to do at this moment; I just know I have to do something. I'm not giving up until I can at least say that I tried.

COLTON

I AM TRYING REALLY HARD to not let myself go invisible. Negative thoughts keep swarming through my mind. I keep seeing her crying on the floor, holding her head. Think positive. "If I ever see that freaking as—"

That's positive.

"Colton, we're all angry about what happened," Liam says. "That pain was excruciating, and I didn't even feel it to the same degree as she did. I just want to know what she saw…" He loudly exhales and looks at me, shaking his head. I can see the anger clearly in his eyes.

"You know it had something to do with us," David says. "She'd only try to go to Dravin if we were threatened."

"It's getting worse. Dravin's getting more persistent. I mean she can't even go to sleep without being attacked," Logan says. "Her body's not going to be able to handle much more of this." On cue, we all look toward the stairs as we see Ryanne stumble down them. On the last stair, she has to grab onto the banister to keep from falling.

"Liam…I'm," her body shudders, "losing control." We all stop. I can feel her magic floating in the air around me. It feels like tiny little shocks are hitting my skin—the feeling you get when a part of your body falls asleep and then you move, waking it up. She collapses to the ground. Liam runs over to her and tries calming her.

"Ryanne, look at me." She shakes her head and starts whimpering. "Ryanne, you need to calm yourself down. Take a deep breath. Concentrate."

"I can't." Her body starts visibly shaking. She cries out. Liam looks back at us. The magic shocks are becoming stronger, so he doesn't have any other choice. He places both of his hands on her back and closes his eyes; his face furrowing in concentration. A couple seconds later, Ryanne stops. Liam lets out the breath he was holding and removes his hands from her back. The magic in the air fades away, leaving in its absence a tension-filled room.

He bends down and picks up Ryanne's limp body and carries her over to the couch. "We need to keep an eye on her."

"Can Adam get to her while she's unconscious?" Emma asks.

"I don't know," Liam says quietly. We don't know anything. This is so frustrating. How are we supposed to help her if we are just as clueless? Tom comes downstairs and looks at Ryanne on the couch. He curses and turns to me, "Adam again?"

I shake my head, "No, Adam attacked her last night. Dravin's the one that attacked her this morning."

"She lost control of her magic again. Liam had to knock her out," Emma says. "It was worse than last time. I could literally feel the magic around me. It felt like I was being shocked…"

"Dravin doesn't know where we are, does he?" Tom asks. "I was pretty sure the enchantment worked."

"Not yet, but he obviously knows that we're close."

"He's not going to stop," Tom says.

"Not until he gets what he wants," I whisper, "or is stopped." I look over toward Ryanne on the couch. I've seen her unconscious or hurt too many times recently. He has to be stopped, and I want to be the one that ends him.

It's been over an hour, and Ryanne still hasn't woken up. However, we know that she's not unconscious anymore. She's been moving and making little noises letting us know that she's asleep—which I'm thankful for. I just hope that Adam doesn't try to pull her into another dream.

I sit down on the couch and wait for her to wake up. Right now, this whole situation is a waiting game: waiting for Ryanne to wake up, waiting for Dravin to find us, waiting. Waiting. Waiting. It frustrates me to no end to think that Dravin's out there looking for her, and there's nothing that I can do.

Liam and Larkin are pacing in the back. Emma keeps glancing out the windows at the woods behind the house. Tom is sitting at the kitchen table, tapping his fingers along the hard surface. David is sitting in the armchair staring off into space. Bragden is flipping through Ryanne's sketchbook, and Logan is sitting in the other chair, keeping an eye on her. We're a very worried bunch.

"Do you think it's possible that there's a limited number to the amount of headaches you can magically get before you acquire permanent brain damage?" Ryanne mumbles. She rolls over onto her back but has yet to open her eyes. "Because I think I'm pushing that number." When she sits up and looks around, everyone stops what they are doing.

"Oh, stop looking at me like that. It's not the first time I've lost control before, and it probably won't be the last," she says while rubbing her eyes.

"Ry, did anyone attack you while you were sleeping?" I ask.

"No." I watch as she walks into the kitchen and opens the fridge. Coming back into the living room with a bottle of water, she continues,

"Though I kind of wish someone did. I really want to hit something right now." She looks over at me and smiles.

"Last time I checked, I wasn't a punching bag," I tell her.

"We could always change that," she says but sits back against the couch. That's it? She's not going to explain anything? She's just going to pretend like nothing happened? She reaches forward and grabs the sketchbook I bought her from the coffee table. She asks for the pencil that is tucked inside the spiral of the notebook from Bragden. He hands it to her without looking away from the drawing. Pulling her knees up, she leans against the back of the couch and rests the sketchbook on her legs. Opening to the first page, she begins drawing.

"Just so I'm clear...contacting Dravin is a big fat NO right now, correct?" Everyone yells a yes at her. "Esh, inside voices, por favor." She mumbles and continues to draw.

"What are you drawing?" I ask her and lean over a little, trying to see her drawing.

"The bench in the forest," she looks over at me and blushes slightly. Thirty minutes later, she sighs and holds the book out in front of her, looking at the drawing from further away. She captured its likeness perfectly. She drew the path in front of it, the small flowers that grew against its legs, and the trees surrounding it.

I open my mouth to compliment her on it when she drops the sketchbook to the ground. Groaning, she grabs her stomach and doubles over. I recognize what is going on. I jump up to grab her, but she has already disappeared.

"Larkin!" I shout. He runs over to me, already understanding what he needs to do.

Liam joins me, "I'm going with you."

Larkin glances down at the sketchbook for a second and grabs both of our shoulders. He closes his eyes in concentration. It's harder to transport more than one person, but I know that he'll be able to do it. A second later, we are standing in the forest surrounded.

Dravin and Adam are sitting on the bench. "Well this is better than expected," Dravin says, smiling at us. Ryanne is lying on the ground at their feet, a dart sticking out of her arm. Dormirako.

"Move!" I yell. Liam and I jump to the side, while Larkin flies to the other one. Two men come toward Liam and me. We jump up and prepare for their attack. One comes toward Larkin. A dart comes out of nowhere and hits Liam in the shoulder. He falls to the ground.

I turn toward Larkin, "Go back. Warn the others." I feel something prick me in the arm. "GO!" I say as I fall, succumbing to the darkness.

CHAPTER
THIRTY-FOUR

I AM SORE ALL OVER. From head to toe, I feel like a giant bruise—like someone deliberately used my body as a shield against a physical attack. I open my eyes and look around the room. Shoot. Before even assessing my surroundings, I know what's happened. I've been captured again. I wanted to do something, but this definitely is not it. Right now, I'm sprawled on a hard cold floor; my body lying at a hard angle. Looking around, I find that I am in a cell similar to the first one. I push myself into a seated position and continue to survey the room. It's completely empty. There's a door in the corner, but there aren't any windows on this one. There looks to be a mirror on one side of the room. That's useless. It's not like I have any reason to make myself look good in here.

I close my eyes and open my mind, trying to hear any thoughts. Like last time, there is nothing. I get static when I try to read anyone's mind. Of course, I don't know if there is anyone near me to even read. I can feel my magic inside me, but it won't come to the surface. Is this what everyone else feels like? I can sense the magic in me, but it's stuck.

With a frustrated groan, I start pacing the room. I wonder if everyone else is ok. I hope no one went into the forest to look for me. I don't know how Dravin knew that I was going to be there...I didn't even know that that was going to happen if I drew that, and *I'm* the psychic one.

I run a hand through my long hair. I never have a hair tie on me when I need one. Hey, they let me keep my shoes this time. I am still wearing my dirty black converse tennis shoes. I wonder how long I've been here. I continue pacing the perimeter of the room, waiting for something to happen. Sooner or later, Dravin or Adam will come in. It is inevitable.

I continue pacing the room for what feels like hours though I know it hasn't really been that long. Hearing the sound of a door opening, I glance across the cell at the doorway. I try to keep a neutral expression as I watch Dravin saunter into the room. Another man comes in behind him and guards the door. Dravin walks into the center of the room.

"Nice to see you awake," he says.

"Well, it's not nice to see you," I lean back against the far wall. Crossing my arms, I wait for his reaction. I'm not going to be afraid of him. I'm trying a different approach here.

"Ha, just as feisty as ever. Is there any situation you're in where you're polite?"

"Not when you're involved."

"You should probably try and get on my good side. It's not very pleasant on the other."

"Do you even have a good side? I find that very hard to believe."

"Believe it or not, I can be very good," he takes a step closer and grins down at me. He reaches out and grabs the end of my hair and runs his hand through it. I reach over and slap his hand away. He laughs and leans forward and whispers into my ear. "You know, *we* could be very good together." With a disgusted grunt, I push him away from me and walk so I am leaning with my back against the mirror. I want to get away from him, but of course, he starts to walk over here.

"Sooner or later, you'll realize I only want what's best for you."

"And keeping me locked up in this cell is what is best for me?" Is this guy serious? I really want to reach out and punch him in the gut, but I need to keep up this charade for a little longer.

"Of course not. This cell is a precaution."

"A precaution? Against a small helpless little girl?" I purse my lips and bat my eyelashes at him. I try to make myself look as innocent and damsel-in-distress like as I can muster.

Dravin starts laughing, "Small, yes. Helpless, no. I can see through this façade you're putting on. You may not be able to use your magic here, but a helpless little girl wouldn't have been able to beat Adam in his own dream."

"I don't know what you're talking about."

"Sure you don't." Dravin takes another step forward until he is standing right in front of me again. "If this magic thing doesn't work out for you, you should go into acting. If I didn't know any better, I might actually believe you. You're good." He smiles at me.

"You know what you are?" I ask him. He smirks at me. "You're a pain in the a—"

"Ah, ah, ah. I wouldn't finish that sentence. See right now, I'm enjoying this little banter between us. You don't want to make me mad."

"I don't? Well then I hope this doesn't offend you." I spit in his face and then smile sweetly at him. I know that he will probably retaliate and hit me, but I don't really care at the moment. He is annoying me with this 'friendly' chat. Like I predicted, he swings his large hand out and slaps me across the face. It's sad, but it doesn't hurt as bad as they usually do. My head swings to the side, but my eyes don't start watering. I guess I'm getting used to getting hit.

"I like you, Ryanne. You have guts for such a small thing. It's a shame I'm going to have to kill you," he says before turning around and leaving the room.

COLTON

"WHAT THE HECK IS SHE trying to do?" I turn around and ask Liam. Looking through the window in our cell, I can see Ryanne pacing again. Dravin had just left after he slapped her across the face. She barely flinched. From where I'm standing, I can see the giant red welt on her face.

"She's trying to show him that she's not afraid of him anymore. It seems to be working. Dravin doesn't know what to do when someone doesn't cower at his presence."

"Does she have to provoke him like that though?"

"Would you rather she sit in the corner trembling in fear?"

"Well no..." I glance back at the window. She is still pacing around her cell. Based on the fact that she hasn't looked our way, I'm assuming that this window is actually a two-way mirror. I turn around and look at Liam again, "Why did they put us together, but put her by herself?"

"I don't know, but I do know that something changed. In the vision she had you were by yourself. I wasn't with you." I forgot about her vision. The vision of my death. I look back at Ryanne and see her mumbling something to herself. I don't think she knows that she does this. She talks to herself. A lot. I lean closer to the window to see if I can hear what she is saying.

"Why Ryanne? Why couldn't you just draw a picture of a bunny? Hmm, no you have to draw the freaking forest! Stupid. Stupid." She hits herself on the head and kicks the wall. Then jumping up and down, she mumbles, "Another stupid decision. Ouch," she stops pacing and leans against the wall to the left of the window.

It is obvious that she can't hear us, but we can hear her. Dravin has a plan, but what is it? Ryanne slides down the wall and sits on the ground. She leans her head back and looks up at the ceiling.

"Do you think Larkin got back to everyone?"

"I sure hope so," Liam says. He looks toward the window at Ryanne. "He's our only hope right now."

A COUPLE HOURS LATER, RYANNE'S cell door opens again. She looks toward it as three people walk in. Adam quickly walks toward her. "Adam, don't touch her," Dravin demands. He stops right in front of her. Ryanne stands up slowly and smiles sweetly at him.

"Hey, Adam. How are you on this lovely afternoon?" she leans around Adam and asks Dravin, "Is it afternoon? It's hard to tell in here."

Adam growls at her. He reaches out and slaps her across the face. The same spot that Dravin hit earlier. Her head swings to the side. I hit the window though I know it won't do anything. They can't hear us. I am so tired of Adam. Liam jumps up when she gets hit. Ryanne takes a deep breath and slowly turns back toward Adam, a red handprint appearing on her face. With a small smile, she takes a step toward him, "Didn't your mother ever tell you not to hit a girl?" Dravin laughs and grabs the back of Adam's shirt and pulls him away from her.

Dravin pushes Adam to the back of the room. Adam leans against the opposite wall and glares at Ryanne. Dravin walks to the center of the room and sits down. "Have a seat. Make yourself comfortable," Ryanne says to him.

I look toward Liam and shake my head. She's going to get herself in more trouble talking to him like that. The corner of Dravin's mouth turns up, but he doesn't smile.

"Now, Ryanne, I'm sure you know why we are here."

"To keep me company? How sweet of you. However, I prefer the solitude. So, you can go. I'll be fine," she walks backwards and leans against the wall again.

"As much as I would enjoy keeping you company, I'm here for other reasons."

"To clean this cell? I've noticed that it *is* a little dirty." She looks around the cell and grimaces before turning her attention back to Dravin.

"What is she doing?" I whisper to Liam. I don't know why, but I feel like someone is listening in on our conversation.

"Stalling."

"Ryanne, dear," Dravin starts.

"Don't call me that, I'm not your *dear*. In fact, I'm no one's dear."

"Oh, I don't believe that," he leans back putting his arms behind him and crosses his legs. "I think you're falling for that boy. You'll be happy to know we haven't tortured him yet." I see a momentary flash of panic cross her face before she recovers. I briefly glance toward Liam. I know they are talking about me.

With an unreadable expression she says, "I don't know who you're referring to."

"Colton," Adam hisses.

She starts laughing. Liam and I can tell that it is forced since we've heard her real laugh numerous times. "You think I'm falling for Colton? That's funny, Adam." With a smile, she returns her attention to Dravin, "You should look for a new side kick. Yours is a little messed up in the head," she taps her temple.

Dravin throws his head back and lets out a laugh. Adam growls again. Ryanne keeps glancing between the two. I can tell that she is scared, but she's doing a pretty good job hiding it.

Dravin stops laughing and looks back at Ryanne. "Just a shame. You sure you don't want to join me?"

"Positive. I'd rather eat a bag of hair," she replies. A bag of hair? Where does she come up with this stuff? Dravin stands up and brushes off his clothes.

Turning his attention to Ryanne, he says, "Alrighty then. Time to get down to business. Now Ryanne, we've been in this situation before. I'll ask you a question. You'll refuse to give any information. I'll try to beat it out of you. You'll still refuse to give any information. I understand that. You're stubborn; I get it," he walks over to her.

"I remember it a little differently. But I don't disagree with you on the stubbornness. I think it's one of my better personality traits."

"However, since torture is one of my favorite past-times, I'm not going to skip that part."

"Hit me with your best shot," she sings. Dravin smiles at her. Then, getting serious, he moves back again. His face furrows in concentration. I watch as Ryanne clenches her jaw. Suddenly, she falls to the ground, landing on her knees. Grabbing her head, she leans forward and lets out a small cry of pain. When she rests her forehead against the cement ground, Dravin crouches down beside her. She screams in agony. I hit the window. I don't want to watch this. I don't want to hear her cry out like that. I don't want her to go through that again, but there's absolutely nothing I can do.

Liam grimaces and collapses to the ground. Dravin stands up and steps back a little as Ryanne continues writhing on the ground. She stops screaming, but doesn't get up. I know when Dravin stops his assault on her mind, because Liam is able to stand back up.

"Now that I have your attention, I want to inform you that we found a way to extract magic from someone. So, once we find out the extent of your magic, we can take it from you. We'll even let your little friends live. What'll it be?"

She looks up at him. I can tell that she's still in pain, but she tries to act otherwise. "You're deranged if you think that I'll give you any information after that."

"I thought you'd say something like that," he says while standing back. He nods to the man standing near the door. At his signal, he takes a step forward and moves toward Ryanne. She backs up slightly as he walks toward her. This man is huge. His size makes her look like a child. He picks her up by the arms and throws her down on the ground, hard. Her body falls like a rag doll. Liam hisses. I slam into the window again.

"Stop watching, Colton," Liam whispers. Ryanne pushes herself up onto her knees and starts giggling. Lifting her head, she runs her right hand through her disarrayed curls and smiles at Dravin again.

"Just like old times, huh?" She takes a deep breath and continues, "That's the way to a girl's heart. My mom always told me that some guy would come along and sweep me off my feet," she sits up and looks at Dravin. "I guess she was right," she dusts of her arms. "Though, I always thought someone would try to catch me. I guess chivalry really is dead," she smiles over at him, though it looks more like a grimace.

I can't watch this anymore. I need to do something. I need…I push away from the window and walk over to the wall and punch it. I hear a pop and pain shoots through my arm.

"That wasn't smart, man. You probably just broke your hand." I flex my fingers and wince at the pain.

"It's nothing compared to what they're doing to her in there." I don't think it's broken. I'm just going to have a nice bruise. Taking a few laps around the circumference of the room, I try to ignore the sounds coming from the next room. I walk back to the window.

Ryanne's alone again. She slowly stands up, grimacing with the movement. Though in pain, it doesn't look like anything is broken. She has some nasty bruises forming on her arms and legs though. Her face is slightly swollen from getting hit. She leans back against the wall—a single tear sliding down her cheek. She shakes her head and wipes it off. Standing tall, she crosses her arms and glares at the door.

Waiting.

CHAPTER
THIRTY-FIVE

I CAN'T SHOW ANY WEAKNESS. I have to show them that they can't break me as easily this time. I haven't even defended myself yet, and they see that I'm not going to take everything as easily as I did last time. There is more at stake now.

Dravin mentioned earlier that they haven't tortured someone yet. Was he referring to Colton? Is Colton here? If he is that means that the vision can still happen. All I know is that I can't let that play out. I look over to the mirror. I wonder if it's actually a two-way mirror. In the crime TV shows, the mirrors are actually windows. Is someone watching me? If so, who is it?

Dravin has perfected the extraction process…or could he be lying? I'm not sure that I want to find out either way. I know that he'll keep coming back if I don't talk soon. I wonder what Liam, David, Larkin, Emma, Bragden and…Colton…are doing right now? What's Tom doing? I need to get out of this cell, but how?

I slowly start to pace the room again. I need to push through the pain. Next time, Dravin or Adam come into the room, I'll do more than just fight with my words. I walk to the side of the room with the window and turn my back to it. My eyes are drawn up to the cement ceiling above me. It looks high enough. I take a couple steps forward and do an aerial cartwheel. I feel a little better when I land it. *Keep pushing through the pain, Ryanne.* I repeat to myself when I feel the aches in my arms and legs from the sudden movements. I can't just stand around anymore. I need to move.

If I am able to get them to knock me out, will I be able to contact Liam? Will he come to me in my sleep? I am afraid to fall asleep here. I don't even know if it will work. What if he was captured as well…would he still be able to go into dreams? So many questions.

Absolutely no answers.

I jump in place a couple of times and pace the room again. Slowly, I start singing "Rescue Me" by Daughtry. When I get to the chorus, I sing louder. I don't care who hears me. I even dance a little.

"Having fun?" I stop and turn toward the door. Adam is leaning against it. Alone.

"Tons. Thanks for asking." I continue singing. He shakes his head and closes the door, locking the two of us in.

"Ryanne, this could all go by so much easier if you just told us what your powers are."

"I have powers? Since when?"

"Do you have a death wish?" Adam walks closer to me.

"Surprisingly, you're not the first person to ask me that. I wouldn't necessarily call it a death wish. I don't really fear death. It's living that scares me."

"That makes no sense." I lean against the wall again and cross my arms. I don't know why I feel the need to explain myself to him. I know that Adam doesn't care, but I feel like saying it out loud makes more sense.

"In life, everything you do affects someone else. Every action has a consequence. It takes a lot to actually live. To feel like you're doing something worth-while. You can choose to make a difference or stand in the background and let life happen around you. I used to be the girl in the background. I was comfortable with that. I didn't like attention. I just wanted to blend in and go on with life unseen. Now, I have a chance to be important—to do something important, and if I die doing that, at least someone can say I tried. At least I can say that I actually lived a little."

I can tell that he is thinking about what I just said. He looks over at me again with an unusual look in his eyes before turning around and abruptly leaving the room.

"What the heck was that about?"

COLTON

"WHY IS SHE TALKING TO him?" I ask Liam.

"What I'm more shocked about is the fact that he hasn't attacked her yet. I mean I don't want him to, but it's shocking that he's just talking to her."

I watch as Ryanne tells Adam why she isn't afraid of death. I never thought about it before, but it makes sense. I'm afraid of dying without doing something worth-while. I don't want my life to be pointless. I watch Adam as she speaks. He is looking at her like he is actually listening. He doesn't have that arrogant expression on his face. He's always been arrogant and didn't care who knew it. In high school, he'd walk around like he was better than everyone else and acted like he owned the place.

Ryanne's not looking at him as she speaks. She's looking in my direction, but I know she can't see me. When she stops speaking, she turns back toward Adam. He is still staring at her. He blinks a couple of times and then just turns and leaves the room. What? That is so out of character for him—even for this newly Team Dravin Adam.

Ryanne is just as surprised. "What the heck was that about?" She shakes her head and paces the room again. When she nears a corner, she turns around and does an aerial cartwheel to the other side of the room.

"Why does she keep doing that?"

"I think she's trying to keep herself busy. I don't think she wants to think about what's going on. She's distracting herself. Also, I think she's trying to prove that she's not going to just let them hurt her. She's showing that she's not weak."

She stops pacing and slides down the wall, leaning her head back, she starts singing "Stronger" by Kelly Clarkson. Fitting. I love her singing voice. I wish I was on the other side of this wall, comforting her. She probably thinks that she is alone in this compound.

"Why do you think no one's come in here? Why are they leaving us alone?"

"I honestly don't know."

I glance back at the window. She is still singing, but her eyes are closed.

"Liam, do you think you'd be able to contact her if she fell asleep?"

"I could try, but I really doubt it. Something in these cells blocks magic."

A small yellow piece of paper flies under the door to Ryanne's cell. She lifts her head and looks at the paper. Moving onto her hands and knees, she crawls over to the small piece of paper. Sitting in the middle of the cell, she reads it. Without reacting to it, she folds the paper up and puts it in her back pocket. What did that piece of paper say? It must be something good. A few seconds later, with a small smile, she crawls back to where she was seated before and sings another song.

It is about wanting somebody to love her. It is much slower than the previous ones. I can imagine her sitting at a piano and singing it. I hope she gets the chance to do that again. She sounds so sad while singing. If only she knew how much I actually do love her. It hurts to think that this could be one of the last times I see her. I still haven't told her everything. I haven't told her how I feel about her yet. I don't know how we'll get out of this situation if we can even get out of this situation.

"She has a beautiful singing voice, doesn't she?" Both Liam and I spin around and face Adam, who is standing in the doorway. I run for him and bounce off an invisible barrier. "Do you really think I'd come in here without protection? Granted, it took a pretty powerful mage to create this little shield, but I'm not stupid, Colton." I pick myself off the floor and back up next to Liam.

"What do you want?"

"Just thought I'd give you two a chance to tell us what her powers are. Dravin's going to go back into her cell and torture the information out of her in a few moments if he doesn't get anything useful here." Neither Liam nor I say anything. We don't want Ryanne to get hurt any more, but we know that she will die if they find out what her powers are. I'd rather see her hurt and alive than dead. It got pretty quiet on the other side of the window; Ryanne stopped singing.

"Fine." Adam leans out of the door, "They're not speaking." He leans back in, "Have fun watching." With one last smile, he slams the door shut and relocks it. With a groan, I turn and watch as Dravin enters Ryanne's cell again.

"Back so soon?" she asks.

"Not soon enough. I'm running out of patience, Ryanne. Do I need to bring your friends in here to persuade you to give me some information?"

"What friends?" She stands up when he mentions us.

"Pretty boy and goth guy over there," Dravin says and motions to the window separating our cells. Ryanne looks over at it. A scared look crosses her face. She bites her lip and turns back to Dravin.

"I'm not quite sure who you're talking about." He sighs and nods to the guy standing near the door. Dravin bends down and punches Ryanne in the stomach. She doubles over, and one of his men walks behind her and grabs her around the waist, trapping her.

I hear the door behind us open, and four men come in. Two walk toward me and two toward Liam. I look at Liam. It's time. We get into our attack stance and wait for them to come to us.

DRAVIN WALKS UP TO ME while I'm being held and slaps me across the face again. "Tell me!"

I lean back against the man and swing both of my legs out and connect them with Dravin's stomach. Pushing outward, I smile as he stumbles backwards. I watch as his face transforms from one of blatant boredom to one of complete anger. The grip on my stomach tightens. I can't breathe. I whip my head back and connect with his. I hear a crunch and then the arms around my waist are removed. I spin around and kick the man in the head, knocking him back into the wall behind me. His head bounces off the wall, and he falls to the ground at my feet unconscious. I turn around and face Dravin, who is watching me with a stunned expression.

Another one of his men comes toward me. I do a quick front walkover and meet him halfway. Dropping down, I swing my right leg out, hitting him in the shins. When he loses his balance, I launch myself at him. Not expecting me, he doesn't have time to defend himself. I jump up, thrust my right leg out, and hit him in the chest. He falls back into the wall too but doesn't hit his head. As he is falling to the ground, I swing around and elbow him in the jaw, thus knocking him unconscious. I whip around at the sound of my cell door opening again. Two large men enter pulling a very angry Colton, followed by two more with Liam. Why is Liam here? Adam starts walking toward me, and I am about to run toward him when Dravin shakes his head.

I fall and scream as Dravin uses his power at full-force on me. Instead of the pain gradually increasing, I feel all of it at once. I don't have time to build-up to it before my head instantly starts pounding. I feel a pair of strong arms wrap around my stomach and pull me up, but I can't concentrate on that. The pain is excruciating—worse than any of the other times. I scream out again as the pain increases further. It is agonizing. I know that if it doesn't stop soon, I will pass out from the pain.

As quickly as it came, the onslaught suddenly stops. I fall back against whoever is holding me. I am panting, completely out of breath. I glare up at Dravin. "That was pretty impressive. You knocked out two of my largest men." I look past Dravin. Liam and Colton are both struggling against the men. I shake my head at them, trying to tell them that I am fine.

With arrogance in his every step, Dravin moves toward me again. "I'm amazed that you're still alive. That amount of power would have killed a lesser individual."

"I'm too stubborn for death," I manage to get out. I am still trying to catch my breath. My gaze flickers over to Colton and Liam again. Both of them look like they put up a fight. Colton has a black eye and blood dripping down his nose. Liam has a giant red welt across his cheek and a split lip. I know that I don't look much better.

"Adam, let her go," Dravin says.

"You sure that's a good idea?"

"I'm sure she'll listen from now on," Dravin says. Ha, like that'll happen. I feel Adam's grip on me loosen. I elbow him in the gut, and when he bends over, I spin around in his arms and kick my leg up. Thankfully I am flexible. My kick connects with the side of his head, causing him to fall to the side.

The pain starts again. I fall to the ground and cry out as another headache comes on. I am glad that neither of these were accompanied by any images. I clench my hands into fists and rest my head on the ground, waiting for the pain to stop. I can hear Colton and Liam yelling in the background. As the pain subsides, I gasp for breath, enjoying the feel of oxygen rushing into my lungs. It is so hard to breathe when you're concentrating on ending the pain. Adam is standing up when I am finally able to get off the ground. He charges for me and slaps me so hard in the face that I fall back to the ground. Dravin yells at him, but doesn't do anything to reprimand him. I catch myself with my arms, so I don't face plant on the hard concrete flooring. Taking a couple deep breaths, I blink the tears away.

With my hand gripping the stinging side of my face, I push myself off the ground and face a very angry Dravin. "You just have to push your luck all the time, don't you?"

"I don't believe in luck," I hiss at him. I can't see out of my left eye because of the swelling. I take a step toward him, "You know what I do believe in? I believe in good. I believe in kindness. I believe that you are a freaking, crazy, psychotic lunatic, who is obsessed with power. I believe that you need to be stopped and I believe in fighting," I pause for dramatic effect, "for what I believe in."

I take my hand off my face. The guys gasp at my appearance. I don't care anymore. I know I probably won't get out of this situation alive anyway. I take another step toward Dravin. I see Adam move out of the corner of my eye. "I will not hesitate to kick you again if you touch me!" I yell at him. He backs up in surprise.

"I've been bullied basically all my life," I look toward Adam. "It wasn't just my senior year. You were not the first person to see a weak girl. I've always had someone trying to tear me down. For some reason, everyone saw me as an easy target. I believed every single word those kids chanted at me.

"However, for the first time, I'm finally standing up to a bully. I have enough courage to defend myself. I've tolerated enough of your crap, Dravin. I've gone through more than anyone should ever go through, and I'm still standing. I'm still not cowering in fear. I'm not afraid of you. Beat me up. Use your stupid mind headachy power on me. Kill me. I don't even care anymore. At least I can say that I tried. Maybe you can't be stopped, but I'm not going to give you any information that will help you further your crazy plan." I swing my arms out to my side. "You're just afraid to fight fairly. That's why you're keeping us here as prisoners without our magic. You're afraid that someone might actually be stronger than you. And you're even more afraid that it could be a girl half your size!" I take a step closer to him.

He grins down at me. "That was a nice little speech. You know, I think you're more attractive when you're mad. Even with the swollen face," he reaches out and grabs my waist and pulls me against him. When I collide into his chest, I start struggling. I'm getting tired of always being put in this position. I see Colton start to fight the men that are holding him. I shake my head at him, and he stops struggling as aggressively but doesn't stop completely.

"Two can play that game," I bring my knee up and kick him in the crotch, the same move that I've done to both Colton and Adam. Dravin lets go of me and doubles over in pain. Even without magic, you can still hurt a guy. "Control her," Dravin groans.

I feel Adam wrap his arms around my waist again. This time, he makes sure to keep my arms at my side, completely containing me. I struggle at first, but realize how futile it is. Dravin stands up, but instead of facing me, he turns around and looks at Liam and Colton.

"Fine, if that's how it's going to be."

No, I recognize this. I start struggling against Adam again.

I scream at Dravin, "I'll tell you!" He shakes his head. Colton hisses and slumps forward. The men holding him let him fall to the ground. Colton grabs his head and starts yelling. Adam's grip on my waist tightens, but I fight harder. Colton is writhing in pain on the ground. I know what Dravin is making him see.

"I'll tell you! Please stop! Stop hurting him," I can't yell anymore. Adam's grip is too constricting. I start crying. I can't see Dravin through my tears. Adam squeezes tighter. I gasp against the pressure and start sobbing. Dravin stands up and walks toward Colton with a dagger. Liam is fighting against the men, but the ones that were holding Colton are now restraining him.

Dravin bends down and plunges the dagger deep into Colton's side. Dark red blood starts oozing out of the wound. I can't breathe as I watch the blood begins to pool on the floor. "Nooo…" I start shaking my head. It can't be true. This can't be real.

"Do you know what I made him see?" Dravin turns around and starts walking toward me. Wiping the blood off the dagger on his jeans, he continues, "I made him see his worst fear. Do you know what that was?" I can't look at Dravin. I keep my eyes on Colton. He is still watching the scene play out in his mind oblivious to his fatal wound. "His worst fear was watching you be killed in front of him when he couldn't do anything to help you." Dravin starts laughing. "Which is kind of funny considering that you now have to watch him die in front of you, while you can't do anything to help him."

CHAPTER
THIRTY - SIX

THE DOOR TO MY CELL flies open, and Tom, Bradgen, Logan, and Larkin all run into the room. Tom goes straight for Dravin, who is too surprised at their sudden appearance to do anything. While he stands there stunned, eyes wide and mouth open, Tom runs straight into him and tackles him to the ground. With one punch, Dravin is out. Bragden and Logan go after the men holding Liam, while Larkin runs toward me. Adam lets go of me, knocking me to the ground. I scurry away from him and crawl toward Colton, trying to avoid being stepped on by the fighters around me. I have to get to him.

I watch as Colton stops writhing. He never opens his eyes. A large pool of blood is forming on the ground beneath him. Tom runs over to me and checks Colton for a pulse. Liam gets free with the help of his brother and Logan. I roll Colton onto his back and lean my ear against his chest, listening for a heartbeat.

Nothing.

There's nothing but silence.

I scream as I fall forward and cry against his still chest. Logan tries to heal him, but like the rest of us, his powers don't work in here. He looks up at me and slowly shakes his head; slow tears falling down his face.

My Colton is gone.

Dead.

THE END ... FOR NOW.

ABOUT THE AUTHOR

Currently a student at Ball State University, Kaitlyn Hoyt is pursuing her passion for writing while working towards a Wildlife Biology and Conservation degree. Vegetarian. Proud tree-hugger. Lover of comic book movies. Avid reader. She has an unhealthy obsession for the soothing music of Josh Groban. She discovered her love for writing during the summer of 2012 and hasn't stopped writing since!

Connect with Kaitlyn:
Stay connected with Kaitlyn Hoyt at:
Kaitlyn Hoyt Writes:
www.kaitlynhoyt.blogspot.com
Facebook:
www.facebook.com/YA.Author.KaitlynHoyt
Twitter:
www.twitter.com/Kaitlyn_Hoyt
Goodreads:
www.goodreads.com/author/show/6940389.Kaitlyn_Hoyt

Made in the USA
Coppell, TX
20 July 2020

31330333R00177